RESET

RESET

NED LIPS

Elliptic, LLC

St. Louis

Published in the United States by Elliptic, LLC, St. Louis, Missouri

First Edition

This is a work of fiction. Names, characters, places and events either are the product of the author's imagination or are used fictitiously. Any similarity to real persons, living or dead, is coincidental and not intended by the author.

Library of Congress Control Number: 2018914128

ISBN 978-0-9980325-0-4

Cover design by Jamie Wyatt, imnotskippy.com

Edited by Karen L. Tucker, CommaQueenEditing.com

Dedicated to my patient wife, Barbara, and my two wonderful daughters, Jessica and Christine

ONE

BANG! BANG! Deafening. Pain exploding. Then nothing. She was falling . . .

Sarah awoke in a cold sweat and sat bolt upright; tears poured from her eyes as she stared into the darkness. Hands clenching the sheets to her chest, she whipped her head from side to side. No gun. No Robert. *Where am I?* She leaped out of bed to run. Stopped, sheets pulled up in front of her, dragged off the bed behind her. Confused, her mind raced to its constant first concern.

Her girls?

Soaking wet, she hugged herself as tears streamed down her cheeks. Her bedroom faded into focus. Another nightmare. Her ex, Robert, and the dread, clung to her. She shivered. The clock read 4:35. There'd be no more sleep. She took a deep breath, snuck into her daughters' bedroom with the slight limp that reminded her of the damage to her leg. Both were fast asleep and safe. Sarah padded into the bathroom and stared into the mirror. Her once shimmering long black hair, now sandy blond and short, was matted to her head. There were bags under her deep green eyes. Her normally golden caramel skin, drained of color, looked as dead and lifeless as she felt at that moment and as she usually felt these days and all too often.

She felt the scar on her shoulder, watching her fingers in the mirror circle the bullet wound. Then she touched the one at her lower ribs—big-

1

ger, star-shaped and more horrific—from the last bullet she thought had killed her. It'd become a sort of ritual after these nightmares.

"Sarah Robinson, you have to forget. You have to move on. He's in jail. We've escaped. We're half a country away. Relax." The affirmation never worked. He'd be back the next night in some other form. He was rich. He'd get out. He'd track them down. He'd kill her this time and take her girls. It was only a matter of time.

Her head fell, shoulders slumped, hands on the vanity bearing her weight. She stared into the empty sink. "What am I going to do?"

She turned to the only thing she knew to do: an hour of intense yoga and a half-hour of deep meditation. It helped. A shower helped even more. By the time the girls began to rise, she was dressed and as ready for another grueling day as she could be.

The morning was routine. She dropped her wonderful girls, Jasmine, 14, known here in St. Louis as Sandy, and Janie, 8, now Sam, at their huge private Montessori school, Mater Dei. She got out of the car, scanned the area as she did every morning, opened their doors and kissed them both. As they ran inside, she waved weakly to a teacher, nodded to someone's mother and sped off.

"MARY RANDOLPH, WHERE HAVE YOU BEEN? It's almost 8:30, goddammit!" She strode past her fat, arrogant, pink-faced boss like she did every morning, hating the name she'd chosen for herself. Like every morning, he followed her, yelling incessantly, until she was back in her cubicle. Sarah nodded dispassionately, waited for him to scream himself out, apologized without conviction and stared up into his pig nose and beady eyes until he left. She was out of explanations. They didn't help anyway. He'd yell at her two or three more times today, without warning or reason. She more than hated him, but she needed this job.

At 11:45, too early for her asshole boss, she strode out of the office for her visit with Asha, her spiritual teacher. Like her guru in D.C. before her, Asha, whose name in Hindi meant "hope," something she so needed, would lead her through deep chakra meditation. It helped her deal with life and prepared her for rejuvenating weekends out camping and exploring with her girls. She needed a change, and soon.

The drive was short, south only a few miles from the spacious downtown office building into an old industrial part of town. A huge storm was churning toward them across the river in Illinois. Sarah smiled. *I love big storms,* she thought. April in St. Louis was famous for huge electrical storms, though this one looked, and felt, different. Very . . . red? *Is it calling me?* A car horn, from behind, brought her back. She'd drifted onto the shoulder. Sarah swerved the car back into the lane, overshot, then back, tires squealing. Heart racing, cars honking, Sarah loosened her grip on the wheel, took a breath to center herself a little. She then looked to her right and waved as the still-honking car passed.

"Learn to drive," the man screamed through his car window. As she guided her car back into traffic, the car radio crackled. She turned it off. She focused on her driving, even as she felt the storm tingling up her spine, strong and powerful.

She half-smiled as she pulled up to the old urban church that had been converted to a sacred temple. The building was old red brick, built in the late-1800s, with white wood trim around the two 8-foot-tall front windows and massive oak doors. The white eaves rose beneath the towering three-story roof as two parabolic arcs that merged at the peak. The building was meticulously maintained, unlike many of the other buildings that surrounded it.

The old industrial area was strewn with randomly sized brick structures, many vacant and crumbling, flanked by cracked grey parking lots with weeds thriving in the many voids. Rusted chain-link fences surrounded them but had ceased protecting the buildings or lots long ago.

As she ascended the three-step concrete stairway, her breath began to steady. This was her urban haven. A place where no one could find her. She came here nearly every day around noon to bring some sanity into her life. In two days, she and her daughters would escape to one of the many parks in Missouri or Illinois for a weekend of solitude and living off the land.

She pulled open the heavy doors and shut them gently, but they still made a deep and powerful whoosh, bang, then a click that resonated within, locking out the world. Somehow that made this place impenetrable. Perhaps it was. She breathed deep and felt the peace that existed here.

The walls of the small anteroom were white plaster with two small hand-painted, watercolor pictures of flowers, water and gardens hanging on either side of the small door opposite her. Sarah removed her shoes and set them on a black rubber mat. She put her purse down beside them on the white tiled floor, removed her jacket and hung it on a wall hook before she moved into the main sanctuary. Her footsteps sounded, and felt, like she was walking on air rather than polished stone.

The interior of the roof was exposed to its peak. She adored the smell of the old oak and decades of stains. She breathed it in. Asha, a wispy woman dressed in soft red silk that floated about her, was standing in the center of the large room. As tiny as she was, her spirit filled the space and enveloped Sarah as soon as she entered. Unlike the stark white of the small anteroom, this sanctuary was adorned with colorful mosaics. On the wall to her right was a sleek black Arabian horse, racing toward the front of the building, his coat glistening in the summer sun just as her long black hair once did. To her left was a mighty black bear, rising on his hind legs, mouth open displaying his bright white teeth, arms wide showing off his long sharp claws, but he had a look in his eyes that conveyed a sense more of love than destruction. Behind her, straddling the standard-sized door from the front room, was a two-story-tall Indian elephant facing the front, trunk held high before her, signifying good fortune and protection. The fourth and most majestic of the mosaics rose behind Asha across the front wall of the church. It depicted a huge Bengal tiger, walking with peace and power toward them, eyes a deep piercing green that reflected a menacing confidence but somehow a warmth that always seemed to penetrate her soul. All around flowed peaceful grasslands, trees, wildflowers, crystal blue rivers and soft cascades. She turned and bowed to each, as was the custom, facing the grand Tiger last, then bowing also to her guru.

She could always feel the spirits of nature embrace her here. This day, however, the four animals seemed more alive, more real. Sarah gazed into the green, penetrating eyes of the Tiger and felt safe yet bold.

It was easily the most unknown treasure in St. Louis, and given both its location and the reclusive nature of its guru, it would remain that way. Asha had sensed her pain when Sarah had first stumbled in a few years back, and since then, other than Asha, Sarah had never seen another person in this place.

Asha greeted her with a bright smile that radiated from her entire being, as it always did. "Sarah, it is so nice to see you." As Sarah approached, however, Asha's demeanor changed. "You are heavily burdened today. I can feel it. Your soul is darker than usual." Asha reached out and took Sarah's hands. Sarah gazed up into eyes so deep, they reminded her of the bottomless mountain lake her parents had taken her to as a child. Dark, soulful, fluid and soothing, but unlike that cold mountain lake, Asha's eyes were warm and deeply comforting.

Just as Sarah was about to share her nightmare, they both heard a guttural rumble from outside. *Thunder?* It grew louder. They both stopped. It was eerie. It pulled at her. Asha's worried eyes let Sarah know she'd felt it as well. She slid out of Asha's grasp, and the two crept toward the front of the temple, craning to see what was going on. When they reached the tall front window, they could see the massive storm coming from the east.

They stood in awe. The churning mass of reddish clouds spanned the horizon and boiled above them.

"What kind of storm is that?" Asha's voice had a faint, uncharacteristic quiver. "It is glowing . . . red." They both could feel the storm, feel it reaching out to them, to her. Sarah shook it off.

"A big one! The red must be the reflection of the sun, maybe?" Sarah felt Asha's gentle hand on her shoulder. The roiling wall of clouds was moving toward them. It appeared to be nearing the city and the Gateway Arch, which she could just see between the two huge oak trees that flanked the walkway Sarah had taken up to the temple. Both were beginning to bud. It wouldn't be long before a view of the Arch would be gone for the leaves. Sarah loved the feel of the storm's fierce energy and let it penetrate her being as she watched it.

Asha broke the trance. "We're safe in this building, Sarah. It has stood the tests of St. Louis weather for well over a hundred years." Asha turned away from the window and glided back into the main room where they would begin their meditation.

Sarah's phone vibrated in the pocket of her coat hanging on the wall. She fished it out. Her old friend from the D.C. police. *What could he want?* She pushed the button, flipped back her hair and put the phone to her ear. "Hello?"

Before she could say anything more, her friend's panicked but hushed voice broke in, "He's out, Sarah. He's escaped. This morning. Not sure when. We have all the routes out of town covered, but he's rich, Sarah. Run. Robert knows where you are. You've got some time, 3 hours at least, but go soon. Gotta go." The phone disconnected.

Sarah's heart raced as she turned and put her hands on the window. Tumultuous red clouds boiled high overhead. She could no longer see the Gateway Arch, but she could feel the energy of the storm growing inside her. She breathed in its energy, thought about her wonderful girls, safe from this storm inside the huge old Mater Dei School, but whose lives she would uproot yet again. Guilt poured through her. *Should I go now?* She closed her eyes and slowed her breathing. *No. This will take only 30 minutes. I need to be centered to do this.* Sarah took a deep breath and started toward the big room along the path Asha had taken. She needed this more than she'd realized.

TWO

S arah looked at the building around her, bowed again to the Horse, the Bear, the Elephant and the Tiger, who seemed to be looking at her. Even a bit worried about her. Sarah shook her head a bit and then looked up at the massive oaken trusses held in place by huge steel plates. Asha was right—this place was a rock, and she felt, with more certainty than made sense, that those four animals, so long now a part of her psyche, would protect her.

Asha sat, legs crossed, her heels on her thighs, the backs of her hands resting, fingers to thumbs, just above her knees, back straight, face forward, waiting patiently for Sarah to join her. Sarah sat opposite her, facing the Tiger, and took the same position.

Asha spoke. She never spoke at this point. "Sarah, it is time." She paused. "Sarah, remember," her eyes were stern, "stay with me." When they'd first met, Asha had explained the importance of doing this only in the protection of the temple and only while with her, a Master, but she'd never repeated it. *Why now?* Sarah only bowed confirmation.

She closed her eyes as Asha began a simple mantra that focused the spirit inward, requesting courage against the world and guiding their focus from the root chakra upward through her energy centers, guiding their spirits eventually from their bodies into the realm of pure spirit. Sarah looked forward to these sessions of total release.

"Om . . . Namah . . . Shivaya," they both repeated in a whisper, two breaths in, one long one out with the final word. Her soul began to come forward as she focused on guiding energy from one chakra to the next.

Om . . . Namah . . . Shivaya

As she neared Ajna, the third-eye chakra, her soul reached out. She could feel Asha with her, even closer, protecting her, their spirits entwining.

Om . . . Namah . . . Shivaya

The rumbling of the storm grew as she slipped into her spirit. She let the storm's energy become part of her, rising toward spiritual freedom. She released herself to the Storm and felt its power course through her.

Om . . . Namah . . . Shivaya

As her energy rose to a new spiritual level, so did the power of the approaching storm inside her. Asha seemed to slip away with a warning, "Stay with me, Sarah!" but the feeling of the Storm was euphoric, dancing, entwining, driving the passions within her soul. Rhythmic. Sensual.

Om . . . Namah . . . Shivaya

She let the huge Storm's energy in, stoking the fire raging inside her, mixing with her angers, fears and desires, as she tried to free her present from the pains of her past, letting go of everything, even Asha, who reached for her.

The Storm was caressing her. She quivered as the feelings soaked into her. Her soul raced out into the vastness of the astral universe, now dark and deep around her.

Om . . . Namah . . . Shivaya

Her nerves were electric as the trance took her out into peaceful, beautiful freedom. She burned with a spiritual heat, a scarlet sense, more intense and ravishing than anything she'd ever experienced, rising, sensual, soft but powerful. Warm reds and oranges surrounded her, enveloped her. Soft. Hot. Passionate. As she approached the peak of her spiritual ecstasy,

Om . . . Namah—the words crashed in her throat!

The soft oranges turned a dark menacing crimson and violet. The powerful, alluring energy now turned on her, ripping at her soul, tearing it from the peace. *The Storm?* The energy was alive, and it wanted her. It had lured her out, out too far, beyond her experience. Beyond her protection. Beyond the temple. Beyond Asha.

Alone.

Blood-red evil emerged from her entanglement with the Storm. She could feel it searching her, scouring her senses, memories, fears and desires. She fought back, but this was ethereal, a spiritual, living being of some kind that was invading her mind, her soul. It ripped her worst experiences, visions, images, feelings and fears from her. She watched as they flowed into the darkness before her, almost as if the being in the Storm were playing snippets of them for her, evaluating them, organizing them. Robert. Her parents. Their coffins. Her boss. Robert's family. Leaving them. Robert hitting her again and again. Gunshots. She was trapped and cold, floating in pure crimson darkness. Disconnected. Watching. She could see her body below. She could feel Asha nearby, somewhere, but trapped as well, restrained. This being was after Sarah, not Asha.

CRAAAACKKKKK! Robert's angry black eyes, murderous visage, clear and real in her face, the smell of bourbon in her nostrils and that deep, loathing voice, screaming at her from inches, "You fucking bitch, you're weak. Die, you whore, die!" Then it laughed his mocking, terrible cackle that echoed through the darkening redness all around her. She recoiled as cold dread enveloped her. The barrel of the gun aimed at her forehead, blaring blasts of gunshots rang through her, searing pain from the bullets ripping holes in her flesh. Fists, bruises, helplessness, pain raked her spirit, became a heavy, penetrating, sludgelike mass, coating her, reaching for her core. Fear, running, escaping, trying to protect her girls, losing their identities, family, friends and lives. His laughter resonated through the darkness, mocking her.

He was there. It, the being, the Storm was there. Right there! Watching. Learning. She could feel it. Then it began sucking, tearing, trying to make her relinquish her soul; every fiber of her being felt as though it would burst apart into oblivion.

The deaths of her parents, falling hundreds of feet from a cliff face, the plain wooden boxes that held their mangled bodies. Alone. Penniless. Frightened to the bone. Pain stabbed, knives of energy probed, dragging her soul out from her physical self. Her body was gone. Asha was gone. She was alone, a spirit only, frightened, cold, horrified, wanting more than anything to curl up in a ball and die.

The invisible being, the Storm, engulfed her in what felt like cold, sticky, deep maroon crude oil poured both over and through her, dragging images into her consciousness. Girls crying, begging to stay. Robert's sisters and brothers reaching out to them. The deep pain and guilt of taking her girls from the only family they knew, Robert's family, ripped at her core. Alone. Penniless. Running. Frightened. Vacuous, endless emptiness. Churning currents of frigid red blood closed in on her. Dark indigo frozen daggers burst through the blood, driving into her spirit, each carrying tears of her girls as they left their home, their screams and protests, their anger at her. She cried out, but as a spirit, she could shed no tears.

The blood exploded as the face of her fat, pink-faced boss attacked, inches from her, screaming, tearing her down, degrading her, demanding more. His horrid breath invaded her senses. She couldn't turn away, couldn't close her eyes. He surrounded her.

Robert's mocking laugh raged through the darkness as entwining crimson tendrils wrapped around her, flying toward her within the swirling tempest that came from outside and from within her own psyche. She was running, running, reduced to nothing. Robert's evil visage replaced her boss's, his voice demeaning her again and again, "YOU DON'T DESERVE THESE GIFTS. YOU DO NOT DESERVE TO LIVE!" The stench of alcohol, the pain of his vicious blows, raining down on her. Curled in fear.

It's ripping me to shreds! She screamed, but nothing emerged. Robert's fists, pummeling her ribs and head, deep bruises, ribs cracking, pain. She was sobbing, trying to defend herself against the huge drunk man, begging for her life. His family holding the girls, loving them, ignoring her pain, laughing at a party while he struck her over and over. Sucked deeper into the depth of the crimson abyss, she felt her life being torn from her, dragged into infinity. She began to resign herself to the swirling darkness, giving in, surrendering to it, feeling only pain, anger and hatred in her soul.

FLASH! White, pure light. From below. From Asha! The light pushed back against the dark torrential maze, fighting for her soul, battling the evil within the maelstrom. Both forces demanded possession of her spirit, of her life, and she was helpless to engage either. The darkness encircled her, images bombarded her, driving only hatred and pain into her consciousness. "DIE!" she heard Robert scream, then that deep, haunting laughter.

Love and peace from the bright light that was Asha tore through the darkness, but just as it reached her, doubt, thick, sticky bloodiness, stoked by her own fears and feelings of failure and inadequacy, squeezed her spirit with vicelike intensity, invading her being, fighting the white energy, pulling her toward oblivion. The energies swirled around her. Lost. Alone. Desperate.

The white light was with her and grew. Images of her wonderful daughters, Jazz and Janie, smiling and playing in their wilderness retreat. She could feel their hugs. They gave her strength to fight. From the light, a powerful Arabian horse, hooves pounding, harder and harder, mane stretching out behind her toward the receding abyss, red swirling winds bracing her. She could feel its power as the muck slid from her sleek coat. She'd become the Horse; it was part of her. The grace of the Horse allowed her soul to absorb the devastating losses of her parents, but she could not outrun Robert.

The crimson being in the Storm refused to release her. Blood-red tendrils grabbed her. A thick, frigid, indigo oil spun in the abyss around her as the Storm dragged her toward it. She screamed into the void as icelike daggers emerged from the goo, separated and flew at her. Like knives they tore at her soul. Her screams had no voice, but Asha heard them.

The white light from Asha brightened, focused, found her. Sarah's spiritual muscles rippled and strained, and in this nightmarish reality, she became the huge Bear. Turning on the crimson evil with a bear's strength, she tore through the sticky, oily mass, ripping huge claws through the clinging tendrils that felt like flesh and exploded in torrents of bright red blood. Her screams hollow, helpless, as the two sets of spirits fought to own her. Her soul, the Horse and the Bear were frantic, detached, confused, ineffectual.

11

The bellowing, red face of her foul-mouthed boss enveloped her vision. Robert's fists drove through it, pounding into her. The Bear clawed at the visions, at the bleak nothingness, at the dark viscous liquid, but they eluded her. "BITCH, YOU'RE STILL TOO WEAK. GIVE IN. YOU'VE FAILED!" Robert's voice was deep, penetrating like frigid steel.

The energy of the being in the Storm, a dark living madness, swirled the visions of panic, escape, the pain of running, the guilt of dragging her children from their lives, the angry red face of her boss. Blackness raged and churned inside her. The Bear within her grabbed at her guilt and loss, enmeshed in the Storm, and crushed bits with his powerful arms, enwrapping each deep into her spiritual core.

The muck and the tendrils were fewer but angrier, and they came for her fear, panic, loss, pain. Robert's menacing laugh continued, ringing through her like a hammer on her heart.

Again, Asha's white light penetrated it all to get to her, releasing the next ally, and she became a pounding, relentless, charging Elephant. She tore through obstacles, ripping the dark crimson energy from its foundations, from its roots, from its core, dragging her back toward the temple. She felt the Horse, which gave her grace and speed, and the Bear, which gave her strength to contain the Storm within her, and she let her soul become one with them. She was also the Elephant, strong and tough, trying to bring her home. Her mind swirled in the chaos, but her soul, for the first time, began to feel a part of the battle for Sarah, for Sarah's life.

More of the energy of the evil being in the Storm became trapped inside the powerful grip of the Bear, tucked safely within her own spirit. Her Elephant's power and tough exterior refused to be stopped by the probing crimson arms of the menace. She allowed her soul, her spirit, her mind to merge and engage with the spirits of the Horse, Bear and Elephant as one. The living spirit of the Storm seemed to grow more alive, focused upon her, thriving and ominous, but now she could feel it, sense it. She could now identify her ethereal enemy.

The oily violet darkness welled up around her. Feeling the Storm rise for another attack, Sarah tried to ready herself. Robert's face exploded into hers: "YOU'RE WEAK. TOO WEAK. GIVE IN. DIE!" The invasive smell of stale bourbon surprised her, overwhelmed her. Intense images followed: beatings, gunshots, searing pain, deep loathing and unrelenting anger, doubt, fear, guilt blasted her subconscious, tearing her apart, breaking her down. She knew it was true. Had she failed them, her girls? She tried, but strength to fight back began to fade. She felt herself losing her connection to the power of her animal spirits. It, the redness, the being, and Robert again had her.

Fading from the temple. The bright pure light of Asha's spirit and her three animal allies were slipping from her spiritual grip as the blood-red darkness began to swirl around her, the images she hated racing past her mind's eye, playing like a horror film. The Storm had learned her weaknesses. Pain, blood, death, loss, guilt, failure, weakness, weakness, weakness. She heard the Storm laugh as it played its trump card.

"YOU'RE A HORRIBLE MOTHER! YOU'RE RUINING THEIR LIVES," Robert screamed into her face, spitting bourbon, echoing laughter through the nothingness.

Sarah felt her girls, their love for her. She'd sacrificed everything for them. She was a GREAT mother! Her soul was incensed and rose from the horror with the power of the Elephant, the Horse reared up on his hind legs, the Storm directly in her sights. The white light and her animals leaped into her spirit. "I LOVE MY GIRLS!" she screamed back, bellowing with a resonant energy she did not know she possessed, echoing deep into the chaos. "YOU'RE THE DEVIANT! YOU WILL NEVER GET NEAR THEM AGAIN!"

CRRAAACKKK! A vicious bolt of white lightning ripped through the darkness. It came from Sarah, surprised her and shook her, but for a second, it blew back the Storm's attacks. In the split second, she focused on her daughters and drew strength and clarity from their love. As the being returned, she was prepared and fought back against the painful images. She rallied her spirits and again became one with them, her spiritual strength growing as they unified. The Storm's evil energy intensified, focused, ready for the final, vicious attack. Sarah could feel it.

Asha's white light, her tether to life, pierced again through the darkening Storm, and her spirits reached for it, the three animals and her soul working together. The light strengthened and helped her bind to the spirits of the three animals, combining their power to tear her away from the grasp of the Storm.

The battle had long ago left her physical body behind, but she could see it now, well below her, floating above the floor of the temple, which appeared to be disappearing. The white light was closer, stronger. Both gave her hope and a sense of bearing in the depths of this churning, empty abyss.

Sarah now focused all her positive energy and strength, meshing her soul completely with her animal spirits and the white light. One vision, returning to her girls, pushing away the swirling nightmare. Tumultuous roars strengthened her, smells of sweat and musk awakened her, bursts of power beyond her understanding raged to her awareness from within her. Entwined with her, one with her, in the battle for her very soul, straining out of the darkness of the roiling clouds, and now, she knew she could win. That she *would* win. She smelled, for only an instant, the sweet flowers of a field, but the memory stayed with her.

The energy of the Storm grew, red tendrils amassing around her. Icy blue spikes at their tips. Oily indigo muck oozing around her, flowing, churning, glowing in places. She could feel the being itself rising in the boiling mass around her. Long and slow and deep, it spoke one word, "DIIIIIEEEE!" and unleashed it all upon her.

She released all connections with reality, focusing on the ethereal battle. Pounding, pummeling and racing forward through the horrid blood-red Storm as it tried to drag her back toward the endless abyss. Bright red flashes torn by her white bolts, slashing claws. Two powerful energies colliding. Thunder blasted her senses. The spirits, *her* spirits, fought to get her back. Holes emerged. Light from below. Her sleek black grace contrasted with the deep, dull maroon muck, tearing her from it. For a brief moment, she again saw her detached body, strained, back arched, toes curled, fingers ripping at the air above the faintest remains of the temple, but it was reaching out to her. The white light grew stronger.

A violent swipe of powerful claws and long white tusks ripped a gaping hole in the blackness below her. The light exploded through it, racing toward her, into her, Asha's vicious, powerful and graceful great Bengal Tiger joining her, joining her spirits, raising their energies.

She sensed a fear in the Storm. It was afraid, she could feel it. She/ they tore through the brightening red morass, radiating a blinding white light in all directions, driving back the terror. The Tiger drove her and the great power of her combined spirits into the final, deadly, ferocious attack to release her from the Storm's grasp.

She could feel her soul taking charge, directing the strengths of the Horse, the Bear, the Elephant and the Tiger into the battle. Oily crimson spikes driving for her soul were repelled. Orange and black streaks, claws, muscles, sinew, grace pushed them back. The red-brown muck was shed off a sleek black coat as she raced through the abyss toward home. The Storm's attacks now seemed more random and unchoreographed, panicked. She repelled the spears of darkness that had penetrated her before with the thick grey hide. From within her, a pure white energy ripped through the darkness, dwarfing the swirling storm. Huge brown claws reached into the chaos and encircled the dark, terrible energy, the visions of Robert, the pains from his fists, the wounds from the gun, the degrading anger, and with the huge bear claws, she dragged all of her own dark terror, the pains of her life that helped to fuel the energies of the Storm, and stuffed them deep within her, enwrapping them, taking control of the Storm's own powers within the benevolent energies of her animal spirits.

Intense heat imploded inside her, sucking, entrapping incredible energy within her spirit. The shock penetrated her consciousness, yanking her violently back into her physical body, out of the Storm, away from the being within it.

The Horse, the Bear, the Elephant and the Tiger spirits exploded with the force of the grand red Storm itself, into and from every aspect of her being, every pore of her physical body, into every inch of the world of nature. A vast oneness united her to the entire universe of the wilds she loved. From the dark, violent abyss, her soul opened into the warmth of nature, the smells of wildflowers, the souls of all living things. She could feel them at once as part of her as it all settled gently within her spirit— stronger, powerful, freed.

She could see it all—vast, expansive, beautiful, hers. Some of the red energy from the Storm was now a part of her. She could feel it, angry and beaten, as its spirit moved on.

It was over. They had won. They were one.

THREE

S arah fell a few inches onto something soft. She was coming back to herself. The energy of the battle she had won settled inside her, releasing joy, ecstasy and even an encompassing physical bliss that reached to every cell in her body like nothing she'd ever felt. Joy beyond joy. The spirits of the animals danced with her soul. They were hers. The energy of the Storm was there, both red and warm, and crimson and terrifying, controlled by the great protective claws of her Bear spirit. The Storm was gone, but she could feel it; she could sense an inner desire for it. Her terrors were confined, dangerously close but trapped.

As consciousness rose, the victory settled into the background, into her memory. A dream, maybe. Her body tingled down her spine to her toes, out to her fingers, through each chakra energy source, a deep warm, relaxing comfort. She was enjoying every moment.

She felt Asha's arms wrapped around her and hers around Asha. They both held on, eyes closed, Sarah savoring the depth of the feeling as it finished surging through her body and then, a few seconds later. . . *What was that?* Her brain raced for a physical explanation. There was none. *I love big storms.*

Sarah opened her eyes, but an unexpected brightness blinded her, and she slammed them closed. A chilled breeze, but sweet. Her side was cold, a little damp. She took time to adjust to the red brightness behind her eyelids as she tried again.

They were somehow not where they'd been. They were outside. The day was brilliant. The air was cleaner than she'd smelled it other than at the tops of some of the most remote mountains. They were sitting on lush green grass, full of wildflowers, butterflies and song birds. These beautiful images, the soft fragrances, sweet sounds, the breath of unbridled nature had brought her back. Her mind was still intoxicated. If there's a heaven, and she didn't believe in one, she was sure this was that place. *What a weird way to have gotten here.*

She hugged Asha close and then loosened her grip. Asha fell away from her, limp to the ground. Then, before her eyes, Asha glowed red, then white and dispersed, swirling as a mist in the air around her, then a brief, almost blinding flash of white light entered Sarah's being, soaking the red mist within her. She felt the Horse, Bear, Elephant and Tiger rise inside her, warm and strong, then a warmer feeling of deep, unbridled love filled her completely.

Just as quickly as the feelings and her spirits arose, they all settled deep into her soul. Sarah's eyes cleared, tears flowed, and she fell toward the grass where her beloved teacher had been. "Asha, Asha," she cried out. But Asha was gone.

The Tiger spirit returned to her, and she remembered the bright light that had sent that spirit to her. She became aware for the first time that that light, the spirit of the Tiger that had saved her soul from the battle with oblivion, had been Asha, Asha's spirit, all of her. She sat back, bottom resting on her legs, and began to sob uncontrollably. Asha had given her soul, her life, to save her. Sarah's head was spinning.

After several seconds, she took a deep breath and remembered the last mantra she'd shared with her teacher and friend. She sat back, took the pose she'd been taught and recited at a whisper, "Om Namah Shivaya." She could feel Asha's gifts, her spirits who were the Tiger, the Bear, the Elephant and the Horse, and the captured spirits of the Storm inside her, and she sat there, breathing in the pure air, sensing her new spirits, the joy of Asha, the power of the Storm and the evil of its darkness. Her pulse slowed. Her mind settled. One last deep breath. Relaxed. She opened her eyes and stared at the world in front of her.

Grass? As her tears cleared and the loss of her teacher became a new reality, the world around her was coming into focus.

Everything was gone. She closed her eyes and rubbed them and opened them again. Still, everything was gone. Everything except nature and people, and they were all naked. She was naked and sitting in the grass. The breeze was cool and filled with soft, sweet smells and the gentle songs of the birds that had recently arrived in the Midwest to prepare nests. The sky was deep blue and cloudless. The sun warmed her body. She could feel it.

Then reality broke into her awestruck mind. "What the—?" she said aloud. The huge temple was gone. She remembered it vanishing during the battle but had assumed it was as unreal as everything else. Was she sitting where it had been? She was sure of it. The two oak trees rose up in front of her, growing leaves. The old concrete walkway and her crappy old car were no longer there. She was sitting in deep green grass, which was growing before her eyes. The roof was gone. Only beautiful blue skies above her. She looked around. The gorgeous mosaics were no longer there because the walls were no longer there. All of the old industrial buildings were gone.

The streets, broken chain-link fences and anything that had been part of the area were gone except for the trees, flowers and plants, and they were visibly growing. She focused for a few seconds longer. Flowers popped open and were brilliant. The two oak trees grew fresh leaves as she watched them. Squirrels bounced through the branches. Rabbits calmly grazed on clover popping out purple and white blossoms. Nature was taking over, taking back its world, and it was doing so quickly—*Twilight Zone, Alice in Wonderland* fast.

She looked to the north. The skyline of the city was gone, along with all of the houses and buildings that would have blocked her view. The Gateway Arch was gone.

She spoke to no one and everyone. "The big-ass St. Louis Gateway Arch is gone?" She paused and looked in every direction. Nothing. She yelled, "What in the hell is going on?"

Buildings were not reduced to rubble. There was no smoke or fire. Everything had just vanished into thin air, or into the huge red Storm, or somewhere, replaced by grass, bushes, trees and wildflowers all growing at speeds she could actually see.

She looked west, and there it was—the huge red Storm, still pushing across the county. She was drawn to it. She could feel the darkness, deep inside her, and felt it straining to escape. She shuddered. *That crazy battle in the spiritual universe with the Storm? That was real?* She stared at it for several seconds then closed her eyes and pulled away.

When Sarah opened her eyes, she surveyed the area. The Storm left behind only nature—beautiful, wildly growing nature. *What is going on? Where the hell am I?*

Screams penetrated her reality. The unsavory characters who frequented the dilapidated buildings across the street from the temple were in a complete panic. They were trying to cover themselves, screaming for help or running. Other people were running past in different directions. Several people were badly injured. A woman knelt beside a man who was clearly dead.

People kept running past her, screaming, panicking, running for or from something, some trying to cover themselves at the same time. Others hid behind trees, embarrassed or frightened beyond imagination.

In the midst of a complete nightmare, she sat paralyzed in the soft grass, staring at absolute bedlam and confusion, in a state of detached observation. *None of this is real. It has to be a weird dream, right? One of my nightmares. An illusion, like the Horse and Elephant and Tiger.* She closed her eyes tightly, shook her head and then opened them. Same. *The wildflowers are real,* she thought as she picked one and smelled it. She felt the grass. Soft and lush, like a Scotts commercial. Very unlike the scrubby, inner-city stubble and dirt that had been here.

"What's going on?" Small tears slipped from her eyes. She closed them and shook her head again to gain some clarity, but when she opened them, nothing had changed.

No fear. No sadness. The tears were more . . . elation.

Sarah gathered her confused senses and stood. The energy of the battle within the Storm and the joy of victory was waning. Something inside her desperately wanted to follow the Storm, to rejoin it. She stared at it as it moved away. She closed her eyes yet again, focused her spirits and pushed all that energy down. Then she centered herself with a deep cleansing breath.

When she opened her eyes again, she could see with clarity. There was an elderly man who couldn't walk, sitting on the ground several yards to her left. His legs were in an awful pose. His wife was lying on the ground in front of him. He was both frightened and peaceful. She felt for them and wanted to help. *What could she do?*

Not far from them, a woman frantically dug at the ground with her hands, screaming, "He was in the basement. Someone, help me." Sarah scanned the area all around her, turning where she stood. People were lost, traumatized. Some stood, some wandered about, while others were searching, running or hiding. Anxiety began to build inside her as well. Screams of complete panic wracked her ears. Injured. Dead. Frightened. Mass hysteria surrounded her. Sarah spun left, then right, eyes wide, the beauty of the place lost now to the insanity, crying and running. She didn't know what to do or where to turn.

She felt like she needed to help, but how? She ran to the older couple as fear began to well up inside her. As she fell to her knees beside them, she asked, "What can I do?"

The old man looked up at her, tears streaming down his face. "Do you know what happened?"

"Did you also win your fight with that demon Storm?" she asked.

"What are you talking about? It was peaceful. The storm came in and shrouded us in a red mist. Then everything began to disappear, to sort of evaporate. We were sitting on our front porch, ready to watch the big storm roll by, and then we were here, on the ground."

Sarah sat back on her haunches.

The man continued, "My wife had a heart attack. She's dying. I guess the storm took her pacemaker. It took my knees and hip. I can't move. I'll die soon too, I guess, without my meds."

The old woman opened her eyes and put a frail hand on hers. "Honey, you can't do anything for us. Don't you have a family?"

"Yes," the old man agreed as he laid beside his wife and took her in his arms. "We'll be fine. Go find your loved ones."

Then reality struck her like a frying pan square in the face. "The girls. My girls. Where are they?" she said out loud. She realized she had to find her girls. She shivered to her core with sudden panic, leaped to her feet and turned in every direction, frantically surveying the area, looking left and right for any sort of landmark. *The sun. Where was the sun?* The wind would come from the west. *Wouldn't it?* The two big oak trees. The red storm is going west. She began to get her bearings. North toward the city, then west along the highway. What highway? She'd find something. She knew north. She had to find them.

She took a deep breath, thanked them, and they nodded. She closed her eyes for a moment and, as Asha had taught her, centered herself and regained control. She could feel new strength inside her, something powerful, part of her and new. She could see Asha smiling at her, holding out her hands. "You are one with this world now, Sarah." The Horse, Bear, Elephant and Tiger appeared behind her in front of a soft red, misty background. "We are with you now as it was ordained. Go. Find your girls. Save the Family. Defeat the darkness. It is your destiny. Trust that we are with you." The vision faded.

When she opened her eyes, her senses were heightened. She could feel the world around her. She was tuned into it. *Who are "the Family"?*

Sarah now had one purpose, and her brain was working fast. She looked at the sun, estimated the time to be about noon, considered the other landmarks and knew which way she had to go. It would be around 10 to 12 miles to the school. Maybe a little more. This was going to be a long run. She ran every night, and at lunchtime, she did a grueling yoga workout with Asha. Could she do this? Doubt. The darkness welled up inside her, but she envisioned Jazz and Janie, and again she pushed it down. Her strength returned. She had to do this.

Hopefully the teachers would keep the children at the school. She sensed danger. Several men began to approach her, first at a walk and then at a jog and then a full sprint. A few veered off after others—after other women, she noticed.

The Horse spirit within her emerged, and Sarah began to run north at a fast pace. Her limp was gone. Her gait was clean, long and fluid. *The Horse?* Though the men increased their speed, she easily outran them, leaving them breathless behind her.

FOUR

As she ran north looking for any evidence of Interstate 44 to take west toward the school, people were running in every direction, screaming, yelling, stumbling, crying, falling to their knees, praying, hiding, trying to help, refusing to see what was happening. People in mangled positions on the ground as their cars had disappeared under them. *How badly would you be injured even at 15 miles per hour?* A few groaned, but most were quiet, dead. Rats and bugs had already swarmed the dead and dying. She turned to avoid them as most had. The horrific smell of death mixed with the sweetness of the flowers exploding all around her.

As she approached downtown, she was forced to avoid growing trees, bushes and grasses. The ground rumbled, then stopped. It became tougher to move. I-44 would be gone. There'd be a lot of dead people along that passage. It was a gruesome thought, but bodies would create a path for her to follow.

She crested a small hill and stopped cold. The area where downtown St. Louis should have been spread out before her. The vision turned her stomach. Bodies in piles, stacked high from the ground where skyscrapers had recently stood. They were swarming with rats, flies, crows and vultures, vines growing from the bodies. The piles of flesh seethed. Some people were still alive. Screams and cries filled the air. She fell to her knees and threw up on the ground. People, screams, panic came from all sides. They seemed to spin around her as she wiped her mouth with her bare arm and spit.

She sat back on her haunches and stared. Even where she was, there were several smaller piles of broken bodies from the many six- to twelve-story buildings in what was once a thriving area around the perimeter of downtown. Those on the bottom floor had been knocked down by those who fell on them from above. Some of those on the bottom were trapped but alive. A few survivors tried to help them, battling the rats, birds and insects that had arrived in force. Her skin crawled. She wanted to help.

Cries came from every direction. Screams and pleas for help. On top of that small rise, Sarah was paralyzed with fear and uncertainty as the insanity boiled over around her.

Focus, Sarah. You can help after you've found the girls, she reminded herself.

A hand grabbed at her. She turned, leaping to her feet. She knew that lecherous look in his eye. His grip on her arm was strong, and he was a big man. He reached for her, but she ripped herself free. He came at her. The Bear's spirit raged inside her. She squared herself up toward the man and drove the heal of her hand, with the force of the Bear's huge paw, through his nose with everything her sinewy 5-foot, 8-inch frame, aided by the 7-foot black bear spirit, could muster. The blow stopped him in his tracks, lifted him off his feet and sent him staggering backward. He was bleeding. He regained his footing and looked at her as though he'd been knocked out of a trance.

"I'm so sorry, ma'am. Something weird came over me." He just stood there.

She wasn't sure, but she thought she felt him change. Something spiritual left him. She nodded, then looked at her hand for a second and smiled at the strength she now possessed. She could feel he was no longer a threat. That clear awareness surprised her.

My girls. I have to find my girls. The visions of death and injury had distracted her, but she was refocused. *West.* She turned left and ran as fast as she could, avoiding bodies, the injured, the swarms of frightened humans and scavenging rats. The wild plants returning with a vengeance grabbed at the skin on her legs, scratching and tearing until they began to bleed. Her feet hurt with each undaunted, shoeless stride. She could push through the pain, she *would* push through the pain. Then the Elephant rose inside her, her powerful spirit healing her legs, allowing her to force her way forward, faster and faster, without injury, skin tough and impenetrable. She now trampled the weeds before her, racing through without so much as a scratch.

Oh my God, she thought, *What about the Zoo in Forest Park?* She wondered what had come of the rhinos, lions, cheetahs and other beasts they'd caged there. Her path would take her not too far south of the Zoo. She saw people chasing other people, their prey screaming for help, and she realized that humans, not animals, were the larger problem. Crazed humans were everywhere, unpredictable. Worse when threatened. What situation could be more threatening? She slowed again, drawn to help, to defend those being attacked.

Find your girls, then help! As she picked up her pace, she traversed areas that had been dominated by multistory, multiple-tenant buildings, all gone. People were helpless and terrified. Many of the injured, dying or dead lay unattended. Survivors were paralyzed with fear, trying in vain to help or just crying out for lost loved ones. A few arrived to hugs from family members only to discover death and injury to others. People ran in every direction, screaming or, like her, intently focused. She was pulled to help, but she was on one mission. She repeated to herself, *Find your girls, then help!*

There was a lot of blood. She passed a lost toddler, slowed and again felt a tug to stop and help. A woman swept in and gathered up the child and then fell to her knees, sobbing. The rats were fewer out here. That was good.

Sarah felt like she was in a war zone. Screams of pain, death, pleas for help, blood and utter pandemonium surrounded her and battered her senses. Her pace had slowed to nearly a walk as she took it all in. The only thing missing were the ruins of bombed buildings. There were none. No structures of any kind. No man-made things of any sort. No cars. No tools. No furniture. No nothing. It was all gone. Taken, she was now completely sure, by the big red Storm that had also invaded her soul.

Her daughters, Jazz and Janie, seemed to call out to her. *Find your girls, then help!* She again refocused, put the chaos out of her mind and began to run. Nature was romping in its newfound freedom as though it had escaped from prison. With the grace and speed of her Horse spirit and toughness of her Elephant spirit, she sprinted west as adrenalin pulsed through her.

One mission, she told herself, *then I'll help,* driving herself forward.

She crossed raging creeks and outcroppings of growing trees, following the guidance of the spirits as her mother and Asha had taught her. She was tiring. The run was difficult, and as the plants grew, even with the power of the Elephant, it was hard to maintain her pace. She needed help.

"Reach to the spirits for help, Sarah," came Asha's voice from within, from somewhere.

Sarah closed her eyes and let go, allowing herself to feel the spirits in nature all around her. Feeling a pull northwest, she opened her eyes and obeyed. Her soul was her guide; she felt connected to this world as though she were a part of all of it, this ravenous return of nature.

For the first time in a long time, she was free of the nightmare that had been her life. This was the sort of reset she and her girls could handle, but her brain fought against her. *Am I really part of this? Did I cause it? Is this still an insane dream? Am I in some weird dimension? Are my girls even here?* The thoughts overwhelmed her, her pace slowed, and she screamed toward the bright blue sky, "WHAT IS GOING ON?"

Her spirit sensed Jazz and then Janie. *They are here!* She shook her head, closed her eyes, centered herself again. *Find your girls!* She knew she was on a bigger mission than simply finding her girls, but that was the only one in focus right now, and so she ran.

She let go, closing her eyes as she ran, and released herself to the spirits, warm and loving. Asha's last gifts. They calmed her. They were her connection, and this realization gave her strength. She could feel nature guiding her. Her deep connection to unfettered nature, to all of this craziness, shocked her almost as much as the human chaos still swirling around her, but the former was deep and positive.

She opened her eyes and said aloud to no one, "OK, universe, we got this."

She crested a hillock. There, walking to the top of a grass-green hill, silhouetted against the bright blue sky, was a grand black Arabian stallion. He was staring right at her, sleek, powerful and, until a few minutes ago, a very pricey extravagance in this formerly high-end neighborhood. Now, he was just a horse. Traveling on him would be quicker and safer. It was still over 5 miles to the place where the school used to be.

As she jogged up to the quiet animal, he continued toward her, a few steps in her direction, then stopped and waited. She felt he'd also been looking for her. *OK, looney, catch the horse.* They reached one another, and she touched his shoulder. The spirit of the horse joined with the one she had inside her, the one from the temple, from the dream, from the battle in the Storm. As she began whispering to him, a warmth flowed between them as though they knew each other. Sarah realized that she wasn't speaking. She'd only thought. She knew the horse had felt her and responded, and she knew they were supposed to be together. She stepped back but kept her hand on the horse and paused.

OK. Get on the horse. He's just a horse. She knew that was a lie. This wasn't just a horse to her anymore. The Horse in her dreamlike battle with that Storm filled her mind. *Was this that horse? This IS that horse! This is HER Horse!*

She'd ridden bareback many times, though not without pants. She grasped his mane, took two steps and leaped up, gliding her right leg over until she was laying forward on his back. The powerful steed felt great under her and responded to her wishes as she thought them. It was almost as though they were one, like she'd ridden him before. The feeling was powerful. He moved forward before she even gave him a kick. He was well trained, but their interactions were more than that. He trotted and then began to gallop in the direction of the school. Without stirrups or pants, the ride was rough, but she would deal with the pain down there to get to her girls. The moment this thought arrived, she and the horse rode in the same rhythm, and the pain stopped as though something was protecting her, wrapping all around her.

The horse's spirit entwined with hers. Her soul was calm, and it calmed her brain, and she let the relationship flow through her.

The horse hurdled a small pile of several people, detached legs and arms entwined with bloodied torsos, empty eyes staring. More mangled bodies lay ahead of them. An open path ran between old deciduous trees to their left and right, a forest growing visibly where houses once stood. Ahead, an opening to hills of grass on their right. This was maybe Manchester Road, but it was changing quickly, plants growing, the earth undulating behind them. Humans, dead or injured, littered the path. I-270 was ahead. It would be worse. She turned southwest toward the school located on the bluffs above the Meramec River.

They passed smaller piles of injured, dead or dying people where cars or buildings had been. Fewer rats, but there were plenty. Sarah rode past hundreds of people who were injured, wailing and crying. They were everywhere. Many were trying to help, to free the living from the smaller piles, while others tried to combat the rats. They'd slowed to a walk as she stared. No buildings. No roads. Nothing man-made anywhere.

The horse took her around some trees and down into a shallow valley. *The girls, Sarah.* As she thought it, her mount increased his speed. She and the horse were thinking—more like feeling—things the same way. Her physical brain again tried to develop some sort of rationality around what was happening, both around and within her. She smiled and dismissed the thoughts, opening her mind to the new world.

She heard the faint sound of children singing. They followed the soft voices. It was more like they *felt* the singing than actually heard it. They increased their pace, and it wasn't long before she and her stallion approached the place where the school had been. The horse was sweating and exhausted. He was not trained to run that sort of distance, but he had. He'd done it for her. She'd felt her way here, following the children, guiding her horse by instinct or that connection her mother had spoken about. Her mother's wisdom never failed her . . . when she listened. She was listening now. The children were singing as they came into view. Those sweet melodic school songs had led them here.

FIVE

✝ he old school building was, as expected, gone. Sarah breathed a sigh of relief; the teachers had kept the children there. They were sitting on the grass in a large clearing surrounded by beautiful tall oaks, hickories, elms and other species that were growing and leafing out even as she approached. The children were singing, tentatively, for sure, but in the midst of this craziness, the teachers at this wonderful school had put the children first and had convinced them to sing.

A few adults had gathered around. It was peaceful on the surface, but she could see the frightened looks in the faces of the adults and children. They, too, were trying to gauge their new situation, concerned about being naked, deeply afraid and struck by a complete sense of inadequacy. Most, she guessed, were sitting there because they couldn't think of anything better to do. They all stared at her as she rode in on a horse.

The place felt different. The quiet, the soft voices of the singing children, the relative calm of the adults she saw here, compared to the insanity, death and chaos she had just ridden through, was palpable. It should have been unsettling, she thought, but it was calming. She could feel Asha's white glow radiate inside her. She slowed the horse, guided him to the stream that ran past the school property, stopped and slid off. He looked into her eyes. She felt his spirit inside her, a positive connection between them. Then he reached down for some water and grass. She patted his big shoulder and turned to look for her girls.

Jazz and Janie were already sprinting toward her, long hair streaming behind them. They both leaped into her open arms. She squeezed them close to her, kissed them and kneeled on the grass. Tears of joy streamed down her face because, of course, her girls were safe, but her joyous relief ran much deeper than that. In the midst of utter chaos, as all around them were people in various states of panic, she was relieved; although confused about all of this, she was somehow relieved and free.

"Mommy, you found us!" Janie's big eyes beamed.

"And your hair is long and black again?" Jazz gathered it in her hands and let the silky strands slide out in front of them, her eyes wary.

Sarah just smiled. Her skin was soft, golden caramel and almost glowed like it used to. She felt rejuvenated, healthy, excited. She took them both and looked deep into their eyes. "I'll always find you. I'll always be here for you! Always!" She hugged them close.

"Mommy, come sing with us," Janie blurted out.

"The teachers say, if we sing, our parents will find us. It worked. You found us." Jazz had been crying but was smiling now. Sarah could sense the tension her older daughter felt that her youngest didn't. Janie took the world in stride, dancing confidently through it, while Jazz carried it on her shoulders, trying to make her way. She'd always been like that.

"OK, you goofballs, let's get up first." Jazz, as tall as Sarah at 14, smiled and stood. Janie, 8, unwrapped herself from Sarah's arms. Sarah rose, and they all walked hand in hand over to the group. The men, women and children were sitting in small groups in the center of the large clearing. They all stared at her. She could see the reaction in each pair of eyes as they sized up the woman who'd ridden in on a horse.

She sat and watched the group as the girls sang. A few of the adults, for the benefit of their children, put on a face of forced peace and comfort, at least as much as possible, but she could see and deeply feel the tension. Then it dawned on her—she could only sense the women. Nothing from the men, even though she could see they were every bit as agitated. A young mother was shaking as she braided the hair of her daughter at the edge of the circle. She was going a bit too quickly. "Ow, Mommy." "Sorry, honey." Most were holding their children close. Some prayed. More were crying. A few stood watch. The children sang.

A woman arrived, gathered up her son and, despite his pleas, was off. *She has to find the rest of her family out in the craziness.* Sarah was so happy both of her daughters were in one place, and she squeezed them to her again.

Another parent arrived. His children ran to him, and he hugged them close. They also left. This happened over and over. Beyond this special clearing was pandemonium.

A young mother and father arrived together, and their two children ran to them. They stayed. A few other straggling groups and individuals, some with children, most alone, wandered in. Some sat down. Some stood. All were confused. The headmaster, Ms. Watson, spoke to each person who arrived. That helped them, somehow.

The children's singing voices were soothing. There weren't many people outside the clearing in this rather secluded area, but those wandering or running past didn't seem to hear the children or even see this group sitting in the grass. Sarah could see a few perk up as they heard the sweet sounds, turn and head into the clearing. Some of those who could hear and see them guided or even dragged those who could not into the group with them. It was only when they crossed into the clearing that they, too, saw everyone, heard the children, calmed a bit and smiled. There was an aura here. She could feel it.

She turned her attention to those around her. The children waiting for their parents to arrive sang the loudest, hoping to be heard. Many would be disappointed. She wasn't sure how they'd deal with that.

The adults could barely control themselves. The desire to do something was so strong. Most had no idea what to do. Perhaps that's why Sarah wasn't panicking. She had her entire family with her, she was out of the nightmare of her old life, Robert would never find them even if he'd survived, and she knew exactly what needed to be done. She'd grown up living in the wild, at least on weekends, and had continued that with her girls. Nature was home to them. More than that, she felt a part of this new world, not stuck in it.

Wings thundered above her as dozens of buzzards and crows glided east. How quickly they sensed the presence of death. They'll tear apart the many human carcasses. The horrors she'd witnessed on her journey here flashed, but she put the disgusting images out of her mind.

She refocused on the girls. What would be best for them? *Can we stay here safely? We can't feed everyone; no way we can get much this evening. Then, what about tomorrow?* She was here in this particular place for a reason. She could feel it. Asha's strange message returned to her: "Save the Family."

"What, Mommy?" Janie asked, as both girls turned toward Sarah as she mumbled these words.

"OK, girls. Come in close. We are going to have to save this group. It's going to be our new family."

Jazz spoke first. "Mom. How can we? All these people?" Her eyes were wide. "Mom, we could just leave and find a nice place like we did on weekends. I can make flint tools. Janie'll find plants. You and I can hunt. Mom, like we do every weekend." Sarah could feel her daughter's heart racing as she pleaded her case. "Mom, we can get out of here and live just fine. Why do we need to save all these people?"

Sarah considered the idea. "We could do that. Does it feel right to you two? I'll do what you think is right."

Jazz and Janie looked at each other, then around the compound, then back at their mother. Jazz spoke. "I guess not. No one else is going to know what to do. We'll have to teach everyone, like everything. That's crazy."

"But Jazzy, they'll die without us," Janie pleaded. "I'll find plants to eat like I always do. You can make great tools and stuff. Mom knows how to hunt and build a camp like no one. We can do this. It'll be fun."

"There'll be some who'll know things," Sarah added. "Military. Scouts. Hunters. Fishermen. There'll be some who can help."

"What about out there?" Jazz asked. "What if all those people come in here? What will happen to them?"

"Jazz, we're going to have to let the rest of the world sort itself out." Sarah tried to be as soft and confident as she could as she gazed into her oldest daughter's deep green, frightened eyes. "Whatever's happening out there, we can't do anything about it. These people are our new Family, and we can help them." Jazz gave a hint of a smile. "That's my girl. Now, what do we have to work with?"

Sarah began to survey her surroundings. She'd seen the hickory-lined stream to their west, wandering southeast past the soft broad knoll they were all sitting on. The horse was still there. The stream must've been contained in a culvert under the streets for decades if not longer. It looked thrilled to be free again. The stream was quite significant and pooled into a good-sized pond before falling over a rocky ledge she couldn't see beyond. The pond was maybe 30 feet across and about the same length.

"Alright, we have water. We'll drink, fish, swim and bathe in that stream."

"I saw flint there when we ran over to you. I can make tools from that," Jazz noted with a little trepidation.

"You, my dear master craftswoman, will help us save this Family. Good thoughts."

Jazz smiled.

"We planted those peach trees behind the school two years ago," Janie pointed out. "We'll get lots of fruit from them in the summer. And we planted that garden. We'll get fresh food from them pretty soon. Look, they're already sprouting. I can find greens out there in the fields and in the woods. We'll have plenty to eat if people like veggies." Her soft blue eyes were alive with excitement.

"We'll gather wood from the forest that wraps around this little haven. What do you think?" Sarah added.

Jazz was visibly concerned. "Can we survive that long—till the food grows? Can we feed all of these people that long, or even tonight, for that matter? Mom, there's dozens, maybe a hundred people, and they keep coming and going, and everyone's scared and crying. They'll be useless."

"Yep, we have a lot of mouths to feed. Let's sort through the things that need to be done to put a dinner on the table tonight."

Jazz broke in. "Table? What table?" Janie laughed a bit too loudly, and the frightened masses turned and stared at them. They all smiled sheepishly back. Janie waved.

"Alright, girls. Fire, greens, protection, shelter, protein. We do this all the time."

"But only for the three of us." Jazz was not quite on board.

"We can do this, honey. We have to do this. What do we need to do?" They spoke, and the steps in the process became clearer and the conversation among them more excited. People stared at them. She realized that they were in their element. Even Jazz began to realize they could do this.

When they had their plan, Sarah said, "Girls, we've been training our entire lives for just this situation. We're ready." They nodded, Janie more fervently than Jazz, but her eldest was now on board.

"Hey, Mom. Can we use our real names?" Jazz asked.

"Of course, sweetheart. We're safe now." She paused for a moment at the thought. In this world where everything man-made was gone and everyone else was in a state of complete panic, Sarah, Jazz and Janie were finally safe. She released a long breath, gathered her girls in her arms and smiled with a joy she had not felt in a very long time. *We're safe!*

The new spirits inside her, the new strengths she'd felt, welled up again. She could feel them—the Horse, the Bear, the Elephant, the Tiger and even the awesome power of the Storm. They were all there. She could feel the wonders of nature all around them. This place was special. Her breaths were deep. Her soul was calm. Her mind was sharp. Her senses were heightened. She was ready. She was exactly where she belonged.

A deep sense of peace settled over her. A peace she had rarely felt. Somehow, something had washed the earth clean. Human pollution was gone. Human wealth was gone. She breathed deep the glorious air, and as Janie reached up to her with a huge smile, they began to sing.

SIX

When the song ended, she gave her girls a hug and stood. It was time. The principal of the school, Ms. Watson, had taken charge. Her right-hand woman, Ms. Jones, was leading the singing, and she launched the group into another simple but sweet and uplifting song.

Ms. Jones was young, maybe mid-20s. She was from California. Jazz had said that Ms. Jones had come to St. Louis for a boy she'd broken up with several months back. Jazz cried for her loss and because Ms. Jones was planning to return home at the end of the semester. Sarah normally didn't remember such details, but Jazz's distress over the impending loss of Ms. Jones burned it into her memory. *Well, that's not going to happen.* The children adored her and she them. Just as she'd watched Ms. Watson miraculously comfort the adults as they arrived, Ms. Jones did the same with the children. She was short and a bit plump, like Ms. Watson, with an engaging smile. A much younger version of Ms. Watson.

Sarah looked over those present and arriving. Most were Midwestern overweight, a few downright fat. They'd at least have useful calories to burn. Some of the old-world country club women with lovely coifed hair were stylishly starved. At least they were used to eating nothing. A few others were well conditioned like her. Their bodies were tuned to operate efficiently. Each body type had its advantages.

Calories would be the number one need. She only hoped they could generate a life-sustaining minimum. Several in the group had already complained about being hungry. *What time was it?* She looked at the sun again and guessed that it was around 2:00. *How many got lunch before the Storm?*

A few of the other teachers were still here, but most had left. Everyone was following Ms. Watson's orders. Parents came and left, taking children with them or arriving with others in tow. Many were crying. Most had no connection to the school. Some arrived in couples, others in small groups, many alone. All were in near panic, naked, afraid, embarrassed, but most of all, glad to find a welcoming group of people. As their numbers swelled, her calculations as to what would be needed to feed them grew.

Ms. Watson greeted each person or group that arrived, tried to comfort them, connected them to family, if there were any already there, and then, if they were staying, asked another teacher to guide them into the gathering. As it had for her, the sweet singing voices were calming for some. Others remained agitated, crying, complaining or wrapped in a state of emotional paralysis.

Ms. Watson and Ms. Jones had created an atmosphere of perceived safety in the midst of the chaos. People were disconnected, freaked out about the red Storm, wondering where it had come from and why. Sarah was pretty sure they'd never know. She had to focus on what she knew and what had to be done next in order to get them all through.

It was a nice day, but this was mid-April in St. Louis, and it would likely drop into the low 40s or even into the 30s overnight. That would be threat number one.

She'd been standing for several moments, observing, a bit paralyzed herself at the breadth of the task she was about to take on. She took a deep breath, patted her girls one more time and strode up to Ms. Watson, who was talking to a tall, strong man. His son was crying and was holding onto his leg as if for dear life.

"Ms. Watson, I have to go try to find my wife and bring her back here."

"Joe," Ms. Watson's voice was calm in the midst of . . . whatever they were going through. Sarah was impressed, and Joe seemed to relax and listen. "You told me Trudy was in Springfield, Illinois, on business. Correct?" He nodded. "To get there, you'd have to swim across the Mississippi River with little Joe, right?" He nodded. "Then the two of you would have to travel the 100-plus miles to Springfield on foot, find Trudy amidst the chaos there, assuming you don't pass each other going opposite directions in the process. Am I right?" Ms. Watson was trying to talk him through the realities of the situation.

"It's much more likely that she'll make her way here to you than you'll find her out there. Am I right?" Ms. Watson concluded. Joe nodded. Little Joe was crying for his Mommy. The situation was irreconcilable, the logic was impeccable, but logic was not a good answer at this time. What was logical about this situation?

Sarah said nothing. What could be said? Joe began to sob. Ms. Watson must have had this same conversation dozens of times today. *How did she handle it? Amazing.* Joe turned to his son and picked him up. They were both crying now. Joe, Joe Jr. in his arms, drifted away back to the group. Sarah turned.

"Ms. Watson?"

"Call me, Shirley, please. I'm no longer the principal." Her shoulders sagged as she exhaled.

"OK . . . Shirley, I'm Sarah Robinson, Jasmine and Janie's mother."

"Yes, it's good to see you. Good, back to your real names. Good. Your girls are wonderful." The small talk came with a quiver in her voice. Ms. Watson was waiting for the crazy demand Sarah was about to make that she would have to deal with. Ms. Watson took a deep breath.

Sarah put her hand on the educator's arm. "Relax. I don't need anything."

"Oh, Sarah, that's a relief. I'm completely at a loss as to what to do other than to try to calm people. But that won't last long."

"I might be able to help. My daughters and I are experienced survivalists, with skills that could help us through this. My parents taught me how to live in the wild without human tools, and I've taught those same skills to my girls. We know how to survive in this situation. I don't know how many others do. We've never tried to feed this many people or deal with all of the other aspects of this nightmare, but we can at least start with what we do know."

Her eyes brightened. "Excellent, excellent. Oh yes, I remember the girls telling me about your weekend adventures." Sarah thought Ms. Watson was about to hug her and, given they were both naked, that wasn't something Sarah was ready for. Luckily, Ms. Watson hesitated as well. "OK, OK, what do we need to do?"

Sarah talked Ms. Watson through the requirements, the challenges and the things that she believed needed to be done. Ms. Watson nodded throughout, taking in the entire plan. When Sarah finished, Ms. Watson took on her principal role once again. This woman was a leader, there was no doubt about that. She was maybe 5'2", grey-haired and portly, but she took on the air of a 6'4" Army general.

As a song ended, Ms. Watson walked with purpose to the edge of the circle of people. She commanded their attention, and an immediate hush fell over those present. "Everyone, we find ourselves in a unique situation. I realize as I say it, that's one of the biggest understatements of all time." She smiled and drew a hesitant chuckle from a couple of the adults. "This is a new time in our history and in our lives. We have no idea what happened and probably never will. What we do know is that everything has changed. Most of us have lost family members to this tragedy. My children and grandchildren live on the East Coast. I'll probably never see them again. Each of us has such a story. We need to grieve. We need to cry."

She paused then continued with a raised sense of urgency to her voice, "We need, right now, to begin to understand that if WE are to survive," and she spread her hands to encompass everyone present, "we have to put those feelings aside and address the challenges that lie ahead of us, right here and right now." She pointed with assertion at the ground in front of her. "We have a long and likely cold night ahead of us. We have food to gather and prepare for all these people and anyone else who arrives. We have shelters to build and, at some point, clothing to create. I know no one wants to look at this old naked body forever."

Again, she received an uncomfortable chuckle from a few. She spread her arms wide. "Yes, I'm naked and uncomfortable. You're all naked and uncomfortable. We're all naked, and it's highly uncomfortable. Now you all know that I don't shave my legs until late May." She looked down, and there were a few more chuckles. "BUT, this is the way it is right now, and we all have to put aside our shame and discomfort and look at the bigger, more pressing issues that face us, like simply living through this first night."

After a pause to let this all sink in, she continued, "Humans are resilient. *We* are resilient. We will survive. This new Family will survive. We'll do so by binding together as one community, one Family."

Family?! Caught by surprise momentarily, Sarah's mind registered the term. Ms. Watson continued, pulling her back to reality. "Beside me is Sarah. She's the mother of Jasmine and Janie, who you all know as Sandy and Sam. Girls, would you join us please?"

Janie sprung to her feet and sprinted around the circle. Jazz looked at Sarah, who nodded to her. She rose slowly, self-confident yet uncomfortable as everyone looked at her. She looked to her mother, and Sarah smiled. Jazz understood the importance of at least appearing strong, so she stood tall and walked around the group to stand by Sarah's side. Janie grabbed her hand, and Sarah winked at her. "Good job. Thanks, honey." Sarah could sense that for others feeling the same trepidation, this display by a teenage girl in front of all these strangers and, worse, her friends, set an example they could follow.

Ms. Watson began again. "Sarah, Jasmine and Janie have some very special skills that I know will help us make it through this situation. She and I have talked through a plan, which she'll share with you now. She's going to put things pretty bluntly, but I think you all realize the gravity of this situation. There are some immediate things that need to be done. Are we all willing to do as Sarah instructs so that we can survive as a group, as a new Family?"

Sarah knew then, with certainty, that this was her Family, the one Asha had told her about, the one she was destined, trained and now uniquely empowered to save and protect. The group responded with a few utterances and chatter among them, all without a great deal of enthusiasm.

A man with black hair stood and yelled from the back, "How do we know that someone isn't coming to rescue us?"

Sarah looked behind her out in the grasslands she had ridden through. Where hundreds of people and utter chaos had so recently been, now only a few random groups of humans were out there, but most were wandering away from the gathered group. A few stopped, seemed to hear the singing, turned and headed into their area. The others seemed not to even notice this growing community.

Ms. Watson was still speaking. "We don't, and I for one am hoping that happens. I think we're all hoping that happens. But we can't just wait around for that to happen. We have to begin to prepare for the worst. We have to begin to prepare to survive if civilization, as we knew it a few hours ago, has changed forever. If we're wrong, wonderful. That'd be so great. But we have to act now as though that won't happen. Does everyone understand that?"

Again, the responses were unenthusiastic. Sarah sensed and knew the Storm was circling the world. There would be no rescue. Ms. Watson knew she had to get the rest of the Family thinking about the future and not the past. "Folks," Ms. Watson said loudly, holding her arms up to quiet the group. Then she lowered her voice and calmed herself. "In a matter of a few hours, everyone who isn't hungry now will be. It'll get dark and cold. Very cold. This is the reality for today. Even if we're rescued, we'll have to live at least until tomorrow. So, let's stop wasting time and begin trying to survive, at least until the morning."

That did it. The Family came to a nonverbal, albeit tentative, agreement that perhaps there was hope of being rescued, and all they had to do was get through one night together.

SEVEN

"OK, again, Sarah knows what needs to be done. Does anyone else feel like they have the sort of survival training that will help?" People looked at one another. No one spoke. The short, dark-haired man seemed about to say something, thought better of it and backed up a few paces. Even if a few might, they weren't ready to volunteer for this job. "OK, then, let's please listen to Sarah."

As Ms. Watson was speaking, Sarah had been reviewing those present. There were about 80 people, maybe more. Most were overweight. Some were fat, some big and strong, a few were slim, while a few others looked reasonably fit. All ages. A cross-section of humanity. A group of much older people had congregated together. She'd deal with them later, but she had duties for everyone.

Sarah took a deep breath, rolled her shoulders and stood tall, then stepped forward to address the new Family. "Hello, everyone. As Ms. Watson mentioned, I'm Sarah. This is Jasmine, who we call Jazz, and this is Jane, who we call Janie. I was raised by two wonderful people who loved the outdoors. They taught me how to survive in the wilderness with nothing man-made at our disposal. I then taught those skills to these two.

"So, we have a lot to do. Food is going to be very rustic. There is no salt or pepper. We'll find some herbs to flavor things. You'll have to eat what we can find, catch or gather, including insects, so no complaining. We need protein, and insects are often the only and best source in this situation." There were expected gasps all around, especially from the children.

"In the future, we'll begin to fish and hunt, but we have no gear to do either today. We'll try. Janie's great at finding edibles in the woods and fields. She'll take a crew to gather anything she can find. I realize that she's just a child, but she knows her stuff, so please listen to her." Sarah selected three men, two women and their children and asked them to come up and stand by Janie. "This will be tonight's food search team. Janie, find a few strong sticks and show the team how to sharpen them, just in case. Make a couple of rough baskets. Got it?"

Janie nodded. She wasn't sure that she could lead this group of adults, but Sarah could see the pride and determination on her face. Sarah squatted to her level, put her hands on her shoulders and returned a look of clear confidence in her daughter. Janie's eyes grew bolder as she stood up straight, ready for the challenge.

"Don't stray too far. There are a lot of people out there, and they're more dangerous than animals." Sarah focused on her youngest. "Be careful." Janie nodded. Sarah patted her shoulder and winked, then stood. "Is anyone a runner?"

"I am." A woman stood. "I run several miles every day."

"Great. Go with them. If anything happens, sprint back here as fast as you can, and we'll get out there to help you." She turned to the group. "Just try to be careful so that doesn't happen. Understood?" They all nodded. "People are nuts. Stay close to camp and watch out, OK?"

"Yes, Mommy, we will. We promise."

"We'll look out for everyone," one of the men tried to assure her. "Our boys are going as well, so we'll all be very wary."

"It'll be OK, Mommy. We'll find some food for everyone."

Like a good team leader, Janie shook the hands of each of her teammates and led them a few feet away for a bit of instruction.

Sarah smiled and returned to the group.

"OK. Jazz is excellent at making tools from flint. There's flint down near the stream. Jazz will take a team down, begin to make tools and teach you how. Don't worry if you can't do it right away. Jazz has been working to perfect this skill for many years. She's excellent. You'll eventually get it. Anything you can make will make everyone else's jobs easier. Thank you for doing this."

She turned to Jazz. "Jazz, first make a shovel, a couple of knives and a couple of axe blades and bring them to me when they're finished. Down and dirty. Fast, not pretty. Got it?" Jazz nodded. "We need to cut some branches, scrape out some fire pits and dig some holes." Sarah could see Jazz knew what tools she was asking for. "Then make as many of each as you and your team can tonight. Rough is OK. We can work on spear and arrow tips tomorrow." She knew Jazz loved to make tips because they were difficult and intricate.

"Yesss, Mommm. I understand. I helped make the plan too, you know." A little adolescent arrogance even in this disaster. Sarah smiled.

Sarah asked for volunteers, and an older, somewhat portly man raised his hand. "I've tried to do this before. It'll be good to learn from an expert." Jazz smiled as the man stood and walked forward. Then a slender woman, whom Sarah felt she should know, nodded at Sarah. She nodded back as the woman and her daughter and son, both near Jazz's age, stood and joined the group. Jazz was all smiles. Jazz pointed to two other girls she knew from school, neither of whose parents had yet arrived, and beckoned them forward. Jazz also greeted each with a handshake and then looked up at her mother. Sarah nodded for her to lead the group, and Jazz guided them down toward their stream.

"OK. We need to build a fire. If we can, we need to build three fires. One there, there and there." She pointed to three corners of the clearing that would put the Family's backs to the relative safety of the fairly large stream to their west, which came to be called the river and ran south and then east. "The fires will keep us warm and help keep predators away. I'm not sure what's out there, but it's safe to say, if nature is back in full force, there are coyotes at least." She didn't want to mention escaped zoo creatures. Everyone was already on edge, and that would alarm them more than she needed right now.

"We need to gather dry wood. Volunteers?" Ms. Watson walked through the group and gently touched a big burly man and a couple about

Sarah's age. As Ms. Watson touched them, they stood and joined the wood-gathering group.

"OK, try to stay close for now and gather wood from the areas right around here. Stay together. We need small sticks for kindling and larger logs, if you can find them, to keep the fires going. Drier and deader the better. Make noise. Animals hate noises they don't understand."

Some among those sitting began to complain until Ms. Watson spoke to them. Sarah wanted to tell them to get over themselves, understand this nightmare and get with the program, but she bit her tongue and let Ms. Watson lead the people.

The short, dark-haired man walked proudly forward and announced, "We can make a fire as good as anyone." Then he turned to a group sitting around him. Sarah remembered that this group had arrived together, almost dragged in by one of the women. The man gave orders. "Get up. We're making fire today." There were six of them, the leader and two big men and three women, slightly heavy but pretty in a sleazy, dive-bar waitress sort of way. *SARAH!* She chided herself at the judgment. They all looked to be strong and reasonably fit.

Sarah had selected three locations for the fires: one near the western tree line that led down to their river. The second, which would become the main fire, was set in the middle of the opening to their woods-surrounded clearing through which everyone arrived. Both would be set several yards back from where Sarah contemplated building a barrier across that opening. The third fire site was to the southeast of the main fire, along the arc of the eastern tree line. In each place, she pushed a stick into the lush green grass.

As she walked, she spoke to them. "We need to clear the grass out of these areas, about 6 feet in diameter, so that the vegetation doesn't burn and ignite outside the rocks surrounding the fire pits." A rough shovel came up from the river. The blade was about 6 inches wide, flat, sharp enough and easy to handle. Jazz was working on speed, not beauty. This would be fine for digging. "Hopefully more of these will arrive. Who's going to dig? The rest of you move the sod out of the circle."

"Where shall we put it?" the woman who'd led them in inquired with a friendly cockney accent.

Sarah looked around, envisioning the completed compound in her mind. "Over there. We'll use the sod to support the wall we're going to build."

She knelt at the location of the center circle with the flint blade and ground it into the grass. "Like this. Just an inch or so to get the grass and top root system. Scrape it off." The grass was soft, the soil moist, and came up in sheets. She handed the axe to the short man, the apparent leader of the group. The man gazed into her eyes, which gave her shivers down her spine. "I'm Tony."

"OK." Sarah was focused, but this Tony ruffled her. "Nice to meet you." His smile made her skin crawl. She pulled herself together. "Down here." Now on her knees, Tony knelt beside her, intentionally rubbing his body against hers. Her body revolted against the contact, while the dark spirit from the Storm inside her seemed to reach out to him. Sarah backed away from the contact.

He pulled through the grass once. Nice clean sheet of grass. Her insides churned. "Perfect." Her voice trembled, and he smiled as he noticed. "Nice work." Sarah backed away and stood. Tony stood and moved closer. She put her hand out. He took it. Her spirits jumped and seemed to be battling one another inside her. She withdrew her hand and took a step back. Tony was smiling at her, which made things worse. "OK, Tony. You got this. About a 6-foot circle around that stick should do it. Not too deep."

As Sarah turned away, the English woman added, "Yes. Let's not make this any harder than it has to be."

Tony ogled Sarah as she broke their gaze. She heard him take charge. "Alright, Harry, you heard the woman, dig us a nice circle so we can build a fire." The dark spirit of the Storm roiled her animal spirits. She felt queasy, staggering a bit as she moved away.

Sarah closed her eyes, refocused her mind and controlled the darkness within her spirits as best she could. Recentered, she opened her eyes, stood tall and announced to the big man leading the wood-gathering crew, "We need wood for each of these fires." She pointed to the center fire. "Bring the wood here first. It'll provide the most protection if we don't get the others done tonight. OK, wood folks, off with you. Be careful and noisy." These woods were new-ish, growing aggressively since the Storm. Would there even be "old" dry wood on the ground? She felt there would be. She hoped there would be. There needed to be.

She turned to three young men who'd just arrived, followed by three young women, all of whom seemed to arrive here because they'd heard the children singing. They were strong, immodest and ready to help. "Follow me." They needed no encouragement from Ms. Watson. Sarah headed west across the compound, through the western woods, down the path that led down a gentle slope, beneath long arching hickory, birch and river willow tree limbs, to the big clear river pond where the stone-cutting team was working.

"We need good-sized rocks to ring all three fire pits. Choose stones like this." The rock was limestone, about five to six inches in circumference had it been round. "Got it?"

"Yeah. We did this with the boys in Scouts. We got this, right?" Sarah patted them on their shoulders and left them to it. She could tell that the three men rather liked the idea of hauling heavy rocks in front of the women. *Anything that motivates.*

"Joe, right?" The man nodded, eyes still moist, and stood with Joe Jr. in his huge arms. "Alright, now for an important and the most dangerous part of our preparations. We have to construct a barrier around the camp. We won't get it done tonight, but we want to get as much done as we can. This barrier is designed to keep animals out during the night. Most predators are nocturnal, which means they hunt mostly at dusk and dawn."

"What about shelter?" a woman asked.

"We don't have time, the tools or the resources to build anything useful for all of these people." The woman looked around. "First, we'll create a barrier to protect ourselves from big predators so we can sleep at night and then build a shelter. Make sense?" That last part was directed at everyone. They all nodded.

"OK. Joe's going to lead this team." Ms. Jones appeared out of nowhere, smiling, said something softly to Joe Jr., who slid from his father's arms. Ms. Jones guided him and several of the youngest off to one side.

They sang as they walked. Sarah listened to, or more accurately, felt their voices. They seemed to touch her like they had on her way to this place.

Sarah smiled, focused, turned her attention to those still unassigned, pointing to several men and women, and asked them to come forward. Ms. Watson glided by, touching each on their shoulders with a pleasant word. Each instantly rose and joined Sarah.

Sarah led the team across the clearing. "We need to find brush with spines and thorns. We have no gloves, so you'll have to be particularly careful. We also don't have a first aid kit, though I'll be gathering some medicinal herbs to create the best kit we can."

Just then, one of the boys on Jazz's team came jogging up carrying an axe blade Jazz had made. "Jazz told me to bring you this. She's amazing." He handed it to her and rushed back to the river. Sarah looked it over. This one was nicer than the one being used as a shovel. Very sharp on one end and nice and smooth on the other. The blade was about four inches wide. Not perfect, but fine for the next task. Fast. That girl was on her game. There'd be no handle, so the person wielding it would have to hold it in his hand and strike.

She handed it to Joe, who turned it in his hands. "Wow. Your daughter made this?" he asked as he guided his thumb along the edge and showed it to the others.

"There are some hawthorn trees over here." Sarah pointed toward the southwest edge of the clearing. They all looked as they struggled to keep up with her, not knowing what they were looking for. "You'll know them because they have very long thorns all over their branches. These are dangerous. You need to cut some branches. Do this as a group to control the branch. These will be the skeleton of the barrier. Cut them about five to six feet long."

She showed them the hawthorn trees, what limbs to select and how to strike the axe at the weakest point at the top of the joint where it met the tree. Each person took a smaller branch stemming from the limb, holding it with a thumb and two or three fingers between the 2-inch thorns. She struck the branch a couple of times, opening it from the trunk, then they ripped it down and away from the tree.

"There's one," she exclaimed. They all smiled. "Joe, you got this?"

"Yes, I think so." He looked at the others, and they returned somewhat uncertain grins. "OK, we got this. Thanks, Sarah."

Then she stopped for a moment and turned toward a strong athlete a bit taller and bulkier than herself. "Erika, right?" The woman nodded. "You, you and you will be in charge of gathering the brush. There are wild roses over there and some bramble bushes just over there. Be careful." The young boy who was about Jazz's age rushed up the hill again from the river with a freshly minted flint knife blade. She saw him looking for her as he reached the bank and called to him. He sprinted over and handed her the knife.

"Nice, huh?" he asked.

"Beautiful. Keep it up," she responded. It was sharp, wide and well balanced. Sarah was so proud of that girl, and it showed as she handled the nice blade. Jazz could make nicer ones, but she realized that this was down-and-dirty work, and Jazz was nailing it. She handed it to Erika. "Use this to cut the brambles and wild roses." Again, she walked them across the compound to a hedge of wild rose vines. "One of you hold the branch being cut right near the knife so that it doesn't spring back and cut someone. The two of you hold onto the other end. It's very important to control each of the branches so that we avoid cuts and scrapes as much as possible. Be patient, take your time and work together. Do you all understand?" She again showed them how to separate the rose branch from the trunk safely and turned it over to Erika. "You good?" They all nodded and looked at one another.

EIGHT

Sarah turned back toward the camp, took a deep breath and watched for a moment. Ms. Watson and Ms. Jones were helping several newcomers. They settled in pretty quickly and, after some water at the stream, seemed ready to work. Sarah strode across the compound to the group of newcomers walking up from the stream.

"Hello. Welcome. I'm Sarah. You ready to pitch in?" They all nodded. Sarah smiled as broadly as she could. "Great. You'll help build our barrier. Are you OK with that?" They again nodded at Sarah like children accepting an assignment from the teacher. "As that group cuts the branches and rose vines, you gather them and bring them to this area here." She walked over to the broad opening into the clearing from the grasslands through which everyone entered. The woods to the east and west were no real protection from animals, but this open area would help address her biggest concern—men.

Several in the group were well behind her. "Come on," Sarah ordered, and they scampered to join her. Sarah's patience was waning, but she pulled herself together. *You got this.*

Ms. Watson intervened to speak briefly to the chosen group. Again, they responded almost as though Ms. Watson had cast a calming spell on them. They looked around to see if anyone was gawking at their naked bodies, which no one was, and followed her. A memory flashed through Sarah's mind of a cruise she and Robert went on with another couple when they were still getting along. They'd stopped at Martinique, a French-controlled island where topless sunbathing was the norm. She took to it eagerly but remembered how hard it was for her girlfriend to remove her top and how it was even worse for her when no one cared whatsoever that she'd done so. *When everyone's naked, no one notices.*

"We'll start at this tree and work across the entrance." She strode in an arc across the opening, and the group followed. "Go about this far and stop." She turned to see if they were paying attention. She put a stick in the ground and walked at a brisk pace to a tree at the other side of the opening. "Then when that's completed, start at this big elm tree and work back." The small group hurried to follow her as she marked an arc to a point several feet past and inside of the first stick. "Overlap the two walls about 6 to 8 feet in this area, with about 4 or so feet between them so there's a way in and out," she said as she pointed with her hand. She then drove sticks into the ground to indicate where the wall should go. "We'll build a gate as well. It'll go about here." They all nodded as she pushed sticks in to indicate each side of the future gate.

Her authority all afternoon came from the clarity with which she understood what to do, how to do it and why. "Start by laying the branches and vines along this path. We'll work on installation later. Got it?" They nodded. She waved them off to begin. "Let's go and be careful!" They all jogged toward Joe's and Erika's teams and began to drag the branches and vines to the area where Sarah had instructed. Sarah smiled at Ms. Watson, who smiled back.

The teachers were still greeting people as they entered the camp area. Occasionally a joyous squeal would indicate a parent had arrived. A few people left. No one tried to stop them anymore. The circle was much smaller, but she still had teams to assign.

The boy came running up from the river, this time with a much rougher but workable axe blade. "My Dad and I made this," he said, beaming. "Not as good as Jazz, but will it work? She said it would."

Sarah looked it over and nodded. "Looks great. Nice job for a first time." It wasn't an axe blade. It was over a foot long. The blade was about 6 inches wide, which was good, but all of this made it heavy. It was rather flat and not terribly sharp. She put her hand on the boy's shoulder. "Young man, this is perfect for the next job. Thank you, and keep at it."

"OK, next team." She pointed to a man who'd just arrived, hugging his ecstatic twelve-year-old daughter. When called upon, she hid behind her father, embarrassed. He was doing his best to protect her. Sarah selected others for the next task as well. As Ms. Watson put a gentle hand on each person and said a few words, they relaxed a little, stood and walked to the front.

Sarah looked at Ms. Watson with a smile. *Magic. That was all it could be.* Sarah considered her own struggles to connect with people on a personal level. She had so few friends. *We'll make a good team, Shirley and me,* she thought.

"Umm, ma'am?" One of the women broke her train of thought, and Sarah refocused on the here and now.

"OK, sorry about that. We need to dig and build latrines." The group returned blank expressions. "Bathrooms, toilets," Sarah explained. They all nodded in comprehension. Sarah began to walk southeast toward the back of the compound while the group tried to keep up with her. "This is your shovel." She handed it to the man with the daughter. He took it and showed it to the others.

They reached the back woods and entered a small clearing near a sharp embankment that led down to a raging section of their river, several feet below. "The hole needs to be about 2 to 3 feet deep, or as deep as you can get it. You get to dig. You OK with that?" He nodded. The young girl had moved beside him, feeling less insecure. She was built like an athlete. Sarah nodded and faced her. "Will you help your father by removing the dirt from the holes? You'll have to use your hands." She nodded and looked up at her father. He smiled.

She turned to a woman with short black hair, about 5'5", stocky but not fat, who somehow looked very professional even naked. "Above the holes we have to build places to sit. This takes a bit of engineering. Marsha, right? Ms. Watson tells me that you're an engineer, correct?"

"Yes, but I build bridges and buildings."

"Perfect. That's what we're about to build." She explained to the entire group the process for building the structure over a latrine. Sarah focused on Marsha, whose eyes became brighter with each piece of the puzzle.

"And without ropes to bind the arms, we'll have to find some green branches and find crooks in the side branches to hold the cross branch," Marsha proffered in support of Sarah's description.

"Right, Marsha. You got this now?"

"Absolutely!" Sarah could see the wheels spinning in her head as Marsha formulated the plan to build a structure that would support anyone in the Family—big and small, male and female. Sarah imparted a few warning tips, and Marsha nodded.

"We need a trough from the hole to the edge of this steep bank so we can wash the waste out into the creek. It runs deep and quick here. Dig the trough as deep as you can get it. Got it?" The man and his daughter nodded. "OK, dig away. Everyone else, follow Marsha's instructions, and let's get this built. We may need them sooner than later." Everyone smiled and got busy.

As Sarah emerged from the south woods, she stopped. It was a busy hive of humans. Nearly everyone was thrilled to have something to do and attacked their chores with maximum effort.

The children were still singing as a few mothers watched over them. A few cared for the injured. People came and left, but newcomers outnumbered those leaving. More workers. More mouths to feed. Ms. Watson was the clear leader of the group. Sarah would be her other right-hand person, along with Ms. Jones, who everyone began to call Molly. No one other than Sarah, even newcomers, called Ms. Watson by her first name.

Sarah walked up to the only person in the group whom she knew well. "Amy, you and I have the next task." Amy was about Sarah's height, 5'8"-ish, but unlike Sarah, Amy was delicate, long and slender. Amy was the owner and executive chef at a swank Clayton eatery. Her claim to fame was that she grew her own vegetables and herbs. As it turned out, she also knew the medicinal qualities of quite a few native plants, better than even Sarah, and Sarah thought she was pretty good. Neither compared to little Janie, whose connection to and knowledge of plants was well beyond her years. To Jazz's chagrin, the three had discussed the topic at some length over wine and juice at Amy's place many times.

Sarah grabbed a middle-aged man, also tall and slender, who had just arrived and asked him to help Amy gather herbs for their medicine kit. Amy was for now the medicine woman. She would also, of course, oversee the cooking, but Sarah believed it would be a while before they cooked anything.

Amy and the man, who was, oddly enough, named Herb, wandered off. "I thought I saw some peppermint over here. That's good for . . ." *Herb hunting herbs.* The thought made Sarah smile.

Sarah gathered five teenagers whose parents hadn't yet arrived and asked them if they could help. The children, all a bit older than Jazz, were huddled together crying. Molly appeared, touched them gently, each on the shoulder, and they turned to her. She whispered to them in her melodic voice. Sarah watched as they were transfigured. Molly turned five smiling teens over to Sarah. *Freaky magic, she and Shirley,* Sarah thought as she watched Molly flit off to solve another issue with the children.

Sarah turned back to the teens. "OK, we need to cut these fibrous plants so the women over there can weave some rope. This is milkweed," she pointed out and then walked a few paces, "and this is Indian hemp. Both are fine." She used one of the rougher knives coming up from the creek to saw through the stems. She turned the knife over to a young woman who appeared to be the oldest. "Young lady, have at it."

The girl smiled. "I'm Brenda." Then she took a bunch in her hand and cut it through.

"Well done, Brenda. The rest of you, please bring the plants to the women over there." They all nodded, and a younger girl jogged off with the first bundle cut by Brenda.

Sarah followed the girl the 15 yards or so across the luxurious grass newly growing in soft soil to the seated older adults. Sarah taught them how to weave the strands into rope. She helped them understand how to break down, combine and twist the long green stems, overlaying a new strand inside the prior ones to create a longer, continuous rope. "Don't taste the sap. It'll help hold all of this together when it dries, but it can make you sick. Understand? Just make rope and lots of it." They were pleased to have something useful to do and thanked her. The rope would be rough, full of bark and the woody parts of the plant they'd later learn to remove, but it would be workable for today.

She gathered two elderly men who moved slowly and asked them to begin turning over rocks to find insects for protein. Later, when she felt safer, she'd get kids to catch grasshoppers out in the fields. The two turned up their noses, looked at one another and snickered, then nodded and set about their assigned task. *Friends, I guess,* she thought.

Tony's firepit crew moved slowly. At least they were doing something. Tony was shorter than she was, dark and swarthy. He turned and smiled at her. Her insides churned. She turned away. *How'd he know I was looking at him?* He'd move at his own pace, and she'd let him. She had no desire to get anywhere near that man.

NINE

Sarah and Ms. Watson were everywhere, helping with each of the tasks and dealing with the various issues that came up. Molly kept the children, along with many of the adults, singing. The music had a calming effect on nearly everyone, but others seemed unaffected, including most of Tony's group. The place was bustling, and newcomers were astounded. Most joined right in once they understood what was happening and Sarah was able to assign them to a task. A few complained and gravitated toward Tony. Morale overall, however, was improving as people began to see that there was a plan and at least some hope. In a short period of time, their nakedness had faded as they focused on their duties and realized that no one was judging their bodies.

It took about an hour, but some useful rope was being finished. Sarah had tested an early effort and instructed them on how to get it tighter and stronger. Sarah asked a couple of the children to bring the finished rope to Marsha and the latrine-building team, and when that team had enough, to bring the rest to the point where the wall would be constructed. People were catching the fever of the efforts around them and wanted to be a part of it. It was better than sitting and worrying about what had happened to them.

When the next rough knife arrived, she directed the boy doing the deliveries to take it to the children cutting plants for the ropes. An older, teenaged boy had arrived and took the knife. He and the young woman were cutting the plants as fast as they could. She could see the teenagers were beginning to talk as they worked. The older or less mobile adults were also chatting and making rope as fast as their fingers could twist. She could see them begin to slide the woody parts out of the rope as they went. They'd figured that out on their own.

As the next batch of thorny hawthorn branches and rose vines were dragged to the barrier, nine newcomers arrived, three of whom were injured. Ms. Watson's team welcomed them and had Family members help the injured to the southernmost part of the compound, under a large sprawling mulberry tree, where a woman was tending to several people. Amy and Herb were also back in the area that became known as the infirmary.

The smallest children who couldn't help were singing louder, with more confidence and emotion. People found this place because of the singing, as Sarah had, and so Ms. Watson had kept it up. It was soothing and helped unite the diverse group. *Brilliant. Simply brilliant. Nothing made people feel better than the power of music. This was good.*

The six healthy newcomers were enlisted to be barrier builders. They were tired but had gotten water at the river and were now ready to help. One of them seemed distant and almost repelled by Ms. Watson rather than soothed by her. He was an older, portly man and refused to help. He wandered back out of their clearing, searching for something. Sarah watched him then turned to her five remaining charges. Two others walked up from the river whom she had not seen arrive, but she added them to the group.

"OK, follow me." Sarah strode to the markers she'd made for the barrier and went through the same presentation as to where the barrier would be constructed that she had given earlier. Three knives had been delivered to her, and she looked them over. Two were made by obvious rookies. They would be perfect for this task. "Young man."

"Mark, ma'am."

"OK, Mark, take this one to those people over there cutting roses and sticker bushes."

"Yes, ma'am." And he scampered off. He was a nice boy. A bit older than Jazz, maybe. He was running all over the place delivering tools from the river.

"OK. The hawthorn branches, these nasty-looking things right here, will be the fence posts of our barrier." She knelt on the ground near the first tree at the edge of their eastern forest. "Drive this knife down into the dirt as far as you can and twist it. Scoop as much dirt as you can out of the hole and get it as deep as you can." They were all circled around her watching. She handed the two digging knives to two of the stronger-looking members of the group, a middle-aged man and a younger woman.

Sarah stood and walked them over to the stack of hawthorn branches. "OK. We need to pick these up *very* carefully. You take the end here. You're the leader. Is that OK?" An older woman nodded. "OK. You sure? OK, you, you and you, each take one of the end branches. You, come here and control this middle area. OK, now together, lift it from the stack. On three from your leader." The woman counted, and they lifted together as Sarah watched. "Good. You two, please help disconnect it from the other branches so nothing pops out and gouges anyone. Move toward the hole I just dug. Put the end into the hole and push it down as far as possible. Guide the branches carefully above her so that she doesn't get nailed by those thorns. Good. Now turn it so that the widest part runs along the wall. Good. Now fill in the dirt and pack it in tight. Over there is some sod. Go get some and wrap it around the base to help stabilize it.

"It'll probably not stay up by itself right now, so you hold it while they put in the next one." She pointed to where the next hole should be. "Make sure that the branches will overlap as low to the ground as you can. Then entwine them so that you have a stable wall. Got it?" They all nodded. "Now take your time. Be extra careful. Work together. No arguing. You good?" They nodded again. "You're protecting this entire community with this. Thank you."

They smiled for the first time, realizing the importance of their job. Moments ago, they'd arrived panicked and lost, and now they were building a protective wall for their new community and listening to music. It was just the right amount of overwhelming.

Sarah sprinted back to the rope makers, chose a nice length and sprinted back to the edge of the barrier. "OK, now tie this around the tree and around the first hawthorn so you don't have to stand here and hold it for the rest of your lives." The group smiled, took the rope and tied up the first branch to the tree. "Great. We'll get you more rope as we can."

She walked back to Ms. Watson, who was greeting some more newcomers and trying to comfort them. Two women backed away from her, turned and left the clearing. Sarah and Ms. Watson watched them then turned to their bustling Family.

Sarah broke the silence, "Well, it's a start."

Ms. Watson nodded. "Good job, Sarah. This is excellent. People feel so good to be doing something that they can see will help. Eleanor Roosevelt said something like this relating to the plight of those in the Great Depression: 'The people felt they would do anything if only someone would tell them what to do.' Panic is about fear and helplessness. You've provided this Family with guidance, something productive to do and, with that, hope to alleviate both. Most, I'd say, have put aside for now that they're naked and in a new world that's beyond anything they've ever known. That's quite an accomplishment in such a short period of time. Well done, indeed." Ms. Watson patted her on the shoulder and turned to address a commotion somewhere in the compound.

Sarah enjoyed the compliment from their leader. It felt so good to be recognized. *How long had it been since anyone gave a rat's ass what she did?* She smiled and gazed at the sky. The sun was heading down, and she figured it was gaining on five, maybe even six o'clock. She took a deep breath and sensed the fresh, pure air.

Newcomers arrived and required her attention. They were sent to relieve others as they tired, to be taught by two-hour veterans. More stone tools came up and were distributed by Mark. The difference in craftsmanship between those Jazz made and those made by others was easy to see, but all had their usefulness and made work easier.

Amy tapped Sarah on the shoulder. "Maybe we can catch a fish or two so we don't have to serve bugs. Can we make some spears?"

"It's a long shot, Ames, but we'll need spears for protection regardless." Sarah gathered a group and, using one of Jazz's better knives, showed them how to clear one end of bark, sharpen the tip, then peel back a bit of wood toward the point to create a barb. She then split the point a bit and jammed a sharp stone chip from the stoneworkers' leftovers into the tip. Before long, they had three decent spears, and the group was left with Jazz, who would teach them how to spear fish. *Maybe we'll catch something after all.*

Sarah returned to the compound. "Tony, the fire circles look great." Tony's team was up to ten. Tony smiled proudly. "Could you carry the sod up to the barrier?" She'd asked before, but most of it was still lying around the circles.

"Sure, sweetie," he said as he moved toward her, eyes scanning her body. For the first time since she had arrived, she was conscious of her nakedness. She backed away as Tony grinned, stared into her eyes and touched his own hardening penis. Smiling, he said, "Boys, move that sod for my future queen here. And do it now!"

As his team moved, Tony stood directly in front of Sarah. The trapped Storm power seemed to reach for him. It made her queasy; doubt and fear crept into her psyche. Tony could sense it—she was sure from the confident smirk on his face.

"Thank you." Sarah turned on her heels from the standoff without another word and headed off. *Macho dick!* Sarah sighed to herself.

TEN

Dry wood was piling up at each circle. Several hawthorn branches were up and entwined on one side. At this rate, the barrier would take days to complete, which she expected. Several selected for their thin fingers were assigned the task of weaving the rose vines into the hawthorn branches, possibly the most dangerous task yet. She showed them how to do it without getting pierced by either the hawthorn or rose thorns, one person on each side, feeding the branches back and forth, starting at the ground. They watched attentively and obeyed.

Amy, with Herb at her side, was already treating minor cuts and abrasions, but Sarah was surprised at how few there were.

The teams were working as nicely together as anyone could expect. A dispute arose involving one of Tony's people. He was challenging Sarah's authority, but before Sarah could get there, Ms. Watson appeared. The instigator backed away from her while the others calmed down.

Sarah caught Tony staring at her with that smile that crept under her skin. Then he winked at her. She shivered and turned. When his cronies returned from causing the disturbance, they were met with a handshake and a pat on the back. *There will be conflict. It's inevitable.* However, she felt there was more than just a conflict with Tony.

Sarah jogged down to the creek to see how Jazz was doing. Jazz had the whole team making various stone implements. She had an assembly line working. Jazz helped each person, giving instructions, and would finish each piece before Mark would race into the compound to deliver it.

Jazz was also showing a young man and his mother how to spear fish. They stabbed at their prey within the little pond, which was teeming with big fish. *Where did they come from?* Sarah wondered. Sarah stood with pride as Jazz guided them through the skill.

Her mind moved to Janie and the group she sent out a long time ago to search for food. *What had happened to them? They should be back by now.* Her heart began to race.

"Joe, Erika, I need you!" she yelled as sprinted up the bank. The two appeared from the back of the compound. "Janie and the food-gathering crew is still out there. They should be back by now. We need to find them."

Sarah grabbed one of the more completed spears then two other sticks that hadn't been started and tossed one each to Erika and Joe. The horse rode toward her, and in motion with it, she grabbed its mane, used its momentum to leap onto his back and turned through the opening into the fields.

Erika nabbed a hawthorn as she ran and yelled, "Joe, thorn branches!"

Joe nodded. "Guys, grab something! Let's go!" Erika was already well ahead, in full sprint behind Sarah.

As Sarah crested a hillock just outside the compound, which hadn't been there earlier, she heard a scream that sounded like Janie. *Oh my God, if something has happened to her, I'll never forgive myself.* The horse reacted to her thoughts, bolting into a full gallop. As they crested the next mound, she saw them in a small glen, surrounded by four hyenas. Their black snouts and eyes made them look mean and nasty. Their large powerful jaws, baring long white teeth, snarled at the Family members. Those jaws were designed to rip away flesh and break bones from animals already dead, but they were very effective killers when necessary.

The three men with the sharpened sticks were holding them off for now. Janie was screaming at the hyenas, trying to scare them as much as they were scaring her group. This was working. These hyenas were, after all, zoo animals and unaccustomed to being screamed at.

She felt the Bear strength well up in her, and she launched herself and her horse, as one, down the slope, hollering at the top of her lungs.

The band of humans and hyenas were equally shocked. She and the horse rode right behind the two hyenas closest to her. She slashed them with her spear as the horse drove his hooves into their sides. The hyenas rolled to their right and yelped in pain. The beasts scrambled quickly to their feet, growling at Sarah and her horse. The men with the spears also began to yell and advance on the now confused and separated hyenas. Erika sprinted past, whipping the hawthorn branch in the faces of the other startled hyenas. They stumbled back.

The hyenas righted themselves, turned toward Sarah, then back to their left at the large approaching phalanx of humans, then at one another. Nearly in unison, they took a step toward the woods behind them. Their final snarl was not menacing but one of fear. The hyenas turned toward Sarah, who stopped the horse several feet in front of them, lifted herself onto her hands on the back of the horse's neck and glared down at them.

Everyone but Erika stopped and watched the hyenas cower before her. Janie screamed one last time, shocking the four beasts, who looked left at her, then back at Sarah and, in the same motion, turned and bolted off into the woods, yelping like wounded dogs.

Erika trotted behind them to make sure they'd retreated. Sarah could feel in her spirit the four animals race through the woods. Erika jogged back to the group and smiled. "They won't be back anytime soon."

The others were now watching in amazement, weapons at their sides. Sarah scanned the area for danger but felt nothing else. The Family stepped back as she came closer and slipped off the horse. Sarah smiled and tossed her weapon to Erika.

Janie sprinted and leaped into Sarah's arms. "Thanks, Mom. I've decided I don't like hyenas very much." Everyone laughed, relieving the tension. Janie squirmed free and, in typical fashion, left the event behind. "Mom, look what we found for dinner!" She opened a rough woven basket, and inside was a large pile of blackberries. "It's early for blackberries, but who knows what's normal these days. We also got piles of dandelion and collard greens, some begonia, marigold, daylily and tons of honeysuckle flowers, and you won't believe what else we found." Before Sarah could answer, Janie pointed to the edibles spilled onto the ground during the melee. "Morels. Gobs of 'em. Well, like ten, but that's lots."

"Well done, young lady."

"We all helped," she responded. "Mr. Bobby found the blackberries." One of the men chuckled at the moniker. "Miss Amy's gonna be thrilled!" They all gathered up the veggies from the ground and began to head home.

"Good work, everyone. And great job fending off those hyenas. Let's hurry home, and we can hear the entire story around the campfire tonight."

Erika led the small band, hawthorn branch in hand. Joe had his spear and hawthorn weapon in back, and the others, armed only with sticks, flanked the group. Sarah remounted and followed behind. The horse gave her a better vantage point. She rode up the small rise to their left to survey the area and was surprised to see nothing but green grass, wildflowers and trees. *Where are all the people? There should be people, shouldn't there be? At least dead people?*

"Mom. This place is weird. Those trees just grew up, like *just* grew up. We watched them. And these hills just changed from flat ground."

"I know, it's hard to believe, but the trees just grew up in a big arc like you see now," one of the men added. "When we left the compound, there were a few trees and lots of growing saplings and then—bang—a forest. The land is changing in leaps and bounds around us. It's weird."

"I didn't so much find the blackberries as the bushes sorta grew suddenly in front of me," the man Janie called Mr. Bobby added. "Then I said, 'Look here, blackberries.' We all chuckled at the time. Then the hyenas came."

"At first, Mommy, the hyenas were as afraid of all that stuff changing as we were."

"I don't think they were hunting us. I think we sort of ran into one another in the confusion, back there in the middle, and neither side knew what to do next," Mr. Bobby explained.

Sarah was listening as she rode across the little dell they were walking in to the rise on the other side. A broad expanse of varied greens covered the gentle slope down to the river and up a long gradual rise from the opposite bank. A few groves of willows, river birch and hickories grew up along the edge of the stream as it wound from the north.

Sarah asked, "Did you guys run into any other people out here?"

The entire group stopped. One of the women answered, "When we first came out, we stayed close to camp, and there were lots of people. Some came closer, seemed to hear the singing, and they went into the camp. The others, which were a lot, seemed not to even notice us. They were all walking or running in different directions, but heading away from us." She pointed out and moved her arm in an arc as the rest of them followed her motion along the horizon.

"That was when there were hardly any big trees yet," another woman added.

Mr. Bobby broke in, leaning on his spear, "Then trees and blackberry bushes grew up fast, like you see 'em now." Sarah surveyed the arc of trees to the east and the north and forests lining the grasslands to their west.

The woman continued, "After that, the hyenas showed up, and we sorta stopped paying attention to the people."

Sarah asked, "So, where'd they all go?" The group shrugged their shoulders almost in unison.

"Maybe they're out there lying in this tall-ass grass," another man speculated. "Should we go look for them?"

Sarah looked out over the grasslands, closed her eyes to see what she could feel. She could sense bustling small animal life, mostly well out in the grasslands. *The dead being returned to nature,* she surmised, then turned back to the man. "Let's consider it with the group later. Right now, let's get everyone home safely. I think we've had enough excitement for one afternoon, don't you?"

"You bet, Mommy. Let's get home." At that, the group continued their trek back to the growing compound.

Sarah rode to the top of the hillock she'd crested earlier. The way was clear back to the camp as far as she could tell. She guided the horse closer to the still-forming forest. It was growing denser before her eyes. She moved close enough to peer into its darkness, but not so close, she hoped, as to encourage a predator to attack. She stopped to listen with her ears and spirit. Her horse was also at high attention, gazing into the woods, ears aimed in the same direction. He'd recognize danger before she would. Sarah lay against his neck. She could sense what he was sensing.

She could feel him become uneasy. Sarah focused her gaze into the woods. Something moved, deep in the woods, graceful and silent. She felt it more than saw it. She knew this animal . . . personally, and its spirit knew hers.

Her horse became agitated, and she took the hint. She turned and trotted back toward the group, which was moving with good speed toward their camp. She glanced behind her and saw the reflection of green eyes near the edge of the dark forest, where the sun low in the western sky flowed into the trees. She stopped the horse to sense who owned those eyes, stared into them and felt something big and graceful in her soul. The eyes lowered and were gone. She felt connected to whatever it was, even though she knew it was a predator . . . a big one.

She rode back and spurred her group on, moving them farther down into the shallow valley and out of the view of those eyes. She glanced back at the forest. Just new trees growing. No eyes. Somehow, Sarah knew he wasn't a threat, at least for the moment.

ELEVEN

Back in camp, the hyena event had convinced more of the Family of the need for the barrier. She'd learned about this sort of natural barrier from a documentary she'd watched on a tribe who lived in Kenya on the broad Masai Mara, a huge African plain known better as the Serengeti. The woman-only camp built this sort of barbed barrier to keep out large predators, like the hyenas and the owner of those menacing eyes, but also as a refuge from male-dominated traditional tribes. They were led by a marvelous and brave woman whom Sarah admired. Hers was based on their unique design. In this world, defending against humans was as vital as protection from predators.

Humans were her greater fear. While the fires would keep most animals away, it would draw men to them. For her to feel comfortable at night, this barrier had to be completed as soon as possible. As would be expected for Missouri and a location near a river, there were plenty of hawthorns, wild roses and other prickly bushes around for the purpose. The job, however, was tedious and, of most concern to Sarah, quite dangerous.

A young man had plucked some thick fuzzy lamb's ear leaves and was using them as makeshift liners for his hands. Every builder followed suit. It was a creative solution for handling the prickly brush that was being added to fill in the structure of the wall.

Marsha let her know that the latrine was finished. Sarah ran back to inspect it and was duly impressed, as were quite a few Family members who were interested in testing it out. Marsha was retasked with overseeing the barrier construction, and her team joined in on the efforts.

There were enough knives and stone tools for now. The stonecutter group joined in. Sarah asked Jazz to help the fishermen. Mark, the young man about her age, volunteered to go with her to "protect" her. Sarah obliged, too focused on the tasks at hand to sense the budding infatuation. The dry wood was piling up, and she hoped there was enough, so she ordered the wood gatherers to the barrier. New rope was directed to Marsha.

No one was surprised to see Tony and his crew sitting in the grass near the back of the camp, listening to Tony who stood before them, gesturing and ignoring the hard work being done by the rest of the Family. Sarah rolled her eyes, and Ms. Watson exchanged a knowing glance with her. The night sky was approaching, and the barrier was the top priority. These issues would be dealt with later.

Three of the older men were sleeping on the grass in the shade. Ms. Watson informed Sarah that they'd agreed to be the nighttime alarm system. While they weren't good for much in these labor-intensive beginnings, they could serve a purpose overnight while the hard-working young people slept. They wouldn't be able to fend off much, but they could awaken those who could. Sarah nodded, adding a thumbs-up. "I hadn't thought of that, Shirley." Ms. Watson appreciated the gesture.

Sarah laid the wood for the main fire. Extra wood lay in piles nearby. Amy was looking over the haul from the gatherers along with the herbs she and Herb had found. Sarah could see Amy's mind working on how she was going to make this into something both palatable and reasonably satisfying to this number of people.

A shock of fear from the horse shot through her like a knife. Tony and his two henchmen were approaching the horse. Tony was wielding a crude, untipped spear. The taller man had one of the rougher knives, and the short stocky man had a stick he'd sharpened. The other seven members of Tony's gang followed several paces behind them. Sarah sprinted through the compound, dashing past astounded Family members, leaped into the air, past the three attackers, slid, spun and stood her ground between them and the horse.

"Well hello, sweetheart. Don't you look sexy. Wanna have a go?" Tony moved his pelvis back and forth toward her, his penis becoming aroused.

Sarah stared straight into his eyes. "Not much to work with, Tony." There were snickers from the gathering crowd. "Now get your sorry asses away from my horse." Two large men stood behind Tony. Five women and two paunchy men stood behind them, unarmed but trying to act tough.

Tony puffed up his chest and ignored the insult to his manhood. "Getting ready to kill our dinner. That horse will feed everyone. We're going to kill it, cut it up and have us a nice barbecue. Now get outta the way!"

Sarah's eyes burned in the fading light as she felt all the spirits well up inside her. "No one is touching this horse. Not now. Not ever. You understand? He is not to be served for dinner tonight or ever!"

The taller man spoke up, "Well missy, what are you going to do to stop it?"

"Yeah, I've had it up to here with your bossing us around all day," the shorter one added. The seven in the rear yelled in support.

"Who do you think you are anyway?" Tony asked as his men began to approach her with their weapons. The others in the camp gathered around. Sarah knew she'd been bossy. Perhaps others felt like Tony and his gang. *Doubt.* She could feel the darkness inside her. She closed her eyes and forced it back down, and the big Bear's claws confined it.

Tony perceived the brief moment of weakness and moved forward, spear raised. Sarah stood her ground, refocused, her eyes boring into Tony's. Then she took a step toward him. Tony raised his spear toward her neck. She could see a hint of fear in his eyes. Even more, she could sense weakness in his soul and something else she couldn't pinpoint.

"Move missy, or I'll cut you up, and we'll have you both for dinner." He reached the spear out toward her, raising it close to her neck. She didn't budge. She could feel her spirits rising, her strength increasing, her rage roiling beneath her skin. Her eyes burned hot. The eyes of her assailants lost their edge as fear crept into them.

In a voice more powerful than any they had heard from her, she bellowed at Tony, moving her neck even closer to his spear, "No one touches this horse!" Sarah snatched the spear, ripping it from Tony's hands, pulling him with it. Tony stumbled. Sarah slammed her bear-strong hand into his chest, driving him back and knocking the breath from him. His two henchmen caught him, gave him the sharpened stick and pushed him back toward her. He gained his balance, eyes glaring at her, and charged. She danced to her left and drove the butt end of the spear into Tony's midsection with both arms, lifting him two feet off the ground. Tony grunted as the sharpened stick fell from his hand. Sarah flicked Tony hard right, sending him sprawling, rolling over in the grass until his butt hit a tree.

Some in the Family laughed. Others were awed. Tony was enraged. "Attaaack," he gasped to his cronies. "Damn it!"

The two henchmen stared at Tony and then at her. She just smiled and beckoned them. They snarled and attacked. As they did, she moved like the Tiger within her, slamming Tony's spear like a baseball bat into the gut of the taller of the two men, doubling him over and snapping the spear. Sarah caught his flint knife before it hit the ground. The far end of her spear spun toward the seven, catching one of the men in his soft stomach. He doubled over and fell back into one of the women, knocking her to the ground.

The tall man, still gasping for breath, stumbled backward several yards and fell into two of the other women. They all fell hard to the ground.

Sarah flipped the spear and turned the jagged broken end on the shorter attacker, the stone knife in her left hand. Sarah smiled as she stepped forward and said in a much softer voice, "You next?"

Ms. Watson, who'd watched the entire scene, stepped to the front, flanked by Joe, Erika and a few others. "OK. Enough!"

"Ma'am," the shorter man said while backing down from Sarah's stare, "this horse would make a great meal for this group tonight. We were going to do our part by killing it, cutting it up and preparing it for tonight's protein. What's wrong with that? It's just a dumb horse, and we're all going to starve to death out here."

Tony scrambled to sitting in the dirt, back against the tree, breathing hard. "And she attacked me with that spear, nearly killing me." She felt

Tony's fear dull his effect on her. Tony's crew was struggling to get back up and said nothing.

The English woman strode forward. "'At's bull, Tony. You 'ad that spear, and you threatened Sarah with it, putting it up ta her neck, ya did. She jus' grabbed it and threw your sorry arse on the ground. You started it with her, and she finished it with you. Tony, you horse's arse, ya lost."

This would be the last time this woman hung around with Tony. She strode defiantly to a position beside Sarah. "I'm truly sorry I led these arseholes in here!"

Sarah closed her eyes for a split second and composed herself, calming her spirits. Nearly the entire Family had gathered around them. The crowd was hushed, awe in their eyes.

"Look, I realize that horsemeat would be an appealing meal, but this is not an ordinary horse. You don't understand this right now, but this horse and I are connected. He's a part of me, of my soul, and I'm a part of him and his. Killing him would be killing a part of me, and I will not allow it. Do you all understand? I knew he was in trouble, and I always will know, well before you can do anything to him. This is a strange new world. The animals are not all food or enemies. We have more allies than you now know."

Tony got back to his feet and joined his friends. Sarah could see the anger in his eyes. She rose tall before him. Tony had felt firsthand the tremendous strength that Sarah possessed—much greater than her frame would indicate was possible. He had no desire to reengage her in front of all of these people, but he refused to give ground. He smiled cruelly at her then winked.

Ms. Watson took over. "OK, these disputes and misunderstandings will happen." Ms. Watson started toward Tony's followers, but they recoiled, turned and followed Tony back to their lair. Ms. Watson walked to Sarah instead, hands open. Sarah handed over the broken spear and knife.

"Everyone, back to whatever you were doing," Ms. Watson ordered. For a few moments, Sarah and Tony stood and stared at one another across the compound. Sarah felt blackness in his soul. It stirred the

Storm's dark spirits in hers. They were connected by it somehow. He'd need to be watched, but right now, she determined that he was harmless and frightened.

He smiled that creepy smile, and Sarah turned away. She connected with her horse, petting his big strong shoulder, but said nothing. The horse bowed his head to her, and Sarah bowed back.

TWELVE

"I'm sorry that happened," Ms. Watson said.

"Me too. It's inevitable. It's even logical." Sarah paused. "Shirley, it's just not an option."

"I understand. Molly and I will make that clearer around camp."

Jazz screeched! Sarah bolted up, then a male voice yelled, "I got one! I got one!" Jazz and a young man came running up from the river. A good-sized rainbow trout was impaled on the end of his spear. After many attempts, he had plunged a chip-tipped spear into the fish and the barbs had held. Sarah and Ms. Watson gave one another relieved smiles and headed toward the victors.

Amy was thrilled. "Excellent. Bring it over. Who knows how to filet this?"

A big hairy man with long, scraggly locks and a full, equally scraggly beard spoke up. "If'n you got a knife, I can filet any fish and not waste nothin'." He strode over toward Amy from the barrier.

Jazz, whose look betrayed her intimidation, handed him one of her knives. He ran his thumb along the blade, then balanced it in his hand and looked Jazz square in the eye. "You made this?" Jazz nodded. "Well done, young lady, well done. This'll do nicely. Sum'a my old steel knives weren't much sharper 'n this."

"OK, then, you filet that one, and you two go catch us some more." Amy was taking charge like she had in her restaurant. The burly man cut the fish off the spear and handed it back to the young spear fisherman, a tall, slender athletic boy with messy brown hair.

Gus reached out his burly hand. "Name's Gus."

"Jamie." And they shook hands.

"And you, missy?"

"Jazz."

"Jazz, is it? More into country m'self, but to each his own. Thanks for the knife."

"Yessir."

"Fine work, young lady, fine work indeed."

Amy interjected, "OK, OK, enough. We're running out of daylight, and we could use another fish or ten to feed all of these people." Amy turned to Sarah. "Sarah, any chance we can get a fire going?"

Sarah strode down to the river with Jazz and Jamie and found a nice piece of flint. After some searching, she found a decent piece of iron pyrite. It was down the river a bit past the lower falls along the base of a three-foot vertical cliff eroded by the river. She noticed yellow and reddish stains on the rocks and touched it. More imbedded crystals. *Iron ore.*

She returned from the river, gathered some dry grasses, some small twigs and some slightly larger sticks and knelt near the fire circle closest to the center of the camp.

She stopped for a minute and stood up. "Hey, Tony."

"Yeah?" he turned and looked at her, his eyes softer somehow.

"Sorry about that. You OK?"

"Yeah?" He was clearly apprehensive, as he stood and walked toward her.

"Lucky break on my part. I understand your thoughts on the horse. Just not an option. We good?" Tony didn't nod, but Sarah took it as a yes anyway. "Any chance you can help me over here with the fire?"

Tony looked at his entourage, nodded at them, and they all strode over. Other members of the Family began to gather around to watch her start the fire, but Ms. Watson reminded them of the importance of the barrier. Several moaned, but they all returned to their duties.

Sarah turned to Tony. "Ever started a fire with flint and iron pyrite?"

"No."

"OK, watch close. I can't be the only person who can do this. Then would you and your friends be willing to tend to the fires? Get 'em laid and started? The other two have to be stacked."

"Sure. I can do fire." He smiled his creepy smile.

Sarah forced herself to smile back. "Sorry we got off on the wrong foot. These times are pretty insane." Tony put a hand on her back. Her skin rebelled, but she overruled it for the good of the Family.

"No problem."

Sarah could sense the dark power inside her pulling her toward him as the other spirits fought against him. The Family needed their dispute reconciled, but she wanted nothing to do with him. Her insides churned in the confusion.

She closed her eyes and took a deep breath. She opened them and knelt down beside the central fire circle. Tony smiled and knelt too close beside her. She explained the process and struck the flint on the pyrite. The second impact from her trained hands sent a spark into the dried grasses. A small flame ignited, and she blew softly on the grasses to heat them up. Her hands protected the smoldering grasses from the gentle breezes as she coaxed the fire into existence.

As the flames multiplied, she moved aside and turned it over to Tony. "Now add the twigs and then the sticks until the fire is strong enough to light the kindling laid at the base of the fire circle." She whispered so it would not seem as though she were providing him instructions. "You got this?"

He nodded. "Of course," *my queen!*

Startled at hearing Tony's thoughts, Sarah staggered as she stood. Staring at him, she backed away a step, stumbling over her feet.

Tony merely smiled back at her. With the main fire lit, Tony stood, turned to his crew and guided them to the circle in back to lay that fire.

Ms. Watson walked over to Sarah and put her hand on her shoulder. "Nice job. Maybe that'll help them assimilate."

"I have a bad feeling about him, Shirley. He makes my skin crawl."

"Me too." Ms. Watson patted her on the back. "I think I have the same effect on them, though. Word is, he has a thing for you." Sarah grimaced. Ms. Watson smiled gently as she left to attend to other matters.

Sarah turned and joined her friend. "How's that, Amy?"

"Fine. Now how are we going to cook on it?" she retorted.

She smiled at Amy. "That, my dear friend, is your problem."

The old men who were sleeping would have to keep the three fires burning all night. She hoped they could. Hopefully there'd be enough wood. Hopefully it wouldn't rain. Their very survival centered on her knowledge and skills, Ms. Watson's calm leadership and a lot of hope right now.

Light was fading fast. Tony and his crew had the back fire going and, to her surprise, actually turned to start on the western fire. Ms. Watson decided it was time to cease work on the barrier. It was farther along than Sarah could've hoped for, but not done by a long shot.

Down by the river, after much searching, Amy found a large rock that had a nice deep indentation in it from water pounding down from one of the more concentrated waterfalls above their pond. "Sarah!" Amy yelled, and Sarah ran down.

"You OK?"

"Sure. Check out this stone." Sarah looked it over. "You know, Sarah, considering this river wasn't here this morning but was, I guess, in a large concrete pipe, the effect of the water on this rock is amazing. It's as if it'd been there for centuries, millennia."

It was about 6 feet long and over 2 feet wide at the center where the indentation was. Seven of the men got their fingers under it as best they could. Sarah took the thicker end, but she couldn't get much of a hold. Erika and four of the strongest women jammed large branches as levers under the edge of the rock. Amy stood above them, "Alright, on three." Sarah summoned every ounce of her animal strength and, when Amy hit three, unleashed it on the rock. The mud acted like a vacuum, but it moved a little. Erika and her team forced sticks under it, and the team relaxed.

"Damn, Amy, big-ass rock," Erika said.

"Take your positions. Get your footing and fingerholds," Amy ordered. Everyone obeyed. "On three." There was a collective grunt as Sarah and the team brought everything they had to bear on that rock. It moved a bit more this time. Water rushed under the edges. Erika's team scrambled to jam sticks and rocks into the spaces, allowing the others to take a break. No one spoke this time as several of the men, fingers bleeding a bit, were replaced by others.

"Everybody good?" They all nodded. "OK, one more time. I can feel it. Ready . . . on three."

Finally, there was a loud sucking sound at Sarah's end as air and water rushed under the stone and the rock jerked up. The onlooking Family members cheered.

They lifted the downstream side from the streambed and turned it up against the falls. Amy and Herb washed the dirt and rocks off as the water flowed over it, and the team regained their strength.

A few of the original men rejoined the team, and Amy orchestrated nine of them to lift the huge rock from the stream and move it out of the river and up the embankment. Sarah took the heaviest end. Tony took a spot next to her, touching his body to hers. His presence weakened her and brought doubt and fear into her psyche, but again, she chose to endure him. The Family stood along the path to help.

Three women, at Amy's instruction, had constructed a semicircular rock wall upon which the huge cooking stone would be mounted.

The group battled the rock up the slope. Several others joined in. As carriers tired, they were replaced. Others cleared the path. As a Family, they wrestled that huge stone the 25 yards from the river to its stone base. They survived several times where the stone nearly fell as someone slipped or lost a hand-hold. Tony gave up early, and Sarah could feel a surge of power when he moved away. Tony gave orders as though he was in charge, but only his crew listened.

When the Family finally guided the stone over the wall and laid it on top, they let out a large collective breath and smiled, shaking hands, patting each other's backs, high-fiving and some even hugged. Sarah put her arm around Amy and pulled her close with a wink. Then Sarah found Tony and shook his hand. His smile was again softer. Sarah turned and walked back to the stone.

Someone, in a businesslike tone, commented, "That was a serious accomplishment." None of those corporate team-building programs could match what was happening in this camp in a single afternoon. A hush fell over the crowd as they stood gazing at the final structure. The group collectively exhaled.

Amy inspected it, ran her hand across it to gauge the angles. Then she asked that they adjust it a little to level it so it could hold a good amount of water for boiling the greens in the indentation created by the falls. Sarah and three young men jumped at the task. Murmurs slipped through the crowd as Sarah handled her end of the rock with relative ease while the three larger men struggled with the thinner end. Some additional rocks were stuffed under the edges to stabilize it. Again, they set the huge rock down to another collective exhalation.

They looked at Amy with anticipation. Amy bent down and sized up the position of the cooking stone. She rubbed her hand over it again to get a feel for it and then stood up.

"Looks great," she announced, ". . . for now." She aimed a grin at Sarah. The group cheered and patted themselves on the backs again. This time they turned toward their mates and children for congratulations and wandered off, chatting with new friends in their big Family. Tony hung around the cooking stone for a few minutes waiting for Sarah to come to him, but when she ignored him, he stomped off in a childish pout. As he approached his group, he held his head high and stuck his chest out.

Amy touched Sarah on the shoulder. "I think Tony wanted to talk to you, or maybe for you to talk to him." Sarah turned, and the two watched him walk off from the cooking stone.

Sarah shrugged. "Ames, I do not have time for that crap, and certainly not with Tony."

"I hear ya, girlfriend. He's a creepy dude." Sarah looked at her friend and smiled. Amy turned to the stone and admired it with her hand again. "What a great combined victory to end a long day, though, eh?"

"Yep. Awesome. Nice stone, Ames. Had to be the heaviest in the stream." Sarah said as she too ran a hand over the stone. "Man, that was heavy." Her right hand was bleeding a little, and Amy reached out to care for it, but Sarah brushed it aside. "I'm fine." Then she looked in Amy's eyes. "Ames, tell you the truth, I'm way more fine than I should be."

Amy smiled at her friend and patted her on the shoulder. "Yeah, thank heavens. Weird day, but nice work."

Amy did her best to scrub the stone as clean as possible with water from the stream, brought up in handfuls. Gus put the split fish filets on the slab. He and Herb then built a fire under the cooking stone in accordance with Amy's direction and lit it from the existing fire.

Amy surveyed their wares for dinner. There were enough berries for each person to have two with a few left over. The berries were held back for dessert. There was a large pile of greens and flowers, six morels and one good-sized fish. She sorted through the herbs. It would have to do.

Herb was adamant that they create small packets for latecomers. They'd be struggling and starving, and he wanted to make sure they had something for them. Amy and Gus agreed.

Ms. Watson instructed everyone to head down to the lower pond, below the waterfall, to wash their hands and anything else they wanted to. She guided them down and kept the line orderly. Tony pushed to the front with his group. Ms. Watson calmed those in line and spoke to Tony, who ignored her and entered the water as if he were king. Two girls splashed and washed him as he stood before the others. The two large men stood guard. When Tony was finished, he walked out of the stream, the two men and two women close behind. Ms. Watson sighed and guided the next group in. She, like everyone else, was too tired to fight with Tony tonight.

Sarah followed at the end of the line. As had so many before her, she walked into the water and rinsed her feet. She hadn't realized how sore they were. She knelt and splashed her face, feeling a sense of joy. The water was fresh and cold. She rinsed her arms, rubbed the dirt out of her small wound, which began to bleed. She focused on it for a second, her Elephant spirit coming forth, and like her legs during her run here through the thistles and briars, the small cut healed. She sat in the stream on a smooth rock beneath the broader falls and let the water cascade onto her head and shoulders. Others had done the same, and she was glad that she was last in the line and able to dawdle there a bit longer. She felt refreshed and exhausted at the same time. The entire day began to replay itself in her mind. *Was it just this morning that she'd dropped her girls off at the school that used to be right here? That was this morning?*

When she returned, she discovered that four more fish had been speared by Jamie, who was getting pretty good, and three more by Jamie's mother. Her young daughter was jumping up and down with joy. Mark had caught two more fish.

They each beamed as they brought their catches up to the cooking stone and each fish celebrated by the waiting Family. Gus took the fish, cut them from the barbed spears and held them aloft before he laid them on a wide log, his makeshift table, and fileted them. The filets were cooked on the flat portion of the cooking stone, seasoned with some herbs Amy and Herb had located not far from the camp. There wasn't much per person. The filets were rationed by Herb to each of the inhabitants as they came through a relatively orderly line.

Again, Tony pushed to the front and received the first portion. He demanded more, but Joe, Erika and two others restrained him, threatening to drag him from the line. Tony's henchmen stood up for him, but when Sarah walked toward them, Tony backed them away with a wink to her. If she'd had anything in her stomach, it would have come right up. She nodded and turned away.

Each Family member was fed one good-sized bite of fish from the end of a flint knife, but that bite was delicious. Smaller portions were retained for the latecomer packets. Sarah underestimated this team and was thrilled to have done so.

Amy steamed the greens, flowers and the crushed insects together. With a few selected herbs and the sweet flowers, the bitter greens were subdued and served by Herb to everyone in equal but substantial amounts, with some again held in reserve. Even the children ate their vegetables.

Amy then boiled the fish heads and bones in some water and tossed in some herbs and the morels that she'd cut into tiny pieces to flavor the soup. Eating the soup, the three realized, was a significant issue. How could they eat it without spoons? A woman found a hardened leaf that was somewhat spoon shaped.

"Will this work?"

Amy inspected it. "This'll have to do." The woman smiled at a friend and they gathered up as many more as they could find. Everyone in the Family had a leafful of the morel fish soup. That, too, was well received. Some remained in the basin of the cooking stone for the latecomers. The fire beneath was doused so that the cooking stone could cool down.

Finally, everyone received their two blackberries to finish the meal. Ms. Watson showed up beside Sarah, who felt their leader's hand on her upper back. "All in all, the first meal in this new world has been a success, don't you think?"

"Better than anything I'd envisioned. It was good."

They heard one of the young boys remark, "That was good, Mommy. I thought we'd have to eat bugs." Sarah and Ms. Watson smiled at each other.

Ms. Watson turned to attend to the group. Sarah smiled. She was proud of what they'd accomplished in one afternoon. *Good start.*

THIRTEEN

After the last blackberry had been savored, Ms. Watson turned to the Family and asked them to circle around the central fire. Sarah, Janie and Jazz found a place on the outside rim of the fire so Sarah could keep an eye on the edge of the woods. Ms. Watson walked over and stood to Sarah's right and addressed the new Family. She called several people by name and spoke to them. Sarah was too tired to pay attention. Ms. Watson sat down and turned to Sarah.

"Thank you so much for everything you did today." Sarah simply nodded.

Once everyone was settled, Ms. Watson rose to speak. The Family quieted. Ms. Watson was a presence. Even Tony's crew quieted. Sarah thought, *How long will this group put up with them?*

"This has, without doubt, been the most bizarre day in the history of humankind. The Wall," Ms. Watson said, giving a name to the Storm, "has changed everything. What I witnessed today was a miracle. Just a few hours ago, we were a small group of frightened children and a few teachers. Others arrived in various states of shock and panic, relieved at least to have found their child or children. We've all lost at least one person. I'll probably—well, not probably—I will never know what has happened to my two children and five grandchildren who live on what was once the East Coast of the United States.

"We're separated from so many, and we haven't taken time to grieve. There was important work to be done, and I, for one, am both amazed and thankful for the work that each and every one of you contributed in the face of this disaster. How, after all that, you worked together as a team to get that huge cooking stone out of the river, up that bank and onto Amy's rocks, I'll never be able to fathom, but it's right there, and you're to be congratulated all around. You rose to the occasion, and you should be proud of what you've accomplished."

She clapped and encouraged everyone to join in, "Celebrate with me the great works of this new Family!" The Family cheered.

When the applause began to die down, Ms. Watson continued, "I want to recognize a few people without whom I'm pretty sure we'd be in grave danger. You've all met and followed the guidance and bravery displayed by Sarah and her two daughters, Jazz and Janie. Please stand."

The three did so and received a rousing ovation. Sarah saw admiration and a little awe in the eyes of those gazing at her. She felt great. For the first time in a long time, she'd done things for people she didn't even know.

The three sat and returned their attention to Ms. Watson, who was looking back at Sarah as if waiting for permission to continue. Sarah nodded for her to carry on and remove this unwanted attention.

Janie turned to her. "Mommy, you're glowing, like when you saved your horse and when you were fighting the hyenas."

"What are you talking about? I'm sure I smiled, of course. I'm happy about all this."

"No, Mom, you didn't smile," Jazz said. "You, like, I don't know, had like an aura or something when you were fighting those guys and just now. Everyone saw it. Like Janie said, you sorta glowed."

"Different colors each time," Janie added.

"Shhh. Ms. Watson's talking." The girls turned back to the circle.

She could feel the spirits moving inside her. She closed her eyes and settled herself down. Thoughts about the day rolled through her mind. She shook her head and returned to reality. Apparently, Ms. Watson had acknowledged several others and was wrapping up.

"Many others deserve recognition, but everyone is to be credited for our successes as a Family this afternoon. Let's revel in a few of our victories today. Janie, would you like to tell the story of the hyenas?"

"Yes." The little 8-year-old leaped to her feet to tell the story. She bent over, put her hand to her forehead and looked both ways as she began, "We were out in the flat grass area searching for food." She reached high as she could, on her tiptoes. "Then out of nowhere, the trees grew tall." She bent down and slowly brought her hands up, fingers wiggling. "But a blackberry bush did too, so we got as many berries as we could." She mimicked picking them and popping one into her mouth. "There are lots." She opened her arms and pirouetted. "Then some hills rose from the flat ground right out there. We were scared. Ms. Caroline moved us to a flat space that wasn't changing, but *then* we ran right into those four hyenas. Mr. Bobby, Mr. Willie and Ms. Caroline were so brave as they fought off the mean ol' creatures, swinging their spears at them. I think the hyenas were as afraid as we were, but they turned at us and bared their big fangs." She imitated them and growled around the fire at everyone. "I screamed right back at them." She demonstrated, and everyone gasped and then laughed.

"And then Mom rode in on that big horse, and Miss Erika and Mr. Joe ran to help us with thorny branches and spears." She flailed in the air as though she had a branch and reenacted the rest of the story with great embellishment, dancing all around the campfire. Then she stood, chest out with pride. "We scared them all away, and they will never come back." The crowd clapped and erupted in cheers. Sarah had to admit that Janie was quite entertaining as her youngest plopped back down with a big smile. Sarah shook her head then grabbed Janie and hugged her close. She was so proud of her girls.

Ms. Watson asked that a few others tell stories of the day's accomplishments. Jazz and Jamie told the story of catching the fish and how hard it was. They were much shorter and to the point, though they told a good story. An older couple told a story about their journey, the insanity they'd witnessed on the way to this compound—the death, panic and futility—and how, following the singing voices that somehow made their way through the din of terror happening around them, they had arrived to find a bustling, cooperative group of people acting like there was a hopeful future ahead. They noted that it was as though only they could hear the music. Many in the Family nodded. Sarah, too, could relate to their story, but she noticed that Tony and his band were incredulous. They'd arrived because the English woman heard the singing. It seemed like such a long time ago.

Ms. Watson then took over. "Now to the hard part. We need to grieve our losses. They're great and very real. I want to go around this circle of new Family members one by one. I want you to provide us your first name and the first names of anyone else you're with, including your wonderful children. Last names are for the previous life, and we'll no longer need them to distinguish one family from another. We're one Family in unity with one another." Everyone nodded. "After you give us your first names, tell us who you've lost and tell us all you can about them. Now is the time to feel that loss, deal with it, get it out, cry and wail if you feel that's required because tomorrow, we have a lot to do in order to survive in these new times.

"Beside me, most of you know my trusted assistant and right hand, Molly. Molly, please tell us your story."

Molly told her story and began to cry as she concluded. She passed the storytelling to the next couple. They had two children who sat in their laps. An older child was off at a preparatory school in Virginia. The woman barely got their story out before breaking down. She held their children close to her and leaned into her husband's big arms. The stories brought tears to everyone's eyes as they moved around the circle. Everyone was crying and trying to be strong for their children and their newfound friends, but it was to no avail. Ms. Watson kept her cool as she guided each family through their story.

The stories of the children whose parents had never shown up were most devastating. The younger ones were sitting with the parents of other children their ages. The young teens who'd cut the rope grasses sat together. The Family often waited in silence several minutes for the speaker to regain control to get the rest of his or her story out. Ms. Watson commanded patience without a word.

The process took hours, but the effect was amazing. It was a washing of the souls of all who sat around the fire that evening. As each shared and then heard the story of those who followed, they cried for them as much as for their own losses.

As the stories progressed, Sarah realized how lucky she was. She had both of her wonderful children in her arms, and they had been marvelous. Her only loss was her husband, who'd tried to kill her and from whom she'd been running for over two years. She whispered to Jazz and Janie to do the introductions and to tell their story. The two girls agreed and began whispering.

When their turn came, the two girls stood, and Jazz began, "I'm Jasmine, but everyone calls me Jazz. This is Janie, my younger sister. Behind us is our Mom, Sarah. We lost our father. We have no idea what happened to him." They left out how terrible he was.

Janie chimed in, "He was far away when the Wall happened. We'll probably never see him again." Sarah smiled.

Jazz finished, "We're so glad to have such a big new Family and can't wait to be your sisters."

What a great end to the circle. The Family rose from their tears and applauded, yelling back various commitments to the new Family.

Ms. Watson stood again and raised her arms. The crowd fell silent again. "Thank you all for sharing. Thank you all for crying for each of your new Family members. Thank you so much, Janie and Jazz, for sending us into this night with the hope for a new and bright future.

"There are no mattresses. There are no blankets. It's still Spring in what was once Missouri, so it'll get a bit cold tonight. Albert, Terrence and Fred will be our night watchmen. They'll keep the fires going and stay alert for anything that could pose a danger. Please huddle as close as you can to your loved ones and even to those you don't yet know. Body heat and the heat of this fire are all we have to get through until morning. Feel free to migrate to the other fires to get closer if this isn't warm enough for you, but stay on the compound side of the fire and huddle together. I don't know about you all, but I'm flat-out exhausted."

Everyone agreed. Only Tony's crew moved to the southern fire. Ms. Watson sat staring into the flames. Small talk murmured throughout the crowd.

Sarah thought about staying up, but she couldn't, for the life of her, keep her eyes open. She and her girls lay down facing the fire, Sarah behind them with Jazz in the middle. For most, this would be a long and fitful night. This new world frightened everyone else. For Sarah, this was freedom. Freedom from the desperation of the old way of human life. Freedom from her ex-husband. Sarah was in her element and was relishing it, and this world was reaching back to her. She felt part of it, not just in it. She patted her children and laid her head on a smooth rock she'd found in the river. She was asleep within minutes.

FOURTEEN

Her Mom. Her Dad. Their faces smiling, then swirling, battered and bloodied. Old brown coffins swirled. Robert, smiling sweetly, like when she first met him, then blew up in her face, screaming, "You're alone! You'll always be alone!" Bourbon. His laugh echoed through her.

Sarah sat bolt upright in the grass. "They're dead. My Mom and Dad, it's my fault they're dead," she said aloud. The sobs came from deep within her. She was sweating and shivering. The cold of the morning gripped her. She closed her eyes and took several deep breaths to center herself. *They've been dead for years, Sarah. It was not your fault.*

The sun's rays were barely peaking above the horizon as she opened her eyes. No one had heard. She breathed in the fresh morning air as she surveyed the camp.

All but the three watchmen had fallen asleep. She was sure that utter exhaustion had overwhelmed the fear. Shivering and shaken, she wiped tears from her eyes. They didn't need to see her crying. She closed her eyes and began a mantra. Asha came to her, through mists of red, her four animals behind her: "We are with you. Defeat the darkness. It is coming. Love your Family." Her spirits engulfed the horrid memories as her breath settled and her mind cleared. After a few minutes, she opened her eyes, ready for the day. Shaken, but ready.

The fire was still going, but the store of logs was dwindling. One of the old men saw her. She put her finger to her lips, and he nodded.

88

She stood and walked over to the watchmen. "How was the night?" she whispered.

"Peaceful and pretty quiet. Heard a few rustles in the woods, and a few people arrived that Ms. Watson helped, but nothing after that."

Sarah realized that by the time they'd gone to sleep, most, if not all, of the predators had called it a night as well. Dusk had been long past by then. Predators might be up now that light was returning.

"Keep an eye out. Now is prime hunting time for things out there." She smiled and patted the old man on his back. He returned the smile, but his eyes betrayed his exhaustion.

The realities of the day pushed her personal issues aside. They'd eaten everything they had the night before. The few who'd arrived had devoured the packets of food Herb had set aside. There'd been one left, and it was divided among the three watchmen as a midnight snack. It wasn't much, but it had helped.

No coffee. Now reality was sinking in. Even on their hiking trips, she brought coffee for the morning. She returned to the girls and touched their shoulders. "Jazz, Janie, wake up."

"Whaaa . . ." Jazz uttered as her eyes opened.

Janie woke right up. "Shhh," Sarah warned, and Janie gazed around at the sleeping Family members.

Sarah whispered, "Everyone's going to be hungry when they wake up. We need to find some food. Janie, where were those blackberries, and were there more?"

"Sure, tons. I know just where they are." The young couple sleeping near them woke up. Sarah put her finger to her mouth, and they stayed quiet.

"I'm terrible with names," Sarah admitted.

"Mr. Willie and Ms. Caroline," Janie interjected.

Sarah nodded, and they returned the greeting. "OK, can you help out this morning?"

"Sure."

"OK, please get a couple of the spears from the watchmen and follow Janie out to gather as many blackberries as possible for breakfast."

"Can we bring our children?"

"Of course!" bellowed Janie, and she reached around their mother, grabbed their hands and pulled them to her. "We're a team. Small in stature, strong of heart." And she stood erect and as tall as possible. Sarah rolled her eyes, and Caroline looked pleased that her kids were being dragged out of their doldrums. The two children, younger students at the school, knew Janie well and were thrilled to be on her team. They started chatting as Sarah continued to enlist several others to join the excursion, armed with three sharpened sticks. Most had children who Janie enlisted in her personal entourage. They had only the one rough basket Janie had made the day before. Sarah kicked herself for not making others.

"Janie, see if you can make another basket as quickly as possible so you can carry more berries back."

The team was off with their duties. Janie found some supple young tree branches, and the adults used one of the knives to cut them. Caroline and Will helped craft some very rough but serviceable baskets for the blackberries and veggies.

As others awoke, it became easier for Sarah to focus. She had a Family. She assigned each person something to get busy on. Nearly everyone complained. They were hungry, tired, frightened or, in most cases, all three. The night had not gone well for most. It came to Sarah, *They probably dreamed of their great lives before the Storm and woke to a nightmare, while I have nightmares of my old life and woke to the wonders of this new world.* She felt a bit guilty about that.

Ms. Watson moved in, calming everyone she touched, then came up to Sarah, put her hands on both shoulders and looked her in the eyes.

"Sarah, it's OK. We're all here for you." Sarah gazed back at Ms. Watson.

"Shirley, I'm OK. I am *so* OK." Ms. Watson winked, released her and turned back to the Family.

Ms. Watson addressed the group. She was as clear as she could be about the importance of this next day's work if they were to survive. Erika joined them, listened to Sarah's instructions and took the lead in organizing the teams, which Sarah appreciated.

Though slow at the beginning, over the course of the morning, peer pressure, fear and the need to do something overcame them, and nearly everyone pitched in. Replenishing the supply of wood. Locating some herbs. Hauling water by hand to the basin. Jazz and her teams headed down to the river.

By the time the last of the sleepy heads was awake, food was being prepared. The fishers caught several. Later, Jazz would make the first fine spear tip and mount it on one of the fishing spears, that of the young boy Mark she "kinda liked a little."

Gus fileted and cut; Amy prepared and cooked; Herb dished out in even amounts small servings of blackberries, greens, flowers and a bite of fish to the Family for breakfast. Not much, but enough.

That morning, Joe and Erika, both former military, began to call this time after the Storm "A-Wall." A-Wall, Joe explained, meant "After the Wall" and, Erika continued, "It's a play on AWOL, absent without leave, since neither of us are returning to duty." They chuckled. Most simply smiled. The name stuck and became the way the days were marked since the Wall, which, Joe explained, was Day 0. So, this first full day was referred to by that afternoon as Day 1 A-Wall.

Sarah grinned at the two of them. "Sounds great." They seemed to have needed her approval for some reason. She smiled a "That's cute, works for me" grin and shrugged to Ms. Watson, who returned the look. It was good to have people begin to buy into the new way of looking at the world and living within it.

Jazz spent the entire day making tips for five hunting and fishing spears. The defensive spears would have to wait. An older man sitting with the women weaving ropes and now baskets put his skilled hands to shaping basic spears with a knife. Jazz's team sharpened and improved upon the tools they'd made the day before. Jazz handled it like a seasoned adult—probably better.

A couple of the other girls her age helped, all the while chattering on about the boys and giggling. A good sign of normalcy. Mark, who was tall, showed signs of future muscles and was very bright, hovered nearby, fishing or sitting by Jazz learning to create stone tools, helping find the right stones or delivering finished pieces to their end users. The girls tried to shoo him away, but Jazz gave him permission to hang around. He'd become a good fisherman and was becoming one of the better stonecutters. He did a lot of the initial shaping work and sharpened some of the tools dulled with use. Jazz enjoyed having him around.

Younger kids threw rocks or sticks at trees or chased one another until enlisted into an actual task. The youngest children drew in the dirt, stacked or laid out small rocks and sticks, frolicked in the big fishing pool between meals and played. The children were acting like children. Molly's team parented the orphans and cared for all the children communally, freeing up parents to do the other pressing chores required in the camp. In one day, a social comfort had grown up in the new community, at least among the youngsters.

In the late morning of Day 1 A-Wall, a big black bear moseyed up to the far side of the pool in their river. Molly and her team gathered the children to the edge of the water and told the children, "That's a bear." Their eyes grew big as they watched in awe. A few of the Family members were bathing below the falls in preparation for lunch. Jazz, Mark and the other toolmakers all stopped and watched. The bear, in turn, stopped at the edge of the pool and watched them, as intrigued as they were.

Jazz sent Mark to get Sarah and Ms. Watson. The big bear waded into the water, splashed around and sat down. The children laughed. Everyone else smiled as he sat there, surveying the water in front of him. Within a few minutes, he swiped a huge paw into the water and speared a fish with his razor-sharp claws. He clutched his other paw to it and ripped off its head with his large teeth and swallowed. The crowd ooooed and ahhhed.

As the big bear ate, Sarah walked down the bank and into the water. Their eyes met. She knew him. He was her bear. He was the Bear in her soul. The bear from the wall of the temple. The one who'd helped her save her soul from the Storm. This was that bear. They both knew it. She sank down on her haunches and sat there, not ten feet from the bear. The Family, even the children, were deathly quiet, but Sarah didn't notice.

The bear returned to the fish, gobbled up another huge bite, raised his attention from the remains of the fish and looked at her. She could feel him in her soul. Everything about him was pleasant and nonthreatening. It was clear that he had no interest in the band of onlookers. She and the bear looked at one another, experienced one another. Sarah knew without seeing her that he had a pregnant mate back in the woods somewhere. They were harmless.

Their spirits were connected, and she could feel her physical strength increase. The bears had the far side of the river protected. She assured the bear that they had his back as well. Then they sat for several seconds without communicating. The bear returned to finish the last vestiges of his meal and licked his paws. He searched the water for another fish, drove his claws into the water once more and speared a good-sized trout. He bit its head off. This one was for his mate.

Soon after the fish was secured, the bear looked at Sarah one more time, turned and sauntered off. Sarah rose, stood tall and turned to the group. "He's safe. He has a pregnant mate in the woods. He has our back over there, and we'll have his over here." Then she bounded up the bank and returned to her duties. Everyone looked at one another in amazement and doubt.

The bear would come down to the river to bathe and grab a meal almost every day. Occasionally, he brought the female bear down to the river. Sarah came down when possible and spent special time to meet her bear's mate, always from about 6 to 10 feet away. The mate was not *her* bear, but they connected. Not as deeply as her and the male, but they connected.

Sarah knew that it was great to have the bears guarding the opposite side of the river. Other predators tended not to invade the familial territory of a big black bear. She didn't immediately relate the depth of her connection with the bear, though after the horse encounter, most realized she was communicating directly with the bear. The story ran through the camp like wildfire.

Sarah's focus turned to feeding this growing family. They needed more protein than they could get from the fish they were catching in their little pond. There were dozens of dogs wandering the grasslands. Sarah carefully selected four and killed them for lunch. Gus prepared to cut them up out in the grasslands. Before he started, Gus looked up and across the field toward camp. "Sarah," he said, pointing his knife.

Sarah turned. Claire, a woman in her fifties of medium height, quite overweight, who ordinarily had a pleasant demeanor, was striding toward them as fast as she could. "Sarah," she pleaded, tears running down her face, "please don't kill any more dogs. It's not right. I raised and trained dogs in the old world. They're pets, not food."

Sarah took a moment before responding. She exhaled. "Claire. This was a hard thing for me to do. Gus and I selected the older, fatter or lame dogs. Actually, they selected themselves. They had no chance to survive in this new world." She put a hand on Claire's shoulder and looked her in the eyes with as much understanding as she could. "The dogs selected were going to be food for other predators or for our Family. We need the meat, bones, fat and hides if we're going to survive. We'll leave the strong dogs alone."

"I'm sorry, but I can feel it when you kill them. It hurts."

"What do you mean, you can feel it?"

"I don't really know. I don't really feel it when a predator kills them, but I know. I can feel it when you do it. It hurts."

"Come with me." She and Claire walked to the four dogs Sarah had just killed. Gus was there, about to skin and cut them up. Sarah waved for him to wait, took Claire's hand and knelt beside the dogs. "Claire, can you thank these dogs for allowing us their bodies so that we may survive?"

Ms. Watson walked up behind Claire, put one hand on her shoulder and took Claire's hand with the other and knelt beside them. Claire knew what she needed to do. She took a deep breath. "We are only humans. We are no better than any of the animals in this world. We need this meat to survive." Claire paused. Sarah could feel Claire connecting to the spirits of the dead and the living dogs. The dogs in the fields gathered around them. Claire continued with more confidence, "Just as you do, we only take what we need. All of us will survive. We will work together to become one. Thank you for your bodies that we might live."

Claire opened her eyes and turned to Sarah, her eyes moist, tears streaming down her cheeks. "Thank you, Sarah."

Sarah spoke from the spirits of her soul, "Claire, you have the gift with dogs that I have with bears, horses and other animals. As long as you are within reach of my spirit, you will have this gift. Use it wisely, as I know you will."

Claire stood, bowed to Sarah and walked out into the grasslands. The other dogs followed her. She spent the afternoon connecting to each one. Sarah could feel it. It was good. For the first time since the Storm, she realized that her connection to this world was bigger than herself.

FIFTEEN

The skills of the various teams improved. The tools they had to work with were improving and becoming more numerous and varied. Jazz could make almost anything. The barrier was farther along, though building it was a slow process. As Sarah sat to tan the hides of the dogs, a young woman, strong and stout, several inches shorter than Sarah, asked if she could help. Her father had been a taxidermist, and she knew her way around a hide. Sarah was happy to turn the job over to her and explained how to use brains from the animals in the tanning process.

Gus handled the rest of the animals. Dog bladders were converted for use moving water. They were small, but better than hands. Amy began to make sausage out of organ meats. Intestines were cleaned well and stuffed with the roughly chopped meat of the heart, liver, kidneys and brains along with some wild onions and herbs. Jaw bones with teeth, once dried, could be used as rough saws. Claws and bones were used for many purposes. The parts that couldn't be eaten or used, Claire fed to the dogs, who devoured them. Nothing was wasted.

Sarah taught a team how to build rabbit traps. Over the next two days, they built a rectangular box of sticks, bound together with thinner rope at the corners. To the frame, other sticks were tied and woven, leaving half- to one-inch squares. One end was left open. Two doors, long enough to overlap across the open end of the box, were constructed in the same woven manner. The vertical sticks in the doors were sharpened. The two doors were attached, sharpened ends toward the middle, with rope to the open end of the trap: one on top and the other on the bottom. Tendons from the dogs were used as rubber bands to pull the doors closed over the opening.

Once the trap was moored in place and sweet clover was placed inside as bait, the lower barbed door was pushed down inside the box, below the clover on the bottom, and kept in place with a small stick with a crook in it. The top door was also forced up against the top of the trap. The tendons were thus stretched and would pull the trap closed when tripped. The two doors were connected so that once the bottom one was tripped by a rabbit, both closed.

The trap was triggered as the rabbit crossed the lower barbs to get to the clover inside. If the rabbit tried to back out, the sharp sticks painfully closed on the rabbit's body, digging into its skin. The rabbit either moved forward inside the box to ease the pain or impaled itself on the barbs trying to back out. Either way, the rabbit was trapped. Sarah selected a young blond man to lead a few others on crafting the traps.

Sarah and Marsha discussed the need for a smoker for extra meat or fish. Marsha and her team created a pretty good design before she went over it with Sarah, who brought Jazz into the conversation.

"It'll be built tomorrow," Marsha announced, shaking Sarah and Jazz's hands before gathering her team and heading to the dinner line.

The first full day A-Wall was fruitful. After a slow beginning, most everyone had worked hard and were exhausted from their efforts. Erika had made sure that they'd rested and drank enough water during the day. The lunch break had been long for many. This was more physical work than most had done in their entire lives. Some couldn't return to work after lunch, while others worked nonstop and had to be forced to take breaks. Roger, who was a performer, was ridiculous. About two inches shorter than Sarah, he was in phenomenal shape and took joy in what he was doing, regardless of what tasks he was assigned. Sarah was thrilled to have people like Roger in the fold.

All spent a fair amount of time in the river cooling their feet and rinsing themselves off. It was spring, so the day was warm but not hot, the sort of day that was easy to work in.

Like the work, meals were not what this group was used to, but few complained. The Family ate three small but healthy meals that first full day. Sarah was happy with the overall mood in camp. Many patted her on the back or took her hands in theirs to thank her for "saving their lives." She could feel how grateful they were and thanked them for their hard work and dedication. Some of the fear was abating, or perhaps they just didn't have time to show it, and by nightfall, all were too tired to think about it.

As Sarah was walking through the compound, she heard a "Psst, psst" sound. She stopped. "Psst." She heard it again and turned to her right. "Down here."

Sarah looked down and to her left. A sweet older lady in the group who made rope, baskets and the like beckoned Sarah over with a long thin finger. Sarah squatted down beside her. "Hello, Miss Sarah, I'm Marge."

"Very nice to meet you. That's a very nice strand of rope you have there."

"Thank you, but that's not why I called you over. I think you should know that that awful Tony guy is trying to spread rumors about you around camp. He's trying to get people to fear you because you can talk to bears and horses."

Sarah looked up and saw Tony and his team lounging by the south fire. Like he always did, he sensed her, turned, smiled and winked. She turned away and took a deep centering breath to calm her spirits. "Marge, thank you so much. I think Tony's harmless," she lied to Marge and a bit to herself. "He's frightened and out of his element, like all of us, and the two of us didn't exactly get off on the right foot. Thank you very much. I'll keep my eyes and ears open."

"Me too, sweetie. You're doing a great job around here. Hate to see a punk like that Tony mess things up."

Sarah giggled and so did Marge. Sarah patted Marge on the back and stood up.

Sarah looked back toward Tony, their eyes met, and he winked at her. As always, the dark power inside her jumped, and she turned away, breathing deeply, but the unrest was suddenly deeper, stronger, more menacing, closer.

"You OK, honey?" Marge asked.

"I'll be fine. Watch that group for me, will ya?" Marge nodded. Sarah did not look back in Tony's direction.

The Family bathed and lined up to eat. Tony tried to move to the front of the line again, but tonight the Family would have none of it. He was forced to wait his turn.

Sarah bathed last, ate last and sat in the same spot around the fire with her girls. Ms. Watson stood to her right and led the meeting. She asked Sarah to speak, so she stood and thanked everyone, then bowed her head to them. Everyone clapped for her, and she sat back down, red-faced. Jazz and Janie smiled, and Sarah hugged them to her.

"Did I glow this time?" They both shook their heads. "Good."

Several additional people had arrived since the evening before. Some were in the infirmary, but those around the fire shared their grief. The Family shared their tears. Sarah tried to pay attention but couldn't, thinking about the next steps. Tony's team slunk to the back fire.

Roger, who it turned out was a marvelous storyteller, regaled them with a wonderful fairy tale that had nothing whatsoever to do with their predicament. His long brown, unruly curls flew about him as he danced through the story. He enlisted Janie and a few other children in the telling. He and his troupe received quite the applause.

Albert, Terrence and Fred served as the night watchmen again. More people fell asleep quickly than had the night before. Sarah lay awake, fearing the darkness insider her and the memories it dragged up when she slept, but exhaustion prevailed.

SIXTEEN

For the second morning, Sarah woke with a start, tears in her eyes, nerves jangled, memories flooding forward. Nightmares. This time it was still very dark. The chill of the night behind her, the warm glow of the fire in front. Her girls lay asleep. She'd taken them from the only family they'd ever known, Robert's family.

She looked around. No one saw her distress. Again, she took refuge in the pose her mother had taught her and fell quickly into a deep meditation. Asha's misty visage appeared, red flowing chiffon, the Tiger, Bear, Elephant and Horse at her side: "You had to leave Robert's family. Sarah, do not doubt your love. You must become stronger. Feel your strengths. You must defeat the darkness. It has arrived. You must become ready. Learn and feel. Love your Family." She was gone.

Sarah opened her eyes, confused and shaking. *What did she mean? What's arrived? What darkness? Where is it?* She could feel the pain of the loss. Tears streamed down her face as she surveyed the compound. More people were up, including both Jazz and Janie. She wiped her eyes as best she could, took another deep breath, focused on the gravity of her responsibilities, pushed her issues to the back.

She breathed deep, smelled the sweet air, let the spirits of this new world envelop her and felt the strength they brought to her. Centered, more relaxed and focused, Sarah rose to begin another day trying to help her new Family survive, but she also began to look for "the darkness" Asha had warned her about, whatever that was.

Breakfast was fish, dog sausage, greens and berries. The trappers promised rabbits would be added to the menu soon.

Erika was now organizing the teams. There'd been quite a bit of shuffling of duties that morning at breakfast. People piped up as to what they could do, wanted to do and didn't want to do. Erika did a great job of keeping them balanced. To his credit, Tony's team maintained the fires, though the task was not terribly consuming. He now had twelve in a crew that did little else but cause problems. The women catered to the men like servants, and the entire spectacle was becoming a source of complaint among the Family. *A people issue for Ms. Watson,* she thought, but something else gnawed at her. He seemed . . . stronger.

Rhonda was a master bowman and took charge of the hunting crew, which still only had spears, but at least now they were stone-tipped. Samantha had thrown the javelin in high school. Marshall had been a small-college quarterback. Samantha taught Marshall how to hold and launch a spear, and Marshall helped her quicken her throwing motion.

The man who carved the spears was called Ol' Mac. A sculptor, he began to craft a bow from a piece of hickory Rhonda had chosen for the purpose. He used one of Jazz's best knives and did his best to make it according to Rhonda's specifications.

As hides were prepared, the older women made rudimentary sandals. Foot injuries were by far the largest issue facing the camp, especially for the wood gatherers. For many, even a layer of untanned and somewhat slimy dog skin under the foot, tied with rope, was better than bare feet. Since they broke down rather quickly, they were not ideal and therefore were given out sparingly to those working in the forests. Bobbi, the young taxidermist, was working on tanning the hides, many now scraped, washed and stretched between trees, as best as she could, but it would be days before they had useful tanned hides.

Sarah was solving problems, crafting solutions and guiding the work. She poured her inner turmoil into her work. She was consulted over the smallest things but remained patient and helpful. It was coming together. People were focused on the task at hand instead of the challenges of their situation.

Sarah met with Marsha, who was leading the design and construction of the barrier.

"Looking good, Marsha."

"Sarah, by this afternoon, the skeleton of the barrier will span the entire opening between the trees." Marsha spread her arms. "I've worked out how to craft a gate in the opening. It'll keep unwanted animals out and allow Family members to exit and enter quickly. Yesterday, we dug those two holes there." The two walked over to the three men working on the gate. "We found those two sturdy hickory limbs in the wood piles. There's a limestone outcropping downstream, and my three young bucks here broke some off and crushed it."

"We hauled it up here and mixed it with sand and pebbles from the river bank and poured it into the holes there," the blond man chimed in.

"Then we dumped in plenty of water," a brunette woman added.

"And, presto chango, overnight it hardened into a passable concrete around the posts." Marsha was beaming.

Sarah pushed on the posts. They were solid. "That's some great work."

"Marsha asked the ladies to make us some thicker ropes for the gate. They're gettin' good," another person in the team said. Sarah knew none of their names. "Here it comes now." Mark arrived with rope in hand.

Sarah looked at it. "Nice." The group smiled.

Marsha said, "So, we're going to cut some 2- to 3-inch diameter branches with these nasty blades Jazz's team is crafting."

"Makes our work much easier," said the big blond man, whose nose looked broken—perhaps from a fight? He was one of Marsha's "bucks."

"That girl's good," said a dark-haired, shorter plump man, who she would find out was a chemist. Sarah smiled.

Marsha was excited. "We'll use the new thicker rope to lash the branches together into a frame with cross members that are strong and solid." She guided Sarah over to the posts. "The gate'll be mounted so that it only opens out. A rope'll be run from the opening end of the gate here and over a Y-shaped branch about here."

"That'll allow an entering Family member to grab the rope and yank the gate open," said the brunette woman, who was quite tall and muscular when she stood up from her work.

Another woman, short and slim, spoke, "Inside here, a rope will run from the opening end of the gate there, across another Y-shaped branch here." She pointed to a small stick in the ground.

"On the end of that, we'll tie a very heavy stone. That one there. I picked it out." The man, another of the bucks, Sarah figured, was short but muscular, like a bodybuilder.

Marsha took over, "This is designed so that once through, the stone can be knocked off a pedestal to pull the gate closed behind the entrant. At night, the stone will be taken off the pedestal, and along with a couple of other mechanisms, the gate'll be locked from the inside."

"It'll be covered in thorny rose vines and stuff like the rest of it to keep outsiders away," the blond man added.

"Brilliant. I love it." Sarah was thrilled, and the group was all smiles.

Marsha looked at her team then turned to Sarah. "The gate'll be finished by the break for dinner today and ready to be tested."

While the building team completed the barrier across the expanse of open ground between the two sets of woods, Erika and Marsha composed a team to work on the barrier within the trees of the two wooded areas: first to the edge of the river and then around the east side of the encampment. Hawthorn branches were roped in between trees, woven with roses and brambles as had been done with the front barrier. By the call to dinner of Day 2 A-Wall, Sarah felt their compound would be protected pretty well.

Although it would take a few days to finish, the skeletal barrier began at the sharp bank of the river at the southeast corner of their compound, about 8 yards east of the latrine, and ran north a few yards deep into the edge of the eastern woods in an arc to the elm that marked the opening into the grasslands. The section of the barrier the group began with on Day 0 ran west in an arc about 20 yards across the opening just past the southern gate post. The outer wall of the barrier began 8 yards east of the northern gatepost, creating an overlap, then arced west to the northwestern woods, then 20 yards or so through those woods to the top of the rapids north of their fish pond. Their river arced around their western flank, flowing south through the grasslands, into the northwest woods, past the western edge of the barrier, then down the strong rapids, over the falls into the 30-foot-wide fish pond, then over the wide 4-foot-high falls that led to the smaller pool in which everyone bathed, then down more rapids and into the rushing trough below the latrine and below the southeastern end of the barrier. Sarah knew that the pools in the river weren't great protection but felt relieved to have her friends, the bears, on the other side.

While many of the Family were resting in the late afternoon, listening to the children and the few adults who were singing, the guard yelled from the barrier, "People. People. There are a bunch of people coming!"

Sarah and Ms. Watson ran to the barrier. There was a good-sized group of people heading their way from the west. They could clearly hear the singing.

"They're Family," Sarah blurted out.

"How do you know?" Ms. Watson asked.

"They can hear the singing." She turned to the rest of the Family and yelled to them, "They're Family! They're our Family. Come on! We have to help them." Sarah jumped off the log, opened the nearly finished gate, which squeaked loudly, and ran out into the field.

Many of the adults came out to meet, greet and help the newcomers into their compound. Sarah stood on top of the big mound, with the soft voices of the children behind her, serving as a beacon for the group.

A little over 40 new residents were welcomed in, which meant more mouths to feed. Luckily, Rhonda and the hunting crew returned with a nice buck tethered across two spears.

"Look what we killed for—" Rhonda saw all of the new people, stopped talking and laid the deer on the ground. "Oh my goodness. I guess we'd better go get something else. Welcome . . . everyone?" Sarah smiled at her positive attitude. Rhonda grabbed some jerky that Gus had dried over coals from the campfire, laying the meat inside a simple four-wall structure made from sticks they'd tied to four corner posts pounded into the ground. The hunting team traded in their spears for newly tipped ones and headed back out. "We'll see what we can catch. Save us some food."

The deer was slaughtered. Fish were caught. Greens, flowers and berries were gathered. As the Family prepared a small meal for them, the newcomers were guided down to the river to drink and wash. Famished, some bleeding, and all exhausted, they returned from the river to some food. More was coming, doled out in equal portions by Herb's team. A few objected to the small portions. One man demanded more for his children, but Joe and another guard made it clear that such behavior wasn't appropriate in this Family. Ms. Watson put a hand on his shoulder, and the man quickly nodded and sat down with the new group.

SEVENTEEN

†heir presence, along with the numerous other small groups and the occasional individual that Family members had found wandering by, would impact dinner tonight. Sarah figured there were over 120 Family members now and told Ms. Watson, "More workers, but more mouths to feed." Ms. Watson nodded.

As the starved newcomers ate, the Family gathered around them. Ms. Watson stood before them. "Welcome to our Family. My name is Shirley, though everyone here continues to call me Ms. Watson for some infernal reason." The Family members laughed, and the newcomers smiled, perhaps for the first time since the Storm. "Beside me is Sarah. Sarah is our guide, our leader. She and her girls, who are around here somewhere, have a unique set of skills that have allowed us to survive. They and those whom they've been teaching will teach you those skills. Please follow Sarah's directions and cooperate with everyone else in your new Family, and we'll all survive." Sarah stepped forward.

"This is Joe. Joe's in charge of security. Do what he says, and you'll have a better chance of staying safe." Joe stepped forward.

"Next to Joe is Erika. She's our organizer. She coordinates all of the workers and details." Erika stepped forward. Sarah hadn't realized how quickly the leaders had stepped into clear roles within the Family.

Ms. Watson introduced Molly's, Marsha's, Amy's and Tony's teams. Tony stood as tall as he could and began, "Welc—"

"Ahh, there's Jazz and her sidekick Mark," Ms. Watson interrupted. The two teens blushed to the further amusement of the crowd. "Jazz is a master stoneworker. Her team makes all our tools. Mark and, let's see, Jamie over there, his mother Maxy, and there's Frank," she pointed out each person she introduced, "and Taneesha, over there, are our fishermen. They fish with spears, but John, over there, is building traps to make catching food more efficient." Sarah began to put names with faces.

"There's Janie. Janie's our resident botanist. She and her team scour our neighborhood for edible and medicinal plants." Janie, ever the clown, bowed and curtsied. Everyone giggled. Sarah rolled her eyes. Ms. Watson had a way of making everyone feel important and special.

"Rhonda's the leader of our new band of hunters. That deer is courtesy of that group. They are back out now trying to bring home something else for dinner to feed this growing Family. Today, which is only Day 2 in what we call A-Wall, is our first real foray out into the woods to hunt with stone-tipped spears. Jazz's new spears have made hunting and fishing a great deal easier.

"This is a true cooperative. Everyone pitches in. There's a great deal to do for us to stay alive, and this group that arrived before you has done a lot of work to create the compound you're now inside. We can't afford—and won't tolerate—complaining, laziness and, most of all, any sort of bigotry or insensitivity." Sarah saw Ms. Watson's eyes move toward Tony, who clearly received the message. He glared back at her. "All are welcomed and loved for who they are and what they bring to the group." She returned her gaze to the newcomers.

"We have a lot more people to feed, and dinner isn't that far off. We," Ms. Watson said, pointing to the team she had introduced, "will be coming around to meet everyone and find out more about you. Tonight, you'll introduce yourself to the entire Family, of which you're now a part, and we'll have some time for you to grieve, which we feel is critical and have all dedicated time to. Stay seated, relax, and we'll be with you shortly." Ms. Watson nodded to Molly, who ran off to lead the children and immobile adults in a song to soothe the spirits of the newcomers. Many others joined in. Sarah loved the near-constant music in this place.

Ms. Watson turned to the leadership. She split up the group of new-comers so that each of the leaders could take part of the group. They each began to introduce themselves to their assigned charges, found out what they could about each newcomer and tried to determine where they could fit into the Family. Of Sarah's assigned newcomers, one of the women had a funny name and taught yoga and meditation. Sarah had an immedi-ate connection to this woman, though almost as immediately forgot her name. As with the horse and bear, the name seemed wholly unimportant.

There was a plumber, an estate-planning attorney, two bankers, a CPA, a couple who managed rental property, a hairdresser, a cosmetolo-gist, a hand model, a computer coder, an electronics technician, a mobile app developer and a television show producer among her group. Sarah realized how many people had spent their lives dedicated to becoming something that'd have almost no translatable value in this new world. In their minds, they were lost. She knew they had skills they didn't yet understand.

She focused on hobbies and other experiences. She evaluated their bodies to determine what sort of physical labor they could do. Most of all, she listened. These people, like those who'd come before, needed to share. They were confused and desperate, and she did everything in her power to comfort them and assure them that they were in a good place, as good a place as there was these days.

As Sarah settled each of the newcomers down and assessed their strengths, she began to assign them to certain teams. The established teams were congregated in various areas. As they were assigned, the leaders point-ed to the appropriate group and the newcomers headed there. They were welcomed with pats and handshakes. Each was assigned to an existing team member who would become their personal mentor in both how to do the assigned tasks and in the cooperative philosophy of the Family. Sarah was thrilled at how much people had adapted in only 48 hours.

Ms. Watson floated above it all. She had grouped the teams, asked Molly and Janie to rally the existing children to involve the few newcom-er children and oversaw all of the interactions, the movement of people and their acceptance by the Family. She was a master at leading without appearing to be doing so. That was so comforting to almost everyone. The Family knew whom to turn to and knew that she'd provide guidance with a strong but steady hand, remaining fair to all.

People had skills that could translate. The hairdresser, Carmen, and the cosmetologist, Candy, found a need helping women with their hair, which had become tangled and uncomfortable. They established themselves in the bathing pond. They used their fingers to help untangle and comb hair. Jazz crafted very sharp but delicate razors by striking the edge of the right piece of conical flint so that it flaked off in long, thin, sharp-edged strips. Carmen and Candy used these to cut hair. They also worked with Marsha and Jazz to create two remarkably effective combs from a rabbit's ribs. The women called it the Boutique by the River.

A newcomer who was a pediatric surgeon, who everyone called Doc, took the lead in the infirmary in the back of the camp. The woman Sarah had seen back there greeted him warmly, and Amy happily passed on the title of witch doctor to Doc, settling herself back into leading the cooks with Gus and Herb.

Among the newcomers was an older fellow and his daughter. "We're pharmacists from Kennett, Missourah. We were at a seminar at the College of Pharmacy," the grey-haired man explained.

"The seminar was on techniques for mixing certain herbs as cures. I guess that'll come in pretty handy now," his daughter added. Sarah yelled to Amy to meet with them. The guy from Marsha's team who was a chemist, the two new pharmacists, Olivia (who Sarah learned was the name of the woman whom she had seen in back and was a military nurse) and a few others joined Doc in the infirmary as the medical team.

Rhonda's hunting crew returned empty-handed to Ms. Watson and Sarah. "We saw a herd of deer, but my throw was short. Weak-ass arm. Marshall was long. Sammy gave it a desperation throw, but the herd had scattered. Got our spears, but that's all we brought back."

Sarah and Ms. Watson patted her on the back. Much of the deer they had killed had been devoured by the newcomers. Herb had the rest reserved for dinner. Some of it was being made into sausage or jerky and smoked. The larger deer bladder made water transportation much easier.

Ms. Watson guided her toward the middle of camp. "I think I can lift your spirits, Rhonda." Rhonda's eyes grew huge, and she sprinted across the camp. Sarah and Ms. Watson watched her with smiles on their faces.

"Oh my God. Ol' Mac, that's beautiful." The old man handed her the bow, and she worked it in her hands. "Strong and flexible. Awesome." She bear-hugged Ol' Mac, who blushed.

Ms. Watson and Sarah met up with them, and Ms. Watson said, "Our good team here, who call themselves the Seamstresses, also made you a bowstring." It was finer and stronger than the rope they'd been making.

Rhonda took it from one of the women. "Oh my God." She held it and allowed it to drape between her hands.

The woman who'd handed it to her said, "It's intertwined with dog gut." Rhonda grabbed her face and kissed her on the cheek.

She blushed. "Thanks." The ladies all giggled.

Rhonda felt the bowstring in her fingers then took her time to stretch it onto the bow. Her smile reached from ear to ear as she tested the reaction.

Ol' Mac then produced a carved piece of hickory. "Thought you'd need a forearm guard." He got another hug from the huntress.

Two of the Seamstresses were next. "We sanded these long straight sticks young Ginger Ann found for us nice 'n smooth with a piece of sandstone." The young lady was maybe 7 or 8 and beamed at the recognition.

"We split the end here," the other woman continued, pointing to the arrows in her friend's hands. "Then we hardened it in the fire as Sarah instructed."

"Then we inserted one of Jazz's tiny stone tips."

"Oh my God, that tip is . . . well, I have no words," Rhonda said as she admired one of the arrows.

The first woman spoke again. "We secured the tip with sinew thread that Florrie there wove from dog gut. Sarah taught us that too."

The woman they called Sandy, also sitting, added, "That sinew stuff shrank and hardened tight. Made a nice streamlined tip."

"The work is beautiful." Rhonda was nearly in tears, and she ran to each woman and to the little girl and kissed them. The women handed Rhonda the other two arrows for the new bow. Rhonda, who was tall, nearly 6 feet, and very strong, with long stringy brown hair and a ruddy complexion, was overjoyed. She turned and picked up Ol' Mac, who was much shorter, grey-haired, weathered and much lighter than Rhonda. He swelled with pride. The three women, all of whom were short and heavyset, giggled.

"I'm itching to get back out there and nail us some real food." She jogged off, pulling on the bowstring, mounting and then sliding the arrows back and forth. She stopped and turned back. "This is awesome . . . AWESOME!"

They'd also tipped two stronger, straighter and more balanced hunting spears for Marshall, whose build resembled Rhonda's, although he was a few inches taller, his hair coarse, bleached blond but dark underneath as it began to grow out, and darker skinned than Rhonda. Samantha was much shorter, but sinewy strong, deeply tanned, with wispy brown hair and deep brown eyes. Several newcomers joined them. Rhonda put the entire team through some practice and taught them some hunting techniques.

Sarah added two young female distance runners, armed with shorter, lighter spears, and instructed them to mark their paths. First and most obvious was so that they could find their way back. Second was to allow a search party to come after them should they not return. They all felt more confident about the next day's hunting venture.

Sarah visited with John the trapper, who'd crafted four new rabbit traps. He showed her a few improvements he'd made. He was confident he would also bring in more protein for the growing Family.

That third evening, Day 2 A-Wall, dinner was fish, the rest of the roasted deer, smoked deer and dog meat sausages, greens, blackberries and a fish and morel soup, but enough had to be prepared for over 120 residents. There were several cooks now, but dinner still took a long time to prepare and eat. Again, the meal was measured in mouthfuls. Tony and his crew tried to encourage some to complain, with little success.

Ms. Watson met with Sarah. "Five more people joined his ranks, a couple from the newcomers. I, and others, think Tony's angling to take over. The rumor's swirling through the Family."

Sarah looked across the fire at Tony who turned, winked, smiled that creepy smile he had and led his team to the southern fire beside the infirmary. The dark spirits inside her fought against the strong animal spirits, and she turned away from Tony to quell them. She was not sure she could do anything if Tony did rebel. "We'll watch him. Watch him closely."

She stood in the middle of the compound and gazed at the small groups of Family members preparing for the next day. Veterans were teaching newcomers the ropes. Janie and her team were chatting and crafting some new baskets.

"Mommy, we think we found a bunch of root vegetables." She held up a carrot. "We're going out tomorrow with a shovel Jazzy made us."

The larger, stronger smoker, similar to the smaller one used to make jerky but with a pit in the ground for the coals, was smoking away. Those responsible for feeding the Family knew that Day 3 A-Wall would be better. They were all very excited. *I hope so. There it is again—"hope."*

As the Family had done the previous two nights, the newcomers shared their stories and expressed their grief. All had lost loved ones, and all needed to grieve. Everyone cried again. For many, it was as cathartic this time as it had been the evenings before. Roger and his troupe entertained again with another fairy tale. Janie was in heaven.

There were too many to fit around the central fire, so many had migrated to the western fire to receive more warmth. Tony's crew of over 15 now hung out at the fire in the depth of the compound, which also supported the infirmary. Tony broke from a woman who was fawning over him, turned with that smile and stared at Sarah. She turned away. It was getting worse. Stronger. That feeling she got when he looked at her.

The night watchmen each received a larger midnight lunch. With the Family more spread out, there were now six watchmen: the three men from the night before, two women and a young man. This night everyone besides the watchmen slept. The day had been long, and the new reality, along with the new community they were building, was settling into a routine. Sarah, curled up behind Jazz, feared sleep, fought it as long as she could, but eventually succumbed.

EIGHTEEN

Pain, dark dread swirled in her sleeping mind. Bruised and bleeding, she pleaded. Robert's mother wouldn't hear her. Smiling, turning away. The girls loved her, their grandmother, Robert's mother. His face, bourbon-laced breath, his loud laugh. Robert's face morphed into Tony's, wearing a creepy smile: *"Join, unite, rule!"*

A deep gasp and exhalation, and she was awake. Sweat poured from her. No tears, but her skin crawled, and her body trembled. She wrapped her arms around herself, rocking back and forth. Robert's gone. Gone forever! She missed her parents so much. And Tony? She forced back tears as she had for so many years.

She breathed deeply, trembling as she did, took a few seconds to calm her nerves, then settled into meditation to regain her spiritual balance. Asha was there, the red mist, her four animals. "The darkness is yours. You must feel it. Expose it, then own it. Let go. Feel again. Live. Love! It is here. It is coming. You must be ready." Sarah reached for the spirits in nature around her, channeling the depths of this world. She felt them dance with her soul, caress it, carry it outward through the trees and flowers. She was one with all of this. She was connected to this new world. She could draw strength from it.

"Morning, sleepyhead. We got rabbits," Janie crowed at her mother as she bound into her lap, shocking her into reality. Just as quickly, Janie bounced off. "I'm taking a group of gatherers out to find greens and fruit for breakfast. Any requests?" Without waiting for a response, she was off with her crew in tow. Sarah smiled and shook her head. Asha's words from her meditation returned. *What does Asha mean? What am I supposed to do?*

Then she saw Jazz was chatting with a couple of the other girls. She smiled as the tremors slowed. *Push them down. There is nothing but trying to survive here to worry about.*

Jazz was looking in Mark's direction but pretending not to every time he looked her way. *Oh, for crying out loud. This is not what I need to be dealing with,* Sarah thought. None of the girls looked like they'd been awake for more than a few minutes, but all had their eyes on some young man in the Family.

She scanned the compound. Tony turned, smiled and winked. *How did he know?* She looked away, closed her eyes, focused to settle the spiritual turmoil inside her, then opened them, took a deep breath and got up to face the day.

Day 3 A-Wall began with more energy than had the previous days. Many were up before Sarah, and some had been for a few hours.

Janie dragged John over to her. "We got three rabbits, Mommy."

"One of the traps sprung but was empty. The barbs didn't close much, and the rabbit escaped," John reported. "We'll fix that trap and make more." Then he squatted in front of her and drew on the dirt. "With some adjustments to the trap designs, I'm sure we could catch some squirrels." Sarah nodded and smiled at Janie. "And the fish trap we made had a good-sized trout in it this morning."

As John stood up, Sarah, still distracted, nearly whispered, "Great work. Keep it up."

Janie, of course, didn't notice and grabbed John's hand to drag him off again.

Erika had also been up for quite a while. Rhonda, anxious to use her bow, had left before dawn with her now larger team.

Sarah wandered over to Amy who was starting the fire under the cooking stone. "We've got to figure out a way to make coffee." Amy nodded, and they both chuckled.

Herb and Gus shuffled up. "Mornin', Sarah," Gus said, taking the rabbits from Amy. Herb never said much. Gus's young female apprentice began on the fish.

The teams of wood gatherers and cutters were many and busy. They brought old dry wood to keep the fires going; young straight saplings for arrows and spears; smaller branches for traps, cooking utensils and baskets; straight pieces of pine for construction of whatever Martha's team was working on; various barks for medicinal purposes, baskets or to enhance the strength of various ropes; and wood for many other needs around the community. It was a constant effort by the 40 residents engaged in these tasks.

"Shirley," Sarah called to get Ms. Watson's attention. "Things are going well in here. I think it's time for some reconnaissance."

"I agree. Good idea." Ms. Watson touched her gently, nodded with a knowing smile and turned back to the Family.

The horse seemed to know her intentions and, to the chagrin of a boy petting him, trotted toward Sarah. Animals sense another creature's spirit and whether it's positive or negative. Sarah loved that about animals. So simple. Humans label everything and make it all so complicated.

Sarah took a few steps and leaped onto the horse and headed out the front gate along the outside of the menacing hawthorn and rose thorn barrier. This was the first time she'd seen it from this side. From this perspective, there were several weaknesses. She rode back to the gate and called for Marsha.

With Sarah's help, Marsha mounted the horse behind her. They rode along the outside of the barrier. "Right there." Sarah pointed at what looked like a wider opening. The barrier was imposing, about 5 feet tall and full of long, vicious hawthorn spikes and shorter, but equally sharp, rose thorns. The structure was tied together with prickly briars.

Marsha was fidgeting.

Sarah asked, "You OK back there?"

"Umm, well, I'm uncomfortable."

Sarah stifled a giggle, twisted on the horse and helped Marsha down. "I'm sorry, Marsha."

"No problem. I'll be fine, I think. How do you . . .? Excuse me." She turned away and checked herself out between her legs, brushed away some horse hair and turned back to Sarah. "Anyway. What if we planted live climbing plants, including roses, at the base of the barrier? That would tie it together with the strength of a living plant. The vines will find all of the holes and spaces. And when they bloom, the barrier will smell nice and be quite pretty."

Sarah stopped the horse and turned around to Marsha. "Girl, that's brilliant. Let's plant climbing flowers on the inside, but maybe some ivy on the outside would be great too. Brilliant, brilliant, brilliant. Let's do it."

"Like roses, morning glory and clematis. It'll brighten up the compound."

Sarah reached down and high-fived Marsha. Marsha trotted inside with a new bounce. *That will look nice.* There were plenty of gardeners in the Family who would jump at the chance to brighten their world and strengthen the barrier at the same time. "See if Janie knows where to find the plants," Sarah yelled after Marsha.

"Already on it." Marsha's experience on the horse, a discomfort not suffered by Sarah, raised the mystery of Sarah even more in the eyes of the Family.

Sarah smiled as she rode out into the pasture and again turned to look back on the compound. The three fires created a huge pillar of smoke above the encampment. She again rode back to the gate. Ms. Watson was there standing on the stump behind the barrier watching her.

"Shirley, we need to tone down the fires. If there's anyone or anything out there, the smoke will alert them to our location. I don't think we want that. The days and nights will be getting warmer. I think we need the fire to cook and to keep warm at night, but it might be better to douse at least two of the fires and tone down the third during the day. Save on wood too."

Ms. Watson saw the wisdom in the new plan. "I'll take care of it. We may as well stop polluting our new planet right now." Ms. Watson stepped down from the stump to find Tony. It didn't take long for them to douse the two side fires. Sarah found out later that Ms. Watson allowed Tony to announce the change to the Family as though it were his decision. When it got around, as it always did, that the idea had come from Sarah, he bristled at the embarrassment, blaming both Sarah and Ms. Watson for setting him up.

Sarah rode to the top of the largest hill in front of the gate. A broad expanse of beautiful green grasses and wildflowers spread out before her, split by their river to her left. The ground was undulating in front of their home. Small hills, dells, mounds and valleys wound their way for several hundred feet out from and in a wide arc around their gate, which faced north, and all the way down to the beginning of their western woods and river. Nearer the gate, the hillocks rose 8 feet or so above a central valley that ran below her. Following the terrain north, the mounds began to smooth out, and the valleys became shallow until the land settled into soft rolling meadows before they reached the imposing tree line that arced around well to their east and then curved dramatically back west to the entrance of their camp and the eastern edge of the barrier. *Could this arrangement be ideal for protection?*

Again, she rode back to the gate. She called for Joe and heard him respond from the eastern woods. She steered the horse along the barrier and saw Joe emerge.

"Joe, got a few minutes? I wanna show you something." She reached down for his hand, but he indicated that he would walk. She trotted the horse to the top of the same highest mound with Joe following.

"I don't know what's out there, but I wonder if we should have a plan of defense."

"Sure," Joe agreed.

"Wouldn't this area be ideal for some sort of defensive setup? You know, just in case. You're the former Marine. What do you think?"

Joe looked over the area. He'd seen it many times in the last couple of days. "Hadn't thought of it in that way before." Joe walked around the top of the mound, gauged the others around it and turned to her. This was also the area where the dogs hung out. A few had risen and followed Joe around as he walked, hoping for a treat. Joe ignored them. "I'll talk to the General."

"Who's the General?"

"The really old guy who sits with the Seamstresses and Ol' Mac but can't really do anything. He tells great stories. The ladies and kiddos love him."

"Really? I'm not sure why that surprises me." He was the guy she'd lamented them carrying into the camp that first evening. She remembered her brief interaction with the man and how he'd touched her soul with his smile.

"Yep. He was all over Vietnam, the Balkans, Iraq and even Afghanistan. He retired about 15 or 20 years ago, but that man is sharp as a tack. Tonight, Erika and I'll get his opinion, and tomorrow we can come back out here and see what might make sense. I was a sergeant, a hard-core fighter. The General and Erika are more strategic. We'll talk to him." Joe's mind had left the conversation. He kneeled down to gain a certain perspective. Then he jogged down into the valley leading to the gate. "This is where we brought Janie and the team through after the hyena thing. I remember feeling like this sure was safe. You rode right up where you are now for a better vantage point."

"I remember. I'll never forget it."

"I'm gonna wander around through this maze for a bit. I'll be fine." He patted his large spear. "Me and Trudy, named after my wife, will be just fine."

Sarah nodded and rode back toward the gate. She called for Erika, who was also in the eastern woods. She and Joe were often in the same general area.

"Erika, so you know, Joe's over across that hill surveying the area. I think it might be wise for us to prepare a plan to defend ourselves. I'm not even sure what we might defend ourselves against, but we should be prepared, don't you think?"

"I'll trot over and help him," she responded, to no surprise of Sarah's. "I think you know I'm a former Navy captain. Military logistics. A lot of what I did was establish strategies for defending territory, with air support, of course. I can look at any terrain and tell you the strengths and weaknesses."

"Is the team in there adequately protected?"

"Sure. Three of our best guys are in there."

How anyone knew who was best or even adequate at this point was up for debate, but three was fine. The wood-gathering group made so much noise, Sarah was sure there wasn't a wild animal for miles.

"OK, have at it."

Erika was off to find Joe. Sarah watched her run through the taller grass in that direction. She was strong and powerful, and Sarah took a moment to admire her physique. Then she turned and guided the horse to the edge of the woods.

"Hey, who's leading this team?"

"I am, Sarah. Jake. What's up?" Jake extended a big hairy hand, which she accepted. She could feel the strength in his grip, but his twinkling eyes gave away his gentle nature. He conveyed confidence and made her smile.

"I wanted to make sure you all knew that I've reassigned Joe and Erika, and they're no longer here to support you."

"OK. I'm not sure we were aware they were even on our detail, ma'am."

Ah-ha! A little rendezvous? she thought as she looked over her shoulder then back at Jake. "OK. Back at it. Just wanted to make sure you knew."

"No problem." And he turned and headed back into the woods. Well, she'd seen that coming. The very first evening, Joe and Erika comforted each other. They were both in great physical shape, former military and had similar levels of attractiveness, which was a weird thing for her to consider. Still, they seemed to fit. Sarah looked back at the hills. Erika was pursuing him more than he was pursuing her. He heads some place, and she follows. Oh well, it was bound to happen and perhaps more likely in these crazy times . . . especially since everyone's naked. She'd really stopped noticing, but she knew not everyone had, including Jazz and her girlfriends.

Sarah shook her head a bit and smiled, then turned to look north. She scanned the broad expanse of varied grasslands in front of the compound. The green, waving carpet was enclosed on the east and north by the darkness of a dense forest. She rode east along the northern edge of their eastern woods to the point where the tree line veered to her left. She then guided the horse along the northwesterly arc of the tree line, keeping the woods to her right.

To her left, the grassland flattened out. She and the horse were in taller, light green grasses with yellow and white wildflowers that reached to the western horizon. The breeze blew across the plain, giving the area the appearance of an ocean, flowing in and out with the never-ending tides. The undulations began up the far slope, crossed the river below her and flowed all the way up the gradual rise to the trees, where the wind was lost in the rustle of leaves above her.

She sat and felt the stillness and peace of undisturbed nature. It was one of her favorite sensations. She could sense everything around her. Small animals scurrying amidst the grasses, birds in the trees and sky. There were hundreds, thousands. Life was exploding around her and within her. She closed her eyes and drank it all in. She felt her connection to the horse and let it sink into her. She felt the bear deep in the woods to the west and let his spirit soak into hers. She felt the predator with the green eyes well off in the forest behind her—a tiger, *the* Tiger—and felt a connection with him. She felt the elephant, somewhere out there as well. It was enveloping, sensual, wondrous. She let them in and felt their spirits become stronger within her.

NINETEEN

Sarah took a deep breath and returned to reality. As she guided the horse northwest, the longer grasses gave way to shorter, richer and darker green grass and soft clover sprinkled with violet flowers and tufts of white. Wildflowers and plants, considered weeds in the old world, decorated the ground in every shade from reds through oranges to yellows. She stopped the horse again for a moment to admire the beauty and breathe in the wonderful scents of nature. She laughed at herself when she reached down for her phone to take a picture.

Rabbits were everywhere. She was certain that this is where Janie and John had set their traps. She kept close to the woods to avoid ruining them.

When the clover ended, the vast field of taller grasses and wildflowers continued, flowing out before her, across the river and up the slope on the other side as far as she could see. She was stunned by the beauty. The tree line continued to curve northwest around the field toward the river. She had found a pretty high place in their prairie.

This land had been covered with acres of subdivision homes. Now small herds, 10 to 20 each, of bison, gazelle, elk and several zoo herbivores whose official names she didn't know, dotted the grasslands. There were an amazing number of babies. Nearly every female in every herd was visibly pregnant. The herds would grow quickly. Like the vegetation, the animals were repopulating the planet at an astounding rate.

To the northwest, on the opposite side of their little river, were about a dozen elephants, both Asian and African species hanging out together. *What an odd herd.* She felt a closeness. *She's among them. My kindred Elephant.* She let their spirits flow into each other.

She smiled then noticed three or four giraffes at the edge of a grove of trees well up the river. It dawned on her that something must have motivated all these disparate animals to travel together this far west, 10 miles from the zoo. Whatever drove them here hadn't come this far. She hoped it wouldn't. *Was that what was coming? The darkness?*

Another forest extended west from their compound, across their river, marking the southern edge of the vast expanse of grasslands. This southern forest was the home of the bears, her bear and his family. She knew from the hunters' reports that it reached well to their south, downhill near them but over a sharp embankment, even cliffs, farther west, with several streams pouring into a large lake that a wide river flowed into from the south. That huge lake was a new feature on the terrain, but so much was these days. She was looking forward to exploring in that direction.

The drier days of summer worried her, but even if their stream dried up, that lake would provide them water all year round. *We'll have to figure out a way to bring water up to the compound,* but she'd deal with that later. As a soft breeze kissed her face, Sarah took a long deep breath and watched as a herd of native white-tailed deer emerged from the woods into the southern edge of the grasslands. There was a lot of wildlife. She felt very good about their fortunes. Theirs was an ideal location.

There'd been plenty of stables for the rich folks who populated what was once West St. Louis County, and somewhere there'd be plenty of horses. They could use several more. There was a herd of cattle penned up along Conway Road, but they were several miles northwest. Reachable, but the trip would be quicker and rounding up the cattle more efficient on horseback. As she surveyed the open plains with the varied herbivores, she decided to suggest that Marshall, Samantha and the spear hunters work out here.

It'd be easier to throw in the open rather than through the trees, and one of those huge elk or bison would provide more protein than two deer. Plus, the hides would be invaluable.

Farther out, there should be pigs and chickens. Being able to raise our own food could take a lot of the risks out of feeding the Family, especially in the winter.

Sarah decided they'd find more horses and then ride out to find other animals capable of being domesticated. *We'll have to make some kind of saddle. It's obvious others can't ride comfortably bareback and naked.* It was a plan. The horse snorted as though in agreement. Sarah patted his neck and smiled. *Thanks, buddy.*

She saw no humans. None. No evidence of humans. No other fires or smoke. *Are we the only survivors?*

Sarah meandered across the broad field toward the river and the end of the tree line. She looked back toward the compound. It was now several hundred yards south of her. Even though she was on higher ground, it was all but invisible.

When she reached the western edge of the northern woods, the tree line ran due north several hundred feet, perpendicular to the tree line she'd been following and parallel with their river. The area looked soft, almost marshy, between the river and woods. It was dominated by short scrubby grasses and plants that loved the wet soil and rotting wood. As she followed it north up the slope with her eyes, the path between the woods and stream reached a high point. She could see only the tops of trees beyond it. The path grew wider and drier to the north.

Her eyes followed their little river from the point where it emerged from the woods far to her northwest to where it meandered east quite a distance then turned southward past her position, across their flat grass-lands, then into their westside woods next to their compound. It was about 10 to 15 feet wide in most places, had several pools, cascades, falls and rapids. Each pool was surrounded by river trees—birch, willow and a few others she didn't recognize. *Janie'd know them all.*

She turned her attention back to the north. This was where she'd first seen the elephants. They'd wandered across the river and were now well up the gentle western slope. A big Asian turned from the herd and looked at her. Their eyes met. She could feel her spirit dance with the elephant's. They shared a moment, and their spirits bonded firmly. Sarah nodded, and the elephant bowed her huge head in recognition.

She noticed a small creek running out of the trees just to the north of her, through the marshy area and down to the river. It met their river at one of the groves of river birch and willow trees around one of the smaller pools. The little creek sprang from an area inside the forest.

Her spirit, so relaxed since she left the compound, grew uneasy. She looked around and opened her senses. She could tell the horse felt it as well, and she instinctively tuned into him. She could not sense any animal threats, but the growing fear was there. *Humans!*

Sarah walked the horse down the gentle grassy slope along the little stream toward the river. His hooves sucked into and out of the soft ground. Halfway down she stopped, looking back and forth for whatever was bothering her. The horse was equally agitated, snorting and looking around, pulling his feet out of the soft muddy ground. She heard a sound and turned. The horse quieted. She heard it again. A human cry for help. It was very weak.

Together they moved in a healthy trot in the direction of the sounds. She heard them again, a little stronger, coming from the river, north of where the little side creek entered it. She veered toward the sound, crossed the creek and quickened her pace. The sound was not the source of their fear. That was clearly behind them now. Back in the forest. She looked over her shoulder but saw nothing.

When her attention turned back toward the river, she saw two teenage girls standing outside the small grove of trees. Sarah and the horse slowed as they approached to make sure the girls weren't trying to harm them in any way. These girls were not the source of her discomfort.

"Help us. Oh my God, people. Help us, please."

"How many of you are there?" Sarah asked.

"Eight. Four boys and four girls. We're from the same high school. Everyone scattered. We stayed together, but we're so tired and hungry and—" The girl fell to the ground weeping. Sarah, still a bit concerned, rode nearer and around a tree to peer into the area beneath the grove of trees. There were several kids with sallow faces lying on the ground.

"Can you walk?"

"Yes. We can all walk. We were just feeling lost and alone and panicked and—"

"I totally understand. We've all been there. Get up. Follow me. I can lead you back to our compound. You can get food and water, and we can tend to whatever other needs you might have."

The small band all got up, and Sarah began in the direction of the compound. The sense of dread arose, and both Sarah and the horse turned toward the woods, then back at the girls as one yelled, "Oh my God. Watch out, it's them!" Then Sarah looked to her left toward the woods and saw "them." Hundreds of teenagers ran at her from the forest edge, screaming and wielding sticks. The horse bolted from the marshy ground into high gear and ripped into the grasses, down the long slope toward the compound. The group was in hot pursuit, but well behind her as she crested the first hillock and entered the maze of hills and valleys.

"Joe, Erika, help!!!"

They were there, lying in the sun, face up in some soft grass with the same look on their faces, enjoying the aftereffects of their sexual encounter. The horse barely avoided running them over as he pounded across the hill. She controlled the horse and stopped.

"There's a hoard of angry people following me. They have sticks. We need to warn the Family and get them inside the barrier."

Joe and Erika leaped to their feet, looked in the direction Sarah was pointing and sprinted toward the gate. Sarah rode hard to the woods, screaming for Jake and ordering everyone into the compound. She then rode to the clover field to make sure no one was harvesting plants or rabbits. No one was. She looked to the northwest and saw what looked like hundreds of teenagers running through the grasses toward her. Most couldn't run straight. Many were yelling things she couldn't understand. *What's wrong with them?*

Sarah raced back toward the compound and saw several of the team running through the gate. She followed the last of them in and slid off the horse.

"Get any weapon you can find. I'm not sure if we'll need them, but just in case." The two fires were cool and no longer smoking. The main fire was burning low. The breeze wafted the smoke off to the east into the trees where it dissipated. She hoped that the maze of hills and valleys and the camouflage the barrier created would prevent them from being discovered. "Everyone quiet. Spread the word."

TWENTY

Ms. Watson was already at her place on the log. Sarah, Joe and Erika stood on the ground beside her.

Soon groups of teenagers began to wander around in the hills and valleys in front of the compound. Some looked right at the compound and still didn't see it.

A young man yelled, "Whoever you are, can someone please help us?"

He sat down in the grass on top of the highest hill, maybe 15 yards in front of their gate. Others came over the hills. Some stood. Some sat. Some dropped their sticks. Some were crying. Some were staggering around. Others stared at the sky.

Ms. Watson turned to Sarah and said, "I'm going out there."

"OK, but we're going with you," Sarah responded. She turned to Joe and Erika, who nodded. Joe held up Trudy. Joe and Erika gathered a few others, and when they were ready, Ms. Watson led the band out through the gate. The screech of the gate opening startled the children on the hill, and they turned in fear.

"What the fuck?" the young man said and stood.

Ms. Watson strode around the leading edge of the barrier. The rest of the team followed in support.

"We're here to help, if that's what you want. Please stand, bring everyone forward to the area between the hills there and have everyone sit down on the slopes. I'll wait."

About 30 teens covered the maze to the end of the little valley. Sarah was sure this wasn't all of them, not by a long shot. The little hills effectively blocked their view of the grasslands beyond. She whispered to Ms. Watson, "There are hundreds. This is not all of them." Ms. Watson nodded.

The young man walked down the hill to the front, then toward Ms. Watson. He politely held out his hand to her. He was unarmed and made that clear.

"Hello ma'am, I'm William. I'm sorry if we frightened you." Then he saw Sarah. "Ma'am, I'm very sorry we frightened you. That wasn't our intention. I'm not sure what it was at the time. Your presence was a surprise. We were all in the woods searching for food. We found some wonderful mushrooms in there and were famished. We saw you and ran out. I'm sure that we seemed crazy. Again, we didn't mean it that way."

Sarah nodded. Something about this group and this guy didn't sit right with her. Something was wrong, like those eerie characters in horror films who are too perfect to believe. Others sensed it as well and were on edge. This group wasn't like any of the others that had come by. Where were their parents? Why were they together and not looking for their families? The boy's explanation of the "attack" was plausible, but she knew what she'd seen. The young girl at the river was clearly afraid—of "them." They were definitely coming after Sarah, and not in a polite way. They weren't frightened, confused or panicking, like the other wanderers. The teenagers sat gazing with emotionless eyes at them or at the sky or at one another. It was like a scene from a 1960's drug-addled peace flick.

Sarah asked one of the Family in the back to get a few more armed Family members to come out from the compound and to find Doc. Ms. Watson felt the tension too. She didn't shake William's hand, but instead asked him to stay where he was and held her ground.

Doc joined them. Sarah watched as his eyes grew big and his face became animated.

"Sarah, we have to get back into the compound! These teens are addicts." Sarah noticed track marks on William's arm. He was becoming unsettled and even losing his balance. "They're addicts who are strung out. They haven't had a fix since the Storm. They're unpredictable and dangerous." Sarah ordered the group to withdraw.

Ms. Watson spoke. "William, you seem like a fine and polite young man. How can we help you? We're a small band of older folks, and we don't have anything of value. We're struggling ourselves."

Doc and Sarah made their way to Ms. Watson, and he whispered his learned opinion into her ear.

Ms. Watson spoke to William. "Young man, you and your band stay right here. We're going back inside to discuss how we can help. Give us a moment, and we'll be right back."

"Why? Wait. We need you." William's speech was beginning to slur, and he stumbled as he took a step forward. He was becoming angry and confused. He mumbled something unintelligible as Sarah guided Ms. Watson and the rest of the Family back.

Sarah turned to Erika. "Is everyone accounted for in the camp?"

"Pretty much. We sent a runner to bring in the hunters, but they went south through the woods and shouldn't encounter this group."

"Alright, Captain Erika, time for that strategic mind of yours. Get everyone ready to defend the compound."

Erika sprinted inside. The greeting party tried to appear calm. They'd made it back to the leading edge of the barrier. William was now moving, staggering forward, as were several others in the group of teens. The Family slid inside and slammed the gate closed behind them.

Once inside, Doc explained to the whole group, "I'm guessing these kids are from the forced treatment center the state ran for arrested teenage addicts a couple of miles northeast of here. I've seen many cases of mushroom poisoning. In addition to my surgical duties, I worked as an internist in several smaller rural towns that have no doctors.

"They're searching for something to ease their cravings. They probably found mushrooms, toadstools, which would tend to act like a drug. Unfortunately, the effects of toxic mushrooms often look the way this boy and others in the group are acting, but they could get dramatically worse.

"Mushroom poisoning, while rare, was not uncommon among drug addicts I treated. When addicts can't get their drug of choice, they'll try nearly anything to get high. They've all heard of 'magic mushrooms,' and when high or in need of a fix, they often try antifreeze, glue, aerosols, prescriptions, common herbs and, of course, wild mushrooms.

"Some mushrooms can create a high similar to that of more common illegal drugs. The problem is they're deadly. The high's the result of the mushroom killing the liver and other organs, resulting in nasty chemicals making it to the brain. For some species, it only takes one or two. I think these addicts have found a toadstool fix. Add in the lack of food these days, and they'd be hungry enough to ignore the taste and wolf down a lot more than two of those mushrooms. Doses that high can be lethal."

Joe returned the group to the issue at hand. "So, we're obviously not letting them in. What are we going to do?"

Erika returned with a small cadre and shrugged. "They're not fighters, Sarah, but they're as ready as they can be."

It was midday. The sun was high in the sky. They had a standoff at present. Joe was peering over the barrier. "Hey, come look at this." Sarah and the others joined him. Most of the kids were sitting, popping small, brightly colored mushrooms into their mouths. Some were staring off into the sky. Others were fiddling with the grass. Some got up and started wandering off.

William was walking to the top of the hill. "Hey, get back here! Where the fuck do you think you're going?!"

"Dude, I'm hungry. I'm going back to the creek."

"Me too." The pair and a few others stumbled off.

A loud gurgling sound rang through the air. William and the Family turned to one of the hills due west of the center valley. A blond girl was throwing up a multicolored mess. She coughed and then dry heaved on all fours. A couple of the other girls and two of the boys came to her aid, but they wobbled on unsteady legs as they tried to ascend the gentle slope. First the taller, darker-haired boy fell to his knees, heaving the same multicolored puke. The other two staggered and each fell, convulsing and vomiting uncontrollably.

William and his audience behind the barrier turned again as a couple of girls began singing incoherently and dancing blindly on top of one of the hillocks before they, too, fell to the ground. They didn't puke but were choking and struggling to breathe.

"They're all turning white!" a young woman from the Family yelled.

A boy screamed in pain, grabbed his stomach and fell down the backside slope of the hill. Several others were wandering around as if lost or began to exhibit similar symptoms, while still others remained strong though disoriented.

"The mushrooms are affecting different kids in different ways," Doc observed. "Maybe they ate different mushrooms, or perhaps different mixtures. Hard to tell." What they were witnessing in the group of teenagers challenged their emotions. The girl who had been vomiting fell to the ground on her stomach.

"Oh my God," Ms. Watson said.

Sarah was still focused on William. She felt a hand take her left hand, the dark fear and doubt rising within her, and turned. It was Tony. "What?" she nearly screamed at him.

"I'll protect you. Don't you worry." His dark eyes were pleading.

"Tony, I'm fine. Thank you, but I can protect myself." She pulled her hand from his and turned back to the scene in front of her. She felt him grab her hand again and turned back to him. "Please leave!" His face fell as he turned and stormed off. She closed her eyes for a second and restored balance to her spirits.

When she opened them, William was looking around, turning violently back and forth atop one of the hills. "We must attack!" he screamed. "Now is our only opportunity. Don't you see it? We must attack now!"

Erika left to speak to her "troops."

"Just defense, Erika. Inside the barrier!" Sarah yelled. Erika acknowledged her, while Sarah grabbed a young boy. "Get me a spear."

Joe ran to join Erika to rally the Family, who were not anxious to get into a battle. Sarah sent as much spiritual confidence as she could muster toward them then turned back to the scene in front of the encampment.

William began running up and down the hills, pushing and pulling various teens, many of whom were struggling to stand. Sarah saw him pop another mushroom and then another.

Doc was studying. "Those are red. The ones the girl and those kids over there ate, I think, were brown and green." Janie joined Doc, fascinated by mushrooms. The two began pointing and talking between them.

William spun and raced to the top of the large hill and stopped. He popped a 'shroom and looked at his empty hand. His body became rigid as though at attention. He bent over and shook his head like a dog trying to rid itself of water. Saliva flew from his open mouth. Then he stopped and slowly returned to attention. He saluted, then turned and marched first left and then right.

William's chest pushed out, and he stood as though he had a weapon, like a rifle or a sword. He perceived growing support around him, talking to invisible men beside him. He marched back off the hill, approached two other boys, yelled something incoherent at them. They stared blankly. He reached down and picked up a large stick that one of the two boys had dropped. William waved it like a sword, placed it at his side and ran to the top of the hill. He stared blankly over their heads.

"Men, fall in. Prepare for attack." He was ordering the boys to his side, though they only wandered around the hill to its base in the little valley, watching him, their eyes seeing something quite different from what Sarah and the Family were witnessing. William didn't notice. He walked to his left and right again, then back to a stop as though surveying his nonexistent troops. He screamed, "Lieutenants, . . . the fourth order. . . uh . . . dress ready, full operations . . . blind pursuit, um . . . arms now good . . . goddammit, soldier." William turned to the Family, looked Sarah right in the eyes, raised his arm with the stick for a sword and screamed, "Charge!" William's eyes were crazed as he ran straight at her, stumbling down the slope toward the barrier, gaining speed with gravity more than form.

"Noooooo!!!" Sarah yelled. She ran to the gate still unarmed. When she reached the outside edge of the barrier overlap, William swung his stick/sword at her and leaped. She jumped from his path and watched in horror as he impaled himself on the hawthorn branches. The thorns ripped his flesh away as he attacked it with anger. One of the barrier's branches penetrated deep into his abdomen. Sarah backed away further.

Blood was pouring from him as he battled his imaginary foe, thrashing at the roses, hawthorn and brambles, which in turn ripped huge gashes in his arms and legs. As he flailed, the hawthorn branch inside him ripped at his internal organs. Fluids spewed forth from the wound, turning his blood brown.

He looked Sarah square in the eyes, angry and vacuous, then saddened and finally bewildered. He swiped at her with his imagined sword one last time, and it fell from his hand, bouncing on the ground at her feet, but she never looked at it. His eyes, still focused on hers, went blank. She could feel his soul leave him. His head lolled back. His body slumped into the brambles and roses of the barrier. He was dead. His weight pulled the barrier forward, it arced and strained from William's weight, but it held. Sarah, and a small band of Family members who'd emerged behind her, stared in shock. Few of William's followers even noticed.

The two other young men, and then a third, however, raised their arms, devoid of any weapons, and came to his defense, running at Sarah with fury in their eyes. *Why me?* Their eyes had the same crazed look. Sarah was paralyzed. Joe, Erika and a few other guards stepped forward. They intercepted the boys and threw them to the ground as Sarah darted out of the way. It took several Family members to hold them down.

One of the other girls who'd thrown up tried to stand but fell to the ground, her face ashen white, blood pouring from her mouth. Others began to fall to their knees or flat on the ground. Some ran in crazy circles, even into one another, sending them swirling to the ground, rolling down hills. Many threw up violently, bleeding from mouths and eyes before turning ashen white. They were dying now, and the small band of Family members stood watching, shocked.

TWENTY-ONE

M s. Watson broke the tension. "We have to try to help them. Try to help someone. Go. See what you can do, but be careful. Bring anyone you can control to Doc, and let's see if we can keep them alive. Jocelyn, get some water up here." A middle-aged, somewhat plump mother with shoulder-length tangled brown hair turned and ran into the complex. Sarah could see the horrified eyes of the Family peering out above the barrier. A few more Family members came out the front gate, each with a spear. No one from Tony's crew were among them.

"Where is my goddam spear?" Sarah screamed. A young woman threw her one and returned inside to get another. Molly kept all the children, even the older ones, well back inside the barrier.

Erika led a few Family members out to help. A big, strong athletic addict grabbed a spear from a large male Family member as he tried to help a young girl. The boy swung it right and left, screaming. It ripped through the neck of a staggering teen. Her blood arced bright red above her as she spun from the force to the ground.

The boy slashed the shocked Family member across his broad chest, tearing open a bone-deep gash from armpit to armpit. The man didn't scream. He focused on the boy, waited and then grabbed the spear as it swung past. Each with both hands on the spear, they fought for control. The Family man pushed him away, secured the spear and drove it through the boy's chest. The teen staggered, the spear lodged all the way through him, but he still attacked. Contaminated blood from the boy splattered into the man's gaping wound as they collided.

"To Hector's aid, everyone!" Erika yelled.

With his gaping chest wound bleeding, Hector staggered back from the boy as Family members arrived. A shorter man caught him, immediately helped by two others. Erika grabbed the spear embedded in the boy, whipped him away and slammed him to the ground, driving the point of the spear deep into the earth, pinning him there. He squirmed for several seconds against the spear before he fell limp in death.

Erika yelled, "Back to the compound!"

Olivia, the nurse, ran to Hector, nearly dragging him back into the complex. "We have to get this treated as best we can right now. We have to get that poison out fast. If we can, perhaps it won't affect you."

Ms. Watson arrived among them, as she often did, and put a calming hand on the man's shoulder. "Hector, go with her. These young people aren't a threat, but that poison is. If you have some in your system, we need to see if we can get it out. We need you alive."

He nodded and walked, one arm around the man who'd caught him and one around Olivia. The Doc's team was already waiting to help care for him and a few others.

Sarah ran to the top of the large hill. From there, she could see the entire area to the northwestern edge of the woods from whence the teens had come. More young people, the hundreds she'd seen stream from the woods, were everywhere. Many were either already dead, in the final throws of the illness or wandering about in the hallucination that led to the final moments. Others had sticks or were acting violently like William had, without focus.

"Oh my God. What did they eat?"

She saw the small band of girls and boys she'd found first at the river. They weren't displaying the effects of the mushrooms and were trying to work their way through the crazed kids and in her direction. Sarah yelled to Joe, Erika and the others to follow her. The boys they'd been holding down had passed.

All eight were there—four boys and four girls. The girl who'd called for her was leading them. Three were limping and had to be helped, but none of them were acting like the other teens. They were frightened beyond description. As their panic rose, they stopped, cowering together in the middle of the field.

Some of the other teens developed the crazed reaction to the mushrooms they'd seen in William. Several turned and focused their imagined wrath on the eight frightened teens.

Sarah raced down the hill toward them. She approached with soothing words. In these eight, she saw abject fear. Joe, Erika and five other Family members arrived right behind Sarah. They encircled the small group, facing outward. Those still alive in the mass of teenagers turned toward them, eyes glazed over, sticks or empty fists raised as though holding weapons.

"I'm Sarah. This is . . ."

"Randi," a tiny, slender woman answered.

Sarah looked at her. *That woman's got guts. So little, yet so brave.* "Thanks, Randi," said Sarah as she touched Randi's soft shoulder with a look of deep pride.

Randi nodded and turned to the eight. "What are your names?"

Before they could respond, Joe yelled, "Incoming."

Sarah wheeled around and saw five boys running at them from the direction of the river, arms raised with large sticks, screaming insults and challenges at the band.

"Randi, keep this group together and safe! Get them up this mound," Erika commanded. "It'll be safer on top. We can defend them from there."

Randi rallied the eight frightened teens and convinced them to move up to the top of the small rise, then dragged a boy, larger than herself, up the slope.

Erika yelled, "Up the hill. Circle the kids."

"More crazies coming," a strong woman yelled from their left. The teens plodded up the rise, screaming profanities and calling the eight traitors and cowards.

Erika exuded confidence as she gave orders. "Stand your ground!" Erika yelled. "I know they aren't well armed, but you saw how unrelenting they are. Even without weapons, they're dangerous. Who knows what their blood will do to us."

"More from this side," a man yelled. Sarah looked his way and was struck by how good-looking he was.

"Six from this side," came a cry from the other woman. That brought Sarah's focus back.

"That's fourteen," Randi yelled.

"I know. We're outnumbered. We won't be able to subdue all of them, and some of them *are* armed," Joe yelled, then quieted, waiting for orders.

Erika took command. "Retreat to the top of the hill. Shoulder to shoulder. Form a phalanx. Hope like hell they all succumb to that poison before they get here."

Their attackers were still a ways away, and given how fast the poison had worked, it was at least a possibility. One of the attackers lost his footing, convulsed and was out. Then another and another. Perhaps they'd get lucky, but the ranks of the attacking teens were swelling.

Whoosh, thud. An arrow pierced the heart of a boy with a stick raised who was ahead of the others. He fell, and two others fell over him. More kept coming.

Whoosh, thud. Another arrow struck an athletic girl in the closest attack group, felling her in her tracks, her stick sent flying. Two fell over her. That slowed them a bit, but they kept coming. Rhonda stood on the next rise over and was doing her best to increase the odds for her brethren. Whoosh, thud, another fell, but Rhonda had no more arrows. The crazed teens screaming and wielding real or imaginary weapons or sticks they believed were swords moved steadily toward them. Family members were streaming over the hills of the maze toward the group, but the crazed teens were near and closing in fast.

"Prepare your spears. Stay close, connected. Protect the kids." They had no training, but they could follow orders. Erika was on her game. "Lower your spears to striking level. Close together. Wait for them. Be strong. Focus. Make your first strike the best strike."

Sarah could feel the fear in her team. They all knew that these addicts wouldn't feel the pain and would fight like William. She could sense their guilt as they prepared to try to kill children poisoned and out of their minds. They were also outnumbered. Sarah raised the spirits inside her and tried to send her team strength.

Erika yelled, "Close your mouths. Don't breathe in their blood."

As the group from the west arrived, Joe stepped forward and slashed Trudy through the first attacker, knocking him sideways into the path of two others, who fell over their fallen comrade. Joe leaped on one, driving his spear into his heart. Erika drove her spear through the chest of the other. Another Family member slashed through the abdomen of a girl, knocking her off her feet. Each teen tried to get up and continue the fight but could not.

"Keep your positions! Maintain contact!" Erika screamed. The poison was beginning to kill some. Faces went ashen. A boy collapsed at Joe's feet. Joe and the good-looking man tossed the body down the hill into the attackers. As the poison took hold, the teens ran with less agility. Several fell over the bodies, while others stumbled over the fallen. Many could not get back up. The Family worked in unison, listening to Erika's commands, to defend the uncoordinated attack of those who made it over the fallen bodies. More bodies were dispatched by the Family or died on their own and were sent down toward the onrushing teens. Still more came.

Sarah stood in the middle, shoulder to shoulder with Erika. She tore through the attackers, stabbing and flicking young boys and girls into others down the hill. She felt a chill from behind her. They had major problems on their unprotected east side. She turned, crossed through the eight and stood alone on the crest of the back of the hill.

Seven attackers were organizing on their eastern flank. Their leader turned and looked directly at Sarah. "Charge!" he screamed.

Sarah glanced back at her outnumbered comrades, took a deep cleansing breath and turned to face the charging teens. Unlike the others, this group was following orders from the young man in the back, a boy who stared at her with the same look in his eyes that William had. Three large boys who looked like linebackers—mean, angry, broad-shouldered and dirty—growled as they began their ascent together. Behind them were two athletic girls, one of whom looked like a rugby player and the other only slightly smaller. All five had sharpened sticks, coated with blood. Behind them stood their leader, with his crazed eyes, and a tall girl, both screaming angrily, bloody long sticks raised, ready to be thrown in the direction of her Family.

She felt no fear as the power of her spirits rose within her. Her strength, coordination and grace increased, and a fire roared in her eyes. For this she needed the power of the Storm, and she let it loose. Rage, fury and explosive negative energy, hatred like she'd never felt, poured into her and from her. The onrushers hesitated as she turned on them, stood tall before them and stared them down with daggers of crimson spiritual energy directly from the Storm. She squared her shoulders to them as the boy in back rallied his attack squad.

Sarah crossed her spear in front of her to take out as many as possible. Her spirit, the Storm and that of all her animals raged as she raced headlong down the hill into them. Sarah drove her shoulder into the midsection of the huge boy in front, over twice her size, and lifted him. The ends of her spear slammed into the two linebackers running beside him, sending them hurtling down the incline. The sudden jolt of the impact drove her spear back into her hip, pelvis and thigh, but she felt nothing. The two-inch diameter branch broke under the force of the blow. She drove the big boy back down the small incline, and with her Bear's strength and Tiger-like balance, she threw the boy crossways into the two rugby girls. The collision sent the three of them in a pile, tumbling down the hill.

The final two had their blood-tipped and sharpened spears high above their heads as they ascended, ignoring the fate of their colleagues. As the tall girl prepared to throw hers, Sarah drove her shoulder into the girl's chest, sending her and her spear flying in different directions. Sarah swung her right leg, driving her knee hard into another smaller girl who she hadn't seen at first, knocking her to the ground. Landing on her right leg, she spun her body around in one motion, driving her heel into the stomach of the leader, wildly sending his spear to the right. Entwined with the attackers, Sarah spun to the ground. Her arms trapped in the mass of people, she could not control her fall, landing hard on her head.

The world became blurry. She lost sense of the spirits and lost control of the Storm energy, which turned on her. The images of Robert attacked her. She felt the terrible pain, and now it was coming from her attackers as well. She heard Robert's laugh in the background. "Die, bitch. You can't control this!" Someone kicked her in the head and her vision blurred, mind fuzzy. In the fog, she could feel the feet and fists of the crazies pummeling her, coming from Robert. He was screaming at her, but she couldn't understand. She was groggy and had no sense of what was happening, fighting back from the confused tangle of bodies. They were strong, and the darkness was weakening her, pushing her animal spirits away. Her body rolled down the hill, and she curled into a ball. The kicking and punching returned. A blow to her head knocked her unconscious.

TWENTY-TWO

Pain, Robert's fists, nothing clear. *Give in, Sarah. Join me.* Gloomy, dark crimson, flashes, Robert's face, bourbon. Robert's family, laughing. Girls crying. A flash. Tony's face. That crippling smile. *Join me, Sarah.* Pounding head, oily daggers, Robert's laughter, searing pain from everywhere . . . *Join me, Sarah.* She was shivering, then crying.

A warmth, a soft gentle soul, strong, new, different. It allowed her spirits freedom. The Tiger ripped through the darkness, Bear claws clamped down on the Storm. Soft red chiffon.

Sarah worked to open her eyes. It was bright, but not Asha's light. Her head hurt. Her vision was blurry. She heard someone call out but couldn't understand. She closed her eyes again, breathed deeply and centered herself. Calming her core, a peace settled around her.

When she opened her eyes, he was there, hovering over her, smiling as her vision cleared. For the second time since the Storm, she awoke to splendor. She knew that she must have died and that *this* was heaven. He looked like something out of a catalog, about her age, tall, strong and well built, with soft brown wavy hair, a strong jaw and bright blue eyes. She was smitten and scared at the same time.

If she could design heaven, this man would be the centerpiece around which everything else was built. Sarah was mesmerized, lost in the beauty of this man who was tenderly looking at her. Her hand moved involuntarily to his broad chest. The touch sent sensual shivers down her spine—something she hadn't felt in a long time. Startled, frightened, she pulled her hand back. But there was something more; she felt the warmth of his spirit encircle hers and caress it. She'd felt it before. Just moments before. *When?*

"Hello, Sarah. I'm Tom. I'd ask how you're doing, but that's obvious. You look terrible." She smiled a little. He reached to her and moved some hair from her eyes with his strong hand, all with a big, gorgeous smile. "That was more than a little crazy, diving into those lunatics like that."

She had no idea what he was talking about until she tried to move. A whole lot of ugly memories came flooding back as the pain wracked her from every part of her body. Robert, Tony, the dark spirit that took her, the crazy teens; she couldn't tell the difference.

This isn't heaven, unless heaven sucks. She closed her eyes, breathed deep, trying to deal with the turmoil inside her, and felt herself begin to cry.

"Hold on, lie back down. Let's see what's going on here." He guided her body back down to the ground. She opened her eyes and gazed into his as he kneeled over her. He took her pulse. Racing. Bent in close to look at her eyes. He smelled amazing. Musky and masculine and sexy. She breathed him in. It cleared her head. He held up a finger. "Follow this without moving your head." She did, but so wanted to stare only into those brilliant eyes.

He moved around her and touched her bruised thigh. She inhaled but didn't cry out, although it hurt enough to yank her out of her fog and into complete consciousness.

"That's one nasty bruise. I was a chiropractor back in the real world. I worked with several of the athletic programs at the colleges." He was making small talk perhaps to take her mind off the pain and perhaps to impress her. She wasn't sure. Didn't care. "Ankle's swollen. Hmmm, nicely sprained. No ice, but the water at the falls may be cold enough to help. It doesn't seem to be broken." She tried to move. He put his soft hands on her shoulders. "Sarah, you were yelling, flailing, squirming and babbling the entire time you were out, so we couldn't examine you, so, please, settle back." She obeyed. "Good. What else hurts?"

"My right knee, my ribs on the right side. Feels like someone kicked me there a few times." The fight returned to her. "Right shoulder, I think from tackling them, or trying to hit them or push them off. I don't know. Everything hurts right now." She tried to smile as seductively as possible, but even that hurt, and she felt like the complete mess she was sure she was.

"OK." He worked her knee a bit. She winced but refused to cry out. "That's badly sprained, but no tear of the ligaments, which would be very bad since this is no place for orthopedic surgeries. That'll heal. We'll have to keep you off both the ankle and knee for several days, but I know some adjustments that should help. Let's look at that shoulder."

He rubbed it a bit, moved it around and then popped it back into the socket. "Ouch!" she complained. It hurt a great deal more than she let on.

"Dislocated, pretty badly. I think it's back in, but we'll work on that. It'll heal. It'll need a sling." He looked up at one of the women nearby, who ran off. "What else?"

"OK, this is embarrassing, but someone hit me hard with something, in my pelvic bone. It hurts, but I don't think it's broken."

She blushed. He blushed a little too. "Well, there's no real way to test for a break." He moved down between her legs and examined the area with his fingers. She winced. "No bleeding. No swelling. It's mostly above your pelvic bone. Looks like it's from the spear because it matches bruising on your hips in the same area. It's amazing you have no breaks, no internal bleeding or serious injuries from the beating you took." She silently thanked her spirits. "It'll have to heal like the rest of you. OK, now we have to get you to the Doc and then down to the river."

He bent down, put his arms under her. "Wait, what are you doing?" she protested as he lifted her in his strong arms and pulled her close.

"How do you think you got here?" he responded. She put her good left arm around his neck and rested her head on it as he turned toward the infirmary in the back of the camp. Her right arm lay across her stomach.

People gathered along their path and touched her and wished her well. The feelings were so genuine. She could feel the love from each person as she passed them. Janie and Jazz, and then everyone else, wanted to know how she was doing. "Not too great, but I'll live thanks to Tom here."

A few women mock-swooned and laughed, which caused Sarah to blush. Tom stood a bit taller.

"It'll take a few weeks, but she'll recover." Everyone was thrilled and relieved that she was going to be OK. She looked terrible, but she'd recover.

"Over here, Tom," Doc called. Doc was checking out a number of wounded from the battle. Tom laid Sarah on some soft grass as Family members gathered around.

"Severely sprained left ankle and right knee, left knee is sore but no real damage, badly bruised thigh, pelvis and hips," he explained, pointing to each area. "Her ribs on her right side might be fractured, but I don't think they're badly broken. Her right shoulder was significantly dislocated, but I popped it back in the socket. Bruises to her face. This one on her right cheek looks the worst. As you know, she suffered a bad concussion. All in all, though, considering the beating she took at the hands of those lunatics, she's in pretty good shape. All of this will heal on its own in a few weeks if she rests and takes it easy. I want to get her to the river to get some cold water on these injuries to see if we can reduce the swelling. I also have a few adjustments and manipulations that should speed the healing process."

"Alright, Tom. She's your patient. Take good care of her." Sarah's heart skipped a beat. Although she'd only recently noticed Tom, certain parts of her were already reaching out to him, even those parts that hurt like hell. It dawned on her that she hadn't had sex in years. *Running from a crazy man can do that to a girl.*

TWENTY-THREE

Ms. Watson stepped in. "Everyone, the show's over. Back to whatever you're supposed to be doing." The Family members moaned, wished Sarah well and walked off. She gave a bit of a tortured smile back at them. That they were all very worried about her was obvious.

"OK, Ms. Sarah. You heard the man. You're in my custody . . . I mean, care." Tom's smile reached something deep inside her, a warmth she hadn't felt in years. She was more than a willing patient. "First, let's get you cleaned up."

He called for Carmen and Candy. Then he picked her up and headed down to the river. The two beauticians hustled after them.

"Oh my gosh!" Candy exclaimed. "Sarah, are you alright, dear? We've been so busy with all the other fighters." Candy had a distinct southern accent, though no one was sure it was real. She sort of dropped the accent every so often, not that Sarah cared.

"Goodness. Bring her down. Bring her this way, it's easier." Carmen had taken hold of Tom's strong right arm and was leading him around to the path everyone took to the river. Jazz and Janie were right on their heels.

Tom set her on the smooth stone under the lower waterfall and guided her swollen ankle into a turbulent pool that was very cold. "Does that feel alright?"

"Much better, actually. Thanks."

Candy began to wash Sarah head to toe. Sarah knew she was disgusting, even by her own standards. Carmen began to work on her hair. It was tangled and full of grass and leaves. There was some blood in it, but Tom had already determined that it wasn't hers. There was no cut on her scalp.

Jazz and Janie spoke with Tom on the river bank. They soon joined Sarah in the river and began to help. Tom had Janie massage Sarah's ankle under the water. "Move it gently back and forth. Then pull on it a little. Then massage it up and down the ankle like this." Sarah loved it the way he did it, but Janie did rather well when she took over, even though her hands were not nearly as strong.

Jazz was put in charge of her knee. He guided her through some manipulations and then turned it over to Jazz, who also did well. Again, she loved Jazz but preferred Tom's touch and strong hands. Jazz and Janie could see it on her face, even though she was trying to hide her fledgling feelings for Tom, which she neither believed nor trusted.

Tom moved up to Sarah's sore shoulder. "You did a nice bit of work on this shoulder. I was amazed at how you handled me putting it back in its socket. Most people cry out, but you just said 'ouch' and grimaced a little. You're pretty darn tough."

"Thank you, I guess."

He massaged her shoulder, moved it around to determine its range of motion. She grimaced so he stopped, then he put her hand in her lap. "Don't move this. I'm going to see if they've found something to make a sling from."

As he left, he slid his hand across her back. She tingled all over. When he was gone, Candy finished cleaning her up. Carmen worked to untangle her hair, which took some time and required quite a bit of her long black locks to be cut. Sarah wasn't as bothered as the beautician was to see her hair float down the stream.

"I'm so sorry, Sarah." Carmen's voice almost trembled as she cut her hair free of sticks and debris. "After a day or so, when you're feeling better, you come back down here, and we'll give you a proper cut and style."

"Carmen, no worries. Thanks so much. You ladies do a great job around here." She felt a bit better. The two smiled, bowed to her and then left.

Jazz looked at her mother with a sly smile. "You like him, don't you?"

"I don't know, honey. We just met." Her heart was conflicted. Men hadn't been good for her, but there was something about this guy.

"But he's soooo cute," chimed in Janie.

"Yes, he is. I certainly agree with that," Sarah replied with a grin. "Carmen and Candy sure like him."

"Oh, screw them, Mom. They'd do everyone in this camp, boy or girl, if they could," Jazz added with a bit of disdain.

"Young lady," Sarah said in a less admonishing tone than she should have, a difference noted by both girls. All three of them broke into laughter. Sarah realized that this was the first time she'd laughed since the Storm. The three continued their inappropriate gossip. Jazz pushed Sarah about liking Tom. Sarah pushed back on Jazz about liking Mark.

Janie threw back her head with laughter as her older sister tried to deny the crush. "You *so* like him, it's ridiculous."

"Oww," Sarah groaned. "It hurts to laugh." But none of them could stop.

Jazz's eyes widened with a girlish warning and then whispered to her mother, "He's coming."

Sarah put her finger to her lips: "Shhhh." Smiling, they tried to act normal but couldn't hide the obvious air of conspiracy among them.

"Hmmm, what nefarious scheme did I just walk into? The three of you were plotting something. Yes?" Tom inquired as he stepped into the water.

They all shook their heads in denial and then broke out laughing. He sat on a rock near Sarah's shoulder, watching with a grin. It was obvious what was going on, but things would move at their own pace, and Sarah was fine with that. She was not sure she was ready for more complications.

"Are you quite done?" Her daughters forced themselves to stop laughing but were still giggling under their breath. Sarah felt like a schoolgirl with a crush. It was fun to be sharing the moment with her girls.

"The Seamstresses made this for you out of a rabbit hide. Posh. It should work for the purpose." The sling was made of some nicely tanned, supple white-and-brown rabbit skins. She admired the work for a minute before Tom put it on her. The soft fur held her forearm across her ribs

147

below her breasts. His arm grazed her nipple as he fitted the sling. Janie saw it and fell into the running water, bursting out laughing. Sarah glared at her, that fake angry-eye stare one gives a co-conspirator daughter who's close to revealing their secret.

Tom backed away and tilted his head. "What *are* you three up to?" Jazz lost it too and began giggling. Janie laughed her way back into the water.

Sarah smiled at Tom. "Don't pay any attention to those two hooligans. How does it look, doc?" She tried to maintain a distance but caught herself gazing into those eyes. Embarrassed, she turned her attention to the sling.

"You'll be fine. It's gonna hurt, and we have no painkillers. We're looking into it, but we've got nothing we can be sure is safe right now." As he worked her shoulder a bit in the sling, he slid his other hand down her back. She shivered, and he continued, "Your daughter there, Doc and a few others checked out the mushrooms those teens ate. They brought some back to see what they can figure out."

"Yeah, Mommy. Some aren't anything I've ever seen. And some were Gyromitra, Helvella, Verpa, chanterelle mushrooms and others typical of the places we camp on weekends, but those were easy to spot. But it's really weird to find them all in one place like that. But that's not the weirdest part. Most of the mushrooms were species none of us had ever seen before."

"And she's seen a LOT of mushrooms," Jazz informed Tom. "She's a plant and mushroom nutcase." Tom's face showed he was duly impressed. They all stopped what they were doing and listened to the third grader. Sarah smiled.

Janie looked at Tom and then at her mother, who nodded. Janie smiled and continued with confidence, "We think those ones we didn't know must be extremely dangerous, the ones that killed all those kids so fast. The others are dangerous, but not that fast, but I don't know what happens if you eat all of them at the same time like they did. Those other mushrooms aren't from here, like, not even North America. I don't know where they came from. Neither did Ms. Amy. Mr.

Franklin thinks he can do some chemistry thing and figure out what they might be good for. Ms. Bethany made him promise to wait for me before he started."

"OK, glad Tom brought that up." She mock-glared at him with as nice a smile as she could, winked, then grimaced from the pain and the confused look on Tom's face. *You're such a dork, Sarah.* She closed her eyes, turned back to her daughter and put on her strong mother face. "Thank you, Janie. That was very informative. Let me know what you guys find out, will you?" Sarah wanted to make it clear she was proud of her youngest, but the words came out so stilted. It'd been a long time since she'd been interested in a guy.

"Suuuurrre!" Janie exclaimed loudly.

"Mom, you're such a dork." Jazz added, rolling her eyes.

Sarah was sure she'd turned bright red, reached for some cold water with her good hand and tossed it onto her face to cool down. Her ribs stabbed her from within, and she froze. Tom's big hands were there, strong, warm and powerful on her back and shoulder, guiding her back down to the smooth river rock.

He flashed his gorgeous smile at Sarah. "So, Miss Patient, that was your ribs, right?" She nodded sheepishly. "Now lie back and rest. How's that ankle?" He stood up and towered above her as he spoke.

Sarah took a deep breath at the vision of Tom's body on full display before managing to speak, turning her attention to Janie to gain control. "Despite the fact that my nurse down there isn't doing her job, it's feeling much better under the cold water." Janie snapped to attention, eyes wide open with mock astonishment, and returned to massaging her mother's ankle. She hadn't allowed a man to get near her in ages, but despite what her head was telling her, she knew her body wanted this man to get near her . . . very near her. A warmth welled up from inside, red and velvety, like Asha's robes.

Tom moved down next to Janie and worked her ankle, "The cold should reduce the swelling. The manipulation will help move the blood through the ankle, reduce pooling in the heel and allow any nerves trapped in the tiny bones to wriggle free. All of that should help it heal faster. How's the knee?" She couldn't keep her eyes off of him but forced herself to look at Jazz, who had a wicked smile on her face.

Sarah smiled. "Jazz is doing fine. It's better. The massaging feels good."

"Keep moving it like I showed you. That'll help the knee the same way it'll help the ankle." He moved around beside Jazz to show her again. Sarah stared at his strong, wet physique. Jazz saw her and gave a sly, "you're busted," smile to her mother.

Sarah shook her head slightly, smiling as if to say, "Yeah, girlfriend, but keep this quiet." When she looked back at Tom, she caught him admiring her glistening body under the cascading water and the dappled sunshine coming through the trees as the sun fell in the sky. She aimed for sexy in that pose, reclined against a rock, clean and in great shape, bruises and all.

His penis started to become aroused. She smiled her approval in a tiny moment of eye contact. He blushed and averted his eyes, shifting his weight to look at the bruise on her thigh, moving his thigh to effectively hide his member from the younger girls. She could feel their souls reaching out for each other. So much of her world these days was centered on her intuition, and it was strong with Tom. Very strong and very positive. It frightened her. The sexual tension broke, and she tried to focus, for a moment, on her situation.

"This looks nasty and colorful, as most bad bruises do." The bruise extended from the front of her thigh around to her inner thigh. "Maybe from a kick, given how long it is." Tom turned to Sarah's oldest. "Jazz, moving your mother's knee up and down like that should also help move the blood through her thigh muscle, and it should also help relieve the pain," he said, as he massaged the bruise. Then he caressed the inside of her thigh, lingering, softly and gently, above the bruise a little too far and a little too long. Sarah gasped and her eyelids fluttered as desire flooded back. She took a deep breath and then controlled her exhalation. "That might hurt longer than anything else." He perceived it as a reaction to pain, but it was so much more for Sarah. If her girls weren't there, she knew where she wanted this moment to go. "How're your ribs?" *He's relentless.*

"Not bad at all. I can breathe fine and move OK." She tried to sound strong and distant as she twisted her torso left and right but was stopped by a sudden and sharp pain. "Auggh, hmmm." He stepped through her daughters' legs and straddled her, one foot in the rushing cold falls, took her shoulders in his strong hands and guided them back to square and onto the rocks.

She looked up into his eyes, both longing for his touch and angry at the pain and her helplessness. "They're not broken!" She wanted to sound strong, but her voice quivered. She could not release herself from those eyes, and he did not look away. She was sure neither of them even blinked. She was putty in those big, strong, gentle hands, and for the first time in decades, she wanted to be.

"Let's hope not, but we can't take chances. Don't do what you just did," he scolded. Still bent at the waist, they broke eye contact as he pulled his foot from the falls and stood next to her. "Alright, as for everything else, keep your weight off your legs for a while. All we can do is massage the injuries to increase blood flow, do these manipulations to increase mobility, try to keep the swelling down with the cold river water and then wait to see how fast you heal." He was towering above her and looked delicious. "How's your pelvis?"

Oh fine, now he decides to go there. "Ummm." She gazed up at his smiling face, sensing the purpose for that inquiry that she hoped was there. "It doesn't hurt sitting here. Perhaps you can examine it later." The water pouring across her thigh was running across her pelvis, which felt nice and helped to hide her own arousal. Suddenly, she remembered her girls were there, and embarrassment raced through her. She turned and looked at Jazz, who had that devilish grin again. Janie also sat smiling. Sarah was not entirely sure her youngest knew what was going on.

Tom diffused the tension. "Again, the cold water should help with any swelling. How's your head?" He knelt down, moved close and gazed into her eyes. She breathed in that wonderful scent. "Your eyes look good. No dilation. Responsive. Follow my finger again." This time she was more coherent and handled the task easily. "Good, better than before. Any headaches?"

"No, I feel great. Alert. Fine, really."

"Doc and I are very worried about that concussion. You were out cold for a long time. You need to take it easy while your brain recovers." She felt that it may have been less a brain injury than her spirits getting the Storm she'd released back into the bottle, but she didn't know for sure. She nodded and kind of batted her eyes. He smiled. "Hang out here as long as you can tolerate it today. Have one of those hooligans come and find me when you're ready." He smiled at the girls, and they gave him a look of mock disapproval. Sarah smiled. He rose, exposing his full and chiseled body to her again. To her surprise, he bent down and kissed her forehead before he left. "You'll be back to normal in no time."

TWENTY-FOUR

om smiled a big smile and winked at the girls as he turned. Both stayed quiet until he cleared the stream. Then Janie said, in a voice she was sure he could hear, "See, Mom, I told you he likes you."

Sarah's eyes got big, and she shushed her youngest daughter. Jazz was watching Tom to see if he'd heard. Tom skipped a step in acknowledgment without looking back and then bounded up the bank to the camp.

"What did he do?" Sarah implored.

"Mom, you are such a loser. He's been following you around for days." Jazz giggled.

"Yeah, Mommy, and you never even noticed him. He totally likes you," Janie added. Sarah hadn't really noticed anyone in particular, and she certainly had no interest in any kind of relationship with a man, but this guy, right now, her body wanted . . . and wanted bad.

The three spent the better part of the next hour giggling and frolicking in the river. Sarah was a quick healer—always had been. This was excellent therapy, and she could feel her body and her Bear and Elephant spirits healing it. Most of all, she was enjoying some frivolous time with her girls. Things had been so stressful, even before the Wall. She was going to stretch this time out. Who knew when it would come again?

She didn't know until later that Ms. Watson had given strict orders not to bother them, except for Tom, of course. The news of their impending relationship spread through the camp. A few of the women feigned sadness. Tony was incensed that Sarah was paying attention to Tom and not him. He receded further with his crew, which had grown larger.

Doc and his medical team were tending to the eight newcomers and the other injured, including Hector. Rhonda, who'd returned just before the fray, had downed a deer with her new bow. Gus and Bobbi, the young woman who tanned the hides, were skinning it. Bobbi took the hide, and Gus cut the meat up for dinner. Everything that could be used was preserved. Claire took the rest to the dogs. Amy and Herb were discussing dinner. Wood was being hauled in. Everyone was excited about the meal, the victory in battle and the budding romance in camp.

These bits of good news were sorely needed. Sarah had no idea what had transpired while she was unconscious, being treated by Tom and now giggling with Janie and Jazz in the river. As soon as they decided to leave, Janie ran to get Tom, screaming for "The big hunk who likes my mother!!" Sarah rolled her eyes, and Jazz shrugged. Janie knew Sarah was helpless. Tom returned with a big smile and carried her up to camp. A few of the Family members who'd returned from their duties moved into the bathing area, smiling at Sarah, touching or patting her to lend her empathetic support as they passed. Carmen and Candy returned to care for the new customers.

That evening, the group dined on fire-roasted deer meat. The meal was by far the largest since the Wall and was very filling. There were no leftovers, other than a few packets for newcomers and a nice midnight lunch for the watchmen. The Family was happy to have fuller bellies, and the eight teenagers, who were famished, were feeling much better, though five were still in the infirmary.

When dinner was completed, Ms. Watson called the Family to gather around the central fire, as had become the tradition. Everyone had their place at the fire. Tom carried Sarah to her place near Ms. Watson. He stood to leave, but to her own surprise, she grabbed his wrist. "I need something to help hold me up. My ribs make it so hard to sit. Do you have anyone else you need to sit with?" He smiled, shook his head, sat behind her and slipped himself under her back as a backrest. She could feel his manhood harden behind her, and she nestled her back against it. She looked forward to feeling up to a more intimate engagement. He kissed the back of her head, and she could feel the sexual energy between them down to her toes.

Jazz and Janie were oblivious to what was happening behind their mother's lower back but knew what was happening in plain view. They were so happy to see their mother happy, and Sarah hadn't been this happy, this blissful, in . . . well, ever, in their memories. Who knew it would take the end of civilization for that to happen?

Ms. Watson stood, and the Family fell silent. "Today, we put to rest a lot of young people. We don't know where their souls will go, but we know they will be cared for. To light the pyre, we used a flame from each of the three great fires that protect us, keep us warm and have helped us remain safe these three days since the Wall. They represent strength, cooperation and love," she said as she pointed left, then right and finally at the fire in the center that remained burning at all times. "Without any of these, we'd be lost. The pyre still burns out in the grasslands. We'll remember this day for all time. We'll honor the dead and those that defended us and our way of life."

She walked around the outside of the circle to where Hector was resting. Tom updated her on Hector. "Olivia scrubbed the huge gash on his chest with some peppermint and hot water. Hector screamed like nothing I've ever heard. There was no anesthesia. There was no alcohol. No pain medication. We had to hold him down. Finally, he passed out. Thank heavens for that. Doc sewed Hector's chest shut. He slept all afternoon."

"I didn't hear him scream," Sarah commented.

"You were out cold, Mom," Janie replied.

"Yeah, we were bringing wet rabbit skins to cool you down," Jazz added.

"You were kinda hot. I mean, like, temperature. You looked horrible," Janie said and ducked as her mother pretended to reach for her. Sarah groaned, and Tom settled her back onto his body. "Ooowwww."

"Alright, no more of that, Ms. Sarah. Be a good patient."

"I'll try," she cooed up at him, then refocused her attention on the girls. "OK, then what happened? He seems to be awake."

"Then nurse Olivia wiped his forehead and chest with cold wet rabbit's fur to try and cool the areas and reduce the redness," Jazz continued. Olivia was a solidly built woman, now standing stoically behind Hector, of medium height with dirty blond hair.

"Like us with you, Mommy. We tried to keep you cool, too." Sarah turned to Janie and gently stroked her hair.

"Thank you, sweetie. Both of you," she said, smiling at both of her girls.

"The cool water helped him rest better, but we don't know whether it'll help him recover," Tom said.

"He was very hot. A lot hotter than you were, Mom," Jazz noted.

Tom continued, "He's a long way from being healed, but he woke up, was adamant about being at the campfire. He ate some and is alert. He's still in a great deal of pain and unable to move much, but he's here."

"Ms. Olivia complained so much that he shouldn't be moved and has been right next to him the whole time. She's still taking care of him and his yucky wound," Janie said. Sarah turned to observe Olivia standing behind Hector. Olivia looked Sarah in the eyes, and they connected—not the way she did with animals, but still spiritually. Her connection to women, like with Ms. Watson, Erika, Claire and now Olivia, were more . . . fuzzy than with animals. She still didn't connect well with men, except now with Tom and in a very disturbing way with Tony.

Ms. Watson gestured to Hector and then to the crowd and called out, "To Hector!" She raised her arms, and there was a loud cheer. Olivia smiled briefly. The gash across Hector's chest was gruesome in the firelight: dark brownish-red and still seeping blood at the cut itself. They had no gauze to wrap it. As disturbing as the gash was the deep purplish-red color of the skin on either side of the gash. Even from across the fire, Sarah could see that it was swollen and had to be incredibly painful. Hector was tough, but she, and everyone else, worried that would not be enough.

Ms. Watson put her hand on Olivia's shoulder. "To Olivia, who nursed him all afternoon and, according to Doc, kept him alive!" Again, a loud cheer arose from the Family. Olivia blushed. Hector reached up and touched her cheek, then cringed and pulled his arm down. This time, the crowd sighed. Olivia left to get more cold water, or to perhaps react to the acknowledgment out of the presence of the Family.

"Are they a couple?" Sarah asked.

"Yeah. Duh, Mom. You are so out of it sometimes." In some ways, Jazz was still a typical teenager. Sarah looked at Hector and could feel Olivia crying in the darkness.

Ms. Watson walked around the group and stood over a slight young woman, maybe in her twenties, with dark hair and dark eyes whom Sarah sort of remembered. She'd apparently also been injured, though Sarah didn't know how it'd happened. "To Randi!" Again, a loud cheer. *That tiny woman followed me out there! She protected the kids!* Sarah nodded her appreciation, and Randi smiled broadly and bowed back to her.

Ms. Watson repeated this for several others, announcing their accomplishments. Each of them looked to Sarah, who smiled and nodded, which was about all she could do. They then bowed to her.

"What's all this bowing crap about?" she whispered.

Tom gently shushed her.

Ms. Watson was including everyone she could, and the cheers of support were strong for each, but she walked right past Tony and two henchmen, and Sarah could see that he was seething.

Tom whispered in her ear, "Ms. Watson had it out with Tony while you were unconscious. He and his two goons ran out among the teens, stabbing those who were already dead or dying, serving only to ruin some valuable spears. Then when some of the crazies turned on them, they ran like little girls back into the camp with the poisoned spears. No one was hurt, and the spears were recovered, but Ms. Watson was livid. I've never seen her so angry. She got up in his face and flat-out laid into him. Though he's taller, had those big guys as backup and you were out of commission, he backed down, and in a hurry." As he spoke, Tony and his now 20-plus followers stood and stomped off to the back fire.

Sarah looked up at him, astonished. "That explains a lot." Tom nodded solemnly.

Ms. Watson worked her way around the Family. When she got to Tom and toasted, "To Tom!" the corresponding cheer was loud.

TWENTY-FIVE

Ms. Watson moved to Sarah's side. Janie, Jazz and Tom all knew what was about to transpire. Sarah didn't. Her story had been told throughout the camp all afternoon. It was already Family legend. Ms. Watson looked down at Sarah with a big smile, then back to the Family and then to Roger.

"Roger."

Roger nodded to Ms. Watson and then bowed to Sarah before he began. "I crossed the ridge with several of our Family and saw our relatives standing strong together atop a small hill in the middle of dozens of crazed teens coming from the west. To the east, however, two of the older teens cut themselves with sharp rocks and, without feeling the pain, smeared their blood on sharpened wooden spears, eyes wild and frantic like William's. They organized six others, armed them with blood-soaked weapons and turned toward the Family on the hill. They began a determined charge up the eastern slope. Sarah broke from her fully engaged brethren and faced them alone. We were coming fast, but we had no chance to get there in time.

"Seeing the heavily armed troops, with insanity in their eyes, determined to kill her Family, she rose and, like she does, glowed bright crimson, crossed her spear in front of her and launched herself, without regard for her own safety or life, into the heart of the phalanx." With grand theatrics, Roger continued telling the story of her battle with the

158

crazed teens and their leaders. He finally stood tall and raised his arms to the sky and yelled, "The last spear flew from his hands, and the Family was saved." Then quickly, his voice fell to a whisper as he turned to Sarah. "But our beloved leader was now in grave danger." All of this she remembered and felt now in her body.

"As we all saw, these zombies wouldn't die easily, and though bloodied by Sarah's superhuman punishment, they regained their footing, along with others, and began to physically attack Sarah. She fought valiantly but was rendered unconscious. Tom and Randi, tiny but brave, broke from the fray and ran down the hill at her attackers. We also arrived, and several of us veered off to help. We descended upon them with strength and determination, spears ripping them apart and our bodies driving them back onto the turf.

"Tom scooped Sarah up into his arms and carried her limp body up to the eight kids still huddling atop the small hill. Though unarmed and weakened by hunger and dehydration, they reached down within themselves, mustering bravery beyond their physical capacity, and circled around our powerful leader to protect their savior." He walked toward them beside the fire as he narrated, pausing to acknowledge them. They all smiled and looked over to Sarah, who smiled and nodded her appreciation to them. They followed the new custom of bowing to her from their sitting positions. Sarah looked up at Tom, who smiled down at her.

"What can I say, they all love you." She could feel it, deep inside her. Robert's family was all she'd had after her parents died on that cliff, but they were shallow. They cared for her. But had they loved her? Loved her like this Family?

"Within minutes, the battle was over. Many in our Family suffered injuries, but when Sarah went down, we all feared for our lives. She was nonresponsive, bruised and broken." Roger moved slowly around the fire toward her with a dramatic stride. "Tom feared she may have suffered internal bleeding, and there'd be very little we could do to stop it." He spun toward the audience. "Sarah lay there on top of the hill, beaten and unconscious."

Roger turned his attention to her. The crowd was hushed. "The eight backed away to allow us in as we climbed the hill." He opened his arms and approached her. "You weren't moving. We couldn't even tell if you were breathing. There was blood everywhere. We were so afraid that you'd perished, that we hadn't gotten to you in time. We were so frightened. We feared that we'd failed you when you'd sacrificed everything for us. What would we do if you were gone? I and others broke down, fell to our knees beside you and cried." He was near her now and fell to his knees before her.

"Your pulse was weak, but . . . you were still alive." He reached down as though he were scooping something up in his arms. "Tom picked up your limp body in his powerful arms," Roger continued, standing up, "and carried you home to us."

He turned back to the Family and raised his voice, arms outstretched in glory. "Sarah, our leader, friend and hero. We're safe because our leader loves us more than life itself." Then he pointed to her with both arms. Except for her girls, she'd never risked so much for others. Warmth flowed through her to a depth she'd never felt before.

Ms. Watson raised her arms to the sky, "To Sarah!" When her name was announced, the cheer was loud and long and rolled across and well beyond the compound. Everyone stood and remained standing, applauding her for several minutes. Jazz and Janie too. Tom held her up as straight and as high as he could. The pain was sharp, but she endured.

Finally, Ms. Watson spoke, quieting the crowd, many of whom sat back down. "We won't ask her to speak. Sarah, please just heal." Then Ms. Watson returned the story to Roger.

"Our luscious prairie was a war zone." He swung his arms to his left and then back to his right to indicate the expanse of the field then opened them wide. "It was unclear how many, but perhaps three hundred children lay dead across the gentle hills and valleys," he said while stalking around the fire, playing to all of the Family, "and the plains leading to the river." His voice softened, becoming reverent. "There was blood, vomit and motionless, twisted bodies everywhere. After the victory, we stood awestruck. Where only minutes before the grasslands had been green and full of sweet-smelling wildflowers, all was now overwhelmed by the stench of death."

Roger's voice dropped to a whisper. "We fell to our knees and sobbed for the teenagers." He bowed his head and paused for effect. The Family followed. A moment of silence.

Ms. Watson tried to remain in control, but like so many, she was moved to tears.

Roger raised his head, speaking barely above a whisper, "Most died from the devilish poison from the mushrooms they'd ingested. Some, however, died from the spears and arrows of the Family members defending themselves and the eight that the attackers called 'traitors' and who we now call Family." Again, he paused as Ms. Watson moved around the fire to them. There was gentle applause and motions to the eight that they were in fact now part of the Family. Their sheepish smiles warmed everyone's hearts.

Roger's tone became mournful as he continued, "The sad duty of dealing with all of the dead in the field fell to Joe, Erika and their teams. The hills and plains were besmirched with poisonous blood and vomit. Rhonda went to retrieve her valuable arrows, but Ms. Watson wisely would not allow it. Ms. Watson made it clear that no one was to touch the blood of any of the fallen teens. We don't know what this poison is. We had seen what it could do to anyone who'd ingested it, and that was scary enough to exercise extreme caution." Sarah could see several looks cast in the direction of Tony's separatist crew.

"All of the bodies were dragged and stacked. Joe and Erika bravely took the task of cutting out the boy entangled in the barrier—a grisly task." Joe and Erika, sitting together with their children, nodded solemnly.

"A lot of valuable wood was carried out and piled all around and on top of the dead. We, the Family, all agreed that the bodies couldn't be allowed to rot or be eaten by animals. They, and the poison they carried, would have to be burned. The arrows and spears were tossed on top of the pile.

"When the huge pile of bodies and wood stood before us, a burning branch from each of the three fires was brought to the site." Sarah was reminded of the scenes in downtown and in Clayton of the piles of bodies who'd fallen from skyscrapers that had disappeared underneath them. Rats had infested them. She closed her eyes and pushed the vision away.

"The pyre was lit on three sides. Most of us returned in tears to the comfort of our Family and to wash in the river. No one knew how the poison would react to fire, though Franklin, our resident chemist, was sure the fire would destroy it.

"It took a long time for the bodies to light. They sizzled as the poisonous blood boiled. Soon the bodies became engulfed in flames. The smoke turned black and putrid."

Darkness had fallen during Roger's retelling, and Sarah noticed a glow in the night sky in the direction of the pyre.

When the story was over, Ms. Watson stood but didn't say a word. The evening's meeting was over. Molly began to sing a song that all the children knew. Nearly everyone joined in. It was sweet, about a child who was lost and afraid but was soon found and grasped to the bosom of parents. It was a song about love, but to Sarah, it was a song about the fate of the teens. Lost in this crazy world and now grasped into the loving arms of something bigger beyond death, free of the fear, addiction and pain they'd endured, not just on this last day of their lives, but for much of them.

Sarah hummed along as she got the gist of the melody. Tom joined in as well. She snuggled back into him, and he wrapped one of his big arms around her. She felt safe and happy. Tom slipped his body down beside hers. She curled over on the side of her bad ribs, which was less painful than lying on her dislocated shoulder, and rested her head on his chest. Within a few minutes, she was asleep in Tom's arms.

TWENTY-SIX

Robert's face. Stench of bourbon. Tom writhing in pain. Tony laughing up, into darkness, lit by leaping flames. Surrounding her. Screams. Cackling. World spinning out of control. Tony, raging fire, closed in upon her . . .

Sarah woke with a start, bolting up to sitting, sweating with terror, pain from the injuries in the fight ripping at her, and she was cold. Another nightmare and, now, rain.

Tom mumbled, and his eyes opened a crack.

"Oh my God, Tom, are you alright?"

"Um, other than it's the middle of the night, cold as hell and raining, I'm fine."

The light drizzle soon turned into a torrent. A violent strike of lightning lit the night sky. It was followed by a huge crack of thunder. The shock ripped through the community, waking everyone. Tom grabbed her into his arms, but she resisted.

The girls awoke and looked at their mother. "Bye Mom!" Jazz yelled as they ran for the trees and their friends. The thunder was followed by another lightning strike and, a few seconds later, another large rumble of thunder. The worst part of the storm was upon them.

Sarah groaned as she gave in and laid back into Tom's arms, her head on his chest, and she whispered, "Why can't we catch a break?"

She couldn't let him know the real reason she was shaking in terror. She couldn't. They'd just met.

He was wet but smiling. "You OK? You seem a little freaked out."

"Yeah, great. Battered and broken, soaking wet and cold, awoken from a nightmare by a storm, and now I sense that you're going to leave me to see what you can do for everyone else. It's what I'd be doing if I could move . . ." She winced in pain. It felt worse. ". . . which I can't."

"Sleeping on the hard ground tends to do that even if you haven't had your ass kicked by a bunch of insane punk teenagers." Tom tried to draw out a smile.

Her emotions were conflicted.

Few had experienced thunder and lightning in the open. They all stood, huddled together and shivering, in the relative comfort of the trees. Moving was not an option. She'd been out in storms before, but never while hurt or lying on the bare ground. Spring in St. Louis meant rain. It rained often and sometimes hard. Now, unfortunately, was one of those times.

Ms. Watson was moving around, comforting those who were struggling. Molly was up gliding through the children. Ms. Watson looked Tom in the eyes and made it clear his job was to keep Sarah comfortable.

"Sarah, I'm not going anywhere," he whispered. She felt his love deep within her. Soft and real and warm. He moved above her to shield her from the rain. She rolled back on her back, smiled up at him and caressed his strong chest with her good hand, watching his chest hairs slip through her long slender fingers as small droplets fell from their tips onto her chest.

Sarah and Tom were alone in the middle of the compound, lying in soaked, muddy grass, smiling at one another as the rain poured off his sides. She reached up and guided him down atop her, although he held his weight off her. She loved the feel of his body close to hers, stroking his strong back with her good hand, gazing into those deep blue eyes.

After a few minutes, he said, "Do you think they're witches? Ms. Watson and Molly." Sarah laughed and slapped him playfully on his back. "I mean the good kind. The Glenda kind. Ms. Watson and Molly *are* magic. You realize that, right?"

Sarah smiled broadly, shook her head and then slyly shrugged her shoulders in tacit agreement, keeping her eyes locked deeply onto his. He kissed her forehead, and she kissed his chin. The Family cheered and yelled for more. The rain softened, and Tom slid off to her side, his left hand on her taut stomach.

Sarah said, "They're great with people. Thank heavens, Tom, because I suck at it. Animals, nature, sure. I'm all over that. But humans. Humans can be a quandary for me." She paused. "They are amazing, those two."

"I've only known them since I got here. There's an air about them, you have to admit. Otherworldly. Maybe they're aliens planted on earth to live among us and study us with special magical powers over us." Sarah elbowed him again and winced. He hugged her to him, and they laughed as the rain again came down in sheets.

There was another flash of lightning followed a few seconds later by a loud clap of thunder. He encircled her with as much of his body as he could. They were lying in mud, being pelted by torrential rain, holding each other close, and she realized that there was no place she'd rather be.

TWENTY-SEVEN

The three fires were doused. She was happy the barrier had proven itself. Sarah knew they would all be very cold over the next few hours. Cold breakfast, whatever that meant, and still no coffee.

The hard rains passed to the east, followed by a steady rain. As the rain diminished further to a light shower, she was able to settle back on Tom's chest and relax. Before the first rays of morning crept into the sky, she slipped back into much-needed sleep.

The dawn broke bright and beautiful, as it often does after such a deep soaking rain. Her eyes opened a crack as Tom moved a bit under her.

She breathed his scent in deeply. No nightmare. The air was fresh and clean. She closed her eyes and became one with it, well beyond them, the Family, the compound, and drank it in. Asha appeared to her in the soft red mist. "That's it, Sarah. Love. Feel the love all around you. Let it in. The darkness is rising. Be prepared." She faded, and Sarah could feel the love from Tom, from her Family, from her four spirit animals and even from the recovering wildflowers swaying in the vast fields beyond their barrier, dancing in the warmth of a new day. Like the stench of the pyre, at least some of the darkness inside her was washed away.

Then the reality of their world crept in. She realized that much of the debris from the pyre, if she was right about where they'd laid it out, would run into the river and would soon float by.

"Ms. Watson," she croaked. Her ribs hurt more this morning. "Tom."

166

"What?" He was sleepy, muddy and cold. He sat up and helped her sit up. The girls were up and about already.

"You have to tell Ms. Watson and the others not to go into the river."

"Why?"

"Because, pieces and parts of those burned bodies probably washed into the river upstream and could be arriving in our part of the river. No one should get into that water until we're sure all the contaminated water is past. Go now. I'm sure everyone wants to wash off this mud."

"OK." He struggled out from under Sarah, who winced again as she rolled off him and laid back on the soft, wet, cold ground. It was not as tolerable without him.

She watched with a smile as that nice buttocks ran off to provide Ms. Watson with Sarah's warning. Sarah began taking inventory of her situation. She moved her left ankle around and tried to get a look at it. *It feels better. It looks less swollen,* she lied to herself. It hurt like hell. So did her right knee. Her right ankle and both hips now hurt as well. With all her injuries elsewhere, these lesser twinges had gone relatively unnoticed yesterday. But now that she had spent the night on hard ground in cold, pouring rain, everything hurt.

She moved her right knee. *OW!* The bruise to her right thigh hurt more than her knee, though both sent shivers of pain through her every time she moved her leg. Her hips hurt. Her back hurt. Her shoulder and side hurt. Her face hurt as she touched it. *Everything hurts, goddammit, and I'm lying here alone in the cold-ass mud.*

There was one bit of good news. As she touched it, her pelvis felt much better. She was happy about that. She had plans for that part of her anatomy in the near future. She let her mind wander off to a daydream about making love to Tom in the soft grass beneath the warm sun.

She made the mistake of moving a little and was yanked back to reality. She hoped that she was mainly sore from sleeping on the ground in the rain and that everything would loosen up as she began to move around a little. She laid back, winced from the pain and stretched out on the soaking wet ground. She moaned through the process until she was flat on her back. That felt better. No more moving.

The woman who gathered food with Janie was nearby. "How ya doin', honey?"

"I don't know. Everything hurts. I bet I'm just gorgeous."

The woman smiled. "You look fine." She reached over and touched Sarah's face. "This bruise under your right eye looks pretty bad. I bet it's sore." Sarah nodded. "The rest of your face looks very pretty." Sarah doubted her but smiled. The woman caressed Sarah's scalp to soothe her. "Whoa. You have a couple of nasty bumps on your head. I guess that's what knocked you out cold."

"How long was I out?"

"I'd guess over an hour. The grasslands were cleaned, the pyre built and pretty much everyone had bathed by the time you came to. It was a long time. Be careful. Concussions like that can be very bad. We thought you might be in a coma. Tom and Doc were afraid to move you again. I have to go honey, but Tom's coming. He'll take good care of you." She winked a girlfriend's conspiratorial wink, kissed her gently on the forehead and stood. Sarah thought, *This woman is my sister. She's a good friend, like Amy, Erika, Joe, Marsha, Ms. Watson, Molly, Doc and, of course, Tom, along with so many others. I'm making friends here, good friends. That's a first.* She gave herself permission to feel the love from her Family, and it felt so good.

Tom returned. "Hi, Caroline. Sarah, you were right, but I didn't have to tell anyone. There were charred bones, ashes and other disgusting things floating in the rushing water, so no one was going anywhere near that river. Some fish are dead. That water's poisonous. The good thing is, the river's running fast."

"This morning's going to suck," Sarah moaned.

"Well, one piece of good news. Amy felt the rain and grabbed a large burning branch from the fire and put it under the cooking stone, and it kept burning. We have fire! Not that you couldn't have made more, but now you don't have to. Good news, right?" Ms. Watson, Joe, Erika and Marsha arrived at Sarah's side. They all waited for her wisdom as to what to do next. She didn't disappoint.

Tom helped her to a sitting position. She grimaced but didn't cry out as sharp pains tore through her from every corner of her body. She closed her eyes, took a deep breath and felt her spirits rise enough to put the pain in the background to allow her to think. "OK. Very good news. Tell Amy 'nice job' for me. Everything's so wet. It'd be a long time before I could have got anything to burn, assuming I could move enough to even do it.

"Marsha, lift as much of the wood as possible up off the wet ground, take it out to the hills where the ground is drier and stack it as wide apart as possible so that the wind can blow through it and help dry it out. The wood on the bottom will stay wet, but hopefully we can get the wood nearer the top to dry out by dinner." *Again with the hope.* "See if Tony's crew'll help."

"Yeah, right," Marsha responded then cracked an exhausted half smile at Sarah. "Don't worry, we're on it." And she left.

"We need to clean out the fire pits. The ashes will have stayed wet, but they often do a pretty good job of keeping the dirt underneath relatively dry. Put the ashes along the barrier. Animals don't like it. It's very acrid. Make sure the team that works with it wears gloves to protect their skin.

"Send the wood-gathering teams out. Even in this sort of rain, there are often dead pieces of wood under the dense tree canopy that are old enough that even when a little wet, they'll burn sooner than the stuff we had here out in the open. Put it out on the hills to dry too.

"Have someone go check the pyre. Not sure what to do with it, but folks should head north of it and wash this nasty mud off somewhere upstream. Get whatever we have and gather some water up there and bring it back so we have something to drink.

"We have to make a boatload of spears and arrows. The points should have survived the fire and should be sterilized from the heat. We need to find them. Get some people on that. If we have another attack now, we're dead. Plus, we have to hunt.

"Everyone else can do the normal stuff. Anything else?" She looked at everyone, but they all seemed satisfied.

"OK, then. Tom, Joe, help me up, for crying out loud. It's cold and muddy and horrible down here."

TWENTY-EIGHT

om took control, and as he had several times already, lifted her into his big arms. Ms. Watson shooed the leaders away and sent them to rally their teams to attend to the tasks Sarah had assigned them. They each did as they were told, gathering their teams and setting off to work.

"Put me down. I need to walk."

"You cannot walk, Sarah! Doctor's orders."

"Down. Now! I mean it." She was stubborn. The entire Family quieted, turned and watched. She summoned the spirits in hopes that they'd help. Tom lowered her slowly, allowing her to put a bit of weight on her better ankle.

She balanced on her right ankle, but her knee and bruises drove nails into her. She switched to her bad left ankle, which hurt but held up better. The knee and hip notified her that they were not pleased with the weight being placed on them. Tom slid around behind and under her good left shoulder and held her. "There is no way you can stand." She glared at him. "You think you can stand?"

"I don't know." She knew she couldn't but needed to try. The Family gathered around her. Silence. She tried to put weight on her ankle, slipped out of his grasp as a wave of intense pain raged through her body, and everything gave out. Tom caught her as the onlookers oohed and aahed.

They sent encouraging words. "It'll be OK." "Don't push it." "We're here for you." She was angry at her situation but did her best to smile at them.

Ms. Watson put a soothing hand on her shoulder. "Let's not risk it yet."

Sarah nodded her agreement. "Just get me someplace warmer." Before Tom could pick her up, she let out a primal yell, deep, powerful, from her soul. The sound resonated well beyond the compound, as though the Tiger inside her was helping to expel her frustrations. She felt her four living animals, and everyone heard them, as the tiger roared in the woods to their east, the bear growled in the woods to their west, the elephant trumpeted to their north in the grasslands, and her horse whinnied behind her by the river, all in unison. The Family members, mouths open in astonishment, took a few steps back.

Sarah turned to her Family. "I'm so sorry. This just sucks. I will be back to full strength soon! I promise you. I promise all of you!"

"Sarah, it's alright. I got you."

She reluctantly put her arm around Tom's neck, and he picked her up. She pointed, and he carried her to a warmer place in the sun and laid her on a slight incline in soft grass near the inside of the barrier. It was still quite damp but much warmer. He laid her back on the soft ground.

"I'm fine. Tom, go see if Doc needs help with the injured. I'm not going anywhere, and laying me here in the sun is probably as much as you can do for me anyway . . . at least for now," she said with a wink. He smiled broadly.

"OK, but stay here, lie flat and don't move. You hear me?" She nodded, but even that hurt. He touched her shoulder, then her face, so gently and then bent down and kissed her on the forehead. She breathed in his intoxicating, musky scent, and her head swooned. Her frustration disappeared. He was in her, in her soul, warm, tender and strong.

"Thank you," she cooed as she lay her head back on the soft grass, gazing up into his dazzling blue eyes.

He maintained the connection for several seconds, then said in such a soft, soothing tone, "You're welcome." He slid a hair from her forehead with his powerful right hand, smiled, stood up straight and tall above her, the deep blue of the sky encircling his angelic curly brown hair like a halo. Tom then winked at her before turning and heading toward the infirmary. She turned her head to watch him stride away, feeling no pain.

Once he was off into the milieu, Sarah took a deep breath, closed her eyes and felt the world of nature flowing around and through her. She could feel him, his soul, his—dare she believe it—love, a feeling she also felt for him.

The thought shocked her. *Love!? C'mon, Sarah. You just met him!* But there was no denying the feelings as a smile creased her face. For the first time since the Storm, she focused on herself, laying on the soft grass, letting the sun warm her cold body and drinking in the elixir that was Tom.

She wasn't sure how long she'd been soaking in this new set of feelings when a young boy arrived with a basket filled with two dried strips of deer meat, a small smoked sausage, some berries and flowers that Amy and Herb had crafted into a solid, albeit cold, breakfast.

"Thank you," she said. The boy bowed to her, turned and scampered off. Sarah surveyed the Family. It was a good thing dinner the evening before had been significant. There was some rainwater in the basin of the cooking stone. It was the only fresh water they had at the moment, and the medical team's needs for it took priority.

Joe and Erika took a team to the pyre to check it out and gather as many spear and arrow points as possible. Jake's wood crew headed out to search for something dry. Janie's gatherers headed out as usual to find greens, roots and fruit. The trappers set their traps for rabbits in the clover fields. After each fisher made themselves a chip-tipped spear, like Day 0, they headed out to fish upstream of the pyre. Others joined them with bladders to gather water upstream.

The Seamstresses served as basket makers, led by a wonderful chatty older woman who'd owned a craft shop in the old society. They contributed some rough baskets lined with large leaves they'd sewn together to help in moving the ashes. This was a slow and dirty job, not done by Tony's crew. Sure enough, however, the ground under the ashes was much drier.

Jazz took her team of stone workers to the river. Even only four days into this new world, most of what the team was doing was sharpening tools instead of making them. The exception was arrow and spear points. If the hunters were successful, they broke points. The battle with the addicts had ruined so many of their points, with only four usable points recovered from the pyre. After a couple of hours, Rhonda left to hunt with one arrow, and Marshall and Samantha left with one spear each. The fourth point was used for a defensive spear.

Many joined the teams making new arrow and spear shafts. Ol' Mac was working on another, even stronger bow, designed according to Rhonda's exacting standards. She'd searched long and hard for the right piece of wood, much longer and fresher than the piece from which her current bow had been carved. Rhonda also had new specifications for the arrows and took to searching out saplings for the purpose herself. She'd brought six home the day before with the deer. Jazz worked hard to keep Ol' Mac and now his apprentice supplied with sharp knives and Rhonda with arrow tips.

That wet morning, the Family used any excuse to get outside the barrier, out of the muddy interior, which was what the ground of the interior needed. The day was breezy, and with so few inside the barrier, the grass began to dry out nicely.

The rains and the slope had driven most of the pyre into the river. There were charred bone and fragments still in the river, but lighter debris and ashes had washed down away from the site. Despite Ms. Watson's warnings, Joe and Erika tossed the remaining charred bones from the pyre into the river. It was running very high, and even the bones were moving downstream. They walked the river, dislodging anything that was catching on the rocks. Once things reached the fast-running water below their lower pond, they were gone.

The fishermen returned before the sun reached its peak. They'd captured and speared several good-sized fish. Enough wood was dry enough to allow a decent fire under the cooking stone.

Sarah noticed Tony was skulking around in back even more than usual. Sarah sent word with a young girl who'd brought her some water to drink that none of the other fires would be lit until enough wood was gathered. Fish were fileted and cooked. Greens were prepared. There were strawberries and blackberries. Gus bellowed that lunch was ready like his grandmother used to from their farmhouse porch.

"Come and get it or we'll throw it out!" He always laughed when he shouted his grandmother's catchphrase. Amy always smiled. Herb always smirked. It had become a ritual of Family life. Of course, nothing was ever thrown out.

TWENTY-NINE

After lunch, Sarah was carried by Tom outside the barrier to some warm grass in the sun. It was a beautiful, warm afternoon. Everything was bright green. Flowers popped up everywhere. The fields were gorgeous. Most everyone was out on the hills or in the fields. A couple of young girls brought her some lunch. She thanked them. The girls bowed to her as they left. She looked at Tom with confusion. He raised an eyebrow. She still didn't get it. People came by regularly to check on her. They spoke softly and bowed upon arriving and leaving. She looked terrible, and they were clearly worried about her.

"We need to get you into some cold water, clean you off and accelerate some healing," Tom suggested. "Plus, we need to get you out of here." Sarah wanted to and had tried several times to get up and help out, but she just couldn't. She could see all the people staring at her.

"Go!" Ms. Watson ordered.

"Yeah, get outta here," Amy demanded. "We got this, and we need you healthy, not lying around while we do all the hard work." She patted her old friend on the shoulder with a smile. "Go."

"OK. Alright. Where're we going?"

"I'll show you." Tom picked her up in his arms again. She was strong and athletic, but she didn't weigh more than 125 pounds—less after the stress of the post-Wall requirements of life. She had to admit she enjoyed being in his arms both because she liked him and it hurt a lot less. She smiled at herself as she realized she felt safe in his arms, even though she could kick his and anyone else's ass if she wanted to, even in this condition.

He carried her past many Family members, all of whom touched her and wished her well, then out across the hills and valleys of the maze, in the direction of the gently sloping field where the pyre had been. He slowed, and they marveled at the beauty of the wildflowers, the butterflies and the way the gentle breeze rolled through the grasses.

How quickly nature recovers.

He carried her past the pyre. She asked him to stop. She felt the power of the place: the mix of negative, confused and positive spirits that swirled above the black scorched circle in the otherwise beautiful prairie.

The lithe woman with the long curly blond hair and the deep crystal blue eyes, the woman with an odd name she'd connected with from the newcomers, was sitting cross-legged in the middle of the ashes, eyes closed. Sarah could feel her, stronger and with more clarity than any other human, even Tom. *That woman is mending nature.* Sarah could feel the spirits responding to her. There were hundreds of them. The spirits of the dead teens. She could feel the woman calming them and setting them free. Sarah made Tom stand there while it happened. Swirling, churning spirits, slowing and gliding before her and then, poof, they were gone. One by one. She knew they were being released from this world by this woman.

The last of the spirits fought against her pull, then calmed and settle before her. It was William's spirit, she was sure of it. She could feel him. Several seconds passed. Only the quiet breeze was heard or felt between them. Then, poof, the last angry negative spirit was gone—to where, she didn't know. The sounds of the Family behind them came back to her, and she turned toward them for a second then back.

The woman rose, sort of floated to standing. She wasn't soiled from the ashes in the least. She smiled at Sarah and then walked—no, more glided—south toward the compound. Sarah could see the new grass beginning to grow through the dark ash.

Tom and Sarah looked at one another. "Done?" he asked. She realized that he hadn't been a part of the experience in any way.

She smiled and laid her head on his shoulder. They headed north, up the river. There he showed her a small waterfall and a nice pool hidden inside a grove of tall weeping willow trees. He waded in and laid her on a long flat rock on the edge of the pool. She was submerged up to her modest breasts, which floated on top of the water. It was cold, but it felt great.

First, he washed her, head to toe, washing the mud and grass from her hair and body. When that was done, he sat on the bank behind her, massaging her shoulders, then combing her hair with his fingers, massaging her scalp, gently around the bumps, then softly around her cheeks, jaw and neck. She closed her eyes and felt his wonderful, strong hands releasing stress from her body.

She focused her breathing and felt her spirits. It was as though she had this moment to get to know them. She sensed the Bear, and his spirit gave her strength and control of the Storm force. The Elephant came forward. Her tough hide was her protection. She could feel her, sense her. Then her Horse, whom she knew deeply and loved, provided her with speed and grace. Then the Tiger strode forward. Deep green eyes, sharp white teeth and claws, rippling muscles and a ferocious fighter, her strength in battle.

Then the Storm, deeper, much less controlled. Evil and good, crimson and red, oily and soft. It was not a separate spirit she'd acquired. It was part of her, *her* spirit, strengthened, heightened, stretched, derived from her own history, fears, doubts, loves and concerns. It was confusing and deep. She shivered in the water as she forced it back down, hiding it, confining it.

She felt Tom react and stand. "You OK? Did that hurt?"

She opened her eyes and saw his strong body glistening in the rippling sunlight above her. "No. I'm perfect."

He smiled and kissed her forehead. "Now for some therapy. Lie back, relax and focus on healing." She closed her eyes again, laid her head back on the soft bank of the river and guided her breathing, feeling her Elephant and Bear spirits come to life within her, protecting her, healing her.

He started on her ankle, and she guided the spirits there. He worked it back and forth, up and down, massaging her foot and ankle and calf.

Though it wasn't as badly injured, he moved to her other foot, massaging it and moving up to her ankle and then her calf. As he moved, she focused her spirits in that area. Then he worked up to her badly injured knee. He spent time adjusting it back and forth, pushing it toward her chest and guiding it back straight. Then he massaged it and moved up her thigh to the bruise. She endured the pain, focused her spirits and thoroughly enjoyed his attention.

The bruise was deep. His touch was masterful. He worked around the edges. "Let me know if anything hurts."

"Nothing hurts," she said in an anticipatory whisper. In reality, it all hurt, but the pain seemed surreal, exterior, beyond her somehow. She was simply enjoying the moment.

He caressed the edges of the bruised area, then massaged in a spiral path toward the center of the bruise, breaking up the stranded and dried blood inside her leg. This sent pain scorching through her, but she closed her eyes, and her Bear spirit absorbed it for her. She felt his strong hands as they caressed her leg. The cold water splashed over her, helping as well.

He moved his body over hers and kneeled, one leg between hers. She felt his growing member on her unbruised thigh and smiled, eyes still closed. He took her arm from the sling, took the sling from around her neck and tossed it on the bank of the river. She opened her eyes, gleaming with joy. He moved her arm so that he could manipulate her shoulder joint: out to her side, up and down, then in a circular motion and then back to her side. He stared into her eyes the entire time. She didn't flinch from the pain, again focusing her spirits on the injured shoulder. His body came closer and closer, his abs skimming her breasts, his penis moving up her stomach and then sliding back in the water as he manipulated her shoulder. She could feel the shoulder loosening up and settling more comfortably into its socket.

He set her forearm down across her flat stomach. Now for her ribs, he moved one leg deftly above her bruised thigh and slid his other leg between hers. Her hand, laid across her stomach, was now inches above his hardened member. She kept it there but knew that wouldn't last long. She felt the sleek Horse spirit inside her, increasing her energy, driving her libido. Tom's strong hands glided along her injured ribs and around her back and then forward, caressing the underside of her breasts.

She gazed into his eyes. Those beautiful blue eyes.

"I think you're going to be fine." His voice was so strong and sexy. The Tiger spirit raged inside her, Sarah's desire for Tom soaring through her from her ankles to the tips of her fingers. She could feel all of her spirits making her stronger, healing her and, most of all, revving her long-ignored sexual desires.

"I'm better than fine." She slid her hand down onto his penis and reached her good arm around his neck and pulled him down toward her. They kissed, and it was as heavenly as she had imagined. Tremors raced throughout her entire body. He stood and lifted her out of the water and carried her into the soft grass in the warmth of the spring sun and laid her on her back. *Daydreams normally don't come true quite this quickly.*

"One place left to examine." He kissed her again and then slid down her wet body, kissing her neck then her chest; fondling her breasts with his hands, he licked and suckled her nipples. She wanted him right now. She reached down and pulled him up to her and kissed him. Then she reached down and guided him into her. He was strong and powerful, and she felt him reach deep inside her with each stroke. Energy grew. Warm. Sarah's spirits danced within her soul, with the pleasure from his touch, his strength, his movements and his love. She released herself to him, completely. She trusted him. All pain left her. Her first orgasm poured through her. The sensation grew. She implored him to go faster, and he obeyed. She could feel his passion welling up, her spirits swirling and raging inside her. She lost her sense of the world around her. The glorious, ravenous feeling raced through every inch of her body, and at the same time she felt him climax, she burst into an ecstasy of orgasmic bliss like nothing she had ever experienced before. He froze deep inside her. Together they lived the joy, the release, the explosion of passion that they'd just shared. In the distance, she heard a tiger roar, a bear growl, a horse whinny and an elephant trumpet into the soft air of that warm spring day. She felt safe and powerful at the same time.

His breath calmed. She was swept away. Her soul and its new spirits blocked all her pain. Her arms fell back onto the grass. He slid out of her and lay on the soft grass beside her. They stared at the sky for several minutes, enjoying the release and complete relaxation that had overcome them both. Her soul and spirits settled inside her.

Then he broke the silence. "OK, my expert medical opinion is that your pelvis is fine."

She laughed as he pulled her over beside him.

THIRTY

The nap was peaceful. No dreams. No nightmares. She awoke as the pains began to return, less severe but present, and she rolled off him. She could see that he had sensed her movement.

He kissed her, stood, picked her up in has powerful arms, kissed her again and carried her back into the pond. The cold water refreshed her, and she lolled back against the river's banks. He floated to the center and somewhat absentmindedly began massaging and manipulating her ankles, calves, knees, the bruise on her thigh and back to her feet and ankles. She loved it and laid back relaxed, staring at the bright blue sky through the willow fronds. A gentle breeze blew them back and forth. She was relishing the moment. *What could be better?* Wonderful sex. This hot handsome man now massaging her feet and legs. Lolling in a cool pool of running water in a gentle creek next to a field of fragrant wildflowers, listening to the birds sing and the wind whisper through the leaves.

Her mind wandered to the spirits inside her: the Storm, the Horse, Bear, Elephant and Tiger. They were so real, so present. They came to her in times of difficulty and joy. However, they still felt outside her control. *Can I control them?*

Soon the plight of the Family returned and the things that needed to be done.

"OK, enough lollygagging. Help me up and get me back to camp. Let's see if I can walk at all. I feel a LOT better." She winked at him.

"Me too, but how are the ankle, knee, thigh, rib and shoulder?" As he lifted her out of the water onto dry land, they both were smiling from ear to ear. He hugged her close and kissed her with the passion of new lovers. "We shall have to do this again some time. Consistent therapy is important for healing, don't you think?"

"Yes, doctor. Whatever you say, doctor." She gazed into his eyes like Audrey Hepburn in a 1950's "perfect world" movie, batted her eyes and gave him an exaggerated wink and a coy smile. Then her demeaner became serious. "OK, hunky genius doctor, let's see if I can walk."

He shook his head, knowing better than to object. She put her good arm around his shoulder, and he wrapped his big arm around her waist. "Easy does it."

She closed her eyes and began to focus her spirits on giving her the strength to walk, to withstand the pain. She opened them and put weight on the ankle; it hurt but held up. Then she shifted her weight to her other leg, and the knee hurt but also did pretty well. The bruised thigh hurt like crazy.

"You have to work that bruise to keep it from calcifying. That can be a nasty result of a deep bruise like that. It'll hurt, but you can't hurt it worse than it is. The more you use it, the better it'll get. The blood will flow through it and gradually take away the nasty stuff making those lovely colors. This is a flat area. Stand here. I'm going right over there. You try to walk over to me."

"Do I have to?" she asked with an exaggerated pout and mock disdain. She took a moment to gain her balance. Then she stepped forward with her bruised leg, extended the knee as much as she could and brought her other leg up to it. Her hip began to complain, as did her ankle as she put pressure back on it. She began to lose her balance, and he leaped forward and caught her.

"OK, OK, too soon. We'll keep working on it."

"Hold onto me. I want to walk a little bit and see if it gets better with some usage. I'm going to try something my mother taught me, so don't get freaked out if it works."

"Honey, nothing you do surprises me anymore." He held her up with her arm over his shoulder as she stepped forward. She made a point of putting as much weight as possible on each leg, feeling the pain and getting used to it. Feeling for her balance. She knew that pain was the body's warning system. She knew what was wrong, so she no longer needed the warning. She took a deep breath, settling her inner self as her mother had taught her. *Feel the pain and dismiss it.* She continued forward, with Tom holding her up with each step.

With each tentative step under the strong support of her lover, she felt a deepening mastery of the pain, of her spirits and of her body. The ground was soft but firm enough to keep her steady under her feet. She stopped and took her arm off his shoulders and instead held his hand, more like a cane now than a crutch. She took a few tentative steps, felt and absorbed the pain, and then began again. One foot at a time. Concentration and balance. The world around her faded. Deep internal focus. Tom no longer there.

"That's it, honey," her mother said, holding her as she had when she'd fallen down an embankment, injured her leg and received her first of many lessons on controlling her body with her mind. "Focus inward, honey. Feel the pain and dismiss it." Sarah did as her mother asked, felt the pain from her ankles, then up her leg to her knee, then her thigh, up to her hips, feeling the pain, sensing it as a warning only, knowing it to be all in her brain, something she could ignore. She felt her Bear spirit wrap the pain within her and the Elephant strengthening her.

"Now up to your side and shoulder and head." Sarah followed her mother's guidance, letting her Bear and Elephant spirits begin to heal each area slowly, breath by breath. Her body was a machine she could repair.

She began to call on all her spirits inside her for help. She stood quietly and focused. She could feel the strength and power build within her. The four spirits swirled with her soul, then became clear to her as if the four animals were right there with her, inside her, part of her.

She began to walk, relying less and less on Tom. She could hear her mother's soft voice guiding her. "That's it, honey. Feel the pain but bring it inside you. Make it part of your consciousness and then let it flow out of you. Own your body with your mind." She also heard a bit of Asha's

Kenyan accent and knew she was with her as well. Her confidence rose. She increased her pace. She felt the spirits adding strength, healing her, taking the pain away. Still slow, but better.

She'd been bent forward from the pain. "Stop, honey. Stand up straight." She obeyed, felt the twinge in her lower back, hips and side. She internalized it, the Bear accepting it into her being. The pain became part of her. Strengthened her. She let weakness flow out of her.

Now more erect, she began to walk again at an increased pace. The pain was there, but it was scarcely there. No longer a warning. No longer preventing her from doing what she wanted. No longer the impediment it'd been.

"Stop limping, honey. Focus on your gait." She felt the Horse emerge. Strong and tall, rhythmic and graceful, he poured into and through her.

"Now, honey, focus on your shoulder." She released Tom's hand and rolled her shoulders back and forth, including her dislocated shoulder. It hurt. It hurt a lot. She felt it as well, letting it hurt as the Bear dragged the pain inside her. The Elephant rose within her, giving her arms and shoulders strength and power. She became one with the pain, felt her spirits take it, then let it go. She stood even more erect, shoulders back, chest out, strong and tall. "That's my girl," she heard her mother say. Sarah smiled at her and reached out. Her mother smiled back. "You'll be fine, honey. I love you. Love everyone, like we taught you." And she disappeared, but Sarah felt her warmth and the depth of her parents' love for her. It had been a long time.

She began forward again. Her Horse spirit guided her gait, improving it with each step. Her movements improved. The pain weakened. It wasn't gone. It remained a subtle reminder, but it wasn't going to stop her.

She opened her eyes and turned to Tom, whose eyes were big as he walked a pace away from her. She held out her hand and he took it, moving next to her.

"Let's head home."

"Sure. Sounds good," Tom answered, at a loss.

THIRTY-ONE

As they crested the first gentle slope that led into the maze of hills in front of their gate, she was channeling the spirits to give her strength and control. They were with her, part of her and now controlled by her. Holding hands now with Tom, Sarah felt so loved and no longer alone.

As the couple stood on the hill at the end of the valley that led to the front gate, word spread through the camp that Sarah was back. The Family came from every direction, gathering in front of the barrier, eyes wide in amazement as they watched her standing strong and powerful, glowing brightly, at the other end of their entrance valley. In front of everyone, she turned and pulled Tom toward her and gave him a deep, passionate kiss. She wanted to thank him for everything that had occurred that morning, but to the Family and to Tom, it was a clear statement of ownership. Tom was hers. She was Tom's, though that felt secondary. All were duly on notice. The Family cheered and applauded as if they were greeting the royal family.

She released him and his hand and turned to the crowd that had gathered. They hushed. Only the gentle breeze dared make a sound. Sarah stood straight and tall, shoulders back, summoned the power of all her spirits, smiled as brightly as she could and marched herself with only the slightest hint of a limp up to Ms. Watson, who stood at the barrier overlap. She absorbed the love that was showered on her from the spirits of her Family. She let it in, and it empowered her. She felt the darkness recede and a softer side of the power she'd received from the Storm, the part that connected her to this new world so deeply, rise within her, and she embraced it.

Asha appeared as she walked toward her friends. "Receive their love, but love them even more in return." And she was gone.

She reached Ms. Watson and took her hands. "Let's get things back to normal and make things happen around here, shall we, Shirley?"

Ms. Watson smiled, and the Family cheered. The two walked inside the barrier. Sarah glanced back at Tom and winked. He'd followed her, but his look was less of pride than of utter astonishment, a look shared by nearly everyone in her Family.

Sarah saw the Doc approaching Tom with an outstretched hand of congratulations. They shook hands, and as Tom was about to relate what he'd seen, she yelled, "Tom, you coming?"

When he hurried to her side, she took his hand, this time for balance. She'd made her entrance. As they touched, she could tell Tom understood that she wasn't completely healed. She needed him to keep the others from recognizing this fact, but she was better, and she now knew how to gather her powers to overcome anything. Everyone stared and smiled.

Jazz and Janie came running from their respective groups of children as they saw their mother return. She summoned her spirits, knelt and caught them in her arms. Pain raced through her, but then just as fast, it left.

"Mom, you're walking!" Jazz exclaimed.

"Sort of honey. Thanks to Tom."

"No girls, your mother's . . . I don't even know. I was simply a support structure for the most amazing transformation I've ever witnessed."

The girls smiled as they saw pure joy on their mother's face, something they'd never seen. They hugged her tighter. She winced as they moved her off her careful balance, patted them on their shoulders, kissed them and told them she needed to talk to the Family leaders and that she'd find them soon.

"Jazz is flirting with Mark," Janie accused with a huge conspiratorial smile.

"Am not!" Jazz retorted.

"Janie, stop taunting your sister. Jazz, be careful with boys; they can be dangerous. OK, get out of here," she joked, patting them to send them on their way. "I love you two."

"Love you too, Mom. Glad you're so much better."

"You feel strong, Mommy. I love it," said Janie.

"Thanks, sweetie, now get." They all smiled. Jazz walked toward Mark, and Janie scampered back to her friends. The pain stabbed as she began to stand. Ms. Watson and Tom helped her back up.

"Dangerous?" Tom repeated.

"You should know. Who's more dangerous than you right now?" She winked. "Although, I'm up for some danger whenever you are." And with that, she grabbed his butt with a smile.

Ms. Watson shook her head with a smile of feigned exhaustion. The main fire was on daylight burn. The other two fires were already prepared for the cold night ahead. The trappers had gotten several rabbits, and the hunters returned with a young deer, much smaller than the one they'd devoured the night before. There were fish being prepared for dinner, and the camp was buzzing with activity as usual. Teams were doing their duties, but it was late in the day, and most of the Family was resting. Erika was moving about managing and organizing teams for various functions.

Sarah asked Tom to check on the infirmary and then walked with authority under her own power to Amy to check on dinner and chat. All these movements caused spikes of pain, but now she could handle them. They were just alerts. Her spirits were with her now. She wanted a chance to show that she was truly independent and to tell Amy all about her rendezvous with Tom.

The two gossiped as Amy prepared dinner. Gus oversaw several people who roasted large chunks of deer meat over the main fire. The fish, rabbit, greens and other morsels were prepared on the cooking stone. Herb oversaw the smoker. The cooking team, like most of the others, had grown and people had fallen naturally into their jobs.

Ms. Watson addressed a few things at the fire. Molly had the little kids sing a song. Roger and his troupe of youngsters and now a few adults enacted an enchanting but silly fairy tale, which made everyone laugh. Janie was in her element and returned to their place by the fire exhilarated, jabbering on. Sarah reached out to her. "Honey, you were wonderful, and we love you, but hush your mouth so we can sleep." They smiled, and she snuggled into Jazz in their normal hierarchy, except now Tom was in back, then Sarah, Jazz and Janie in front. Sarah sensed a disturbance in the harmony of the Family somewhere, but she was too exhausted to even consider it and fell asleep quickly in Tom's strong embrace.

THIRTY-TWO

She awoke, feeling stronger, more confident. She turned and kissed Tom, and the two hugged for several minutes before they got up. She was letting herself feel. She could feel herself beginning to let go. She could love beyond her daughters. A revelation.

After breakfast, Ms. Watson met with Sarah and Tom and then called for the rest of the leaders. Joe, Erika, Amy, Marsha, Rhonda, John, Molly, Doc, Carmen and several others left their groups and walked over. Tony, despite the size of his following, was not invited.

The meeting began. Erika had increased the leadership, and Sarah thought it was great. She introduced the new members of the council and what they were in charge of.

"Thank you all for coming over. Let's go down to the river to talk."

They each found a reasonably comfortable rock or outcropping to sit on. Sarah sat on Tom's lap.

Ms. Watson opened the meeting: "OK, we have a couple of things to discuss. Nothing earth shattering, but just things to deal with as a team.

"First, of course, people have issues with other people, and this haven, while lovely in its way, is no different." Ms. Watson addressed some internal issues between a few of those in the leadership group, none of which involved either Tom or Sarah. They both listened, though Sarah struggled to care. Carmen had flirted with Rhonda's "boyfriend," and that had to be settled. Carmen and Candy were a constant threat to the other women. They were pretty, sexy, flirty and they hand-washed and combed the hair of nearly everyone in camp, including the men. There was a discussion, which got heated for a few minutes. Carmen's argument was that no one was committed to anyone else, and that until they were, they were fair game. Then Carmen turned to Sarah, "Except for Tom, of course."

The reference was unexpected. She looked at Tom quizzically. He knew full well what Carmen was referring to and why, but Sarah was quite unaware as to how clearly she'd staked her claim to him. She was respected, honored and feared. Her status had increased even more after she'd left broken and bruised in Tom's arms and returned walking under her own power, erect, strong and glowing. Sarah was, in fact, a woman to be reckoned with, and even Carmen and Candy would make a wide berth around Tom going forward.

The issue was resolved or left unresolved, Sarah didn't know which, but she still didn't care. Regardless, overseen by Ms. Watson, Rhonda and Carmen shook hands. They seemed OK to Sarah.

"Good. That's settled," Ms. Watson reported. "Now . . ."

A few other personal relationships, some among the leadership and some between their teams, were addressed. The effort of some of the Family members was addressed, and a plan to deal with that was formulated. Sarah was offered a role in each resolution, but she let the others handle them.

A scream emanated from somewhere in camp. Erika, Ms. Watson and the others raced out of the river bed and into the camp.

"Help me up!" Tom put an arm under hers and guided her to a standing position and then, as quickly as she could, she limped up the muddy bank. Each time her feet slipped, pain ripped through her body. "Hold on." She closed her eyes and focused on her spirits, took control of her body and her pain, stood up straight, stretched to the sky and back, and then took Tom's right hand in her right hand. He put his left hand on her lower back. "OK, now."

She moved much more quickly up the bank now, and once on the grass of the main area, she was able to amble toward the confusion. As she arrived, she heard Ms. Watson dressing down a man, who was quivering under her verbal attack.

"That kind of behavior is simply not acceptable," Ms. Watson screamed.

To Erika's right was the English woman who'd left Tony to stand beside Sarah in the battle over the horse. She was of medium build, a little plump, medium height, with sandy brown hair. Sarah nodded toward her, and Tom helped her walk up beside her. "What happened?" she asked.

"That bastard snuck up behind me and grabbed my right breast. When I turned around, he tried to reach down between my legs. I slapped him. Arsehole!"

She glared at the man on the ground, cowering beneath the onslaught from the women in power now encircling him.

"Well, what do you have to say for yourself?" Ms. Watson demanded.

"I'm sorry. Tony told me she wanted me to touch her there. He says she would like it."

Most of the Family had gathered around by now, and all turned toward Tony's group in the back of the camp. Tony was laughing hysterically, as were most of his crew. One man was lying on the ground holding his gut and laughing loudly.

Sarah released herself from Tom, summoned her spirits and moved as quickly as possible toward Tony and his crew. Tom, Ms. Watson, Erika and the others followed close behind. Tony stood, smiling broadly, facing her straight on. She could feel the Storm's crimson side grow inside her as she approached.

Tony opened the jousting. "That British bitch deserved it. Leaving me for you and your weak-ass Family. Marv's harmless. He has no idea what he's doing."

Sarah wasn't sure how to respond. Her skin crawled as the crimson darkness inside her came to life. She stood in front of Tony, standing as tall and powerful as she could. She couldn't speak, and the Family could see a fit of uncertainty, maybe even fear, cross her face. This was not lost on Tony.

Ms. Watson stepped up for her. "Tony, this is NOT funny. Do it again and there will be serious consequences. You need to get in line around here and become part of our survival instead of being such a consummate asshole."

"I should be running this place, bitch. There'd be more food and better conditions for everyone. Soon, you old biddy, soon, and no one will be able to stop us!" His crew stood tall behind him, chests out, exuding confidence. Several others joined his group. The Family was much larger, but Tony's numbers were now formidable, and Tony's followers were palpably angry and, Sarah sensed, possibly even evil. Sarah understood their advantage and could see that Ms. Watson felt it too.

"Alright, Tony, you've had your fun and your revenge on Holly, but this stops now! Do you understand?" Ms. Watson stood firm in his face.

"Fuck you." Tony laughed, turned and guided his ebullient crew back to their fire, which he'd lit. Sarah was incensed, as were Ms. Watson and Erika. She could feel their anger, but she could also sense confusion and uncertainty from others within the Family.

Murmurs spread through the Family. "Why'd she just stand there?" "Why doesn't she just kill that bastard?" "Is she really back?" "What's wrong with Sarah?"

Sarah listened as she followed the others back to the river. *Why can't I? What's wrong?*

"Alright, it was on the agenda, but let's discuss Tony and his crew's behavior now," Ms. Watson began. "Sarah, until you walked back into this compound under your own power, I had felt like he was going to try to take over with force."

Erika continued, "They've been trying to recruit more members to their group. They're secretive, don't follow the rules, do little around here and are generally unruly."

No one spoke for a few seconds. It was clear to Sarah that the feeling was shared among the group. Finally, a woman Sarah didn't know spoke. "They're disrespectful of women, demeaning. They demand that we do things for them. They make sexual references and flaunt their junk. They try to touch you. Grab your butt or boobs. No one else does that around here. We may be naked, but we're respectful. They're disgusting. We need to do something."

"They absolutely don't fit in," Marsha agreed.

The lithe woman who'd freed the teens' spirits in the charred field spoke in her soft melodic manner. "They cannot hear the music. They are not Family. The spirits here are rejecting them."

Again, silence. They all looked to Sarah. She looked down for several seconds and closed her eyes. She listened for an answer from someone—Asha, her mother. Nothing. She looked up at the leadership, all still staring at her. She took a breath. People were not her strength. She cleared her throat and looked at each person, then spoke. "I agree, they're not Family. We can all feel it. Is it right to kick a person out because they're not Family? Because they didn't get here following the singing?" There was no response. "OK, when I'm better, feeling stronger—and I am getting there fast—I'll speak with Tony. I think we can talk. We'll see."

There was a long pause before the tension settled out of the issue. Sarah would handle it. Ms. Watson finally held up her hand.

"OK, enough about Tony."

Sarah spoke, and everyone listened. "One more thing. Joe and Erika, secure the weapons, especially at night, just in case. We don't have much at the moment, so get the teams on rebuilding our arsenal as quickly as possible. I'll talk to Jazz about tipping more spears and arrows with at least flint chips as her team catches up on making true points. This will not be the last we hear from Tony and his crew. We need to be smart and ready. That's all I have."

Ms. Watson returned to the mundane issues in camp. Children, food preparation, issues between people, allocation of resources, etc. As the rest of the Council spoke, she realized how few of the Family members she even knew. Heck, she'd just met Tom, and he was the hottest guy around. *I've got to get around more. Tony's getting around. If he is up to something, I may need my own army.* If it wasn't for Tony and his threats, she knew she'd remain aloof. She'd deal with the leaders and let them deal with their people since she wasn't a people person. It's not that she didn't care; she did. She cared deeply about her Family and had proven it. She hadn't felt a need to know all of them on a personal level. That was Ms. Watson's job, who was incredible at it. But Sarah needed to learn.

Doc spoke next. "The infirmary is full of sick people. Flus, colds, budding pneumonias. Infections are a constant problem. Some who built the barrier sustained minor cuts but are dealing with nasty infections.

"Hector's in dire trouble. He may not survive. The sutures are holding, but even in a sterilized hospital, postsurgical infections aren't uncommon. Hector's been ripped open. Blood, possibly poisoned, splattered inside the wound. There's little we can do. Olivia's working around the clock. We have others recovering from their addictions, convulsing and in pain. We can't do much for them. It often takes the entire medical team to subdue patients. A few are better, but others are still struggling. Of the eight teens, three are still wrestling with heroin convulsions."

He was venting more than providing new information. Everyone knew the problems. Sarah felt for Doc and his team. They must feel so helpless. She vowed to try to help.

Ms. Watson paused and took a deep breath. "Thanks, Doc. Let us know how we can help. Any other internal news or issues we need to get ahead of?" Ms. Watson asked. "You all have marching orders. Those of you with personnel issues, let's try to keep those in order or address them. Anything else?" She paused. "OK, meeting adjourned. Off with you. Love to everyone."

The leadership chatted in small groups as they left the riverbank meeting.

THIRTY-THREE

Tom helped Sarah to a standing position.

"Thanks, Tom." She smiled at him as sweetly as she could. "I need a minute. I want to walk out of here on my own." He let her go, and she again put herself into a near trance, gathered her spirits, pulled herself erect, rolled back her shoulders and stood straight. She worked her lower back into a natural position. Gained her balance. Felt the pains. Weaker now. Let them flow into her, then out. She took a couple of very deep breaths and exhaled. "OK, I think I have this now. I know I do. I'm perfectly healthy."

She took a few steps but slipped on the sandy wet soil next to the river. Tom caught her and helped her up.

Ms. Watson always had the right words. "Let Tom help you dear. It'll be OK with the Family if you need some assistance. I dare say, they were pretty impressed when you walked back in here under your own power, young lady. Quite a feat. That one display was enough. Let's not get you hurt again, thank you very much." Tom and Sarah nodded.

"I'm OK. Tom, just give me your hand so I can use it for balance if I need it." She held his right hand with her right hand, summoned her spirits, felt their power and was ready. With new confidence, she stepped up the grade of the river bank and into the compound. She was getting good at this. He had his left hand on the small of her back to reassure her. She appreciated it.

"There's nothing you can do here. Let's go out and lay you down in the grass and work on those injuries."

"I want to visit the infirmary first. Tom, I've never even been back there. Is that horrible or what?" Sarah's worried voice demanded reassurance.

"Nah, it wasn't your area, and you've had plenty to deal with, so not to worry."

"I'm going."

"OK." Tom nodded and held his arm out toward the back of the camp with a defeated smile.

As they walked, people rose to greet her. She stopped, almost like a politician, and spent a few minutes with each person. She asked their name, what they did within the Family and who was with them. Children ran up to join parents. Some had examples of work they were crafting. She admired each one. Time slowed down, and she took the opportunity to enjoy it. It was that sort of day.

Each person valued their time with the local heroine. Each conversation was nearly reverent. Each person tried not to look at her bruises and swollen joints. All ended their time with a bowed head. Talking to so many people about themselves was so new for Sarah, it took effort to keep going. More difficult than walking. These were her Family, and she had vowed to herself to protect them. At the end of each conversation, Tom acted like her handler and moved her along. She took each person's hand in hers, spoke their name, hugged them and stepped to the next person.

Members of the Family began to line up along her path. By the time they'd reached the infirmary, she'd spoken with over 35 people, each for several minutes. It'd taken well over an hour to walk less than 40 yards across the back of the compound from the river to the infirmary. She was fine with that. Tom was fine with that. She wasn't sure she could've moved any faster, and it allowed Tom to help her control her balance and stay erect.

Several of the women winked at her. "Nice catch." She smiled each time and replied, "Tom was not caught. Maybe he caught me?" She'd wink back. Tom would feign a blush. That always got a little chuckle, especially with the older women.

The gauntlet, as Tom referred to it once they'd arrived at the infirmary, had been good for her. It was good for her confidence, but most of all, she'd connected to each person. She cared about what they were saying. Would she remember any of it? Knowing her memory and how it worked, she doubted it. It was not the sort of information that she reserved much space for in her brain's databases. Plants, animals, rocks, paths, tools and the like, sure, but not information about people, at least individual people. She was determined to try. What she would maintain were the connections, the spiritual connections she'd made with each person. Those were real.

The Doc came out to greet them. "So, Thomas, my boy, how is our favorite patient coming along? Pretty well, it seems. Nice work!"

"Like I started to tell you outside before I was ordered inside," with that, he gave Sarah a wry smile, "she did most of this on her own."

"Just following the doctor's orders," Sarah replied. "So, who are you treating and for what these days?"

"Well, sadly, we aren't able to do much treating of anyone. We're only trying to make their lives less miserable. Bethany and I have concocted a few meds, but I'm not sure they're doing much.

"Over there are the eight new kids, three still going through withdrawal. Five are mostly through theirs. They should be out of here and contributing to society by tomorrow. Erika's already spoken with them and assigned them to teams. Ms. Watson sat with all of them and explained how things work here. They're genuinely grateful for having been saved, fed, cared for and allowed to recover.

"The other three aren't so lucky. They're going through full-fledged heroin withdrawal. The boy is very frail. I'm not sure he can handle the trauma. We'll see."

"Try bone marrow broth. Lots of iron. Might help," Sarah suggested, her brain working quickly.

"Good idea. It ought to help their blood work more efficiently. We'll try that." The Doc paused and spoke to a young woman who ran off toward Amy. "Behind them are a few of the previous arrivals in the final stages of their withdrawals. Heroin, cocaine." He was pointing. "A few are recovering from severe alcoholism, which can be every bit as bad." Doc pointed to another man. "He was a crackhead—his term. So, we have our work cut out for us, but the team handles it well, and most are recovering, which is great."

"Not much choice. There are no dope dealers anymore," Sarah noted. Doc nodded.

"Over here, the news isn't so good. This is where I spend my time. Infections are a huge problem." For Sarah's benefit, they took several steps to walk the short distance. "You remember Hector?"

"Yes, hello Hector. You were valiant in battle the other day." She reached down and stroked his shoulder. He was very hot and sweaty. His face was flushed, and he was incoherent. She reflexively pulled her hand back off him and took a stuttered step back.

"He isn't contagious. Severely infected and perhaps poisoned," Doc explained as they moved away.

"I'd heard. He looks terrible."

"I personally doubt he'll last the night. Olivia," he pointed as she rushed up from the river, "has been tending to him since he was wounded. Cold water compresses. Washing the wound with peppermint water to keep it as clean as possible. It's about all we can do. We tried a poultice made from the ashes of the fire, and that helped a little, but not enough."

Sarah was aware that the acridity in the ashes could help kill the bacteria infecting the wound. Sometimes carbon could suck out poison, but it needed to be clean and activated, which ashes weren't. She heard Hector moan as Olivia put several cold compresses on his head and on the wound itself.

Bethany, the young pharmacist, arrived. Sarah was now focused on the problem. "We need to find some juniper berries. While they provide a pretty nice flavoring, they also have significant antimicrobial capabilities. Shrubs have berries through April and then sometimes again in the fall. I'll get Janie and her team on finding some as soon as possible. Just mash them up and apply them right to the wound. They probably won't help Hector, but they may work for some of these lesser infections."

She turned and called out for her daughter. In mere seconds, Janie came running.

"What are you doing back here Mom? You never come back here."

"Yeah, I know. Well, I'm here now. I've had a lot on my mind, young lady. I need you and your team to do something very important, you hear me?"

"Yes, Mom."

"These patients need juniper berries. Do you remember what they look like?"

"Of course. You know they aren't berries, but little seed cones."

"Right Miss Know-it-All," she responded smiling. "What can they be used for?"

Janie looked around at the people in the infirmary. "Fighting infections!! Why didn't I think of that?" She struck her head with her hand and exaggerated a look of shock. "What was I thinking?"

"Alright Miss Dramatic, now go get us some. Gather everything you can. We're late in the season and need to store up."

"I know just where they are." And with that, she was off, calling for her team and yelling, "Emergency, emergency" at the top of her lungs.

"Oh, for crying out loud. That's just what we need. That girl can't do anything quietly."

"She's some girl, that one," the Doc replied.

"She knows her plants," Bethany added. "As good a botanist as I've ever met, and what is she, nine or ten?"

"Eight and a half," Sarah corrected, "and don't get that wrong around her."

Sarah spent the better part of the next hour talking to patients.

As they were about to leave, Janie came running through the camp. "Make way, make way. Valuable medicines coming through."

Sarah rolled her eyes while the others giggled.

"Savior Janie, at your service, your heinie-ness," she said as she bowed and presented Sarah with the basket full of juniper berries.

"That's cute," the Doc commented as he took the basket from the young girl.

"It is not. She knows precisely what she's saying, don't you, you little rascal?"

"Yikes!" Janie bounded off a few feet.

Onlookers laughed. "Don't encourage her," Sarah implored, but everyone knew Janie was one of the more entertaining members of the Family, and they all loved her. She was no wallflower, as many of the children were.

Sarah turned to Bethany. "OK, juniper berries, which as Janie pointed out aren't berries, are rather hard. They need to be crushed, ideally with a mortar and pestle. We don't have one, so a couple of flat rocks should do."

Bethany showed her a water-smoothed, concave stone and a similar spherical rock. "This is what we use."

"Perfect. That's great. OK. Mash them up in this and then add a little water to make a paste. Add some peppermint. That can help as well."

Bethany took the juniper berries, and Doc nodded and returned to his patients.

Tom took her arm and walked her north. "Outside the gate to the soft grasses in the sun where I can work on your injured joints and that bruise. You need to get off your feet. This has been a lot for a first day."

They started toward the gate. Before they got very far, Family who had never been able to speak with her hustled to her path. Tom ran interference, but she could only move so fast, and she really wanted to connect with more of her Family. Tony was building his army. She needed hers. She stopped and chatted with each, felt their love, which settled her. Tom moved her along, but she needed this time and took it with each person.

It took a couple of hours. Some she'd met earlier brought friends and loved ones to meet her. She enjoyed talking to and learning about each person, their names, relations, their jobs and backgrounds.

The walk was subdued. Rhonda and her team returned from a hunt, and Sarah greeted and met each member of Rhonda's team. "We got us a wolverine," a young man named Fred explained as he held it up.

Rhonda corrected him. "It's a badger, not a wolverine, Fred. We got it more out of self-defense than anything else. Marcy stumbled across its path, and it reared its very sharp claws."

Marcy followed. "Then Rhonda drew her bow and killed it with one arrow."

"The meat's for lunch," Fred said.

"That hide will be great," Sarah added. Gus fileted the beast, and the pelt was cared for by Bobbi, the taxidermist, whose name Sarah had made it a point to learn.

As the gauntlet continued, Sarah noticed a few others migrate toward Tony's group. She needed allies.

When they cleared the gate into the beautiful grasslands, Tom helped her down onto the slope of the first, biggest hill. It was arced to the contour of her body, so she rested her head back on the grass and gazed into the sky, trying to center her spirits.

"Damn it," she exclaimed. "Look." She pointed to the west where the sky was dark. Another thunderstorm was coming . . . and soon.

"Not again," Tom lamented.

"Spring in St. Louis. Tom, stand me up and get Ms. Watson, Erika and Joe for me!" It wasn't a question.

"OK, but you stay right here," Tom said as he helped her up. "Moving is good to a point, but I think you may have overdone it. Just promise me you'll stay right here. I'll bring them to you. Got it?"

She was exhausted. "Agreed. Just go!" As Tom jogged off into the compound, Sarah closed her eyes and focused her spirits on healing and strength.

Tom, Ms. Watson, Erika and Joe raced through the gates. She watched the rain approach. It was still quite a ways off. Joe and Erika jogged past, up to the top of the hill. Tom and Ms. Watson stood beside Sarah.

"Rain," Joe sighed.

"Maybe two hours max. It's coming, and based on those clouds, it's a doozy," Erika added.

"I hope that's all," Sarah said.

"Oh my God," Erika remarked, "hail. What if it's hail? What if it's big hail like we got a few weeks ago? I remember watching that storm out of our front picture window from the safety of our nice suburban home. We were going to have to replace the entire roof, although all this stuff happened before they got around to it. What are we going to do now if we have hail like that? We aren't ready."

"We still don't have shelter to speak of," Marsha noted as she arrived.

"Hail's gonna hurt regardless," Joe stated the obvious. "Damn!"

If it was golf ball–sized, as happened with some frequency in the spring, to the joy of roofers and car repairmen and the chagrin of the insurance companies in the old world, it would be devastating to her unprotected Family.

"Being out here is not an option," Joe lamented.

Ms. Watson called to the guard at the gate and ordered him to get the rest of the leadership team. As the other members heard the weather report, most walked up to the crown of the hill to see for themselves, returning with several expletives.

Sarah spoke, and they all listened. "Get everyone into the woods. The canopy's dense. That should slow down the hail."

Jake, of the wood crew, spoke up. "We've cleared out an area near the outside of the barriers, and we have a lot of wood stored there. We should all fit there."

"Great. It won't be fun, but better than getting pelted." Sarah was in charge. "Amy, gather up our food stores and get them out of the compound and under the trees. Use the skins. Talk to Bobbi about whatever she has. Grab some rope, and we can tie some up in a tree if we can't cook it. We have to make sure that an animal doesn't get to it." With that, Amy took off running back into the camp.

Sarah doled out instructions to the team, her hand on captain Erika's shoulder. Joe stood on the hill staring at the storm. "This is a huge one. Might have tornado activity in it. Damn." He jogged farther north to get a better view. "My God, that looks scary. Huge thunderclouds. Wow."

"Move, everyone, NOW!" Sarah screamed. "Erika, take charge!"

THIRTY-FOUR

Sarah could hear her captain screaming her orders with regard to the fire, the wood, the injured and the older Family members who struggled to get around, and the various tools and raw materials they'd been working on. Spears would be brought with them to the woods to protect them, though Sarah assured them the animals were no more interested in being caught out in this sort of storm than they were. None would be hunting in this.

Sarah stood alone, watching from her perch on the hill as various members of the Family moved out through the gate and into the woods. Nearly everyone nodded to her, almost in deference.

The spear hunters returned from the fields with their prey and their own warnings that the storm was approaching. Samantha and Marshall had made their first kill, a good-sized elk. Samantha had felled it with a strong throw, and Marshall had driven his spear through its head to put it out of its misery. Sarah summoned Bobbi and Gus, who followed the team as it dragged the elk by its antlers and hind legs into the woods.

Sarah ordered Tom to find Jazz and Janie.

To his credit, Tony's team was moving the dry wood and the fire. Erika, Olivia and several of the others were helping or carrying the infirm. The Seamstresses were helping Ol' Mac.

The grey storm, punishing the leaves of the woods to their west like military fire, held her attention. This was a hailstorm. Her hair whipped in the wind, and the gusts nearly pushed her over. Pain raced through her as she stepped back on the slope, but she maintained her balance. She knew inside that she was a beacon for her Family and needed to emit a sense of strength and calm. Light rain hit her arms as she watched the last of the Family race out through the gate, across the front of the barrier and into their eastern woods.

Olivia ran back into the compound. "Olivia, what the heck are you doing?"

"I'm staying with Hector. He can't be moved." As she bolted back inside the compound, Sarah heard her arguing. Tom emerged, pulling the gate closed with a screech behind him.

Hector's not going to survive this, she thought. As the hail began to pound across the grasslands, Tom swooped in and lifted Sarah from the hill. She was happy he did. Her walking speed right now would not suffice.

"Sorry I'm late. Hector can't be moved. Olivia's refused to leave him. She's a veteran military field nurse. I tried to make her leave. She says that she's tended wounded in bigger storms where the incoming wasn't only hail. She's staying." They reached the edge of the woods as the hail reached them.

"Put me down. I can walk. Are they protected?"

"She's got him under a large tree limb. I hope it'll protect 'em from this storm, at least a little. I told her she was crazy, but she wouldn't budge."

Sarah smiled as she considered the love Olivia had for that man. The hail was big and pounded the leaves above them. By the time it reached the Family at ground level, its velocity had been slowed by branches and leaves, though being struck on cold skin by the falling pieces of ice still stung.

The Family had saved the fire and moved a good amount of dry wood to the forest to be added to the wood stored in this area by the gatherers. To his credit, Tony's team had built and lit a fire, which was now blazing. *He may be an asshole, but he isn't stupid.* Even though rain was getting through in significant quantities, the fire was strong enough to withstand it, vaporizing drops in the air. They knew this was dangerous, creating a huge fire inside a forest, but the risks were outweighed by the benefits.

The elderly, ill and injured were moved closer to the fire to keep warm. They didn't need any more people getting sick from exposure. It wasn't pleasant, but it was more bearable than the evening before had been.

Tom placed Sarah near the fire at the base of a big tree and made sure that she was comfortable. Her girls soon snuggled in against her. He kissed them all. They all smiled at him as he left them to help with the affairs of the Family.

Joe returned from the edge of the wood. "This is going to be a bad one, folks. We're in for a long afternoon and evening, it looks like." A thunderclap shook the group, followed by a bright lightning strike. The Family murmured, almost as though they were witnessing something holy.

Sarah whispered to the girls, "Remember back in the old life, when we'd sneak out onto our big covered back porch and watch this kind of rain pound down on the ground and on the trees and plants in the backyard?"

They nodded. "That was fun, Mom. This is icky," Jazz noted.

"Mom, can I go to the edge of the woods and watch the rain out on the grassland?" Janie asked. "It would sort of be like sitting on our porch."

Tom returned. "Tom, my dear, we have a request. We'd like to go to the edge of the forest and watch the rain come down."

He had that sort of *Really?* look on his face. "OK. Sure, why not?" And he reached down to help Sarah up.

"Carry me?" she cooed and kissed him on the cheek. He did, of course, and many in the Family ahhed. She winked at them over his shoulder. She could tell he still didn't have a complete read on her yet, and she liked it that way.

They got to the edge of the forest, and he found a big old, full weeping willow. They slipped under the branches and sat gazing out at the pouring rain. The hail had largely passed, and the big willow did a remarkable job of lessening the rain that reached them, even though they were still drenched.

"Mommy, this really is a lot like watching the rain from our back porch. Thank you, Tommy," Janie said. "When we would be camping and it rained like this, we'd sit at the edge of the tent, just like this, and watch the rain. We got almost as wet then as we are now."

"You did, you little nutcase, because you sat outside the tent and got soaked." Sarah grabbed her goofy youngest and dragged her close and tickled her mercilessly. Jazz and Tom laughed as Janie squealed, "Mommmmmyyyy." Tom feigned a rescue, grabbing Janie from the clutches of Sarah's tickling fingers. They all laughed.

"I've laughed more with the three of you in the yuckiest of conditions than I've laughed in years," Tom admitted.

She realized that she knew almost nothing about him prior to the Storm except that he was a chiropractor and a good one. They'd talk later. Right now, he lifted Janie onto his thighs, slipped her close to Sarah, and they all cuddled together and watched and listened to the rain, the crack of lightning, the now far-off thunder and the sounds of the whistling wind rustling the feathery frondlike branches of the weeping willow. Janie curled up on his chest and put her cold hand on her mother's stomach. It was fine. Everything was cold. Jazz climbed up on her mother's lap, and Sarah gathered her in and wrapped her up in her arms. Tom and Sarah tried to keep the two children as warm as possible while the children served as blankets for them. The rain kept coming.

CRACK! A huge lightning strike and the immediately ensuing burst of thunder shattered the calm. It hit on the far side of the northern bend in the woods. They all jumped. Tom snatched them all closer in his bear-like arms.

"Yikes," he exclaimed. Everyone laughed once they settled down. "Wow, that was close by, wasn't it?"

Jazz, "Yeah, right over there."

"That was loud. I jumped practically into the tree, but then Tommy squished me into everyone."

"I liked it. It made me feel safe," Jazz said, looking into Tom's eyes the way a daughter looks into her father's.

Sarah smiled, "Me too. It made me feel safe too. I haven't felt that way in a long time." The way she looked into his eyes was much different. He returned the look with the soft assurance that he was feeling the same way. He squeezed them close again simply because he could. Janie squealed. Sarah and Jazz sighed. And then he released them a little while keeping a tight grip on his new family.

They sat quietly, staring out at the rain. Janie fell asleep on his chest. Jazz and Sarah smiled at Tom and snuggled closer into him as well. Jazz had worked her way into the crevice between them where it was warmer. Sarah was spooning her, with the help of Tom's strong arms. She reached across both daughters and around his left bicep. She was feeling no pain. Well, things hurt, but she was ignoring them. This was bliss. Rainy, wet, cold, yucky bliss, and she loved it. *I am so weird.*

She'd met him two days ago, knew almost nothing about him, and was completely and totally in love with every bit of him. She chalked it up to the crazy new world and laid her head on his shoulder. She could feel his breath even out and his grasp loosen. He'd fallen asleep. Jazz was sleeping. Sarah was awake. She daydreamed of lovely summer days, romping in the wildflowers with Tom and her girls—a greeting-card life, but it was her fantasy right now. Then she, too, drifted off to sleep.

THIRTY-FIVE

"Dinner!" The bellowing call from Gus meant it was time to eat. "Come and get it or we'll throw it out." She still smiled every time. Maybe someday it'd get old. Everyone, awakened by the bellow, began to stir.

"Arrgh! I was sleeping so well. That was one of the best rests I've had since that stupid Storm. Well, I guess I have to say, wonderful Storm. I wouldn't have met you two knuckleheads and your lovely mother had that thing not come through, whatever it was," Tom said. They all smiled at his endearing words and the sense of completeness within their family. "Alright everyone, let's eat."

Janie popped up. Jazz squirmed free and scrambled to her feet. Tom rolled sideways, slipping his arm from behind Sarah as she moved forward, and got to his feet. When he turned, he stretched his arms high over his head. She was struck again by the view of him standing strong and powerful above her. She liked it. Everything she saw. The girls ran off toward the dinner call, and she watched them around the tree trunk. When they were out of sight, she returned to her man.

She reached up and took his member in her hands and began to stroke it. He looked down with wide eyes, then around the tree toward the raging fire and over a hundred of their closest friends, and numerous enemies, then back down at Sarah. She pulled herself up and licked him. He got hard immediately. She slipped her mouth around it and could see him smiling down at her. He slid down the tree in front of her, her hand still on his penis, and kissed her deeply and passionately.

She released him and put both arms around his broad shoulders and whispered into his ear, "Stand up."

He lifted them up and leaned her back against the tree. She guided him into her, and they made love, kissing, caressing and feeling the depth of their relationship growing. Warmth and energy began pulsing through her body with each stroke, reaching from her toes to her fingers. It grew, and she could feel the energy in him. Her spirits raced inside her, driving the passions, encircling her and taking her spirit out of her body and into his, their energies joined together and dancing wildly, spinning, leaping, flying. Then ecstasy exploded between, into and through them as they climaxed together.

The feeling flowed to every corner of her being. She could feel his love reach deep inside her, but most of all, she could feel herself release completely to him, to his spirit, to every fiber of his being. She let herself love him, trust him, be his as she knew so deeply that he was hers.

Then they leaned against the tree, rain cascading down upon them from above, bringing them back to their senses. As he slid them down the tree, he rotated so that he was seated and leaning against it. She straddled his strong legs. His arms pulled her into him, hers wrapped around his powerful shoulders.

She sat there, feeling Tom with her, loving every sensation that raced through their bodies. She had never been so in love in all her life. She knew it was time to let him know. She lifted her head from his shoulder, smiling as she looked into his eyes.

"I love you so much." It felt so good to say, but more to mean it so deeply. She'd never felt that before.

"I love you too." She gazed deep into his eyes for several seconds, safe in his big arms. She took a deep breath.

Asha appeared to her. "Now is the time to let it all go. Love, Sarah. The darkness is becoming stronger." Sarah sank deeper into Tom.

After several minutes, she said, "Whenever you're ready, and there's no rush, you can take me to dinner. I know this great spot about 15 yards that way if you're in the mood for . . . whatever Amy's making."

Tom gathered her in his arms, stood and carried her toward the rest of the Family. Gus had sliced huge sections of the elk, put them on the end of some spears, and his team had roasted them over the fire. He watched over the meat like a hawk.

The couple snuck into the fire ring. As they approached, Tom set her down, guiding her onto her spot at the base of a tree. Ms. Watson had taken her usual position to Sarah's right. He secured them some nice pieces. There were berries aplenty, and the basket was passed around to them to choose from. They were more than satisfied in so many ways.

That evening, the Family chattered, the rain lightened but kept falling, and the fire blazed, warming the area. Marshall and Samantha told the story of their first kill. Everyone applauded. Sarah decided to use the moment to find out more about Tom.

"Soooo, I know you were a chiropractor before the Storm, but tell me about the rest of your life." They spent the evening sharing stories about work, spouses, girl- and boyfriends, college, what they did for fun and a whole host of other things. She tried to stay away from the horrid details of her battles with her ex. He was married. He loved his wife and missed her. They had three children, two girls about the ages of Jazz and Janie, and a boy in between them. He pined for them. He'd never get over them, and she knew that. She hugged him as he teared up.

After he regained his composure, he continued, "We lived in a beautiful small town called Tolland in Connecticut, about 20 miles northeast of Hartford. It is, well, I guess, was, an old New England bedroom community, with stone houses and stacked stone walls that were over 200 years old. We lived in a haunted two-story. I'll tell you the ghost stories sometime. I had a nice little practice there in town. I was in Rotary club and served on the City Council. We were comfortable. It seems more like a fairy tale now than a reality that's gone forever." He teared up again. She realized why he didn't talk about it much.

"I was here on business when the Storm struck, attending a conference for chiropractors at Logan University. It had ended, but I was staying with a friend for a few extra days. I could have been home with my family." Tears reappeared, but he brushed them away, and she kissed him on his salty cheek. "My friend was at work when it hit. I was lying on the couch on the first floor in my underwear watching television. First, the picture went haywire right before the Storm hit. Then as it enveloped the apartment complex, everything got hazy—the walls, floor, ceiling, everything—and then it all faded like a mist, sort of, until it dispersed into the air and was gone.

"I fell several feet onto the ground. A woman from an upper floor slammed into the ground beside me and broke her neck. She was dead. Other people from the complex fell too. Broken ankles, arms, sprains, people screaming and crying for help. It was crazy, and I had no idea what to do. I didn't know anyone or the area. People were running around, struggling to figure out what to do. I helped as many as I could. I reset a compound fractured leg but had nothing to splint it with. The guy passed out. We finally used a tree branch and some bark some woman brought over.

"I wandered from injured person to injured person and did what I could, which in most cases wasn't much. I had nothing to eat. I found a small creek and got a drink. When it got dark, I leaned against a tree, hungry, exhausted and frightened like I've never been in my life before. I maybe slept an hour.

"In the morning, a small group asked me to join them. It was a struggle. We were lost. Scared. We ate dandelions and bugs. It was horrible. We continued to walk until a few of us heard the kids singing. The others didn't. Weird, right? We asked them to follow us. Most didn't. We arrived at the compound at night. There were six of us. We were accepted immediately by the watchmen and given small packets of food. Ms. Watson walked us all down to the river and explained how this community was going to work. Ms. Watson brought me to the reality that I would never see my wife and children again. I was devastated, like so many others.

"In the morning, she found out that I was a chiropractor and sent me to Amy, who guided me to a few injured folks in back with Olivia and Hector, who, by the way, was also a nurse.

"I was struck by you the moment I saw you. I told my story at the campfire that evening." She sort of remembered something about a guy from Connecticut.

"I saw you from across the fire, the light dancing on your face. I saw the love you shared with your two girls, who remind me so much of mine. Though you don't look like her and are way more passionate, which I like, you remind me of my wife. She was strong but soft, a leader but able to let others do things their own way. You're both beautiful, but in different ways. Both long and lean and in great physical shape. I love that. I worked hard to keep my body in shape."

"That's obvious," she responded, rubbing her hand on his strong shoulders and down his muscular arms. "I like that about you too. Go on."

"That's it. All of that's lost, and now, by the grace of something, I found you out here in the middle of nowhere. I began to shadow you. I stayed out of your way, and you were so focused and busy, I couldn't keep up. That guy Tony followed you around as well for a while. I wasn't sure what to make of him, and still don't. Then Doc arrived, took over the medical duties and created the infirmary, but every chance I got, I found a reason to get away and check you out."

She feigned a blush of girlish surprise.

"When you ran out into that fray, I freaked. 'What does she think she's doing?' I grabbed a spear and ran out after you."

"I thought you were part of Joe's guard team."

"Nope. I ran out there to protect you, which was a huge fail."

"No. You did not fail! I was going to protect those kids and our Family. No one was going to stop me."

"Yeah, I got that. You were masterful. Crazy and insane, but it worked, and you saved a lot of lives."

"And you were there, my knight in shining armor—well, my knight in a gorgeous body—to protect me and help coax me back to health. You're a wonderful man. Your wife was a lucky woman to have you. I can't imagine not knowing the fate of my children. I'll never replace her. I never want you to forget her. But I'm also so glad that I found you. I've known you for only a couple of days, and I've never loved anyone as much as I love you."

"Alright, Ms. Sarah, you know all about me. Let's talk about the 800-pound gorilla in the room: you and Robert." He looked with stern certainty into her eyes, and she cowered from his glare.

"How do you know about Robert?" her voice quivered.

"Your nightmares. You babble, but Robert comes through clear," Tom replied. "You're scared to death of that guy!"

The crimson darkness churned inside her, but she closed her eyes, felt it, controlled it and guided it back down into her soul. Asha appeared to her. "Release it all. To love, you must share. To defeat the darkness, you must free yourself of it."

She opened her eyes and took a deep breath. She told him about her parents and how they taught her all her survival skills. She explained how she'd been dating Robert when she heard her parents had died horribly in the wilds of Montana. An old frayed harness she'd known about but had forgotten to tell her father about had broken and they had fallen. She was devastated and alone.

Robert had swept her off her feet, whisking her around on private jets to pick up their bodies, have a funeral in her hometown and then back to D.C. His family had taken her in at her lowest point and made her a part of it. She got pregnant with Jazz, and they married. She hesitated as she remembered those positive times, wiped tears from her eyes and looked across the fire. As if he could sense what was happening, Tony was staring at her. Cold, icy shards raced down her spine as she caught Tony's eyes. She turned away.

"Damn," she murmured.

"You OK?"

She turned and cuddled deeper into Tom's arms. "Yeah, I think so."

"Can you keep going?"

She took another deep breath and spoke into the void, to no one in particular, feeling Tom's warm strength beside her, the spirits inside her, the red energy churning deep, the freezing cold of the rain as well as Tony's troubling presence. It took several seconds for her to sense it all, feel it all, put each energy, spirit and part of her life in its place, and begin again.

She told him about the beatings he gave her, the deepening relationship to his family but their refusal to see what was happening to her. The battles in public. His drinking. The night, in a drunken stupor, he'd tried to rape Jazz. The day he chased Janie around the house trying to hit her.

The car crashes. The darkness began to release from inside her, churning, sending out crimson tendrils. It fed on her fears.

She closed her eyes again and stopped. She felt herself gather her spirit allies to control the darkness, but instead of pushing it down, she held it there, right at her consciousness, until she could continue.

She'd never told anyone. She'd kept it all inside, deep inside her. Even the girls knew only a fraction of what she had endured. She spilled it all out to Tom and hoped against hope that it wouldn't scare him away. "Tom, I was trapped. I had nothing. I was an only child. My parents were dead. They'd spent everything they had on my law school. I had no uncles, aunts or cousins. I was alone, penniless and scared out of my mind when I got involved with Robert. He was handsome, rich and had a huge, wonderful family that took me in. It was a trap, and I fell right into it.

"They became the only family the girls had. I knew what it was like not to have a family, and I was sure that if I left Robert, I'd lose them. I might even lose the girls. They were rich. I had nothing.

"Then I decided to stand up for myself. I took some of our money and rented a house far away in Maryland and moved the girls there one morning. Then I returned to our house and waited. He came in drunk and tried to hit me as usual. I ducked and drove my right arm through his face with everything I had, which was not that much back then. I knocked him backward, and he fell into a glass coffee table. He was scared. I told him we were leaving and stormed out of the house.

"He apparently got into his car and crashed it into the side of his favorite bar. He was arrested and treated at the hospital but then put in a security psych ward. I thought he'd never get out. We began to settle in, but he escaped. He stole a car, drove to his brother's house, stole his gun, demanded to know where we were, and when he wouldn't tell, Robert shot at his own brother, who then told him our location. Robert stole his brother's car and some booze and headed out to our place. I couldn't get us out in time.

"He stormed the house. I got the girls out my bedroom window. I scrambled out just in time, but he followed. As I ran, he shot me in the leg. He shot again as I was sitting on the ground and hit me right here in the shoulder. The police were coming. He heard the sirens. I was able to pull myself around the house and lean against it." Tears were streaming down her face, her voice halting as she spoke. "He and the police shot at one another. I was losing control, going into shock, they told me later. I saw the huge gun barrel pointed at my forehead. I talked to him. He fell to his knees. It was a blur. Then a bang and pain, and I was out. He'd shot me here." She pointed to the lower left side of her abdomen. "Later I woke up in the hospital. I guess he'd been shot and was in jail."

"You were shot, but you don't have any scars or wounds. I should know. I've checked this hot bod out myself." She instinctively felt for the gunshot wounds, but she knew they were gone.

"What are you looking for?" Tom asked.

"Tom, I wasn't a happy person in the old world. I loved my girls dearly but hated nearly everything else. After the shooting, we escaped to St. Louis to get far away from Robert." She put her head in her hands. "I took my girls from the only family they'd ever had, Robert's family. They cried. They were mad at me. I felt so guilty. I'd ruined their lives. I made them change names. They couldn't contact their grandmother, who they loved so much, or their friends. But Robert's family loved him. I have no parents, no siblings, no family." She paused. "I missed his mother too." He held her close and said nothing as she sobbed, the rain flowing off her long black hair, puddling in mud around them.

Then she turned to look at him with deeply sorrowful eyes. "I found out that he'd been released . . . the day of the Storm. He would find us, somehow. I knew I had to yank my girls out of their lives again." She told him about Asha, her insane battle inside and with the Storm, her four animals spirits and her associated powers, the Storm inside her, dark and powerful, and winning the battle. Then losing Asha, who had sacrificed her soul for her. "Tom, that horrible Storm was the best thing that has ever happened to me, and then you came along. How terrible is that? Billions died, probably, and the living, like your lovely family, are suffering, and here I am, happy about it. What does that say about me?" She began to sob. Tom held her close and tried to soothe her. It was out there—the blackness, the darkness, the terror that included her joy in a tragedy that killed so many.

Finally, he spoke, "All of that's so far in the past, it's in a different reality. That's not you. It never was you. It was your circumstances. That mess is gone. Completely gone. You didn't cause this. That Storm is from something else. You and I live in a new world, one in which you're ideally suited, one with over a hundred people who love you, honor you and literally owe you their lives. You have your daughters, and they're truly wonderful. Amazing. It took a phenomenal mother to raise two daughters as tremendous as Jazz and Janie, and a strong woman to do it under all of the stress and negativity you were facing every day."

He raised up onto his knees, straddling her legs and looking straight into her eyes. "Honey, I love you with every bone in my body. There are no comparisons. I loved Maryann with all of them as well, but this is different. Not better. Not worse, for God's sake. Just different. Wonderfully different." And he lowered himself to her and kissed her with passion. Whispers raced around the fire, and the Family fell quiet.

Then the Family cheered and applauded as Sarah guided Tom off of her. Tony and his crew booed and hissed from the far side of the fire. As Sarah blushed, she caught a glimpse of sadness, perhaps regret, in Tony's eyes.

Ms. Watson smiled and shushed everyone, "Alright, alright, the show's over." Then she turned to the couple and said loud enough for all to hear, "It's over, right?" Everyone laughed. Some hooted and hollered for an encore. "More, more!" Ms. Watson sat back down. The teasing dissipated and then ceased as everyone returned to their respective conversations.

Sarah's face was still pink as he moved in behind her, and she leaned back into his strong embrace. She let her head fall to rest on his shoulder as she gazed up into the trees, letting the rain fall into her face.

The rain picked up, and Tom spoke, his words resonating deep within her, as though mixed with Asha and her mother somehow. "Let this rain wash all of that hatred, fear and guilt away. Let it wash away everything from that past life except you and your girls and how they are right now. Feel it wash you clean and new and free in a new world." She felt Asha smile. It was like a Sandhyopasana ritual that her guru had taught her, a sort of Hindu baptism for purification. She closed her eyes and opened her mouth, drinking the rain. She let the rain wash over her, down her body and off onto the ground as she controlled her breath and silently recited the Gayatri. She felt the evil darkness flow out of her, mixing with the rain, sinking into the ground. She settled into a low meditative state and let the rain carry away her sins, failures, mistakes and terrors from her previous life. She could feel the water take the Storm's dark side from her soul, pulling it into the earth below.

After many minutes, she didn't know how long, she sat up and shook her head, scattering water from her long black hair everywhere, including Tom's face. Tom let her have this moment to free herself from her prior reality. She needed to do that. She was amazed at how much of that life she'd been holding onto. She let it all go. For the first time in her life, she was free and honest with herself. She'd let herself love. Sarah settled against his chest and released a long exhalation, sending her remaining negativity into the universe. She felt Asha glow inside her.

THIRTY-SIX

The rain stopped sometime during the night. The fire was still burning, but much lower as the day was breaking.

Sarah was awake and cold. No nightmares. No fears. Only joy. She was lying on Tom's chest. Jazz and Janie were curled up on top of them. They were all still asleep, and Sarah couldn't move without disturbing them, so for several minutes, she lay there awake, surveying the area, watching her big Family sleep, and thinking until her injuries began to bark at her. She moved, and Janie woke up.

"What?" she yelped.

That, of course, woke up Jazz and Tom. She kissed Janie and Jazz. "Girls, you have jobs to do, right?"

They both nodded, took a moment to stretch and then kissed their mother and were off. Janie bounded off to round up her vegetable- and fruit-gathering party, rousing them from sleep if necessary. They ran into the compound to grab their baskets, Janie singing at the top of her lungs. Other kids woke and joined in. It was a pleasant way to wake up and begin the morning.

Jazz trudged over and poked Mark. "Get up, lazy butt." He grumbled but then sat up and got to his feet. "Gotta catch breakfast, dude." Sarah laughed at the interplay. They liked each other but were young. The courting rituals of 14-year-olds was interesting. They both plodded into the compound, roused a few other reluctant teens, and all of them moved as slowly as humanly possible, heads down, shoulders slumped, to the pond in the stream to catch fish for breakfast.

Tom and Sarah shared a small laugh. He reached down to pick Sarah up, but she stopped him. "Let's see if I can walk again. I'm sore, but overall, I feel better. Another therapeutic trip to the river pond may be in order later today." She smiled.

He reached down and helped her up. They were both muddy. Everyone was. She was also cold and still a little tired. The sun was out, and it was likely a lot warmer out in it than in these woods. She tested out her ankle. It felt a lot better. She put her full weight on it without problem. Then the other leg. She felt a twinge with her knee, but it was functional. The bruise was painful but dull and manageable. She spent a moment going into her meditation, drawing on her special spirits to give her strength, quell the pain and heal her injuries. She felt only the warm but powerful nature-creating side of the Storm, now her ally. Joyous!

She took a moment to straighten herself out, stretching upward to the sky with both hands together. Her shoulder was much better. Then she arched her back as far as possible. Her ribs were also handling this well. Then she stretched forward to the ground in front of her and back up.

"Wow, I feel great. Much improved. You're a magician." She turned and threw her arms around his neck and planted a big kiss on him. He wrapped his big arms around her and lifted her up in the air and kissed her back. Sarah felt more alive than she could ever remember.

He let her down, held her hand, and she tested out a few steps. Not bad. Her balance was back. The pain in her ankle and knee were reduced, and her range of motion in both was better. The bruise was still ugly, but easier to touch without pain, though of all her injuries, that one, as Tom had predicted, still hurt the most by far and would give her trouble for a while, she guessed. She held Tom's hand, but more like a couple of school kids than like a doctor aiding his patient. As they left the woods, she released him. He knew she was determined and independent, and she knew he liked that about her. That felt wonderful. She refused to allow comparisons or thoughts from the old world to creep in.

The day was beautiful. The sky was cloudless. She closed her eyes and felt the soft warm air, guided by a subtle breeze, wrap around her. She smiled at Tom as her eyes returned to reality. Like the day before, Marsha's team was stacking wood on top of the hill to dry. Unlike the day before, they had plenty of fire, ten fresh fish, elk and deer sausage, and four rabbits for breakfast, along with a big basket of berries, which were starting to pop up all over. They had mixed field greens adorned with numerous edible and tasty flowers and small carrots. The breakfast was wonderful.

The camp was muddy but drying out. Everyone headed down to bathe. The water was cold but refreshing. Carmen and Candy were washing and combing hair; they stood in front of the younger men to do their hair. *Just let it be.* That became a way of looking at the world. It was cooperative. It wasn't just tolerant. The Family's way was set out by Ms. Watson from Day 0 and still stood: simple recognition that everyone is unique, and each person should be loved for who they are, and each person's differences should be recognized and respected, not merely tolerated.

It was a powerful message, and the Family embraced it. Other than the one incident, there'd been no other serious problems.

After a bath, where Sarah and Tom washed each other, and breakfast, they each attended to a few things in their parts of camp and then went out for a walk in the grasslands. The work that needed to be done was lessening, and people were getting it done faster with the new teams and better tools. There were quite a few people out for walks, and Sarah noticed quite a few relationships developing, whether long-term or simply sexual, she wasn't sure. She saw Candy and Jake disappear into some tall grass and guessed what sort of relationship that would be.

"Those two are something out of a porn movie," Tom observed. "He's hung like a horse, and obviously those boobs are real because they're still here." Sarah slapped him.

"Behave, you! You're not supposed to notice other women's breasts!" She glared at him with a smile and then agreed, "They seem to be made for each other."

Sarah's gait was improved, and she engaged the Horse's spirit as though it had been part of her all her life. The pain was decreasing with each passing hour as she released her Elephant spirit to take charge of her healing. The feeling in the air was unbelievable. The lightning brought life to the plants. Something about the electricity in the air. Regardless, they were bright green, strong and beautiful. Tom picked her a few wildflowers.

She smelled them and put one in his hair. He put several in hers. She took the one out of his hair and told him it didn't work with his outfit. They both laughed. He preferred not to be festooned with flowers anyway.

She was feeling great but also a bit guilty. "I haven't been able to do much of anything for the Family. It's driving me crazy."

"Are you kidding? You raised the spirit of the entire camp. You spoke to everyone, many of whom needed to talk to you. This situation is very hard on them. Everyone's former reality was so much better than their current one. You're a beacon to them. You're their savior. You're their leader. Sure, Ms. Watson is the administrative leader. She's masterful with people, and I still say she's a witch. But everyone, even Ms. Watson, turns to you when anything is astray. You gave all the orders when the hail was coming, and you saved the food, the fire and who knows how many bruises from that nasty hail with your quick thinking. No one else thought of all of that.

"How many people will recover from their wounds because of your juniper berry concoction? They all simply execute your orders. You're the CEO. Ms. Watson may be the president, but you're the Chairman of the Board. And I'm proud to be the First Gentleman."

She didn't even smile but stared straight into the ground. She was too deep into computing these revelations to take in the humor. She'd always thought of herself as Ms. Watson's first mate. But he was right. Everything the Family did, they did because she told them to. Ms. Watson executed her orders.

"Sarah," Tom continued, bringing her out of her trance, "for everyone else here, this situation is beyond their wildest nightmares. In every horror film ever made, there was the opportunity to defeat the beast or aliens or madman, and when that happened, everything returned to normal. Sure, people die, and horribly scary stuff happens, but in the end, the bad guy or thing is vanquished, and life returns to normal.

"This is way worse than that. Everyone's lost someone, and in most cases, many someones, who were near and dear to them. Spouses and children like me. Parents, friends, relatives. They weren't killed visibly on screen, either. They're lost. We have no idea what's happened to them. They're dead or suffering and getting close to death. People wonder and talk about their loved ones all the time."

"Really?" she replied.

"Sure. It's still so recent and still all so out there and uncertain. There's nothing worse than the combination of uncertainty, hope and realization about what's happening, and a complete inability to do anything about it. It's horrible." He paused. She said nothing.

"And it's miserable. Cold, wet and slimy. Children are whining. The food is edible but nothing like what they're used to. Amy's doing a great job, but she doesn't have much to work with—nothing that she or her diners are used to. And, of course, there's nowhere near enough for most people. Everyone is hungry, tired, cold and afraid . . . and *naked*, which is a new way of looking at the world. None of the rules they grew up with apply. Married couples have fallen apart here. Life is crazy.

"Then add in the hyena event, which I've only heard about, the crazy attack by the zombie teenagers, which is what everyone is calling them now, and the Tony problem. Then Mother Nature soaked us to the bone and pounded us into submission last night."

"Wow" was all she could say.

"And here you and your two daughters are. While they're all struggling, complaining and wishing with everything they have that they could get back to their previous lives, you're living, thriving, laughing and leading them. You know what to do. You know *how* to do it. While their children are whining, your children are leading teams on critically important missions. You don't care that you're naked. You don't care that it's cold and there are no hot showers. It doesn't even affect you.

"Then you prove you're brave beyond measure and invincible. None of them would have taken on that many armed crazy people on their own, much less defeated them, all to your near destruction. Even if they had been that brave, they'd still be back in the infirmary licking those many wounds you have and whining about the pain."

When he paused, she turned and looked at him, and he continued. "When they saw you go down, their spirits fell. Without you, they knew life was hopeless for them. But you wouldn't let them down. When you returned with me, standing tall and defying everything, especially the pain, which had to have been excruciating, they were thrilled. When you let go of me, stood with an emanating power that literally glowed around you, they were in awe. Then you walked tall and strong into camp; the people who saw you leave in my arms, bruised, swollen and helpless, were astounded. You showed your people that you and they can't be defeated. Not by 300 delusional nutcase zombies. Not by Mother Nature. Not by anyone or anything. It gave them hope. It restored them. You, their fearless leader, were back, and back with a vengeance. It may be the most important thing you've done for this Family, and you've done a lot."

After a long moment, as she considered everything that Tom had said and took it all in, Sarah realized that he was right. She turned to him. "OK, First Gentleman, let's get back to the compound and pull our weight around here." He smiled and nodded. She quickened her pace, still with a little limp caused by her bruise, but she was getting around quite well, employing her spirits as part of her instead of as uncontrolled tools at her disposal.

THIRTY-SEVEN

As always, the place was bustling. All the teams were doing their things. As she moved through the camp, the people around her stopped and turned to greet her. She smiled back, and if she remembered their name, she added it to her greeting. Tom whispered several to her. Each person bowed as she left.

She started to see her handiwork everywhere. She had taught the Seamstresses how to make a needle from a piece of bone. She'd put the three fires in their places, orchestrated the barrier construction and was even the architect for the latrines, which worked and drained well. *OK, enough self-congratulations.* Though it did make her feel good.

The next steps, she knew, were major ones. They had to build some shelter. They had to protect themselves better from the elements and eventually from the frigid cold and snows of winter. They needed to cover the wood and build a bigger meat smokehouse so they could better preserve proteins.

The area inside of the compound, while wet, was still grassy. As the ground dried, the compound became bearable again. The soft, short grass restored itself quickly. *Please, no more rain. At least for a while.*

Doc arrived wearing a sad expression, Olivia right behind him. Although wearing a more matter-of-fact expression, Sarah could feel her pain. Doc delivered the news. "Hector died last night. Not unexpected, but still a blow. Our first death. There will be more. We have some sick folks back there." Sarah reached out and touched Olivia's arm, and they shared a moment. The nurse nodded, sniffled then headed back to the infirmary. Doc stayed.

Sarah stepped up in her role as their leader. "Hector will be remembered as our first fallen hero, defending our community against dozens of crazed attackers. Do we have any way to keep track of what day this is? Is anyone keeping some sort of calendar?" Sarah asked. "Shirley?"

"I heard," she said as she joined the group, anticipating the conversation. "Hector's dead." Others on the leadership team gathered. When they saw Sarah and Ms. Watson come together, they knew something was up.

"I think we should honor him as our first fallen hero. We should commemorate this day as Hector Day, and each year on this day remember those who died in the previous year," Sarah suggested, and everyone nodded. "We'll have to create a calendar. It'll be good to keep track of growing seasons and other things we decide to celebrate."

"Like birthdays!" Janie offered with her typical enthusiasm, startling everyone.

"Where'd you come from?" Sarah reached for her youngest, but Janie scampered off.

"Can't catch me, your heinie-ness!" That made people smile and kept Sarah humble.

When the adults turned back from watching Janie bound up to her friends and then off somewhere, Ms. Watson spoke. "I know just the person for the job." *Of course she did. She knew everyone. She was a marvel.* "Helen was a teacher of astronomy. For centuries, days of the year were counted based on what was happening in the heavens."

"Perfect. If anyone can create and maintain a calendar, Helen can." Sarah had met Helen the day before. She wasn't certain which woman she was, but she remembered the name and that she was a science teacher. *I can do this.* "OK, Shirley, can you take care of the funeral arrangements and stuff like that?"

"Sure." Ms. Watson nodded at Erika, who nodded back, and Ms. Watson headed off. Both things would get done. She watched as Ms. Watson walked over to Helen. *Oh yes, that's Helen.* Helen looked up at her with a huge grin. Sarah waved. Helen waved back. She realized that it was an honor to have been chosen by Sarah for a specific duty.

"How are the other patients, Doc?"

"The juniper berry-peppermint compress does wonders. It works best if we change it frequently. Sucks the infection right out. That could save some lives, young lady. Nice work. We have six people down with nasty cases of the flu and one with pneumonia. Last night didn't help. High fevers. Not much we can do for them. Anything in your bag of tricks for the flu?"

"I'll think on it, but fevers are good, right? And the flu is a virus, so it just has to run its course, pretty much. The pneumonia is another thing. Bacterial, right?"

Doc nodded. "All we can do is keep them comfortable."

"I'll talk with Amy and Janie later about an internal antibacterial. I'll let you know if we can think of anything. An internal juniper won't work, and we can't afford to waste them. Try making a peppermint tea. Peppermint has antibacterial properties. Might help the flu victims as well. Amy knows where it grows." With that the Doc nodded, turned and headed back to the infirmary.

"See, you were laid up and still saving lives and making other people's lives better, including mine," Tom reminded her. Her eyes told Tom how much she appreciated him.

"I hope I'm up to it."

"You are. The girls and I will keep you humble, your heinie-ness."

She slapped him playfully. "I bet you will. I just bet you will." She pulled him to her and kissed him. "You're mean as a snake, you are."

His face made it clear he wasn't sure what that meant. *Good.* Lunch was called. They were served last as usual. She wolfed her small portion down and was ready to move on. Tom was always amazed at how little Sarah consumed considering her boundless energy. He was, however, happy to have the extra helping.

After they ate, Sarah looked around and noticed there were more people lying about doing nothing than there had been the other days since the Storm. Tony was lounging on soft grasses with about 30 others around him. He was holding court.

"Shirley, got a minute?" Ms. Watson gave a parting comment to the young woman she was speaking to and strode over. Erika, Joe and a few others followed. "Looks like we're starting to have a complacency problem."

"Well, that's one way to put it."

Joe chimed in, "It's been very difficult. This is the sixth full day of hard work since the Wall. These people are not used to doing this much. Most worked in climate-controlled buildings and then headed home to the safety of their homes to watch TV all night. Maybe a few went to the gym or for a run or walked the dog, but they didn't haul wood or make stone tools or any of those things."

"And they're almost all out of shape," Erika added. Erika was a chiseled athlete. "They're fat. Their muscles are underdeveloped. They have no stamina. Their skin is soft and can't handle the strain. And, of course, they're so vain. The women especially. They can't stand it that hair is growing out on them everywhere. They've never had underarm or leg hair. Most had perfectly waxed pubic regions. Not anymore. Their once beautifully coifed hair now gets messy fast, and they're spending a lot of time at the Boutique by the River. For a few, looking good was their life. They have nothing here they used to value."

These revelations always surprised Sarah. She was so interwoven into this world, even though she had worked in such an office all day and returned home to a comfortable home.

Joe continued, "Carmen and Candy have steady work down at the river. Jazz showed them how to make those razor knives, and Candy's getting pretty good at shaving with them. They use a grease from the animals that we kill. Carmen's great at using them to cut hair. Women are spending a lot of time being styled rather than working."

"And, shockingly, the guys are doing things for the prettiest women," Erika added. "Not to be crude, but they're doing things in exchange for things that guys want from women. It's human behavior 101. Girl gets pretty for boy. Boy bends over backward for the girl in hopes that she'll have sex with him. It's happening all over the place."

"The bad thing is we've gotten close to some fights among the guys over the prettier girls," Joe noted. "Guys are starting to preen too and try to one up one another. Fights are one of the ways men prove themselves to women. You know, Tony has a crush on you, and he's threatened to take down Tom several times, not that it would matter. He's so full of it."

Before Sarah could respond, Erika breezed past that bit of information as though it was common knowledge. "And women hate it when Carmen and Candy flirt with 'their' men down at the Boutique."

Amy added, "A bigger issue is the 'married' couples. People who were married before, are they still married? If their marriage was a mess before the Wall, it's way worse now. Guys are fooling around with other women. The 'wives' are getting mad at both their husband and the other woman and are frustrated."

"People who used to garner prestige through money or political power are starting to consider ways to insert themselves into the power structure around here. That's a real concern. We weren't exactly elected, you know," Joe said.

"Early on, fear kept people in line. As people get used to this new way of life, interactions are getting messy," Ms. Watson said. "Molly and I've tried to address it, but it's tough. It's a strange place. Everyone is fed, has lost weight with our diet, is stronger from the work and are feeling better about their bodies, which are out there for everyone to see. It's spring. People are starting to get frisky."

There was a pause as everyone looked at Sarah.

Finally, Marsha pointed out the obvious. "Sarah, you're special. You have . . . powers or something. Everyone looks to you as some sort of mythical figure. They fear you. They don't understand you, but they know you talk to bears and horses and who knows what else."

"And glow sometimes," Amy interjected.

Ms. Watson turned to her. "Sarah, everyone else feels disconnected and lost. You seem to love this world, for some reason, and it loves you back."

"You can fix all of this because you're Sarah," Marsha said in a reverent manner, like someone referring to a deity of some kind.

They all got quiet, waiting for her to speak.

She took several seconds to consider everything that had been said. There was a lot to do. There were chores that had to be done for the Family to survive. They were about to embark on an ambitious project, building the winter house. That huge undertaking would require everyone working in concert, for a benefit that wouldn't be enjoyed for months. And it wasn't like she was Miss Purity around here.

"OK, I don't think we want a puritan lifestyle." She paused and scanned the group. "Flirting's going to happen." Sarah closed her eyes for a second as though looking for answers. She opened them to staring, pleading eyes. "Perhaps we have to make a clean break from the old world. If a marriage or other relationship from the old world is dead, maybe it should be put to rest." The leadership looked at one another then back at Sarah. "There are no legal documents keeping couples together anymore."

Erika blurted out, "Yeah, make everyone earn their partner's love every day!" The team nodded, one by one.

Ms. Watson seemed to count the votes and turned to Sarah. "Can you announce that tonight?"

"OK, sure." Sarah felt sure it was the right answer in this new world, though she didn't really know why.

THIRTY-EIGHT

S arah continued, "As to getting things done around here, that has to be everyone's obligation, but we don't need people working 12-hour days anymore. I think we need to break down the tasks into smaller bites, with smaller teams working shorter shifts, and then perhaps doing other things that are less taxing so that they can recover. Perhaps a before- and after-lunch schedule. Perhaps we can schedule workers so that combatants are seldom together. How complicated would that be Erika?"

"I'll try to work that out. Ms. Watson, can you help?" Ms. Watson nodded.

Sarah said, "And we can get certain groups to do the tasks that benefit them. For example, the hunters love to hunt. That's pretty easy. What we're going to do, however, is make the hunters responsible for making their own arrows and spears, including the points." Sarah looked at Rhonda, who nodded her agreement.

"I want the wood team, especially the teams cutting wood, to begin to at least sharpen their own axe blades. Again, high-quality axe blades benefit them." Sarah turned to Jake, and he agreed.

"Gus can make and sharpen his own knives, or he can get one of his apprentices to do it," Amy said. "I'll let him know."

Marsha agreed to similar tasks for the engineering and construction teams.

"Jazz can continue to make them for Ol' Mac and the Seamstresses," Sarah concluded, "but even they have young helpers who can take over for them, don't they?"

"I'll tell them and send them to the river to have Jazz work with them," Erika offered.

"It'll take a few days, but it won't be long before they're proudly making their own points, relieving that dwindling group of that obligation. Let people know that came from Ms. Watson and me. You OK with being included Shirley?" Ms. Watson nodded. Sarah was still the only person who called Ms. Watson by her first name. To the others, it was a display of Sarah's superiority, even though Sarah used it out of respect.

"OK, Erika, more for you," Sarah continued. "To organize smaller crews to do smaller sets of critical tasks in shorter shifts, we'll have to identify more natural leaders. Do you have any ideas?"

"Yes."

"OK, put them at the heads of each of the groups. Try to find people who feel a need to lead, are competent leaders but won't be authoritarian. Let's get ahead of those who are trying to compete for leadership here by including them right now. Make sense?"

Erika and Ms. Watson nodded.

"OK, get as much input as you can so that people value their leader. Lots of leaders, and everyone has to follow someone sometimes. More importantly, everything gets done.

"As to me being special, well, I guess I am. I'll tell you all about it sometime. But for now, let's use that to our advantage. Your authority comes from mine, whatever that means to people. Do you think that will work?" Everyone nodded.

"Now the issue of people being out of shape. Work and our diet will resolve that, but in the short term, the troops are struggling, and I get that. Tom, would you open your chiropractic office somewhere in the compound so that we can start caring for the larger Family members and get them feeling better and back to work?"

"Sure. That's a wonderful idea. There's not much I can do back in the infirmary anyway. Doc and the nurses have it pretty much under control, and you're doing great. I'm just a glorified helper. Yeah, helping people using the theories of chiropractic care would be awesome. So much of illness is about nerves and how they're affected by stress." He continued on about how chiropractic care is misunderstood and that it's great for so much more than backaches, helping to resolve issues anywhere in the body where nerves are important, "which is everywhere."

Sarah gently cut him off. "That should help with overall healing and with some of the aches and pains and stuff. There are some massage therapists, right?"

Ms. Watson named four of them.

"Any physical therapists or athletic trainers or things like that?"

"A couple."

"OK. Take them off whatever they're doing, put Tom in charge of them and have them start giving massages and doing whatever they do to work out muscle soreness. Tell them to keep it nonsexual when they're working on someone, just to keep the stress levels down a bit. Shirley, Erika, Tom, can you handle that?"

They all nodded, and Ms. Watson answered for all off them. "Sure. On an earlier point, if you don't mind, I'm also going to ask Doc to talk to the beauty ladies and ask them to stop shaving people. It's dangerous and unnecessary. I've seen a few people get cut and get infections. Nothing bad."

Sarah added, "And, more importantly, we have limited supply of medicines to treat infections. The juniper berry season is almost over, and while we have a store, it'll have to be rationed until the next crop. We have enough accidental injuries. We don't need to create them."

Tom added, "Plus, there's no real way to sterilize those stone tools. They can cut hair with them, but close shaves need to stop."

"I agree," Sarah said. "We also need to somehow convey to women that it isn't healthy and not a required look anymore. Who would be good to convey that message?"

"Carmen and Candy," Ms. Watson replied. "They need to start by not shaving each other."

"OK, please join Doc in talking to them to make it clear that this is serious. Shall we make an announcement on that tonight?" Sarah asked.

Ms. Watson nodded. "OK, one more question. Who is the woman who flits about here like a nymph or fairy or something?"

"She was a yoga instructor in the old world. Into meditation and relaxation techniques. She's also very spiritual and into positive thinking and stuff like that," Ms. Watson replied. "She's hard for me to talk with."

Erika said, "Her name is Daffodil. She's fascinating. Very positive. Very into nature and going with the flow of things. Very reassuring. Some people don't know what to think of her, but she could be helpful, I think."

"OK, Tom, can you ask her to lead some 'classes' on yoga and meditation and, most of all, relaxation. Let's formalize her contribution. Erika, since you have that connection, can you talk to her and connect her to Tom?"

"Sure, I'd be happy to."

Sarah nodded at Ms. Watson. "Let's make these changes. We'll go over them again at the fire tonight, but let's try to get things organized and agreed to before then. Sound good?"

Everyone nodded and headed out to talk to their teams except Tom, who stayed with Sarah.

THIRTY-NINE

"**O**K, big guy, next thing. We need to find Marsha." Marsha, the engineer, had left the meeting early to meet with her team.

Sarah called, "Marsha, got a minute?"

"Sure, Sarah. Whatcha got?"

As they approached the team, Tom spoke up, which shocked everyone. "Marsha, if you don't mind, I don't know everyone on your team. Would you mind introducing them?" Sarah realized he was covering for her and allowing her to learn names without admitting she hadn't known them already.

Marsha went around the group, introducing each person and giving a brief synopsis as to what their roll was. Sarah paid close attention.

"Thanks Tom, Marsha." Sarah took charge. "Alright, I think we can all agree, this rain totally sucks." She saw Jazz and realized she needed to be in this conversation. "Jazz, come over here, would you?" Jazz came running and plopped down in her mother's lap. It hurt a little as she landed partly on her thigh bruise. She winced but sucked it up.

Marsha piped up, "We all know our little toolmaker, Jazz. Her team's amazing. We've already talked to her about teaching us how to make our tools." Jazz smiled up at her mother, who smiled back at her and gave her a big hug.

"OK, back to business. We need to start building a shelter. We need to build something that can house everyone, keep them dry and keep us all warm and safe, especially in the winter." Everyone nodded their agreement but looked to Sarah for instructions. "Outside the barrier is the large clearing where we were last night. If we use that clearing as the living area of the house, we can use the trees as the main structural supports for the walls and ceiling."

Marsha nodded as did several of the others.

"That's going to take a lot of wood and thatch for the roof and exterior walls. Do any of you guys know how to craft a thatched roof?"

Emma, a short, angular, middle-aged woman, raised her hand. "I do. Well, I read about how to do it in a class once and then saw a documentary on it. It's pretty cool and fairly simple from an engineering standpoint."

"Great. Jazz and I can help if you want. We built one once. You're right, it isn't hard conceptually. It can be hard to make work in real life, though.

"Now for the tricky engineering part. We'll have a big fire in the middle to keep warm. The fire draws air to operate, right?" Everyone nodded. "If it just burns in the center of the building, it will literally suck the frigid air into the building through the imperfect seams in the walls, defeating the whole purpose of having a fire inside." Eyes lit up as everyone nodded and began chatting among themselves.

"Soooo," and everyone quieted to hear her speak, "we need something to create pipes to the outside."

"Something hollow or hollowed out," Marsha noted, her mind beginning to whir, "to create pipes from outside the structure to the base of the fire so that the cold air is drawn from outside the walls to feed the fire. Maybe cutting a branch in half longways, hollowing it out and strapping it back together? We'll need a tool to hollow out the limb. Jazz?"

"Sure. We'll figure it out together," Jazz replied, smiling.

"OK, Marsha, do you guys get this? It'll take a long time, but we need this. Another thing we need is a smaller structure designed to cover the wood so that it doesn't get wet," Sarah added.

"Great idea. We can use it to test out our ideas and work on thatching," one of the others interjected.

"I'm getting very tired of hauling that stupid wet wood out onto that hill in front to dry out, only to haul it right back in again," another person admitted.

Marsha said to her team, "Let's do that first. Jason, please get some charcoal from the fire. Sheila, find some birch bark we can write on. Then everyone join me in a few minutes at the wood pile." Jason and Sheila took off. "Sarah, can you walk around and show me where you envision this house being built?"

Tom helped her up, and she stretched a bit less than usual. "Tom, I can handle it from here. Why don't you work on setting up your clinic somewhere and start caring for people?"

Tom nodded and kissed her. It was one of those cute, off-to-work kisses.

She and Marsha walked around the inside of the barrier, out the gate, to their right down the barrier wall and into the eastern woods. The two walked around, pointing and gesturing to branches and trees and spots on the ground. Marsha grabbed a stick and began to draw the walls around the trees.

"We'll need a chimney for the cooking stone as well. Are we going to move that one or get another?" Marsha was standing in the middle of the area, near the remnants of the fire, staring up into the trees, then she turned and walked farther away below another opening in the canopy.

"Your deal, Marsha." Sarah thought about it. "Probably will. This'll be the place we meet, eat and do most things, even in the nicer months. Measure it out and build a proper support for it." She watched as Marsha was already drawing the cooking area on the ground with her stick. "You're right about needing a chimney for the cooking fire."

They discussed every aspect of the construction for the better part of the afternoon. Marsha summed up by saying, "Lots to do."

"Yep. Can you handle it?" Sarah asked.

"Sure. We'll get lots of help. We can divide up the chores among the various teams. We should be able to get it built by the time the air gets too cold at night to sleep outside. Hopefully a lot sooner."

"Spoken like a true building planner." Sarah winked and shook Marsha's hand. "Make it happen. Let me know what you need or if you have any pushback. I'd like to understand your plans as you dream them up, if that's OK?"

"Of course, Sarah, of course."

She turned to walk away, and Marsha called out, "You know what would make this so much easier?" Sarah turned, but Marsha didn't wait for a guess. "Bamboo. Bamboo is a phenomenal building material. Easier to work with than wood. Thinner but stronger. Lasts longer, grows nice and straight. Bamboo would be easier to hollow out and would be good for pipes. It would be perfect. Know where we can find any?"

"Umm. Possibly. The lady who lived behind us had a big Japanese garden, full of those stupid plants. They kept sprouting up in our yard. Who knows what that looks like now? Bamboo's a weed. Since those woods weren't here the day of the Storm, maybe there's a bamboo forest out there somewhere." *Another adventure ahead of me. I may be CEO, but I also still have to do the dangerous stuff.*

"Good luck," Marsha said, distracted, more focused on what she was doing than Sarah. "We could sure use it."

Sarah took a deep breath. *Now for the talk with Tony.*

He was where he always was, near the back. She gathered her spirits, raised her courage and strength, focused on her walking to reveal as little weakness as possible and headed in his direction at a strong pace. He saw her coming and sat up a bit, smirking with confidence.

"Look who's coming."

The others turned and watched as she approached.

"Tony, may I have a word?"

The darkness that usually roiled up inside her when she was around him was calm. Tony no longer made her skin crawl.

"Talk."

"You sure you want to have this conversation in front of everyone?"

"Talk." His voice was arrogant and disrespectful. "Woman."

"OK. Ladies and gentlemen, and Tony, your behavior over the last several days has been unacceptable."

They all broke into laughter. "Who the fuck made you queen?" Grunted one of the big hulking goons.

"That, my friend, is the point. There is no ruler here. We respect everyone for who they are, pitch in to the best of our abilities, take our turns and receive equal shares. You are shirking your duties and acting with disrespect toward the women and others in this community, and it is not acceptable." Sarah's voice was measured and reasonable. She hoped to simply convince them.

One of the older men, erect but portly, a businessman or politician, said, "Miss Sarah, if you are not in charge, then we do not have to listen to you, and your rules have no force or affect over us. You were not elected, at least not by any of us. You have no authority, save for your unnatural powers over which you have little control. We will simply wait until people realize that you are a menace and then take control of this place. But for now, you are dismissed and may leave us."

Sarah was not shocked by the disrespect.

Tony rose and walked up to her, so close his chest touched hers. "Woman, you had your chance to be my queen, my consort, but now you will find yourself my servant when the time comes. Leave us." He stepped back and waved her away.

She stood her ground, looking calmly down at him, then surprised herself by asking, "Tony, are you evil?"

He puffed out his chest, moved back so that his chest touched hers again, then spoke with deep confidence, "I am Anthony Scarfiero, the most feared man in the City of St. Louis. I ran the largest and most lucrative crime syndicate in the Midwest. We ran drugs, prostitutes, gambling, whatever, and if anyone got in my way, and I mean anyone, I either killed them or had them killed. I killed my own father to take his position. I killed my own brother. No one fucked with Tony Scarfiero. No one. Am I evil?" he hesitated and broke the connection between them, looking at the crowd that had gathered around them and then he leaned back into her face. "Yes, Miss Sarah. Yes, I am evil . . . to the core. And I will own you and this sorry excuse for a community!"

"Be careful, Tony. I defeated you once, and if you rise against the Family, I'll do it again. And this time, you will not come through it with only a few bruises to your foolish pride."

FORTY

Ms. Watson stood near the main fire and waited for Sarah to arrive. "Tony's evil," Sarah said in opening. "They will not be intimidated. We'll need to watch them. Use your sources." The two nodded at one another.

"Come and get it or we'll throw it out."

Dinner was pretty standard. Tony's entire team ate at the back fire. After dinner, Ms. Watson laid out the new work strategy and introduced Erika to go over the teams. Most people already knew the new deal, having been told during the day by Erika, but she went over it anyway to make sure it was common knowledge and became part of the Family culture. Sarah lost track of the monologue at some point, leaning back against Tom, staring into the fire and feeling a warmth she'd never felt before. There was polite applause and clear agreement among the Family.

Then Marsha spent several minutes going over the construction plans for improving the current meat smoking area into a true smokehouse and why they needed that, the lean-to they'd build to keep their firewood dry, and then she turned to the much more ambitious project, the house. She explained all the basic concepts. Marsha finished by asking for any help and ideas for making this a reality. "Come to me tomorrow with anything. Thank you," she said before sitting down. There was nice applause and a lot of positive-sounding chatter from the group.

Doc addressed the shaving issue, then Ms. Watson turned to Sarah, who decided to see just how strong her position in the Family was.

Sarah stood strong in front of the Family and looked each person in the eyes before she spoke. "This is the new world that calls for new traditions and ways of looking at life. We are a community. We share and expect everyone to be part of making this new world bearable, to allow us to survive together. No one person is above any other. We all will, from this day forward, expect all others to pull their weight according to their abilities." She stared directly into Tony's eyes, and he glared back at her. Everyone felt the intensity of the challenge.

"Now to another issue—relationships. We will not recognize legal fictions in this world. Relationships must be real. Whatever legal ties you had in the old world are gone forever. No one is married to anyone else, as of right now." She turned her attention to Tony's group. Several behind him were seething, but she stared them down before returning to the Family. "There will be no divorces because there will be no formal marriages. Each of us will have to earn the friendship, respect and love of everyone, including chosen partners, from this day forth. No longer will anyone rely on a piece of paper, or any other kind of a legal commitment, to slack off in their efforts to love a partner as deeply as humanly possible so that they, should they choose, will return that love.

"Tom is not mine. I am not Tom's. We are with each other because we both want to be. I hope that never changes, but that is as much up to Tom as it is to me. Does anyone have any questions or a problem with this?" There were murmurs, but no one spoke. "OK, that's settled. I love you all. Love each other." She sat down.

Roger wrapped up the evening with a little story that he told alone and quite well, but which Sarah didn't pay attention to. The tales were designed for the children to help them think of good things and to adjust to this life. Janie and Jazz loved him.

FORTY-ONE

The night was nightmare and rain free. She felt rested, healthy, relatively pain free and excited for the new day. Tom was just waking. "Alright, Tommy boy, if you're up to it, we have an adventure to go on. We need to find bamboo. We'll take the horse. Do we know where he is? I presume someone is using him to get some work done somewhere."

"Ohhh, no way." Tom was astonished at how little she was aware of in the Family.

"What do you mean?"

Tom smiled and shook his head. "Girlfriend, that is the queen's horse. No one rides or uses that horse but you. He's been cared for, groomed, fed and walked by various members of the Family. It's considered an honor to be chosen to do so."

"Shut up, you." She slapped him playfully. This had become a ritual, and he'd begun to expect it and defend himself. She was a physical woman. They were standing now.

"See for yourself." And he pointed toward the river. The horse was being groomed by a young man and a young woman. He looked magnificent. He was standing in the nicest patch of green grass inside the compound. "Janie brings him oats and wheat from the fields every day. She named him Latifah, after the Queen."

"Oh, for Christ's sake. He's a horse and a male horse at that. He's big and strong. He could pull wood and stuff. I had no idea. Well, we'll change that, but after we take a ride to see if there's any bamboo out there. Do you ride?"

"Umm, no. Not really fond of horses, actually."

"OK." She took his hands and pulled him close. "You don't have to go. In fact, you should run your new clinic. There are a lot of ailing and sore people. You, the therapists and Daffodil will be very busy and should be. They need you."

He held her hands. "Sarah, you shouldn't go out—", but he knew she had already decided to go and stopped short.

She pulled him close and gazed up into his deep blue eyes. "Really, I'm invincible, right?" She kissed him and backed away, still holding his hands. "And I'm not going out there alone. I'll take Erika. She's tough as nails and an excellent rider." She lifted herself up on her toes to whisper into his ear. "I'll be back, and you'll need the rest, my dear." She licked his earlobe. It sent a tingle down his spine. She could feel him shiver.

"Alright, go help our Family. Ask Janie to talk to Amy and see if they can think of any concoction for the flu. Honey helps coughs. It makes them more . . . productive, and that's good. Crushed mustard seed is good, but there won't be any until fall. That's all I can think of." He nodded, and she let him go.

She saw Erika partway across the compound and called to her. When she arrived, Sarah asked, "Wanna go on an adventure?"

"Sure. Where to?"

"We need to build some structures. Marsha mentioned that bamboo would be a great building material. The lady who lived behind us had a ton of the stuff, and it kept coming up in our yard. Maybe it's grown up and we can find it."

"Bamboo isn't native to Missouri."

"Well, my good friend, neither are hyenas, elephants nor giraffes, not to mention those strange mushrooms, but we have them now. We're apparently not in Missouri anymore. Plus, I want to see if we can find any other domesticated animals that we can bring back here—cows, chickens, pigs, more horses. If we can, it'll make finding food a lot easier."

"We taking Latifah?"

"Yep. I'm driving."

Erika got the spears and some jerky for the trip. Sarah grabbed Latifah's mane and leaped up onto the back of the big stallion. She reached down and helped Erika slide on behind her. "OK, Erika, I'm going to connect to the horse, to Latifah, and I need you to get completely into the connection, otherwise this ride is gonna hurt in a place you don't need to be hurting."

"Yea, I can already feel that."

"OK, deep breaths. Slowly exhale; feel the horse's spirit enter yours." She and Latifah were already deeply connected, and she guided the horse's spirit into Erika's, and Erika's together with the horse. She could feel them intertwining.

"Wow, I can feel him. I feel like I'm on air."

"A lot better, right? OK, let's get outta here."

Erika put her left hand around Sarah's waist and held the two spears in her right hand.

Latifah handled so well under Sarah's guidance. Rider and mount felt and acted simultaneously. Sarah thought, *Go right,* and Latifah was already on his way. It was so cool. She could feel Erika's spirit as well. As they rode, her thigh bruise hurt. She brought her spirits forth and ended the pain. She could sense that Erika felt it.

"What the heck was that?"

"Painkiller."

Once outside the barrier, Sarah glanced behind her. "You ready? Hold on tight." Erika leaned into Sarah and wrapped her arm farther around her as Sarah thought Latifah into a gallop—not a full gallop, but a good strong pace across the valley and up across the hills at the far side of the maze. Family members rose from whatever they were doing and waved. She rode straight for the edge of the northern reaches of the forest. Latifah was a smooth runner—probably a racing or dressage horse in his day. She knew from experience that he had several more gears than this.

They relished the beautiful day. She loved the wind whipping through her hair. Within a few minutes, they reached the edge of the forest, and she guided Latifah to the center point between the woods to their right and the river to their left. She turned the horse around and looked back. They were at a higher elevation than the compound, and she wanted to see if anyone could see it from here.

It was very difficult. Erika even asked, "Where's home?"

Sarah pointed to the south. "You can kinda see the maze of hills and valleys in the grassland area right there."

Erika tried to follow her arm. "Yeah, sorta."

"They're very hard to see. Everything blends together and is so green. But the compound is just over that larger hill there."

"Wow, we're completely invisible. If you didn't know precisely where you were headed, there's no way you'd find us," Erika said, then paused. "What if Family, someone still out there, is looking for us?"

After several seconds, Sarah said, "I guess, if they're Family, they'll hear the singing."

They both stared back at the invisible compound. Erika broke the silence first. "Alright then, that makes sense. Let's go find us some bamboo."

"That's the spirit." Sarah had been checking the area in front of them, and it was uninhabited by humans. The growing herds of grazing animals were across the river to the west, where they seemed to always be. She sensed her elephant, who nodded to her. Latifah launched into a nice gallop across the flat grassy spit of land between the river and woods. It was a good distance to the north edge or "back" of the woods, maybe 150 yards, Sarah guessed. Maybe more.

She stopped as they reached the gentle ridge she'd noticed before the teens attacked her. There was no way to see the compound from here. Sarah also noticed that her connection to the Family was very weak, even to Daffodil and her girls. They'd be out of range soon. *What would that mean?*

Erika seemed to respond to the unspoken question. "We won't be long."

The ridge ran eastward, parallel and about twenty yards north of the back edge of their forest. She wondered, *Did the teens chase all those animals out here, or did something else move them both in this direction?* Hopefully they weren't riding right into whatever it was. She pushed herself up to get a good look at what was coming up.

"Uncharted territory," Erika whispered. "I feel like Lewis and Clark or something."

The woods on both sides ran as far as she could see, though the grassy passage, centered on this ridge, grew wider to the east.

Erika suddenly pointed to the right. "Horses." There were four grazing in the shade near the northern edge of the woods. "Shall we get one more, for me?"

"We can try." As they got closer, she could see that there was a male and a female quarter horse, both deep reddish brown, a good-sized lighter brown draft horse with a long soft tan mane and large hoofs, and a young brown colt, still quite slender, without the reddish tint to his coat. She stopped Latifah and watched them for a few minutes. It wasn't long before the horses spotted them.

Sarah whispered over her shoulder, "Let's see what'll happen if we move. I want to see if an alpha's been established. That'll be the one we'd ride. The others will follow the alpha."

The quarter horse moved first, west down the edge of the woods, toward the river. The others followed.

"The quarter horse is the leader," Erika whispered.

Sarah nodded. "Maybe they're as tame as Latifah." She guided Latifah toward the four horses, but the four picked up the pace.

"The mare's pregnant," Sarah whispered.

"The big draft horse is putting himself between us and the colt," Erika whispered. They were still about 100 feet north of the other horses.

Sarah could feel the spirits of the horses. She pulled Latifah to a stop.

"What're you doing? Aren't we going to try to catch one?" Erika whispered.

"Not now. The big guy there isn't going to let us. That's his colt. We need to let them become comfortable with us first."

The quarter horses settled in and began eating. The big draft horse stood tall and kept an eye on them. Sarah's spirit poured out positive energy so the big horse would know they weren't a threat. He relaxed.

"This is good enough for today. I calmed the draft horse a bit, but we need to leave them for now. This is their grazing lands. They won't go too far until winter perhaps. We'll come back later more prepared to guide them back to camp. They're frightened. They're not wild."

Erika nodded.

Sarah felt the hairs on the back of her neck rise. Latifah and Erika could sense it as well. Sarah looked back and forth, then toward the other horses.

"What?" Erika asked.

"Shhh," Sarah responded, raising her hand. Erika quieted.

The four horses were also agitated. The orange flash was sudden and decisive. The three adult horses bolted away. Behind them they saw the colt on its side and atop it was a huge Bengal tiger. The tiger stood with both front paws on his kill.

"Oh my—"

Before Erika could continue, Sarah shushed her again and raised her hand. "Lower the spears out of view." Erika obeyed. Sarah climbed up so her knees were on Latifah's shoulders, put her hands on his neck and glared at the tiger. The tiger met her eyes, and they locked onto one another. This was him. Her Tiger. She could feel his spirit rise in her. She could feel her spirit connect to the big Bengal. Sarah leaned in. The tiger stood taller.

Sarah could feel Latifah gain confidence under her and lift his head to support her better. The tiger's spirit was inside her, intertwining with her soul and her spirit entered his, just as it had Latifah's, the bear's and the elephant's. There was no analysis, only knowledge of the connection. She looked deeply into the tiger's eyes—the same big green eyes she'd felt a connection to that first day and several times since. She felt his power merge with the spirit inside her. She nodded. The tiger lowered his head, almost in a bow. She settled back down onto the horse, and the tiger grabbed his meal by the neck and dragged it into the darkness of the forest.

"What was that?" Erika asked.

"We've reached an accord. We help him, and he'll help us."

"Shut the F up. You talked to that tiger?"

"Communicated. You can't talk to tigers."

"And that big draft horse?"

"In a different way, but yes." She was coming down from a spiritual high. Returning to reality. She took a deep breath, reached back and touched Erika's leg.

"OK, enough about that. Refocus, we have a mission. Two good things accomplished, but we still have to find some bamboo, if we can." Sarah was in command. Erika wrapped her arm around Sarah's waist and held on. There was a new energy between them, coming from Erika. Sarah could feel it, pleasant and powerful.

"I felt the quarter horse, I think?"

"What do you mean, you think?"

"Well, when you were communicating with the draft horse, the quarter horse looked at me. We looked into each other's eyes. I felt him inside me. It was so weird. Then when the tiger leaped out, I felt his fear. I still do. I don't know Sarah, but it sorta came from the horse and from you at the same time."

"Good. When it's time, you can connect with him and bring them all in. Wonderful. I could feel something, but there was a lot going on in me right then."

"Yeah, girlfriend, a big-ass tiger. That's pretty cool."

FORTY-TWO

"OK, back to the mission." There was a significant rise ahead. She slowed to a walk as they approached the apex. "Never run across a hilltop like this without knowing for sure what's on the other side."

Erika nodded.

As they reached the top, more grassland spread out before them. There was a small stream, smaller than their own, but heading eastward at the bottom of the rise to their left. It was surrounded by willow and birch trees, as one would expect, and then turned and flowed into the woods. The grass was a little higher on the south side of the crest.

She stopped on top of the long gentle ridge and surveyed the woods that flanked it north and south, the horizon toward the Mississippi and then up and down the small stream. The ridge separated their river from it, but as the land rose to their northwest, she thought they might come from the same source. She was looking for anything the least bit threatening, anything that might incite that feeling she was getting lately when trouble was near. Nothing.

Then she began to survey the woods for any indication of the light green color of bamboo. *Where the hell did we live?* She realized that she had no idea what was where anymore. No landmarks remained. Huge forests existed where none were before. Streams ran that were probably there all along but had been corralled by human-made barriers.

"Over there," Erika pointed. "That light green area in the woods. What do you think?"

"Could be. That's pretty far away." Sarah was a bit worried still over her disconnection from the Family. She took a deep breath and closed her eyes. *Nothing from Daffodil or Jazz.*

"Come on, Sarah, we've come this far. We have to check it out. Then straight home!"

Sarah surveyed the sun and gauged the time of day. "We have time. Not a ton, but I think we can get there and back home before it gets too dark. Ready?"

"Let's go." She felt Erika squeeze her around the waist, a little tighter and then a slight release. Erika's spirit embraced hers as well. Latifah understood Sarah's wishes and rode quickly along the ridge. Sarah realized that she also didn't want to lead any more crazies to their camp. "Watch to our left, OK. Keep an eye out for anything unusual."

"What's usual?"

"Good point." And she leaned back into Erika's body to indicate she appreciated the comment.

"Oh my," Erika squealed. "Bodies. Lots of them. Well, just skeletons."

They stopped on the ridge and looked south and east along the back side of their eastern woods. Rising from the grasses to the southeast, for as far as they could see, were skeletons, bones, white and bleached, devoid of skin or clothing or anything. They dotted the landscape. There was no smell.

"The grass is brown over here. Right to that line." Erika pointed. There was a blending of green and brown, but there was a distinct border. Their side was bright green. The other side was tan, with only hints of light green. "It didn't seem to infect the woods."

"That's weird," Sarah said. "Why would the Storm make nature grow in abundance and then kill it like this?"

"Maybe this is something else. Not the Storm. Or maybe part of the Storm . . . an evil part," Erika added.

They stared. The place was full of negative energy, but they were just outside its edge.

Erika broke the silence. "So that explains why all of the animals ended up in our grasslands. Something nasty got about this far and killed everything."

"Give me a second."

"You going to do that connection thing?"

"Shhhh." Sarah closed her eyes, took a deep breath and could feel death in that air, but she could also feel life. Tiny life. Mice, rats, insects, and in the distance, she felt the hyenas, buzzards and vultures. She opened her eyes, calm. "I don't know what did this, but it came from that Storm. The carrion eaters are taking care of the dead. They'll clean the earth, and it'll recover, and from the feel of it, pretty soon. The hyenas we saw are in there. Over there." She pointed.

"Whatever, but I ain't going that way."

Sarah smiled back at her and patted her leg. "Me neither."

"Latifah agrees," Erika added. Sarah laughed and patted the neck of her steed.

They headed northeast along the ridge through the grasses, quiet, skirting the edge of the dead zone, as they called it. When they got to a point where they hoped the bamboo stand was, in the woods to their north, she stopped.

Erika whispered into her ear, "No heroics, Sarah. No telling what we'll run into down that hill."

"I'm with you." Sarah took a deep breath, and Erika did the same. "You ready to head down and see what we can see?" Sarah whispered.

"May as well." Erika hoisted the spears just in case, and Sarah took one. "Let's go, girlfriend."

Sarah turned Latifah down the hill and headed down at a trot. "Keep an eye out." That was an instruction Erika already knew. They were again extremely quiet. Latifah slowed. The native deciduous trees wrapped around what could be bamboo. "We'll have to go through the woods."

Erika objected. "Let's try going that way," as she pointed down the line of trees. "Maybe there's a path or something."

"Good idea. I've no desire to go into that blackness either." Latifah turned to the right. She increased the pace and rounded a peninsular out-cropping of trees. They took a wide berth and looked back.

"Look!" Erika yelled. "Is that bamboo? It is, isn't it? That's bamboo. Big, tall, straight bamboo trees. Oh my God, we found some."

Sarah's smile was brief as she took a moment to survey their where-abouts. "It's far from home but perfect. Huge. Our neighbor's bamboo was never that big." She paused. "OK, let's get clear bearings as to where we are so we can find this again."

She turned Latifah and rode up the hill from the entrance then back down to the stand of bamboo. She headed out a little east and then up to the ridge and stopped on top to look in every direction. She noted the peninsula of trees and what it looked like and carefully observed the backside of their woods. There was a huge oak inside the woods that rose up well above the other trees. It was right at this location. She could re-member that. She pointed each landmark out to Erika.

She turned Latifah around and back toward their river. She observed how far away the stand of trees along their river was from them. She walked Latifah, counting down the time it took to get back to the edge of their woods. She committed that to memory and told Erika to remember it as well.

"OK. Let's head home."

Erika agreed and then did something unexpected. She put her right hand on Sarah's head and turned it, reaching around her. "Thank you," Erika said and kissed Sarah square on the lips. Sarah was taken aback at first but felt their connection, settled into the kiss and returned it. When they separated, Erika gazed into Sarah's eyes with love and commitment. It wasn't a sexual kiss. It was a kiss of deep bonding. Sarah could feel Erika's soul entwining more deeply with hers, similar to what she shared with Daffodil, almost as deeply as with any of her animals. Sarah gazed back into Erika's eyes then reached back and kissed her, a simple peck on the cheek but just as meaningful. That kiss sealed their bond as mutual.

"Sisters," Erika said. Sarah nodded. Perhaps more than that. It was good to have another ally.

Erika broke their gaze first. "Let's check out the horsepower of this thing, shall we?"

Sarah turned toward home. She could feel that Latifah knew what they wanted and was excited to give it to them.

"Kick it in, Sarah." They both smiled. Latifah took off and in a few strides was racing at full speed. Latifah was thrilled to go all out, and he could fly. They held on tightly and enjoyed the ride. Latifah knew exactly where they were headed and ripped down the length of the ridge, down through the grass around the edge of the woods and across the flat prairie, and then across the first several hills of the maze before slowing and pulling up to a walk as they approached the gate.

FORTY-THREE

"Wow. That was amazing. Exhilarating. We have to do that again!" Erika exclaimed as she slid off the horse's back. "Where is everyone?" The hair stood up on Sarah's neck. Erika could feel it and whispered, "Something's wrong."

Sarah turned to Latifah and ordered him into the grasslands toward the elephants. She turned to the fields and felt her Elephant, who turned and walked away from her herd. Sarah guided Latifah across the pastures to the elephant, who led him back to her herd.

"You have an elephant too?" Erika whispered.

"You have a horse." Sarah winked. "OK, let's figure out what's going on. Give me a spear."

They snuck toward the gate. Silence.

"This is too eerie, Sarah. What the—?" Sarah raised her hand.

The gate was open. Spears raised, they walked through, eyes peering left and right.

"Sarah!" Erika yelled as a swarm of Tony's team raced from the woods behind them, spears in hand. Erika and Sarah turned, then turned again only to find several others now in front, all with spears pointing at them. They were trapped in the overlap in the barrier she'd created for their protection.

Tony confidently strode through his soldiers and greeted the two women. "Welcome home to your new world. We have taken control, and

253

now I am your undisputed ruler. Lest you consider objecting, I want you to be aware of our assets."

The phalanx parted again, and one of Tony's henchmen walked forward, Jazz and Janie in tow, both bound and gagged.

"You shouldn't have run off without your children. You behave, and we might not kill you, or we might just take care of your lovely daughters. You do understand? You know what I'm capable of." Tony's voice was distant, evil but different.

Sarah's mind raced to Tom. Was he OK? Would Tony harm him or, worse, kill him?

Sarah laid down her spear and Erika followed. The soldiers in the back pushed forward, poking Sarah with their spears, forcing them both forward. Inside the scene was overwhelming. Ms. Watson, Joe, Amy, Herb, Rhonda and several others were tied up with the ropes she'd taught them to make. They sat in a circle, backs together, facing outward, in the middle of the grasses, far from any of the fires. *Where's Tom?* She scanned the compound. There were clearly two groups, and Tony's was armed with all the weapons the Family had crafted.

Sarah's heart sank. She'd left her Family knowing Tony was set for a revolt. She'd left her girls and her lover unprotected while she was out gallivanting in the wilds.

Tony's group walked the two of them into the compound. Erika was separated and tied up with the other leaders.

Tony turned to Sarah. "OK, missy, now for you. Tie her up to that tree over there, the one she threw me into." Two men were already there, holding the ropes. She walked, head held high, toward the tree.

A woman from the back cried out, "You fucking witch."

Tony grabbed her girls by their hair and dragged them in front of Sarah. "Now how powerful are you? Now how mystical and strong are you? You could have been my queen, my lover. Well, bitch, we're all going to watch you die a slow and gruesome death, tied to this tree until you wither away to nothing." He turned to the two with the ropes. "Tie her up." He pulled out one of Jazz's long knives and held it to the girl's throat. "Don't try to fight back or your oldest dies."

Sarah was bound tightly and gagged with a rope, which was then tied behind the tree. She could barely breathe. Tony walked up to her and began to fondle her breasts. "Turned on, my sweetie?"

She felt nothing. Not the weakness she had felt earlier when he was near. Not violated by his behavior. Nothing, and her eyes showed it. She then closed them and focused deep. Asha came to her: "The darkness has arrived. Relax. You are ready."

Tony stroked his own member and then tried to put it into her, but he was too short to reach. Several of his own men laughed. He turned, bright red, and jammed his long knife into the gut and then up into the chest of the one closest to him and held it there, watching the life drain from the man's eyes as his blood flowed from his body. Tony removed his hand without the knife, and the man fell to the ground at her feet. One of the other men reached to move him, but Tony bellowed, "Leave him there to rot at her feet." The man backed away, and Tony grabbed his spear. Tony turned to the rest of the crowd. "Now we celebrate a new life, a new world, a new dominion, the reign of Tony the First!"

There were shouts from the crowd as Tony strode toward the main fire, the highest point inside the relatively flat compound. Two guards were left with spears beside Sarah.

Tony returned the girls to the big man who dragged them to the far side of the compound. She could feel their fear and struggled against her bindings, but even with her strength, she couldn't budge.

The evening progressed with revelry. Tony ordered Ms. Watson to be brought before him. Two women pulled Ms. Watson to her feet, her hands bound tightly behind her. Ms. Watson spat on the women. Sarah squirmed against her bindings and tried to yell through her gag as Ms. Watson was thrown before Tony.

"You're a fucking witch, and you deserve to be punished for your blasphemy."

The group began to chant at them, "Witches, witches, witches." Moving forward with their spears, faces angry, they aimed their spears and chants at the Family's leader.

Tony raised his hand, and his crew quieted. "We are sick and tired of being pushed around by a bunch of bitchy women and pussy dickheads. As of right now, we are taking over this compound. You will now answer to me and do as you are told or suffer the consequences. Do you agree to be my subject?"

Ms. Watson shook her head calmly, fire in her eyes. "I will never bow down to you, you evil bastard." Tony slapped her across her face, knocking her to the ground.

"Stand her up!" His henchmen pulled her back to her knees. He returned his attention to Ms. Watson. "Oh, soon, witch, very soon, you will beg to be my slave. He slapped her again. This time she retained her balance and spat on his feet. Tony punched her, blood spattering from her mouth as she again tumbled to the ground. Tony stood over her. "It will be such a pleasure to see you grovel at my feet for mere morsels of food and beg to serve me." He paused as he watched her struggle in the grass, bound by both her hands and feet. "Drag her back to the group. We'll have our fun with her later."

He raised his spear into the air, and the crew behind him yelled "King Tony" into the sky.

The crowd continued to chant. She could feel Tony pouring his evil spirit across them. Those who were not Family responded. Sarah worked to counter it by sending positive spiritual energy toward the Family.

"Drag the Army bitch up here." Two men yanked Erika to her feet, while another held a spear at her back.

"Men, step forward. We're going to put this bitch in her place!" Men walked forward almost in a frenzy, women patting them on their shoulders. The Family stood back, petrified around the outside. Most couldn't watch. Tony raised his hand, and his crew quieted. "You will now answer to me and do as you are told or suffer the consequences."

Erika spat on his feet. "NO! I'll never bow to you. Never. You will pay dearly for this."

"Shut her up!" A big man smacked her, while a woman dragged a rope through her mouth, gagging her, pushing her forward onto the ground. Tony raised his spear into the air, and the crew again yelled "King Tony" into the sky.

Sarah closed her eyes and whispered her mantra, leaving her body, entering the universe of souls. She'd never tried to find another spirit in this state. She let her soul guide her, the spirits guide her. She felt Erika's soul, frightened and defiant, and moved toward it. She connected spiritually with her friend, entwining her spirit with Erika's. "Erika, close your eyes and let go. They are going to brutalize you. Breathe slowly and come with me." She could feel Erika's spirit slide from her physical body and rest in the soft ether with Sarah's.

As Sarah's spirit held Erika's spirit away from her body, they watched together, just above the fray. Tony's women laughed, running around to the front of Erika's body, which did not respond to the punishment. Tony's followers ran around the leaders tied in the center of the compound, laughing in their faces, almost cackling. Dancing and swirling near the fire.

Erika's body was beaten and bloodied when it was finally dragged back to the other leaders. Sarah guided Erika's spirit back into her body, and Sarah returned to hers.

Joe tried to comfort Erika, but Tony's men jabbed him with spears, drawing blood from his shoulder. Joe scowled at his attacker, who knocked him to the ground with the butt of his spear.

FORTY-FOUR

"Let's eat!" Tony yelled. "We can play with our new toys more tomorrow!"

Tony and his henchmen and chosen servant women ate first from the food killed and gathered that afternoon prior to the uprising, which apparently was well executed and swift. It didn't appear that anyone had suffered any injuries. Tony's crew danced into near frenzied states. Family members in the circle were slapped and kicked, while the rebels laughed and danced around them. It was as if they were on some sort of euphoric drug.

Sarah could feel the eerie cold she'd felt out near the dead zone flow through the compound. Was it coming from Tony, or beyond him? She could see it follow Tony's evil spirit, penetrating his followers' souls. Family members, however, reacted as though they smelled something horrible, backing away, sneaking deeper into the compound. As the Family backed into the woods, Tony's followers were guided by the force closer to him, almost in reverence. She could sense the division of Family and non-Family being orchestrated by Tony. Allies and enemies. Tomorrow would be a very bad day for the Family. She reached out for them from her spirit but could not find her girls.

The grass in the compound was turning grey, beginning on the far side, near Tony. Was he the embodiment of the darkness Asha mentioned? Tony stared at her and laughed, as though he felt her longing for Jazz and Janie. Her glare was menacing, causing Tony to turn away.

Tony's party roared into the night. Only his allies were fed. As the night progressed, the festivities seemed to rise to new levels of insanity. Orgies erupted. Screaming and chanting, demanding blood. Sarah worried for her Family. Perhaps tomorrow would be too late. She closed her eyes, gathered her spirits and pulled forth everything she had. She struggled against her bindings but still couldn't free herself.

Tony rose before his people. "Today is the first day of the dawning of a new era. We have slaves we must punish into doing our bidding. They are weak. Passive. We will kill any that will not bow to our authority." The crowd went crazy.

"Some need to die NOW! My fucking, cheating husband needs to die NOW!" The woman was very heavy. Tony ordered her husband dragged forward, hands bound behind him. Tony had known this was coming. The woman stood him in front of the raging fire and bellowed at him as he tried to apologize, tears flowing down his face. Sarah felt Tony's evil pour into the woman as his followers chanted, "Kill him, kill him." Her eyes became crazed and she raised a knife, grabbed his penis and sliced it off. He screamed into the night air as blood flowed onto the ground before him. She held his penis in the air. Tony's people cheered. Then the woman danced before her husband, then with two arms to his chest and more power than one would expect from her, she shoved him back into the raging fire. Tony's crew again cheered as the man screamed until the fire consumed his life.

Tony orchestrated two more sacrifices that evening, both former wives of men in the group. Both were killed in barbaric ways and tossed into the fire. Sarah tried to pour positive energy into more of the souls around the fire, but the rebels were unaffected. Tony smiled at her, as though he knew what she was trying—and failing—to do. He wanted to make sure she saw his power. Sarah glared at him.

When Tony returned to his followers, she turned to hers. She poured out positive energy into her Family. Most were back, away from Tony, in the woods surrounding the compound, reeling in what they had witnessed and, worst of all, unarmed. She turned her attention to her lover but still could not find Tom.

Tony marched over to Sarah and stared up into her eyes. His eyes rabid and full of hate. Hers calm. She could feel their two forces battering one another. Tony smiled as Sarah saw one of his henchmen walking toward them with a long switch. As he got to her, Tony stepped aside and offered her to the man. Tony turned to the Family's leaders in the middle of the compound. "All of you who follow this witch will see in a minute that she is a mere human. Remove her gag! I want to hear her screams."

Sarah brought her Elephant spirit forward, strengthening her skin in preparation for the beating. The man reached back, whipped the branch forward and struck her bare stomach, ripping the branch across her skin. It didn't so much as welt from the strike. Tony was incensed. "Hit her harder, you big wuss." The large, muscular man reached back and hit her as hard as he could over and over. She didn't scream out from the pain. Her skin reddened briefly at each strike but then returned to its normal color. Tony yelled with blood-curdling anger, took the large spear he'd been carrying with him and drove it deep into the man's belly, knocking him to the ground, screaming and squirming around the staff. He stopped for a second and looked up at Tony, as if to ask, "Why?" Tony and Sarah watched as blood pooled on the ground around him and the life drained from his eyes. Sarah had managed to reduce Tony's army by two large men while tied to a tree.

Tony marched over and grabbed the switch from the twitching hand of his former minion and turned on Sarah.

"You want me to hit you, don't you? Well, I have something much more enjoyable to show you, my dearest." Tony turned and ordered his men, "Bring him up here."

It was Tom, dragged between two of Tony's larger men, slumped and bleeding. When they reached her, the two men threw him onto the ground at her feet.

"You bastard! I am going to tear you apart, limb from limb, bit by bit for this. You hurt him anymore and you'll wish to hell that you'd never been born." Sarah turned the power of the deep red Storm toward Tony's followers. "That goes for all of you."

Tony merely leaned his head back and laughed. What emerged was shrill and hollow. It sent shivers down her spine and strengthened the resolve of those around her.

She returned her gaze to Tom, who looked up at her, his blue eyes stained red, bruised and blackened, but so loving. "I'll be OK. Save the Family."

Tony turned and drove his foot into the side of Tom's head, sending him reeling.

She pulled against her bindings, but she couldn't free herself, no matter how much of her powers she brought forward. "You asshole!" she screamed. Then she centered herself, an eerie calm falling over her. As though warning a child, she spoke, "Tony, let this be clear, you will die today. You will die, and it will be worse than anything you've inflicted on my Family or on Tom. You have messed with the wrong woman!"

Tony pointed to Tom, and the two men drug him back toward the fire. "He'll be dead long before daylight, and then we'll bring his corpse back here to rot in front of you as you slowly wither away to dust against that tree." He slashed the switch across her face. "Now shut up, bitch. I'm tired of your complaining." He turned to a large woman. "Quiet her."

The woman pulled the large rope through Sarah's mouth, tying it tightly onto the back of the tree, holding Sarah's head back.

"You won't need that mouth for anything anyway. May as well fill it with something to keep your filthy trap shut." He walked over and fondled her breasts. She tried to squirm but was tied too well. She couldn't move. "You'll like this, my sweetie pie." The feeling of his finger inside her nearly made her vomit, but she knew that she would suffocate if she did and forced it back. She took a deep breath and relaxed, realizing that she had no choice but to let him do his worst.

"Johnson, beat her until she cries. Boys, drag that piece of shit back to the fire and let's have some piñata fun with him." Turning back to her, Tony said, "Sleep well, Ms. Queen of the Family." The crowd laughed loudly.

Tony tossed the switch to the man called Johnson, holding his arms up in the air in triumph. "Now that's how you take care of an enemy!"

Tony did not look back but stormed off. "Let her die, long and slow," he screamed, then demanded the services of two young women, who dutifully ran to him.

The large man approached her, eyes vacuous but deadly. She felt him touch her and then pull back the switch and rip it across her stomach. She realized he would not stop until she bled, so she pulled her powers back. The next blow stung and drew blood. She closed her eyes and entered her mantra. Within a few seconds, she was in meditation, the trance that allowed her soul to leave her body. She slid above and felt the warmth of her mother and her guru Asha wrap her in comfort as the huge man continued to whip the body she'd left behind. Her body went limp, and she could see him decide he was finished.

He laughed and slapped her face. "Thank you, Sarah. Be back for more soon."

She allowed herself to reenter her body as the mantra came to an end. Her Elephant and Bear spirits healed the flesh wounds within seconds, though her body remained streaked with her blood.

FORTY-FIVE

Sarah watched as the compound fell asleep. Tony's guards were leaning against their spears, eyes heavy if not already closed. They'd not slept during the day as was the Family's custom for night watchmen. Within a few minutes, the two guarding her were fast asleep.

She closed her eyes and focused, connected with Daffodil, who was with the Family members in the woods. Sarah asked her to gather the Family at the southern end of the compound.

Then she connected to Claire and asked her to bring her dogs around through the river and stage them at the path to the pond and to keep them quiet.

Next, she found her girls, sensing them in the compound. They were on the opposite side, very close together. They were still awake and distressed. She had to assume they were bound and under guard.

She connected to Erika and conveyed her plans. She only hoped she could escape, that her peace-loving Family would fight because she knew Tony's would and that his evil powers were no match for hers. It was a lot of hope, but they'd survived on hope. It had to work.

Sarah took a deep breath and turned her mind inward to her spirits. She used them to reach out to her four animal allies out in the woods. Latifah was with her always. She felt her bear rise and attend. Then her elephant and tiger. She laid out her plan and guided them as they approached.

She felt her bear crossing the forest and emerge at the river. He pawed across the waterfall, and she was amazed at how quiet he could be. He rose behind her, and she guided him to tear his huge claws into the ropes as they ran around the back of the tree. As he weakened them, she brought her Bear-spirit strength forward. *Nothing.* The bear ripped at the ropes. The guard next to her moved, snorted. The bear froze as she told him to with her thoughts. She then released him, and he scratched at the ropes. Another try, her Bear strength focused, and snap, the main rope broke, loosened, unwound. Her hands and arms could move. She stopped the bear and freed herself.

The guards sniffled as she slipped to a squat on the ground, reached into the dead man and retrieved the long knife. Sarah glided close to the ground beneath the waking soldier, rose behind him, put her hand over his mouth and, as his eyes got big, drove the knife deep into the back of his neck, into his brain, pithing him like a frog in biology class. She helped his limp body to the ground and slit his throat through his voice box. The other guard snorted and moved. She froze, but he didn't awaken.

She moved to the other dead guard and pulled the sturdy spear from the ground without making a sound. Her hands were full of blood as it came free, and she marked her face and body with it.

She moved in front of the other guard, drove the spear up through his neck and vocal chords, into his brain in one motion, scrambling the soft grey matter. She caught the body in her bear-strong arm and pulled it into the woods. Sarah gathered their two spears and gave one to Claire, who'd arrived with the dogs, quiet as church mice. Claire nodded.

As Sarah turned and slipped into the darkness, the bear followed her part way around to the southeast. She stopped and asked his spirit to stay and wait. He nodded.

Her feet made no sound along the southeast arc of the water, the gurgling of the river hiding her movements. The Family members who'd escaped were gathered near the latrine. She saw their big white eyes as they reacted to her blood-stained face, and the relief in them as they recognized that their leader was loose and in charge.

She handed the two remaining spears to them. "We need to take out the guards near the back. That guy and that one. Can you kill them?" she looked directly into their eyes.

Little Randi stepped forward and spoke for them all, "After what we saw tonight, no problem."

"Good. Grab some sticks to use as clubs—big ones—and get ready. Daffodil will guide you when it's time." She paused and saw only determination in their eyes. Daffodil bowed to her. The others followed her lead, but Sarah didn't wait for their acknowledgment.

Sarah returned the way she had come past where the bear was waiting. She gave him guidance, simple and clear.

She reached Claire in the woods, with the dogs surrounding her. "Your job is to free our leaders. Got it?"

Claire nodded and closed her eyes. She could feel her connecting with her allies around her. Sarah moved across the path to the river without a sound, entering the northwestern woods, then within the shadows of the barrier, close to the ground, around toward the gate. There were three weary guards who appeared to be asleep, two still standing up.

She approached the first and rose behind him. She drove the bloody knife deep into the base of his skull, severing his spinal cord, shutting down his heart and lungs immediately, turning it back and forth inside his brain. She guided the pithed man to the ground.

She then slid into the space between the two barrier walls to the gate and moved back along the inner wall behind the sitting guard. She reached around and slit his throat, hand over his mouth, then she dragged the guard silently behind the barrier and finished him.

Her elephant was quietly waiting on the other side of the gate. She asked her to dispose of the third guard. The elephant reached her trunk over the barrier, wrapped it around his neck, squeezed tightly and yanked him off his feet and over the barrier, dropping him at Sarah's feet. His eyes opened wide with fear as Sarah drove her dagger deep into his voice box, silencing him, ripping his neck wide open. Blood spurted onto her chest.

She lifted the gate and opened it in silence. The elephant sauntered through behind her and stood in the overlap. She gathered the three spears and waited. The tiger slunk below the elephant inside the barrier up to her and bowed. She bowed to him as well. They did not touch. It was not that sort of relationship.

He took the three spears in his huge jaws and moved along the western tree line, silent, hidden in the darkness, his natural camouflage blending with the trees. One of Claire's dogs barked, startled by the big cat. Claire silenced it quickly. The tiger stopped. Sarah, now moving east inside the barrier, froze. A guard sitting near the Family in the center of the compound, his spear across his lap, looked up and pushed on another.

"Dude, I heard something."

"No shit. It's the middle of the night in the middle of a jungle. What'd ya hear?"

"Sounded like a dog. A yelp."

"Well, dufus, we got dozens o' dogs out there." They looked at their charges. "Jack, you're hearing things. Go back to sleep."

The Family and their allies stood in absolute silence for several minutes as the two guards' heads lolled back, and they were soon sound asleep.

Sarah let everyone know the coast was clear. The tiger continued. She could feel him deliver the spears to the startled Family.

FORTY-SIX

Now to free her children. The tiger moved north from the back through the woods inside the eastern edge of the barrier as Sarah moved with the same stealth east to the woods and then south within their shadows. As she approached, the tiger joined her. She nodded to him and he to her.

She closed her eyes and felt Claire and the dogs amassed at the opening to the river. The bear was in the woods to the south of them. The Family members listening to Daffodil, now better armed, assembled at the far south end of the compound. Her elephant stood at the gate to her right, the north end of the compound. Latifah was to her right, outside the barrier. All were waiting for her signal to launch their attack.

She snuck through the darkness to the edge of the woods. There were her daughters, tied together, back to back. Two guards were dozing against their spears on either side. They were the targets. She nodded to the tiger and launched the attack. Claire and her dogs raced forward. Two German shepherds tore into the two guards. The other dogs surrounded the Family leaders, and Claire began to free them, starting with Erika, who took charge.

The group in back moved quietly toward the smaller gathering of Tony's allied forces around the back fire. The bear sauntered from the woods, filling the gap between Tony's crews. Sarah hoped for a quick victory over the southern team so the Family could arm itself and the freed

Family leaders with their weapons for the next phase of the battle, an attack on the main fire from the south. It would be Sarah and the tiger's job to engage that larger group from the east, keeping them from supporting the smaller southern group. The elephant would attack from the north, hopefully helping to deflect the main group's attention.

As the first phase began, Sarah sprinted from the woods, ripping a gaping hole across the front of the startled guard's neck, throwing him to the ground. The tiger tore the other guard apart in two huge swipes of his big paws. She silenced him quickly with a dagger to the larynx.

Sarah could hear the other attacks begin from all sides; several armed soldiers were approaching them, backlit by the northern fire. The tiger dodged to his right just in time to avoid a spear-led lunge, turned and tore massive gaping wounds across the man's lower back. His scream startled the other attacker, whose hesitation cost him as the tiger snapped his neck with a huge right paw.

Latifah leaped over the barrier and ran to Sarah, who was cutting the girls free. She helped them both onto the big horse. "Hold on tight girls. He's taking you out of here."

Sarah turned to the battle. The Family was engaged to the south with that group of Tony's tribe. She could feel them through Daffodil, valiant and winning. The bear's roar carried across the smoky sky to her left. She heard the yelps and barking of the dogs amid the Family leaders.

Sarah and the tiger moved into the gap north of the southern battle and faced the mass of Tony's allies, most of whom were struggling from slumber to understand what was happening.

The elephant stomped around the barrier and into the compound, trumpeting loudly. The dogs tore at the guards, barking and snarling, Claire close behind. Erika freed Joe, who took Claire's spear. Claire released Ms. Watson, Molly and the others and guided them back to safety. Erika grabbed a spear from a guard and connected to Sarah.

Sarah, the bear and the tiger began their northward assault, protecting those to their south. The startled southern flank fell quickly as she'd hoped. The dogs tore into groggy revolutionaries as Joe and Erika drove their spears into those who'd risen with arms.

Sarah and the tiger ripped through the startled traitors, who'd grabbed their weapons. Those near the outside could not respond quickly enough. Sarah could see the elephant throwing Tony's crew right and left, stomping on a few who got in his way. The bear's powerful claws sent blood into the air as he ripped through one rebel after another, driving deep gashes into them.

Some of the Family from the south remained to guard their prisoners. After being freed, Amy and Herb ran south with the ropes that had bound the Family leaders and helped to bind their southern captors. Some, led by tiny Randi and graceful Roger, grabbed weapons and followed the bear into the battle. Rhonda emerged, as did others. Her Family was rallying.

Erika's voice was strong above the din, giving commands and orders, leading the troops into a more ordered attack.

Sarah raced forward, feeling for Tom and knowing precisely where Tony was. He was driving his dark energy into his followers. They awakened, enraged, grabbed their weapons and began to fight back. He'd lost many, but those he now controlled were his inner circle, formidable and well-armed. Sarah battled toward Tony near the big main fire. Cold crimson tendrils, invisible to most, reached from Tony and connected to his followers throughout the crowd.

Two men jumped in front of her with spears and attacked. She moved left, grabbed the lead attacker's spear and yanked it past her, driving her dagger deep into his neck as he stumbled forward. She ripped it out, blood spurting everywhere, and pushed the man into the spear of the other. As he tried to manipulate it around his dying colleague, she leaped and drove her long knife into his neck, tearing it wide open.

A spear sliced her back, and she whirled to her left, grabbed the spear with her left hand, swung her right leg up, driving it into the side of her attacker's head. Then she spun to her right as another approached and smacked the spear with her knife, landing balanced, her feet shoulder width apart, facing the man. Sarah forced her strong left arm into his right hand, held up to defend, and into the bridge of his nose, breaking it. Blood spewed forth, and the man cried out as he staggered back, dropping the spear.

Erika appeared at her side, and the two raked spears and knives through attackers, each having the other's back. They were connected deeply and acted as one. It helped Sarah focus.

She felt Molly guiding the children away into the woods. They rallied to her as though she were the pied piper. Then, to Sarah's surprise, the children began to sing their sweet songs as the adults fought. The tiny voices rose as more arrived, and Molly encouraged the frightened young-sters. The Family members drew strength from the music. Tony's crew couldn't hear it.

She could feel the tiger knock an armed woman down, tearing his claws across her chest. Rhonda had located her bow and a few arrows. Sarah guided the elephant to her, who lifted Rhonda onto her back where she could take better aim. *Shoop.* The arrow flew through the air and drove itself deep into the heart of her target, a man running up behind the tiger. Then another into a man engaged with the bear. Joe, Randi and Roger fought valiantly by the bear's side, and a few others fought, but most flailed in defense against the crazed rebels, backing down. A man went down. Dead. Another injured. A woman. Then another.

The few Family members who were fighting were winning, and as they acquired weapons from fallen rebels, they passed them to their brethren, but most of the Family was passive. They defended themselves but struggled to attack. The battle was turning Tony's way, she could feel it. She had to find Tony and cut the head off the beast. It was their only hope. She could feel him, dark, cold, menacing. She and Erika battled their way through the crazed soldiers, eyes glazed over as they were con-trolled by Tony.

FORTY-SEVEN

Sarah fed positive energy into the Family and could feel the children's song guide her strength into them, but they were losing, and losing badly. She knew she had one mission—she had to kill Tony, to fight the darkness with darkness. She stopped in the middle of the fray.

"Sarah, what the hell?" Erika screamed.

"Erika, take command. Save the Family. They won't fight. Get them out! I'm going after Tony!" Erika gave Sarah an encouraging pat and ran off, yelling commands, as Sarah closed her eyes to focus. She released the positive red power of the Storm from inside her. She could feel herself getting hotter as she also lost all track of the battle beyond.

Her eyes were bright red, her aura, which glowed so often, was crimson and strong. Those around her stopped dead in their tracks. Sarah turned toward Tony, who could feel her rage. He was smiling. She could feel him loving the battle.

"Come to me, my queen." She could hear his voice inside her head. "That's it. Let the rage build inside you. Come to me. Join us. We can rule the world!"

Sarah smiled. Doubt invaded Tony's confident face. She owned her spirits now, all of them. She raced through the fighters, tearing into those who opposed her, dispatching them with ease, until she stood ten feet in front of Tony. She had her long flint knife. He had a solid, nicely tipped spear and a shorter knife. His remaining soldiers, men and women, disengaged from the Family and gathered behind him.

She felt Erika move the Family back into the woods. The bear and elephant stood with Erika. The tiger arrived at Sarah's side. Tony's army was smaller but still heavily armed. She could see and feel the evil in their souls. The Family had lost several in the battle, and she felt Daffodil guiding their spirits. No one moved. Sarah's concern centered on the Family.

Tony felt her distraction but misread it. This time he spoke with a deep, haunting voice, "Feel the hatred. Robert is your enemy, not me. He lives in you. Join me! I will rid you of him forever, and we can rule this new world together."

Sarah turned her attention fully toward Tony and stepped forward. "How do you know about Robert?"

Tony didn't respond but took a small step back. He smiled that smile that had made her skin crawl in the past and stood his ground.

But Tony no longer affected her. The spirits were burning inside her as her strength and power grew. She controlled the awesome power of the Storm within her. She no longer feared Tony and could sense his confusion.

Sarah stepped forward and said, "Tony, are you sure you want to do this? Again?"

Tony looked at his gang. He could see they saw the aura that surrounded her, now brighter, stronger and bright red. Tony stood as tall as he could, pointed his spear at Sarah and said, "I own you now, you broken-down bitch. Minions, show her what we have."

"Jazz and Janie are free and out of your reach, Tony. So are Shirley, Joe, Erika and the rest of the Family leadership. You're done. Give in, and I might let you live."

The group parted and there, bound and gagged, beaten, bloodied and kneeling on the ground at spearpoint, was Tom. "Give it your best shot, bitch! One move and your beloved Tommy boy's dead meat."

His entire gang rose up behind him, raised their spears and chanted, "King Tony!"

Her heart sank for a moment as she saw Tom, slumped and breathing heavily. His eyes were puffy, and he bled from cuts to his body. He'd endured a brutal beating since they'd dragged him away earlier. Her heart was heavy, and her shoulders slumped a bit as she watched the love of her life nearing the end of his.

"Oh, Sarah, you so underestimate me. I knew you were coming. I let you have the weak among us. Each blow to one of them was inflicted on your beloved Tom by my strongest soldiers. As you thought you were winning, dear Tommy, here, was losing. He is close to death, but I can save him. I have the power to heal him. You need only join forces with us. Release yourself to the forces of the Storm within you. They rule this planet now. I am part of the future. Together, we can rule the world. Sarah, together, we can make this new earth a haven for all. Join me. Join us."

Her world became foggy as she felt the evil of the Storm, the darkness, surrounding her. She fell to her knees, tears flowing down her cheeks as she gazed into Tom's eyes. Crimson tendrils approached her. From Tony.

In the midst of the confusion, she could feel Tom and the love he poured out toward her. She could not lose Tom, and she completely released herself to the love she felt for him. He was several feet away, but she could feel his embrace as though they were together.

"Save them, honey. Defeat this menace," she heard him whisper. Her head and eyes cleared, and a warm white light radiated from her, lighting the onlooking faces as though it were midday.

"You are ready." It came from inside her. "It is time." Asha did not appear, but Sarah could feel the guru, guiding her, providing her strength. She gazed into Tom's eyes one more time.

Her spirits rallied inside her. She heard her great bear roar from the edge of the trees and the horse whinny from beyond the barrier, and she knew her Family was safe. The elephant's protective strength repelled the tendrils of dread emanating from Tony, and her elephant trumpeted into the night sky. Her massive Bengal tiger moved beside her, his muscles rippling, shoulders well above her waist. She felt his fur against her skin as he growled through his teeth at Tony and his crew. She was one with all of them.

Sarah stood tall. She gave a confident smile to the Family standing back in the compound and could feel their relief as they realized their hero was there for them. Erika strode from the edge of the woods. They had a plan. Joe and her bear led a small band behind Tony's crew.

Sarah turned on Tony, staring at him with different eyes. The darkness no longer controlled her; he had no power over her. "You think I'm broken, do you?" She rolled back her shoulders and stood taller still. "You think your darkness makes me fear you, don't you?" She took a step closer. The tiger followed. Still engaged with Tony's black, soulless eyes, she took another step forward. Then she turned her glare to his group of chanting followers. The chanting stopped as she moved from one to the next. Tony was becoming agitated. Sarah smiled. "Alright then, but remember, you evil asshole, you asked for it."

Sarah reached down and scooped up two rocks; in one motion, she sent them hurtling through the air at the two men holding spears pointed at Tom. As the rocks sailed toward their targets, she, with her Tiger spirit, leaped over the three men between herself and Tom, stomping Tony's henchmen aside, propelling her forward. The tiger attacked behind her, ripping into the startled soldiers staring at the woman sailing above them. The bear tore into the phalanx to their left, who were also mesmerized as they watched Sarah rise over their comrades. The elephant trumpeted from her right. Claire released her dogs from the back of Tony's army.

Sarah bounced once off the ground, and as those guarding Tom diverted their attention to avoid the rocks flying at their skulls, she grabbed Tom in her bear-strong arms and raced with the grace of the horse through the back of the astounded crew, knocking over several fighters focused on dealing with the dogs. She emerged on the north side of Tony's rebel army and released Tom safely to Joe, Randi, Marshall and Olivia, behind the protection of her elephant.

She bent down. "Tom, don't you leave me now. I'll be right back." His eyes opened, and he smiled a weak, pained grin, which vanished quickly. She kissed his head. "Take care of him. Get him out of here." Then she turned back toward Tony.

FORTY-EIGHT

Tony screamed at his troops something she could not understand. She could feel him pouring evil energy into them. Their eyes glazed and their faces focused, menacing. They began to run with reckless abandon, swinging spears, throwing knives and rocks. Sarah connected to Erika and ordered her to back the Family and the animals into the woods. Tony's group would not retreat. They would fight to the death. She had to cut off its head.

She heard Erika giving orders. Erika had a plan. Lure them in. Let the smaller, crazed rebel gang move forward and disperse, then take them out a few at a time in the darkness of the surrounding woods. Sarah conveyed the ideas to the animals, who moved into formation with the humans. Retreating, leading them deeper into the compound, spreading them out. The Family moved more quickly into the shadows around the edges of the compound, separated into squads of humans and animals, waiting for the rebels. Erika had this. Sarah cut the connection to focus on her mission.

Tony was imploring his minions to sacrifice anything to kill Family members. He was surrounded by three loyal subjects, a woman and his two large sidekicks.

"Tony," she yelled as she began her approach. The two men turned on her. "Tony! You little pussy. Turn and face me yourself, or are you too frightened?"

Tony turned to her, his eyes deep, empty pools. His voice was low and guttural. "You will die. You must die! They all must die!"

Tony's scream was shrill and bloodcurdling as he lunged past his crew, spear pointed toward her, then stopped. "Kill the animals!" he screamed to those out in the compound. Sarah warned each animal and ordered them to move behind the Family. Erika was moving her forces, and against their nature, the Family members were forced to kill Tony's possessed rebels. Sarah could sense the difficulty her Family faced but also their determination to repel this evil at all costs.

Tony turned to his two remaining, most loyal henchmen. "Attack her with me." The three turned their spears toward her. As they approached, she felt the evil emanating from Tony, who was focusing more on her, leaving less for the rest of his army.

Tony stopped eight feet in front of her, spear raised ready to strike. "Now, kill her." His evil spread around her, but it could not penetrate her aura. She poured positive energy out, repelling his power. He focused even more, pulling it away from his army. More and more of his energy redirected toward her and away from them. She could feel his ire and frustration grow as he forgot all about the others. Sarah focused entirely on repelling and penetrating Tony's energy.

Dark crimson and maroon tendrils crept toward her, dark misty energy surrounded her, out at the edges of her bright white aura . . . but no closer. Tony's face cringed in pain.

Sarah stood tall, the bright white force encircling her body, lighting up the night sky. "Tony, face it, you've lost. You can't get to me. It's over."

She felt the bear. He'd been wounded in the shoulder. It caused her to back up as she, too, felt the impact. It shook her focus, and she could feel the dark tendrils begin to penetrate her spiritual shield.

Tony could sense the moment. One of his henchmen threw a spear at her. It struck her on the calf, ripping a gash in her skin and muscle. She lost her balance and stumbled to her right with the intensity of the pain, both in her leg and in the shoulder of her bear.

One of his men ran toward her, spear held high, eyes radiating evil, all drawn from Tony. She could feel Tony feed the man. She limped back quickly, parried the spear with her long knife, then slid it up the shaft and off, across the neck of her attacker. He stumbled past her, writhing on the ground, blood spurting from his neck.

She closed her eyes and guided the healing powers of her Elephant spirit through her Bear spirit and into the bear itself. She saw, in her mind's eye, Ms. Watson pull the spear from the sitting bear's shoulder. She could feel the wound healing. She healed her bear first, loved him more, and the pain in her shoulder improved.

Sarah leaped backward, avoiding a spear thrown at her, and gained her stance, ignoring the pain in her own body. She could no longer distinguish her blood from that of those she'd vanquished. She smiled at Tony as she stood strong to face him, extending the white shield again, repelling his crimson attacks.

She connected with him and could feel him. Feel his thoughts. Sense his fear. The woman and three more from his crew arrived, bloodied from the battle, aligned behind him, spears facing her, eyes glazed, faces awash in anger.

She saw with such clarity, as though the Storm inside her gave her a view into his soul and his next move. As the tip of one of Tony's soldier's spears approached, she grabbed the shaft in her left hand, turned and allowed it to pass her as she spun on her left foot, whipping her right elbow around, driving it into the side of his head. The crack rang out through the camp, and the man fell.

Sarah turned to the next two men, who ran at her, spears raised, trying to act in unison. Sarah grabbed the shafts behind their stone blades, pulled them apart and yanked them down, tip first, into the ground on either side of her. The spears stopped short, but the momentum of the men propelled them forward. She drove from her squatting position up into the two, swinging her arms into their stomachs, lifting them upward and throwing them over her shoulders, head over heels. Joe and Randi appeared behind her, each driving a spear into their chests.

Another ran at her. She grabbed his spear and threw him sideways. He sprawled on his back in the grass, disarmed, writhing, screaming obscenities at her, deep, unseeing evil eyes staring back. As he tried to rise, the elephant emerged and stomped on his chest, then on his head, crushing his skull.

Several dogs, teeth bared, snarling, encircled Tony's few remaining men and women nearby in the compound before they could rally to his support. Tony screamed, and two men ran, spears raised at Sarah, through the dogs, who tore at their legs. This time she attacked them. As they closed in on her, Sarah leaped, twisting between the two spears, and drove her elbows into their Adam's apples, carrying them hard to the ground as she landed gracefully on her feet. The dogs leaped on them and tore them to pieces.

Sarah turned on Tony, who was visibly shaken, one last man and the woman standing behind him.

A few members of the Family raced in behind her, but she didn't notice them.

Sarah could feel Tony trying to use the anger to turn Family members to his cause. The songs of the children rose across the compound. The sweet voices penetrated the Family, as they always seemed to, strengthening their resolve.

Sarah squared up against the three remaining rebels. Outnumbered now by enormous odds, Tony's own aura kept the Family members at bay. They could not approach him. It was, again, up to Sarah.

"Tony, you have no power over me. Give up, and I might let you live."

The aura around Tony grew, anger emanating from every pore, forcing the Family back, creating a circle for the final battle. Tony's last man and woman moved in opposite directions, flanking her on three sides within his aura. They began to move toward her, behind her and on either side, far enough back so as to be beyond her peripheral vision, but they struggled at the edge of her white aura.

She had to kill Tony. There was no other option. He was the darkness, the power that drove the others, that repelled her allies, that violated her Family and besmirched the magical peace of their compound and this new world. He had to die. Whatever else happened would take care of itself.

Sarah ignored the two behind her and raced toward Tony, her long knife in hand. As she got closer, her white barrier thinned, and razor-sharp crimson tentacles pierced her skin. Small pricks, then deeper cuts that bled. She countered his defenses with the protective and healing powers of her internal spirits. The bleeding slowed as she focused her white energy forward. She carved a seam in Tony's defenses, moving toward him, reaching for him, but as she got closer, his frozen spikes intensified. He laughed as he watched her struggle against his focused evil. She kept it from penetrating her, but it kept her from getting close to him. He seemed to be just out of reach. He laughed, reveling in his perceived victory.

"Who's the loser now, my dear?" She felt the point of a spear enter her right shoulder from behind. Focusing forward had opened herself to attack from behind. She recoiled and turned, ripping the spear from the man's hand but dragging it through her flesh and then out onto the ground. She slashed him twice, the second time fatally, across his neck. The woman was fast approaching, but Sarah couldn't worry about her.

She turned toward Tony, closed her eyes and focused her entire aura on Tony's field of energy, controlling the soft red, nature-creating Storm force within her. Her glowing power and his darkness came from the same source. She realized that it alone could pierce his armor, and she focused the Storm's positive power forward with every ounce of her strength.

His eyes grew wide as he felt her breaking in, breaking him down, fending off his cold tendrils, getting closer. She smiled at Tony.

A whoosh of orange flew past as the tiger pounced onto the remaining soldier, ripping into her as the Family members scrambled back from the barrage of conflicting energies they could not understand.

The tiger was part of her, and she felt him take the life of Tony's remaining ally. Then the tiger turned behind her. The bear arrived, as did the elephant. She could feel them following her, guiding and supporting her as she forced Tony back.

The elephant grabbed one of the dead rebels in her trunk and threw him at Tony. The body deflected off the energy force that emanated from him. Tony turned, a moment of distraction, and that was all Sarah needed.

Sarah forced every ounce of positive Storm energy she had into the breech, slashed her long knife across Tony's chest, tearing his skin in an 8-inch, blood-gushing gash. Tony's scream pierced the night, his defenses weakened. Sarah ripped her blade again through his chest, then across his stomach. Tony's evil energy dropped, and the tiger flew past her, driving his long claws into Tony's shoulder, tearing his left arm nearly from his body, knocking him to the ground. The dogs tore at his arms and legs. She could see Tony's eyes widen as the huge cat stood over him. He looked left and right, as if for help.

The tiger turned to her, and she nodded her permission. Tony screamed, "Nooo!" as the tiger grabbed Tony's head in his huge mouth, ripping back and forth until it tore from his neck. Blood spurted onto the dogs. The tiger turned like a proud cat who had caught a mouse and carried the head back to Sarah, dropping it at her feet.

FORTY-NINE

As the energies of the two spiritual forces faded, the sky cleared, and the first hints of golds and pinks of the sunrise peaked over the horizon. A fresh, soft breeze rose from the west and seemed to cleanse the world, wafting away the stench of death, the weight of evil and the caustic, cremating smoke from Tony's raging fires. The Family, despite their exhaustion, cheered with joyous excitement. The children, protected from the violence and its aftermath deep in the woods, were singing their wondrous songs as Molly led them into the compound. Parents streamed toward them.

Sarah bowed. The tiger bowed. They shared a moment during which Sarah thanked him. The tiger loped across the compound, turned through the gate and was gone. She bowed to the bear, now fully healed, and the elephant, and they bowed back. She thanked them, then the two huge animals wandered their separate ways, out of the camp, returning to their families.

The surge of evil energy was dissipating into the air. Sarah felt what little was left of the darkness inside her flow off with it, leaving only a benevolent, loving red strength and the power of hope and knowledge in the bright white light. As she had after her battle with the Storm, she felt all of nature in this world flow into her soul, but this time, she had the power to receive it, to love it, to feel it and to release herself fully to its beauty. She stared at the glowing morning sky and deeply breathed in the crisp morning air.

She looked down at Tony's body as the Family gathered around her. It burned translucent blue and orange, as from a gas flame. His body turned red and then began to blacken, turned to ash, drying up before their eyes; some of the ash seemed to be sucked into the ground, into the bright green plants engulfing his body, and the rest turned to dust, blowing off with the gentle breeze. He seemed to Sarah to have been devoured by the energy of the earth itself.

Sarah returned to reality. Her forces settled inside her. The pain from her unfelt injuries manifested themselves. Nearly everything on her body hurt, and she was bleeding from many wounds. She nodded to her Family.

Ms. Watson arrived. "Oh my." She turned and called for Doc.

"No, Shirley, he needs to tend to the others, to Tom. I'll be fine."

Latifah rounded the barrier wall with Jazz and Janie on his back. They were helped off the horse and came running for their mother. Both stopped short as they saw her, bloodied and bruised.

"Mommy!" Janie blurted out, but for the first time in a long time, her youngest was speechless.

Jazz walked over to Sarah and put a hand on her shoulder. Sarah could feel her spirit and her concern.

"Girls, I'll be fine. I just need some time to heal." Sarah turned to the Family, opened her arms to them and announced, "I'll be fine."

Then Sarah turned to Ms. Watson. "Shirley, how's Tom?"

"I don't know, Sarah. He's badly injured, but he's alive."

Sarah closed her eyes. "I can feel him." He was in pain but fighting for his life. "Girls, check on him for me. Tell him I'll be beside him soon."

Jazz nodded, stood and turned to take her sister's hand. "Janie, let's check on Tom." Sarah watched as the two most important people in her life left to check on her most dear love.

Sarah slipped to the ground. As Ms. Watson guided everyone away, Sarah took her lotus position, closed her eyes and began the healing mantra Asha had taught her.

Om Trayambakam Yajamahe Sugandhim Pushti Vardhanam
Urvarukam Iva Bandhanan Mrityor Mukshiya Mamritat

As she repeated it softly, she could feel her spirits begin to care for her physical body as her soul settled into the universe of spirits. There before her, in the lotus position, appeared Asha, misty but real. The temple solidified around them, the mosaics of her animal spirits and friends became clearer.

Her soul left her body as it did when the two had meditated as one. She could feel the spirits of her parents, smiling and proud. It was the part of this experience she enjoyed the most and looked forward to. In the past, they were empathetic, concerned for her safety. Now they were confident in her, proud of her and, as always, so deeply in love with her. Her soul smiled as she felt the depth of warmth from them.

Then a different feeling emerged within her. A broader love, deeper and warmer than anything she'd ever felt before, in out-of-body meditation or in physical life. The love came from dozens of spirits, human and animal. Tom emerged in her universe, smiling and happy. Then one Family member after another appeared behind him. Her horse was there. Her tiger, his mate and two cubs were there. Her bear, his mate and their cubs were there. The elephant, her mate and herd were there. The dogs were there. Her Family was there, pouring love into her soul from the universe and beyond.

Asha opened her eyes. "Well done, Sarah. You have won. You are loved, and you love back without conditions. Evil hates, but like the darkness is always defeated by light, no matter how black it may be, so too is evil always vanquished by love. You have released me to the universe of spirits, and we will not see each other again. I, like all spirits who love you, will be with you forever, but you no longer need me in your physical life. Lead, Sarah. Lead and love. You have a new Family."

Asha's spirit leaned over and kissed her on the forehead. As she did, Asha and the temple disappeared, replaced, as she opened her eyes, by bright greens, clear deep blues, reds, yellows and violets, the sweet smell of flowers bursting into bloom, the songs of birds, the rustle of leaves. But most of all, she felt the love from her Family, the deep connection and wonder of her relationship with Tom, and the warm embrace of her girls.

ACKNOWLEDGMENTS

*R*eset is my first novel, and I owe a great deal to many people for its completion. I have learned so much and met all of my editors and most of my mentors from my memberships in the St. Louis Writers Meetup Group, St. Louis Publishers Association and the St. Louis Writers Guild. I recommend these groups to any aspiring author.

I have employed three editors in the crafting of this book. Andrew Doty of Editwright had the unholy duty of reading and critiquing my very first manuscript. Without his care and input, this novel would not have gotten off the ground.

After much work and help from my organizations and beta readers, whom I am so thankful for, I brought the next version to Meghan Pinson of My Two Cents Editing. She helped me refine my voice, craft Sarah and the other characters, and understand how to begin and end the book. I am deeply in her debt.

This book would not have been finished were it not for Karen Tucker of Comma Queen Editing, who worked through the "final" versions of *Reset* with me patiently but firmly, helping me craft better prose and bring the story to life in so many ways. She and my book cover designer, Jamie Wyatt, put the book in final form. Thank you, Jamie, for your excellent cover and diligence in getting it there.

I want to thank my family who served often as the guinea pigs in reading those early drafts. They, especially my wife Barbara and daughter Jessica, were incredibly invaluable in getting this book to where it is. Finally, I want to thank my many beta readers who read all or parts of *Reset* over the last two-plus years and to my advanced readers for agreeing to take time out of their busy schedules to read and provide me with honest opinions of *Reset*.

Thank you to all. Without you, this book would not have reached this point.

ABOUT THE AUTHOR

Ned Lips is a father, serial entrepreneur, attorney and dedicated writer. This is his first published novel, though he has written myriad poems, short stories, magazine articles and even a previous book that he will eventually get around to polishing and publishing. *Reset* is launched as the first of a series. Ned is a columnist with *The Moderate Voice*, an e-zine, and has ghostwritten more than 25 articles for well-known experts in their fields. Ned is involved with several not-for-profits and dedicates a great deal of time to helping others. He's been married to Barbara for over 11 years and has two wonderful daughters making their own names in the world.

To learn more, visit www.nedlips.com.

Made in the USA
Lexington, KY
02 January 2019